FLYING WITH ANGELS

Part Five
of the
Angel Mountain Saga

Brian John

Greencroft Books
2005

First Impression 2005

Published by Greencroft Books
Trefelin, Cilgwyn, Newport,
Pembrokeshire SA42 0QN
Tel 01239-820470. Fax 01239-821245
Email: greencroft2@macunlimited.net
Web: www.books-wales.co.uk

ISBN 0 905559 84 3

Typeset by the author in Palatino 10 pt and designed on
Apple iMac computer using Appleworks 6

Printed and bound in Great Britain by Biddles Ltd,
King's Lynn, Norfolk PE30 4LS

CONTENTS

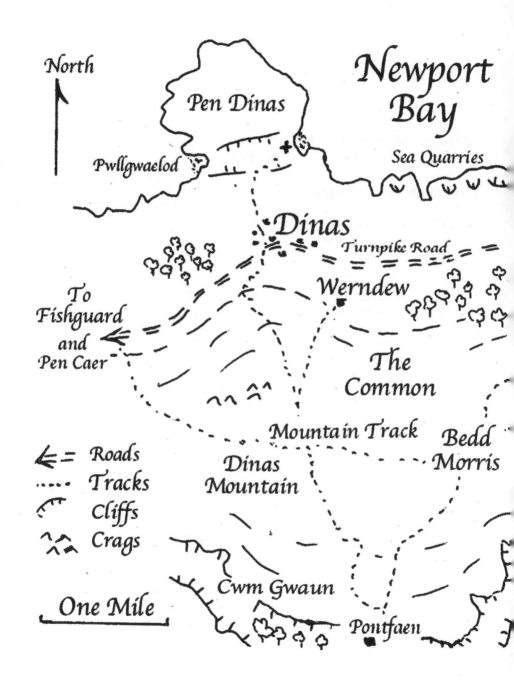

To Moylgrove

River
Nevern

To Cardigan

erry Sands

Nevern

Cwmgloyn

rrog

Llwyngwair

Henllys

Newport

Pentre Ifan

To
Eglwyswrw

Carningli

Ty Canol Wood

Plas Ingli

Chapel

Mill

Cilgwyn

Carnedd
Meibion
Owen

Dolrannog
Penrhiw

Church

Brynberian

Llannerch

Gelli Fawr

To Haverfordwest

**To Inger
Irene, Ian, Robert and Lorna
and
all the others
who love Angel Mountain**

KEY CHARACTERS IN THE STORY

The Surviving Morgan family of Plas Ingli
Martha, born as Martha Howell on 12 May 1778 at Brawdy. Married to
David Morgan on 21 August 1796, widowed 1805. Never remarried.
Died 27 Feb 1855, aged 76. Her surviving children:
Betsi, b 1798, married Ioan Rhys of Cenarth 1818. Three sons, Benjamin
(b 1821), Abel (b 1823) and Owain (b 1829).
Daisy, b 1801, illegitimate children Amy b 1822, John b 1826, William b
1829. Married George Havard 1846.
Brynach (adopted), b 7 April 1807, m Anne Edwards 1830, inherited
Llanychaer estate 1832. Children Rose (b 1831), David (b 1834).

The Howell family of Brawdy
Betsi (Martha's mother), b 1748, m 1765, d 1841.
Morys (older brother), b 1770, was Baptist minister in Haverfordwest,
married Nansi 1797. Three children, Edward (b 1799), Jane (b 1802)
and Robert (b 1805). Took over as Squire of Brawdy 1817.
Elen (oldest sister), b 1773, emigrated to USA 1807, m Tom Bradshaw 1810,
children Susanna (b 1812), George (b 1815).
Catrin (sister), b 1776, moved to Castlebythe as tutor 1797, m James Bowen
1800. Two children, John (b 1803) and Mark (b 1806).

Plas Ingli staff
Bessie Walter, b 1776. Maid. Worked at the Plas in 1795-1799. Moved
back after death of husband and son. Housekeeper from 1812.
Gomer Jenkins, b 1812. Son of Shemi and Sian. Started at the Plas 1827,
tenant at Penrhiw after 1844.
Gwenno Jenkins, Liza's daughter, housemaid from 1827, m Gomer 1840.
Will Owen, b 1780, started at the Plas 1806, head man after 1836. Married
Tegwen Gruffydd 1823, three children, b 1824, 1828, 1831.
Gerallt Owen, Will's oldest son, b 1824, taken on as cowman 1845.
Myfanwy Owen, Will's oldest daughter, b 1828, housemaid in 1845.
Liza Philpin, Martha's "lady's maid", b 1784, m to Tomos 1806, two
children, b 1807 and 1810. Came to the Plas 1807 as wet nurse.
Blodwen Bebb, illegitimate daughter of Rosie Bebb from Newport, b 1797,
taken on as dairymaid 1846.

Other Key Characters

Skiff Abraham, respectable smuggler, waggoner and merchant after 1807. Married 1812, three children b 1814, 1816 and 1820.

Thomas Campbell Foster, b 1813, *Times* reporter 1843-44.

Elijah Collins, Llysmeddyg, b 1760, old friend of the family.

Aeron Griffiths, b 1773, tenant at Dolrannog Isaf from 1835.

Wilmot Gwynne, b 1895, m Delilah 1820. Industrialist from Swansea.

Joseph Harries of Werndew, known as "the wizard", born 1761, died in 1826. Doctor, herbalist, sleuth, and Martha's friend and mentor.

George Havard Medical, b 1790, local doctor.

William Howell, b 1805, illegitimate son of John Howell, who was executed in 1807. Last of the Howell line.

Madoc Huws, Squire of Bayvil, b 1780. Took over estate 1823.

Shemi Jenkins, wizard and healer, from Werndew. Born 1782, m to Sian Williams 1810, 3 children including Gomer. From 1797 to 1836, was a servant at the Plas.

James Jobbins, Squire of Holmws and local magistrate.

Jacob Jobbins, senior deacon, Brynberian Chapel.

Amos Jones, b 1785, known as Jones Minor Prophet, itinerant evangelist.

Dafydd Laugharne, Squire of Pengelli, magistrate and leading light in the Society of Sea Serjeants.

Owain Laugharne, b 1780. Betrothed to Martha. "Lost" 1807-1822. Died in 1825.

Nicholas Lloyd, took over as Squire of Cwmgloyn in 1833.

Stephen Lloyd, deacon at Capel Brynberian.

Patty Nicholas, Martha's friend, living on Parrog. Married fisherman Jake in 1807. Two sons and two daughters.

Brendan O'Connell, b 1801, Irish itinerant labourer.

George Price, Squire of Llanychaer, b 1742, m Susan 1768, d 1832 aged 90.

Iestyn Price, b 1771, d 1822, son of George Price and father of Brynach, who became Martha's adopted son.

Richard John Rice, b 1815, last of the Rice family. Ex-Army officer.

John Thomas, deacon at Capel Brynberian.

Llewelyn Thomas, Rector of Newport 1824-1875.

Thomas Watkins, b 1795, Squire of Ffynnonddofn, last of the Watkins line.

John Wilkins, young Newport lawyer in 1843.

Gwyn Williams, b 1782, tenant at Gelli after 1818.

Hugh Williams, b 1796, solicitor based in Carmarthen. Died 1874.

GLOSSARY OF WELSH TERMS

Aber: river mouth, estuary
Aderyn y gorff: corpse bird, harbinger of death
Bach: "little one" (used as a term of endearment)
Bara brith: literally "speckled bread", traditional currant cake
Cariad: darling
Carn: heap of stones, rocky hill summit
Cawl: leek broth made with mutton, potatoes etc
Ceffyl Pren: wooden horse (used in folk traditions including mock trials)
Cnapan: old ball game, thought to be a forerunner of rugby football
Coed: wood or trees
Cwm: valley or hollow in the hillside
Diawl, Diawch: devil
Duw: God
Dyn hysbys: literally "knowing man", wise man or wizard
Ffynnon: spring or water source
Gambo: a flat two-wheeled cart with no sides
Gwylnos: wake night or vigil, before the funeral
Hen Galan: the Old New Year, January 12th
Hiraeth: longing or belonging, nostalgia. Refers to a special piece of land
Hwyl: fervour, passion, mood
Ingli: uncertain, but probably an old Welsh word meaning "angels"
Mam-gu: grandmother
Mari Lwyd: grotesque figure with a horse skull, used in folk traditions
Parrog: flat land along a shore or estuary (the name of Newport's seaside
     community)
Plas: big house or palace
Plygain: candle-lit Christmas service ending at dawn
Simnai fawr: big chimney, large open fireplace
Toili: phantom funeral, interpreted as an omen of a death to come
Tolaeth: a death omen, usually heard as the sound of coffin making
Ty unnos: "one night house". A hovel built on common land
Twmpath: jolly evening of song and dance (literally "tump")
Wrach: witch or hag (**y wrach** is the name given to the last tuft of corn cut
     during the harvest)

The Angel Mountain Saga

The Story so far........

In *On Angel Mountain* (Part One) eighteen-year-old Martha Morgan arrives at Plas Ingli, a small and vulnerable estate on the flank of Carningli (Angel Mountain) in North Pembrokeshire. The year is 1796. She is pregnant and suicidal, having just been forced into a shotgun wedding. She is saved from harming herself or her unborn child by Joseph Harries the Wizard, who later becomes her mentor and friend. Joseph realizes that Martha has special powers, and she is very frightened when she experiences a number of visions and premonitions. She loves her husband David, and as she settles into the Plas she also learns to love the house and its extended family. But then she loses her baby and suffers from deep depression, and her resolve is further tested when there is a short-lived invasion by the French in 1797. Martha is increasingly concerned by the activities of a strange and sinister manservant called Moses Lloyd, and she becomes convinced that he is intent upon the destruction of the estate. After a number of misdemeanours he is sent packing, but Martha knows that he is not far away. Three local squires become increasingly antagonistic towards her and the estate, and matters come to a head when one of them, Alban Watkins, claims that the estate is rightfully his. David and his grandfather Isaac have to rush off to London to fight this claim in court. While they are away, Martha, who is pregnant again, has to face a trumped-up charge of theft. She is found guilty, and whipped through the streets of Newport. Then she is incarcerated in Haverfordwest Gaol. At last she manages to obtain her release through the good offices of Lord Cawdor. She returns home and receives a message to the effect that the court case is won, and that the estate is safe. Two of the villains are sentenced to transportation, and the other commits suicide. Martha needs space and peace in order to recover from her ordeal. She goes up to her secret cave on the mountain, and is captured by Moses Lloyd, who knew that she would eventually come. He is intent upon raping Martha and then killing her, but in a frantic struggle she kills him. She disposes of his body in a deep crevice and crawls home, more dead than alive.

In *House of Angels* (Part Two) Martha learns much about the brutality of the world, and about the devastating effect that her beauty has on the men with whom she comes in contact. She also learns a good deal about her own strength in the face of adversity. In the year 1805, her husband David is killed in the annual *cnapan* contest on Newport Sands, leaving her with three young children to bring up alone. She is also pregnant. She is helped through the crisis by her servants and friends, and her fourth child is born. Joseph is convinced that David's death was not an accident, and his investigations lead him to the conclusion that four men – Matthew Lloyd, Joseph Rice, John Howell and Ifan Beynon -- are guilty of murder. The four villains, together with two strange Londoners and a squire's son named John Fenton, are intent upon the destruction of the estate because they are convinced that there is treasure hidden on Plas Ingli land. Indeed there is, but only Martha knows where it is. As the story proceeds, Martha falls in love with Owain, the younger son of a local squire, and their love affair is anything but smooth. Alban Watkins, the dastardly squire who claimed the estate in 1797, suddenly returns from the colonies, also intent upon finding the Plas Ingli treasure. Martha orchestrates a treasure hunt, which results in the capture of all of the villains. In the court cases that follow, David's murderers are all sentenced to hang, and the other treasure hunters to transportation. But two of the villains manage to escape. One of them, Alban Watkins, is murdered by an Irishman in revenge for atrocities committed in the penal colonies. The other, John Fenton, abducts little Sara, and entices Martha to a lonely cottage where she hopes to obtain her daughter's release. Fenton has always lusted after Martha, and he attempts to rape her; but Owain intervenes in the nick of time, and following a ferocious struggle Fenton escapes, only to be sucked to his death in a nearby bog.

In *Dark Angel* (Part Three) the story starts in 1807 with Martha and Owain deeply in love, and engaged to be married. Martha has premonitions of dark and tragic events to come, and her unease is increased by sightings of a mysterious figure in black on the mountain. He appears to be watching her, and when others see the figure as well he is given the name of "The Nightwalker." Martha is uncertain whether he is a man, or a ghost, or the Devil himself. She becomes quite paranoid, but her attention is diverted when a small baby is left on the front doorstep of the Plas. Martha names the child Brynach, and arranges to adopt him. Plans are made for the wedding, but then Owain goes out on a fishing trip and disappears without trace. Joseph investigates, and deduces that a squire called George Price has arranged for the sabotage of Owain's boat. Again Martha becomes depressed and paranoid, and very possessive about the baby. She gets some straight talking from her nearest and dearest. Over the years that follow the Nightwalker appears over and again, and Martha suspects that Joseph Harries the wizard, and even her servants, know more about the creature than she does. Her daughter Daisy goes off to London and breaks off all contact with the family, and her son Dewi is drowned at sea. In 1822, under pressure from family and friends, Martha agrees to marry again. Squire Ceredig ap Tomos proposes, and she accepts. On the night of the wedding Owain returns from the dead, and Martha has no option but to choose him over Ceredig. She is horrified when the man she has rejected commits suicide. Owain is also ill, having experienced appalling hardship in North Africa and Spain, and she tries to nurse him back to good health. Exhausted by all this emotional turmoil, Martha goes to her cave for silence and contemplation, but comes face to face with the Nightwalker. He is terribly disfigured and injured as a result of an accident in the Napoleonic Wars, and he proves to be Iestyn Price, the son of Squire Price and the father of the child left on the doorstep of the Plas fifteen years earlier. Iestyn is reconciled with his father, but he dies within a few days of his encounter with Martha, and is buried secretly in his father's walled garden.

In *Rebecca and the Angels* (Part Four) Martha is a mature and confident woman in charge of her own destiny. The story covers the years 1832-1844. She recounts the loss of Owain and Joseph, and finally the death of her daughter Sara. She becomes increasingly aware of political issues, and decides to fight for social justice in order to make her mark on history. She is dragged into the controversy involving the corrupt turnpike trusts in West Wales, and at first tries to mediate between the labourers and the squires in order to minimise the suffering associated with unjust tollgate charges. But she gets nowhere. Hardship increases, and the Rebecca Riots commence. Men with blackened faces and dressed in female garb ride out and smash down tollgates all over West Wales. Martha becomes more and more involved behind the scenes, and eventually finds a role as one of those orchestrating events. As the turnpike trusts and the authorities seek to enforce law and order, the Army is called in, and Martha starts to cooperate with solicitor Hugh Williams in her attempts to keep one step ahead. She also develops an unlikely friendship with Tom Foster, a reporter from the *Times* newspaper. Spies begin to operate in the area, and some of the rioters are arrested as a result of information provided by a traitor. He is identified and hunted down. Martha is suspected by the authorities of involvement in the riots, and a complex game of cat and mouse develops. With matters building towards a climax, Martha makes a foolhardy gesture and takes part in a raid on the Boncath tollgate. She is lucky to escape relatively unscathed, and thinks that it is time to retire from any further involvement with the rioters. But in a final terrifying twist to the story a gang of criminals moves into the area and Martha has to confront its leaders in the kitchen of the Plas. She saves her female servants from rape and kills two of the thugs. She fears that she will be charged with murder, but is deemed by the magistrates to have acted in self-defence. Finally, her long-lost daughter Daisy returns from London, and with her assistance a new Act of Parliament is passed which addresses all of the abuses associated with the turnpike trusts.

ΩΩΩΩΩΩΩΩΩΩΩ

Note

All of the stories in this saga are told by Martha herself, in her own diaries which are written in the archaic Welsh Dimetian dialect. This dialect was once spoken widely in parts of North Pembrokeshire, but has now entirely died out.

The Death and Life of Mr Jenkins

Western Telegraph, 9th March 2005
Obituary

MR ABRAHAM JENKINS
NEWPORT

The death occurred on 27th February 2005 of Mr Abraham Jenkins of Waun Isaf, Cilgwyn, Newport, Pembrokeshire, after a short illness. He was 85 years old.

Mr Jenkins was a native of Cilgwyn, and he was born -- and died -- in the cottage on the flank of Carningli which had been in his family for many generations. He lost both of his parents before he was five years old, and spent most of his childhood in the home of an aunt in Cwm Gwaun. He was an outstanding pupil at Newport CP School, and from there he obtained a scholarship to Haverfordwest Grammar School. He displayed natural ability as a sportsman, but his greatest talent emerged in his studies of language and in his compositions in Welsh, which brought him success at an early age in *eisteddfodau* all over Wales. At the age of eighteen he won the bardic crown at the Wrexham National Eisteddfod of 1938. He won a scholarship to Jesus College Oxford, but was prevented from taking it up by the advent of the Second World War. As a young man who held strong pacifist beliefs, he refused to bear arms and was for a time imprisoned; but he later agreed to place his formidable intellect at the disposal of his country and spent the rest of the war working at Bletchley Park on secret translating and decoding work.

Mr Jenkins never married, but after the war he pursued a teaching career which took him to various parts of Wales and eventually back to Newport. He was a feisty defender of the Welsh language, and this occasionally brought him into conflict with the law. He also remained active in the field of Welsh literature, and he won the coveted bardic chair at the National Eisteddfod of 1973. In 1980 he became a member of the Gorsedd of Bards, with the bardic name "Ingli". Then he inherited the very cottage in which he had been born, and gave up his teaching career to run a smallholding of twelve acres. In recent years he was a respected member of Newport Town Council, and he served on three occasions as Mayor. Up to the time of his death he remained alert and

The Death and Life of Mr Jenkins

active, and in 1998 his linguistic skill, and his detailed knowledge of the Dimetian Welsh dialect, were brought to bear in the translation of the extraordinary diaries of Mistress Martha Morgan of Plas Ingli. It gave him particular pleasure, a few years ago, to be appointed Official Translator to the National Library of Wales, and with his death the world has lost the last fluent Dimetian Welsh speaker.

Left to mourn are cousins William and John, nephews Harry, Matthew and Nicholas, and nieces Eleanor, Rebekah, Sally and Martha. Mr Jenkins will also be sorely missed by a multitude of friends from all over the world.

The funeral will take place at 2 pm on Friday 11th March 2005 at Caersalem, Cilgwyn, followed by interment in the adjacent churchyard.

❀❀❀❀❀❀❀❀❀❀❀❀❀

1. The Death and Life of Mr Jenkins

When I found him Abraham had been dead for maybe twelve hours. I had been pulled to Waun Isaf by the pitiful whining of Megs, his old border collie, as I walked along the Cilgwyn Road on a bright and frosty February afternoon. I knew that he was dead even before I reached the cottage. I opened the front door, which was never locked, to be greeted by the dog. He was in his kitchen, still sitting in his favourite chair, slumped over the edge of the table with his head resting easily on a neat pile of paper. His arms were stretched in front of him on the table top, with the palms of his hands flat on the scrubbed pinewood surface. To my unpractised eye, he looked relaxed, as if he was fast asleep. Later on, when Doctor Tom had examined him and satisfied himself that he had died from natural causes, we removed him from his chair and tried to lay him out on his bed, which was not easy since he had been effectively doubled up when he died and since *rigor mortis* had now well and truly set in. As we struggled to take off his boots, to unbend him at the waist and to lower his arms, I imagined him enjoying the joke and grinning down at us, old devil that he was, from his newly-acquired place in Heaven.

Doctor Tom left when he had satisfied himself as to the time and cause of death, and I stayed on in the cottage until Jones Bones' fellows came to take away the body. I fed the dog and tried to comfort her, and then I went through Abraham's notebook of telephone numbers and rang up all those whom I thought might be relatives. There were some who had the surname Jenkins, and I rang them first to tell them the sad news; and after an hour or so I was content that I had reached at least some of those who might have an interest in the old man's affairs and who might take responsibility for organizing a funeral. His nephew James, who ran his own business in Cardiff, immediately offered to drop everything and to travel down to Waun Isaf, to liaise with Jones Bones and with the Caersalem pastor, and to ensure that all other relatives were informed.

There was not much more I could do while I waited for the hearse to arrive, so I turned my attention to the kitchen table. Intuition told me that Abraham had finished his task, and that he had been fast asleep when he was struck down by heart failure around 2 am. The fountain pen which

The Death and Life of Mr Jenkins

he had insisted on using in these days of fibre-tips, ball-points and laptops had its cap screwed tightly on, and lay close to where his right hand had been. The pile of paper on which his head had been resting was tied up with crossed strings. On the front he had scribbled the words "For Brian -- Martha's Last Testament." I flicked quickly through the pages and found that there were over 700 of them, filled with Abraham's dense handwriting and with many crossings-out, arrows, revisions and insertions. Then I noticed that the three bound diaries that he had translated were also on the table, alongside various Welsh dictionaries and reference books, and Meredith Morris's familiar 1910 *Glossary of the Dimetian Dialect.* I concluded that when he died Abraham had been contented and possibly even happy, having lived a rich and rewarding life for 85 years, having completed the fifth and final volume of Mistress Martha's diaries, and having made one last colourful contribution to the literature of Wales. Also I realized that the last thing he saw, before laying his head down on the pile of paper which I now held in my hands, was the landscape through his kitchen window -- Carningli dusted with frost crystals, illuminated by the white light of a high February moon, and silhouetted against a glittering starlit sky. It had been a calm and beautiful winter's night; not a bad night, I thought, for an old man to leave the place which he loved with a passion which I would never fully comprehend.

Then I had a further thought. Abraham had died early in the morning on the 27th day of February 2005 -- one hundred and fifty years to the day (to the hour?) after the death of Mistress Martha Morgan. The date of her death is inscribed on her memorial stone in Cilgwyn Churchyard, and I can remember with perfect clarity the excitement with which Ben Phillips and I discovered it some years ago, at the beginning of this adventure.

A strange coincidence of dates? Knowing both Abraham Jenkins and Martha Morgan, I doubted it.

They came to take Abraham's body away just before teatime, and when they carried him out of the house poor Megs needed more consolation. I could not leave her alone in the empty cottage, and in any case I needed to walk on the mountain and to try and come to terms with the loss of a very dear friend. So Megs and I climbed up across the rocky slopes of the common, brushing our way through brittle and broken bracken stalks and

The Death and Life of Mr Jenkins

gorse bushes glowing gold with winter blossom, until Waun Isaf was far away and far below. I was fitter than Megs, and I had to stop frequently to wait for her; but in spite of her arthritic joints ground out during twelve years of honest toil, she battled on gamely until at last we reached the lichen-encrusted rocks of the summit. She lay down panting on the grassy patch beloved by summit campers and summer picnickers, while I sat on a boulder and scanned the wide horizon. There was not a breath of wind, and although the temperature was not much above freezing I could feel a gentle warmth in the sun's rays. So Abraham Jenkins was gone -- that kind and gentle man with a wicked wit and a fierce intellect; that funny old bachelor with the blue eyes and weatherbeaten face and wispy white hair; that fellow who was said by the locals -- and who am I to disagree? -- to have had "special powers"; that pacifist who is said to have attacked reservoirs in mid-Wales in his fight to save Welsh water and the Welsh language, and who is reputed to have been in jail no fewer than five times; that bookish bard who wrote poems and translated strange diaries into Welsh and then into English.............

And that brought in to my mind the strange relationship between Abraham and Mistress Martha Morgan. I recalled that I had asked Abraham once, some years ago, why he had never married, and that he had told me without a hint of embarrassment or evasion that he had been passionately in love with a young woman during his time in Bletchley during the War. She had been a fluent Greek speaker, and had been sent by British Intelligence into the chaotic conflict of 1944 in the Balkans, to help with the coding and decoding of partisan messages. She had never been heard of again. "At the end of the War I hunted through all the records I could find, and even went to Greece and Italy to see if I could find out what had happened to her," Abraham had said, with a break in his voice and with tears welling up in his eyes. "Nobody had met her or even heard of her. No trace of her. No trace of her........" After that, having suffered so much pain, he vowed never to fall in love again, and to turn his attentions to the great causes of his homeland -- home rule for Wales, Welsh ownership of Welsh resources, and the rescue of his precious language from the onslaught of English. But I realized now that in his twilight years he had truly fallen in love with Mistress Martha, and that having completed his task of translating all five of her diaries he had concluded that his contact with her was at an end. Had he not said to me,

The Death and Life of Mr Jenkins

a fortnight before his death, that the last seven years -- spent in the interesting and passionate company of the long-lost Mistress of Plas Ingli -- had been the happiest and most fulfilled years of his life? And had he not said, several times over, that he really did not know what he would do with himself after the completion of this last translation? I had laughed with him, and had told him to take up a new career as a brain surgeon, and had failed to appreciate that as an old man he had looked into the future and had seen a life of empty horizons and grey skies and parched earth. He had not committed suicide -- of that I was sure. But I became convinced that in the quietest hour of the night he had simply let go of life in the manner of Papet in Pagnol's novel *Manon des Sources*.

Was it not more than a little weird or even perverted, I thought, for an old man to fall in love with a woman who had died in 1855 and who had left nothing but words -- and one small painting -- behind her? But then I remembered that Mistress Martha had in fact left behind a great deal more. The old buildings of the Plas, for a start. They were more ruinous now than they were seven years ago, but they were created by her husband David until the time of his death, and thereafter by Martha herself. She was the one who caused the old stone walls on the side of the mountain to be maintained and new ones to be built; she was the one who instructed her servants and labourers in the digging of drainage channels and the clearing of trackways. She planted the white lilac tree near the wall of the ruined garden. Some of the peat pits on the high common are hers, as are six or seven of the little cottages around the fringes of the Plas Ingli estate which housed poor people in 1840 and which are now deliciously-appointed holiday homes worth more than a quarter of a million pounds each. Fragments of the clothes that she wore and of household items that she made or handled must surely still be contained within the Plas Ingli rubbish dump. She built the cottage at Werndew for Shemi Jenkins the Wizard, one of Abraham's ancestors. The little quarries on the mountain are hers, and it would not be too fanciful to imagine that many of the footpaths that criss-cross the mountain were made by her during almost sixty years of walking and exploring. Many of the old blue rocks were anointed by her perspiration and her blood. Through her offspring and her friends she helped to fashion the landscapes of Brithdir, Llanychaer, Parrog and Cilgwyn, and some of the stones in the Old College in Newport were put there with the aid of her money. The rotting hulk on

The Death and Life of Mr Jenkins

the estuary is reputed to be that of the *Mary Jane,* of which she was part owner in 1844. She travelled in one of its cabins, and walked its decks. The old tenant farms of Dolrannog Uchaf and Dolrannog Isaf, Gelli and Penrhiw must still carry her footprints in their fields, and her laughter must still echo around all of the farmyards of the neighbourhood. Do echoes and footprints really disappear, or do they simply fade away slowly to the point where they are beyond our hearing and seeing?

Abraham certainly knew Martha in a way that no other person could possibly know her. He handled almost all of the thousands of pages of hand-written manuscript on which she laboured during a lifetime of diary-writing. He said to me once that he could still smell traces of her lavender water on some of the pages, and he also said that he could see where tears had smudged the ink and where she had occasionally spilt wine or dropped bits of food onto the paper. Some pages were stained with perspiration, and on others there were drops of something that Abraham presumed to be blood. He claimed that he could interpret her moods from her handwriting alone, with large lettering and deep impressions when she was angry or agitated, small and careful lettering when she was pensive or puzzled, and a confident and flowing style when all was well with the world. I had not appreciated until now that the great majority of the pages of Martha's diary had not been seen, let alone read and translated, by anybody until Abraham had opened them on the table in front of him and allowed his eyes to pass from word to word and line to line. I see now that for him, it must have been both a physical experience and an almost mystical one, creating an intimate relationship between a lonely old man and a long-lost woman. For him, it might even have been a passionate relationship. However he experienced it, it must have been quite different from the bond that exists between the writer and the reader of a printed book, for no other reason than that the reader of a book might well be one of a thousand or a million other readers. If a multitude can be aroused or irritated, or moved to laughter or tears, by the words set down before them, how much more intense must be the relationship between the secret writer and the first translator of a hand-written and ancient diary? And how much of Martha's soul did Abraham really lay bare through the words of his translation? He was the last native speaker of Dimetian Welsh, and no matter what scrutiny may in future be brought to bear on Martha's original hand-written texts, nobody will ever again have the

The Death and Life of Mr Jenkins

same subtle appreciation of nuance, and light and shadow, and word selection and sentence construction, as Abraham Jenkins of Waun Isaf. Maybe Abraham heard Martha's voice and saw her face and shared her deepest emotions as he read her words; and maybe, in passing on his translations to me and the rest of the world, he used words intended for public consumption, kept most of her secrets to himself in life, and will now take them into his grave. May God bless him, and may he now be together with his Martha.

I must explain how the three volumes of this latest diary came into my possession and at last ended up on Abraham's kitchen table. The hunt for them started about eight months ago, when Abraham told me that he had recently been unwell, and that after tests in the hospital in Haverfordwest he had been told that it was a wonder he was still alive. "A congenital heart deformity," he said. "Mr Khan told me that I should have died as a child and that I could have dropped dead through heart failure at any time during my life. So here I am, my friend, hale if not hearty, confronted by the prospect of imminent death."

"Oh, Abraham, I am so sorry to hear that.........."

"Misery is not an option," he said, with a wry smile on his face. "I have clocked up eighty-five years, which is not bad for somebody who should never have crept out of the cradle in the first place. So I have enjoyed something of a bonus already on this good earth. Mister Khan told me that he could not operate, since at my age the trauma involved would certainly kill me. But he gave me six different sorts of tablets, which I have to take regularly. Probably one of them works, and the other five counteract each other's side effects. But if they keep me going for a bit longer, I will not complain."

"I admire your courage and your equanimity, Abraham. If I had just received such news, I am not sure that I would be smiling."

"Life itself is something to be grateful for, my dear fellow, especially if it is lived in a place such as this. And I have truly enjoyed six or seven blessed years in the company of the Mistress of Plas Ingli."

"Enjoyed? I think I would put it higher than that, Abraham. You have been a man refreshed and rejuvenated, if I may say so. Her company has done you a world of good."

He laughed and slapped his knees , but then his grin faded away and was replaced on the craggy landscape of his face by a look of infinite

The Death and Life of Mr Jenkins

sadness. I reacted straight away. "But? But? What more do you wish to say, Abraham?"

There was a long pause as he turned his face away from me and gazed through the kitchen window towards the south-eastern slope of the mountain. When he looked at me again I saw that his eyes were glazed with tears. I put my hand on his arm and waited for him to speak.

"There is another diary out there somewhere, my friend. You know that, don't you?"

"How can you be so sure, Abraham? Last time we had to hunt as far afield as Australia for the text of *Rebecca and the Angels*, and had to depend upon pure luck in order to find it."

"I learnt a long time ago that one makes one's own luck. Or maybe Martha makes it for us! She was sixty-five years old when she finished that last diary in 1844. She was still as bright as a button and still aware of the joys of sex. She did not die until she was seventy-six -- and I cannot imagine that an inveterate diary keeper such as she would have left her pen lying idle on her desk for the last decade of her life."

"I cannot disagree with you on that, and you know her better than I do. And you feel that you have more work to do before............"

"Correct. Before I go to my Maker. But if we do find further volumes of her diary, and if I do find the strength and enjoy the good fortune to translate them for the world, I think that I shall die a happy man."

So Abraham Jenkins, an old man stalked by the Grim Reaper, convinced me that it was my duty, as a personal friend and as a student of the human condition, to engage in a new hunt for papers or bound volumes written in the hand of Martha Morgan. But where on earth should we start? Had we not already explored every avenue, opened ourselves to every intuition, and pleaded for every intervention from the spirits of the mountain in previous hunts? Should we not be satisfied that four volumes had already come into our hands from a tin box in the Plas Ingli attic, next from the library of Plas Pontfaen, then from the National Library in Aberystwyth, and finally from the suburbs of Melbourne on the other side of the world? Every diary had been found further away from Cilgwyn than the last; was there **anywhere** on Planet Earth further away from the centre of attention than Melbourne?

I articulated this concern to Abraham when we met up a few days later, over a cup of herbal tea, for a morning thinking session. When he

The Death and Life of Mr Jenkins

had stopped cursing Mr Khan for telling him to give up coffee, he had one of his sudden inspirations, and his scowls and frowns disappeared. "Yes indeed!" he chortled. "I think I see what is going on. Now then, think about it, my friend. Distance is not what this is all about. Think about our previous discoveries another way. Come along now -- prove to me that you are not as stupid as you look!"

I refrained from assaulting him, for fear of bringing on heart failure and being arrested for murder, but I could not for the life of me work out what he was on about. At last I had to give in. "All right, Abraham, you old scumbag. I bow to your superior intellect. Tell me all."

After enjoying the moment for longer than I thought polite, Abraham delivered his interpretation of the latest -- and last -- of Martha Morgan's little games. "It is blindingly obvious, my dear Watson. The first diary was in a box just up the road, in the attic of the Plas. That was her home, but also the home of her husband and her adopted family. The second diary was found in the home of Owain Laugharne, her lover. The third was found (before its removal to Aberystwyth) at Plas Llanychaer, the home of her son Brynach and her grandchildren. The fourth resided for maybe thirty years (before it was bundled up with other family possessions for shipment to Australia) in the home of Tom Foster, who was clearly a very dear friend. So where is the mysterious fifth volume likely to be?"

No matter how much I wrinkled my brow and hunched my shoulders and gazed into Abraham's mischievous eyes, I could not work out where his mind was going. I shook my head in resignation and defeat, and he roared with laughter. "Compared with the cracking of the Enigma code, this is a doddle," he said, looking very smug. "Husband, lover, son, and friend. David, Owain, Brynach, and Tom. Each one of them loyal, brave and selfless, and each one deserving of a special place in Martha's heart. But is there nobody else, my dear fellow, who deserved her special thanks through a lifetime of joy and tragedy? Who saved Martha from herself on more occasions than she -- or we --dared to count? Whose shoulder did Martha weep upon when the men in her life went, one after another, to premature graves? With whom did Martha share life-threatening moments? Who laughed with Martha when times were good, who giggled with her and played foolish pranks with her like a silly little girl? And who knew Martha better, and over many more years, than any husband,

The Death and Life of Mr Jenkins

lover, son or friend? Come along now!"

"Her daughter Betsi?"

"No, no. Betsi was greatly loved, and certainly knew her mother very well. But remember that she married in 1818 and thereafter had her own life to lead, mostly away from the Plas."

At last the penny dropped. "You can't mean Bessie, her beloved handmaiden?"

"Of course! Who else? We know that Bessie was at Martha's side from the day that she arrived at Plas Ingli as a frightened and pregnant teenager in 1796. They grew up together, and although her mistress kept secrets from her, there can have been nobody who knew her better. She was still at Martha's side in 1844, at the end of the Rebecca Riots, and was apparently still in good health in spite of the traumas that they experienced together. When last we heard of her, she was still in service, as housekeeper. If Bessie was still alive when Martha died, I would not mind betting that she was the one to whom the last diary was entrusted. If you have a better idea, I would be pleased to hear about it."

I admitted defeat, and slapped the old rogue on the back, and then we set about discovering the whereabouts of Bessie Walter's personal history and personal possessions. We knew relatively little about Bessie. She had been born Bessie Gruffydd in 1776, probably in Nevern, for that was where her father Robert lived when Martha was newly arrived at the Plas. Perhaps her mother died young. She started at the Plas as a housemaid or a dairymaid in 1795, before the tragic fire that burned down the old house and consumed the bodies of five members of the Morgan family. She left to marry a merchant called Benji Walter in 1799, and had a small son, but suffered a double tragedy in 1802 when they both died. Thereafter Martha encouraged her to return to the Plas as her personal maid, and she continued in that role until she took over as housekeeper on the retirement of the formidable Blodwen Owen in 1812. After that, Martha and Bessie grew old together, as comfortable in each other's company as a pair of twins, with occasional squabbles and disagreements, and periodic misunderstandings and episodes of mistrust, but in general providing for each other a wonderful mutual support and affection. So far as we knew, she had no brothers or sisters, and the only relative to have been mentioned in Martha's chronicles was a female cousin who worked at Cilgwyn Mawr in 1806.

The Death and Life of Mr Jenkins

So what had happened to Bessie after 1844? Of course, she might have died before her mistress, but we decided to work on the assumption that she had lived to a ripe old age. At the time of Martha's death she would have been around 79 years old -- a good age for a servant in an era of hard labour and inadequate medical care. If the Plas had remained in the Morgan family, maybe the new master of the estate would have kept her on, or at least provided for her, as a reward for long and faithful service, through the provision of a cottage. But if the estate had been sold or incorporated in some other, Bessie might have been treated as a disposable item -- in which case she might have ended her days almost anywhere in the Newport area.

Together, Abraham and I could do little more from his cottage under the shadow of Carningli, so I took my leave and promised that I would dig into any records that I could find. I treated this task with some urgency, since I was aware that Abraham was a sick man and that his days were numbered. I would find more volumes for him, as a sign of my affection for a good kind gentleman. But I would also find them for myself, for if truth be told I was caught up in the chase again, and adrenalin was coursing through my veins. For the fifth time in as many years, Mistress Martha was out there somewhere, floating unseen among the blue rocks of the mountain, with an enigmatic smile on her face, beckoning me to join her in some secret place.

But where should I start? My first instinct was to immerse myself in the worldwide web, and so I returned home and gobbled down a quick lunch. Then I switched on the computer, and hunted through the information held by the Public Records Office, through Census data, through Family History and Ancestry sites, and through people searches. But the most detailed information I could find for the inhabitants of the Newport area related to the 1871 Census, and when I hunted through the returns I could find no record of a Bessie Walter. I assumed that by 1871 Martha's beloved handmaiden must have been dead and buried. The data for the 1861 census was much more patchy and difficult to get at, and I spent more than £50 looking at assorted pages which gave me nothing. I hunted for her by entering in her supposed address -- Plas Ingli, Newport -- but to no avail. I filled in as many details as I had about her, on people searches and advanced people searches, and on place searches and occupation searches. No luck. So she was probably dead by 1861. I turned

The Death and Life of Mr Jenkins

to the 1851 Census, and there I found her, in the right place at the right time, on the record for Plas Ingli. Her real name was Elizabeth. Up she came on the screen: Elizabeth Maria Walter, nee Gruffydd, age 75, domestic servant, single (widow), born Glasfryn, Nevern.

Invigorated by this success, I found that in front of me on the screen were the records for all the other residents of Plas Ingli as at the date of the 1851 Census. I found Martha Susanna Morgan (my first encounter with her middle name), nee Howell, age 73, single (widow), farmer, head of the household, born Brawdy. And there were others too. Three of them were Owens. Will, her head man, was there, shown as single (widower). Then there was Gerallt Owen, aged 27, and Myfanwy Owen, aged 21. They were both single and were both shown as servants, and since they were not man and wife I assumed that they must have been Will's children and the grandchildren of her crusty old housekeeper. There was no sign of Daisy Morgan, Martha's prodigal daughter, on the census return, leading me to conclude that she might have moved back to the familiar streets of London following her spectacular return to the Plas in 1844. Then again, maybe she had married, and moved on, or even died in the preceding six or seven years. Finally there was another resident at the Plas in 1851: Amos George Christmas Jones, aged 66, single (widower), pastor, lodger, born Pontypridd, Monmouthshire. A minister of religion under the roof of Plas Ingli! And from faraway Pontypridd! I could hardly believe it, given Martha's somewhat ambivalent attitude towards the Church and all things religious. What on earth could have been their relationship? Could he have been a distant relative, simply passing through at the time of the Census? I knew that in 1851 the countryside of West Wales was being set alight by the fervour of a great religious revival, in which harsh self-discipline and respect for the teachings of the Old Testament were virtues valued more highly than kindness and humility. Maybe the reverend gentleman was an itinerant evangelist? If he really was in residence in 1851, what risks had Martha run, as a widow in a big house with a widower more than ten years younger than herself, installed as a lodger? I could imagine the wagging tongues and the rolling eyes and the whispered innuendoes in the pews of Caersalem and Ebenezer and Bethlehem..............

But Martha was not my immediate concern, and neither was her lodger or her reputation. No doubt discoveries about the Reverend Amos

The Death and Life of Mr Jenkins

Jones might follow in due course, but first I had to find a diary. Tired of gazing at a square screen and hitting keys with my index fingers, I took an afternoon walk on the mountain. It was high summer, in the month of July which in Martha's time would have marked a lull between the hard labour of the hay harvest and the even harder labour of the corn harvest. Now, with virtually no corn being grown in the Newport area and with the hay harvest but a distant memory, the sounds that echoed around the *cwm* as I climbed were those of heavy traffic on the main road to the east of the town, and half a dozen tractors, some nearby and others far away, involved in the cutting and carting of the second silage crop of the season. Passenger jets whispered high overhead, outward bound for New York or inward bound for Heathrow, leaving a tracery of wind-blasted vapour trails and an invisible cloud of combustion products directly above the sacred summit of Carningli. Sacrilege, I thought, but then I realized that the sky was still as blue as it had been in Martha's day, and that the skylark chorus was still in fine form, and that there were still lizards scuttling among the warm blue rocks and grey wagtails hunting for flying ants. There were still sheep and ponies on the common, and the rough patchwork quilt of stony fields and boulder trails and gorse and sphagnum and bracken was probably not that different from that observed by Martha on her frequent expeditions to her secret cave. As I climbed the sun beat down on me and I had to remove my sweatshirt. I went off the track and scrambled across the rocks, seeking the most direct route to the summit. An old dog fox started up from a swathe of tall bracken just a few feet in front of me, and ambled off across the bouldery slope in a state of high dudgeon. I apologised for disturbing his siesta, and continued to climb.

I was the only person on the mountain, and once on the summit I removed my rucksack, poured myself a cup of tea from my vacuum flask, and settled down to think. Downing the contents of my cup, I then drank in the beauty of a landscape that I knew as well as my right hand -- scanning through three hundred and sixty degrees, from the stubby fingers of Pencaer, Pen Dinas and Pen Morfa thrust into the blue expanse of Cardigan Bay, thence across the rolling wooded lands of the Nevern Valley to the crags of Carnedd Meibion Owen and the distant summits of Mynydd Preseli, and round again to Mynydd Morfil and the hazy outline of Ramsey Island, almost thirty miles away on the edge of a vast ocean. This was my land, I thought, as it was once Martha's land. I closed my eyes and tried to

The Death and Life of Mr Jenkins

think of Bessie rather than Martha, having quite convinced myself that one good woman would lead me to another.

I knew that I was not alone, and when I opened my eyes there was the old black raven, perched not on her favourite crag but on a tilted slab of rock maybe twenty feet in front of me. She was as beautiful as ever, in spite of her great age. She was quite unafraid, and even nonchalant in her behaviour. She preened her anthracite-black feathers for maybe ten minutes, pausing occasionally to survey her domain. The landscape of wild moorland and rocky outcrops on the south side of the mountain was hers, as indeed was the lower land of fields, farms and copses. Every day she soared across this landscape, sometimes so high up that she was virtually invisible from my house, and sometimes down at treetop level. If buzzards or kites or kestrels appeared in her air space she might send them packing, or if she was in a benevolent frame of mind, she might tolerate them and allow them to stay for a while. They might, after all, spot some carrion that she had missed. Now and then she might take a mate and raise a brood. Now and then she might be alone, as she was today. Strange, I thought, that a big black bird could rule a territory quite so comprehensively, and yet in a relatively quiet and undemonstrative way; she hardly ever seemed to become agitated, and she hardly ever made a sound. Occasionally I would hear the dark raucous call of a raven on the mountain, but were those calls coming from her, or from one of the younger birds? Was she indeed REAL, or simply something created inside my own mind, and invisible to all but me?

Before I could get too involved in my speculations on the nature of reality, she looked me in the eye and launched herself into the air. I expected her to catch a thermal and to soar high above the mountain as I had seen her do a hundred times before, but no -- today she flew north at considerable speed, heading away from her own territory and onto that of the raven pair who owned the estuary and the Newport cliffs. That was a risky thing for her to do. I thought she was heading for the castle and the town, but then I realized that her destination was the Parrog. At last I lost sight of her as she flew low against the backdrop of buildings and trees. Was she trying to tell me something?

Was this old black raven trying to tell me that the last of Mistress Martha's diaries was located somewhere on the Parrog? But that was absurd -- how could she have known that I was thinking about a diary, of

The Death and Life of Mr Jenkins

all things, as I sat on the summit in the sun with my eyes closed? I might as well have been dreaming of Wales winning the rugby Grand Slam, or sex, or planting potatoes. But then I had to suspend my disbelief, since that old black raven had given me signs before, and they had always been eerily significant. So I focussed on the Parrog, the old trading and fishing port at the mouth of the estuary, now well and truly silted up but once a hive of activity with boat-builders, merchants, seamen, lime burners, fishermen and fishwives rushing about in the process of earning their honest and dishonest livings, not to mention vagrants, drunkards and prostitutes............. Prostitutes! Suddenly it came to me that there had to be a link with Patty Nicholas, ex-prostitute and later fisherman's wife, who had been a dear friend to not only Martha but Bessie. She had saved Martha from her enemies more than once, and in partial repayment of her debt the Mistress of Plas Ingli had managed to organize a church wedding for her and her devoted Jake. I knew from Martha's previous writings that the marriage had been a happy one, and that Jake had prospered as a fisherman and later as a shipowner and merchant. I also knew that they had had three or four children, although I could not for the life of me remember their names.

More research was needed, so I got up and thanked the old black raven in her absence for her latest blessing. Then I scrambled back down the mountain, slipping and falling several times in my haste. I trotted past Waun Isaf before reaching the road, and there was Abraham, leaning on his gate and eating an apple. "You are in a great haste, my dear fellow," he shouted. "If I were you, I should take it easy. No broken legs if you please, until you have got that diary for me!"

"Nothing more than a few bruises, Abraham," I shouted back. "Can't stop. It may not look like it, but I am on the trail. I'll talk to you tomorrow."

Back at home, I switched on the computer, entered my password, and dived straight into the 1851 Census returns. The members of the Nicholas family had clearly made a lot of money and had risen in the world. There they were, safely installed in Bettws Mawr, one of the larger houses on the Parrog sea-front: Jake Nicholas, head of household, merchant, age 71. Patty Nicholas, nee Ellis, no occupation shown, age 75. At the same address there were also two young servants whose names I did not recognize. The children had all left home, but I soon found them elsewhere

The Death and Life of Mr Jenkins

in the Newport returns -- Mary Williams, nee Nicholas, age 43, resident at Green House; Jack Nicholas, age 41, resident at 3 Springhill; Hubert Nicholas, age 38, resident at Ty Glas, East Street; and finally Amy Ifans, nee Nicholas, age 35, resident at Y Felin. As to occupations, Mary had none so was obviously a housewife or lady of leisure, Jack was a shipbuilder, Hubert was a groom, and Amy was a seamstress. There was nothing very unusual about all of that, but then I looked at the other entries for Green House, I found three children who were still at home in 1851 and found that Mary's husband was one George Williams, age 47, who made his living as an attorney.

A possible breakthrough at last. If there is one place in this world where one might find bundles of legal documents, buff folders piled on the floor, and cupboards bulging with box-files and bound volumes, it is the office of a family solicitor. Several years ago, when I had first started searching for the diaries of Mistress Martha Morgan, I had asked all the practising solicitors in the area whether they had any records relating to the Plas or to the Morgan family, and I had drawn a blank. But I had not thought of looking for **retired** solicitors. I hardly dared to hope, but I could not resist it. When my wife and I first came to Newport almost 30 years ago, I now recalled, there was still one practising solicitor in the town. The firm was called "Williams and Williams, established 1815." Nobody could ever remember there being more than one Williams, but before his retirement in 1990 the business was run by a strange fellow called Billy Williams, universally known as "Billy Thrice". The house was still there at the western end of town, looking very dilapidated and surrounded by a bramble jungle that must once have been a fine garden. The office sign could still be seen from the road, almost obliterated by ivy. I did not know whether Billy was alive or dead, so I rang up the Post Office to find out. "Oh yes," said Jackie Postmistress, as helpful as ever. "Alive he is, but only just. The social services go in to look after him four times a day, but he refuses to leave the house. They say it's like a pigsty in there. Bottles everywhere. He's more pickled than Mr Branston, and they say he has drunk his fortune away. Not that it matters, since there are no relatives......." She went on to tell me that the old house was now owned by a trust, and that as soon as Billy died it would be cleared of all the old papers and junk and converted into flats.

I thanked Jackie and decided that I had better get a move on while

The Death and Life of Mr Jenkins

the old fellow was still alive. But I needed to do one more check on the Census data. I turned back to the computer and called up the information from 1861. As I suspected -- no Martha Morgan, no Bessie Walter, no Jake Nicholas, and no Patty Nicholas. All of them had gone to their graves between 1851 and 1861, carrying their secrets with them. But maybe not **all** of their secrets.

I jumped straight into the car. As I drove into town I feared that I was chasing after a will o' the wisp. Was there even a one-in-a-million chance that Martha had entrusted her last diary to Bessie before she died, or that Bessie had found it and taken possession of it; that Bessie had moved to the Parrog for the last years of her life, and had possibly been given shelter by Patty and Jake; that on her death her estate, such as it was, had been looked after by Mary's husband; and that somewhere in a Dickensian solicitor's office in a ruinous Newport townhouse there was a file tied up with red ribbon with "Bessie Walter" written on its front cover? But the more I thought about it, the more I thought that the odds were shortening, and by the time I arrived at the front gate of Green House I was quite convinced that I was onto a winner.

My knock on the front door was answered by a bellow from somewhere deep within the house. I answered the invitation and stepped inside. It was dark and musty, and the passage was partly blocked by cardboard boxes full of empty bottles, waiting no doubt for somebody to come and take them to the bottle bank. "Come inside, come inside!" said a good strong voice, with just a hint of an alcoholic slur, from a room at the end of the corridor. "Early for a change!" I found the one open door, popped my head round the corner and gazed into the kitchen. There was Billy Thrice, settled in to a deep armchair, with a rug over his knees, surrounded by cats and bottles. He was a small thin man with a sallow complexion, sunken eyes and a few traces of white hair. He was obviously disappointed to see me, having expected Blodwen Rees. At six o'clock every day, he said, she came to make his hot supper and get him off to bed.

I apologized for disturbing his equilibrium and introduced myself. "Ah yes," he said, perking up. "You'll be that editor fellow who writes about Mistress Morgan Plas Ingli. Pleased to meet you I am. I imagine you'll be the sort of chap who is interested in everything. Interested in birds, are you?"

"Interested, but not very knowledgeable. I know some birds, but

The Death and Life of Mr Jenkins

would not call myself a twitcher."

"Funny thing, this afternoon, earlier on. This old crow....."

"Do you mean raven?"

"Could be. How should I know? Big it was, at any rate. And pitch black. Perched on my window-sill, it did, and stayed there for about ten minutes, bobbing its head up and down, and looking inside. It even tapped on the glass with its beak, to attract my attention. I thought I was imagining it. Never seen such a thing before."

"You did not feel frightened?"

"Good God no! It seemed to me to be a perfectly friendly sort of bird. Almost as if it was somebody's pet. If you find somebody who has lost a raven, please be so kind as to let him or her know it was in my garden."

I agreed that I would do that, and with my heart beating wildly I decided to broach the purpose of my visit, before he died from liver disease or before his supper arrived, whichever might be the sooner. "Mr Williams, I'm aware that your time is valuable, so I will come to the point of my visit........"

"You should have come before, sir," said he, making it increasingly apparent that his vocal chords had been well oiled by the contents of a half-empty whisky bottle perched on the edge of the kitchen table. "Yes indeed you should. On this Mistress Morgan business. Some years back, when that first book came out and before age started to get the better of me, I was on the point of asking you down to see if you would like to go through my office in your hunt for things to do with that Martha woman. Never did get round to it. But I had a hunt myself one day when the urge came over me, and found nothing. Obviously she and her family were never sensible enough to entrust their affairs to Williams and Williams, Family Solicitors of Repute. The Morganses always were sadly lacking in judgement. A small dram, perhaps?"

I declined, explaining that I would shortly be driving home. "Do you mind if I........?"

"You go ahead, Mr Williams," I said as he poured several drams into an ugly glass tumbler. I thought that if he wanted to kill himself that was his privilege, so long as he did not do it within the next thirty minutes. "I have indeed called about Mistress Morgan and her diaries. This morning I had a long talk with Abraham Jenkins........"

"Jenkins Waun Isaf?"

The Death and Life of Mr Jenkins

"Yes indeed. He lives just up the road from me. A dear friend, although I am sad to report that he is not in the best of health these days." There was a long silence from Billy Thrice, and I noticed that he was gripping his tumbler of whisky so hard that the whites of his knuckles were showing. I got to my feet and asked "Are you all right, Mr Williams?"

At last he said: "No, I am not all right. Can I tell you something in the strictest confidence?"

"Please go ahead. I promise that my lips are sealed."

"I have always paid my debts, sir. Strict motto of Williams and Williams, Family Solicitors of Repute. All debts cleared, and long since. Except one. It goes back a very long way. Jenkins Waun Isaf and I were at school together, and good friends too. Bosom pals, you might say. When we were about thirteen, I had one book which was my pride and joy. A beautiful edition of *Pilgrim's Progress*, with a calfskin cover embossed with gold. Given to me by my grandfather it was, as a reward for getting into the Grammar School. One day it disappeared without trace. Nobody knew where it had gone, and I never did find it in spite of appeals, and threats, and thunderings from the headmaster about morality and guilt and punishment, in front of the whole school. I was distraught, since that book was the only valuable thing that I owned. Then Abraham did a funny thing. He took me to one side and said: "Billy, do you want me to help?" I gave him a funny look, and I remember that I shrugged my shoulders and replied: "All right, Abe. But what can you do?" Then he gave me a little grin, and went and sat in the corner of the room. He closed his eyes and just sat there for about ten minutes, breathing deeply and not saying a word. Then he opened his eyes and said: "Frank Gibbon has got it. In his bedroom at Number Fifteen Hill Street. Under the bed, wrapped up in a green cotton table cloth." I remember that I stared at him with wide eyes, but he just grinned again and said I should go up to Frank's house and ask his mother if I could go into his bedroom to recover something that was rightfully mine. I did just that, and the book was there, exactly as Abe had predicted, wrapped in a green table cloth. Frank's mother went mad, and his father was even madder when he came home from work, and Frank had one hell of a hiding and never stole again."

"What a wonderful story of friendship, Mr Williams! I can see that you felt a sense of debt after that, but surely Abraham would have

32

The Death and Life of Mr Jenkins

received reward enough in the happiness of a friend?"

"Ah, that is where you are wrong, sir," said Billy, with tears welling up in his eyes. "You see, that was not the end of it. After the recovery of the book I did the most stupid thing I have ever done in my life. I do not know why I did it, and I have reproached myself ever since. Perhaps I was jealous of Abe, and perhaps I wanted to ingratiate myself with some of the older boys so as to become "one of the lads." At any rate, instead of keeping quiet, I went around whispering to all the other boys in the class that Abe was a witch, and that if they did not watch out I would get him to put a curse on them. One thing led to another, and after that they made his life into a living hell. I do not know how he survived the rest of his time in school, for thirteen-year-olds can be pretty brutal if one of their number speaks Welsh better than English, writes poetry in his spare time, and is said to be a witch. I betrayed him, and although I am sure he has forgiven me long ago, the guilt from that moment of madness still presses down upon me, to this day........"

He looked embarrassed, put his glass down onto the table, and wiped his eyes. I did not know what to say or where to look, but then I had a rare moment of clarity. "I think I understand your feelings, Mr Williams. In your position, I am sure I would feel the same. But perhaps there is something you could do to repay your debt to Abraham, and at the same time make a good many other people happy."

"Oh yes?"

"Abraham and I are looking for the final diaries written by Mistress Martha of Plas Ingli. As I mentioned before, he is not too well, and he is the same age as you. I think it would be a wonderful thing for him to devote his time to a final translation from that old Welsh dialect while he is still fit enough to do it."

"You sound very certain of its existence, sir. Have you got proof that this diary actually exists?"

"None at all. But I am increasingly convinced of it, and I think it may be here in this house."

"That sounds very fanciful, if I may say so. Did I not tell you that I looked once, and found nothing remotely connected with Plas Ingli or Martha Morgan?"

"Indeed you did. But I now think that the papers or volumes, if they exist, might be classified under quite another name."

The Death and Life of Mr Jenkins

Billy, having wept, now started to laugh. "Classified? Classified? Have you seen my office, sir? Classification never was a strong point in Williams and Williams, Family Solicitors of Repute. The only one who knew how to organize his papers was my great-grandfather George, who was by all accounts a meticulous fellow......"

"Wonderful! The smell of success becomes even stronger! Can I explain further? George Williams married one Mary Nicholas, the eldest daughter of Patty and Jake Nicholas who lived on the Parrog. I know that from the Census returns, although I dare say I could find it in the parish registers as well. I have a theory that Mistress Martha wrote a diary covering the last years of her life. She died in 1855, and I have another theory that her diary was entrusted to the safe keeping of one Bessie Walter, who was both servant and dear friend. I think that something happened to the Plas on Martha's death, and that Bessie, as a very old lady herself, had to leave. Where did she go? I think she might have gone to live with Patty and Jake in their posh new house on the Parrog. She probably took with her all her worldly possessions. She died some time between 1855 and 1861 -- I dare say I could find the date in the parish records with a little help from the Rector. Bessie must have known George and Mary, and when she died, my last theory in this sequence of theories is that George would have sorted out her estate, such as it was. He might even have helped her to make a will."

Billy frowned. "I am afraid this is all very confusing, my dear fellow. Too many theories and not enough facts. My father taught me that one must have the facts."

Just then there was a brief knocking on the front door, and Blodwen Rees swept along the passage and into the kitchen, laden with a basket of good things intended for Billy's supper. We exchanged greetings, and I thought it best that I should take my leave and perhaps return next day. But Billy would not hear of it. "Now then, sir. This is all nonsense, of course, but on the slim chance that I might be able to do something to make Jenkins Waun Isaf happy, I want you to look in my old office. Back along the passage, and the last door on the left. If my memory serves me right, there is a wooden cupboard to the left of the window, with *George Williams* written on the front of it. Have a look inside it. You never know your luck."

"Why, that's most generous of you. Will you not come and help?"

The Death and Life of Mr Jenkins

"No no. Liver problems, you understand. I find that it is very difficult to walk after three in the afternoon." He grinned, and Blodwen Rees rolled her eyes, and I understood.

I entered the study, and it was every bit as Dickensian as I had anticipated. It had clearly not been touched for twenty years. The cobwebs were truly spectacular, and simply by opening the door and entering I raised so much dust that I was overcome by a sneezing attack. But I battled on through hostile territory, determined to achieve my objective. There was the cupboard with *George Williams* written on its door. To open the door I had to move away several piles of buff folders and cardboard boxes, and then I had to pull away a number of trailing fronds of ivy which had entered through a crack in the window-frame and which had colonised a sizeable area illuminated by the rays of the setting sun. The door swung open after the removal of all obstacles, and I saw maybe sixty box-files, a few larger cardboard boxes tied with string, and even a few small wooden chests.

There was nothing for it but to hunt through one box after another, and I had just started on the task when I realized that they were all arranged in alphabetical order. There was Bessie's box-file, down in the bottom right-hand corner of the cupboard, after the Tuckers and the Vaughans and before the Watkinses and Williamses. The name "Mrs Elizabeth Walter, Parrog" was neatly inscribed both on the cover and the spine of the box. Hardly daring to breathe, and almost overcome by dust and anticipation, I pulled it out and opened it. There were assorted papers and letters, some still in their envelopes, but no will. And there, on the bottom of the box, in three bound volumes, were Martha's last diaries. I flicked through each in turn, and recognized at once the handwriting and the strange Dimetian Welsh script that Martha had always used to confuse her enemies and protect her secrets. I could not resist shouting "Aha! Found them!", to which Billy responded with a burst of applause from the kitchen.

I put the box file back into the cupboard, minus the diaries, closed the door and restored the office to something like its previous disorder. Then I went and showed the diaries to Billy and Blodwen. They were both greatly entertained by the fact that my convoluted mental processes had led me to three diaries whose very existence had been a matter of pure speculation; and I though it best not to try and explain how I had been led

35

The Death and Life of Mr Jenkins

to them as inexorably as a train is led towards it destination by the tracks upon which it runs. Billy thumbed through the diaries, and was fascinated that even he, as a fluent Welsh speaker, could understand hardly anything. "Perhaps if you drank less you would understand more," said Blodwen, showing a distinct lack of tact. Billy scowled at her. Then he brightened up, and said: "God knows who these belong to. Do they count as treasure trove, I wonder? I dare say that if they had belonged to somebody, they would have come to collect them a long time ago. Since 150 years have passed since the completion of these diaries, I hereby declare them to be mine. And I hereby make a gift of them to Jenkins Waun Isaf, a man whom I sorely wronged many years ago and from whom I now seek forgiveness." He then asked me to write out a little note on his behalf, as follows:

> *To Jenkins Waun Isaf from Williams Green House.*
> *When you were thirteen and I was a fool, I did you great wrong and lost your friendship. May God forgive me, and may you find it in your heart to do likewise. May you find great pleasure in recording and interpreting the last words of Mistress Martha ----*
> *Yours truly*
> *Bugs Billy*

"Bugs Billy?" said Blodwen.

"That was my nickname when I was thirteen," said Billy, with a surge of colour into his pallid cheeks. "I was a great one for collecting caterpillars and beetles and things. Mind you, that's my secret. Please don't tell anybody.........."

We both swore secrecy on pain of death, and since Billy's supper was ready I thanked him profusely for his patience and his help, and took my leave with the three bound diaries tucked under my arm. I promised him that I would return before too long with a report on Abraham's translation work, and left him to his liver and onions, green peas and mashed potato.

There is not much more to tell. I went straight from town to Waun Isaf, and found Abraham at his supper. He was astonished when I placed the three slim volumes onto the table in front of him, and even more astonished when I described how I had tracked them down. "You are getting quite clever at this, my friend," he grinned. "Just like parenthood.

The Death and Life of Mr Jenkins

Not that I know anything about it, but I am reliably informed that people get good at it just in time for it to be too late." He was very touched by the dedication and by the gift of the diaries from his old school friend, but when I asked him about the circumstances under which he and Billy had fallen out and gone their separate ways, he claimed that it was long ago, and that he had forgotten all the details. I did not press him, and left him to his supper and his thoughts.

So eight months passed, during which Abraham worked hard on the diaries and effectively gave up farming. He kept his land, but sold his sheep and his younger sheepdog, and let his good fields to his neighbour from Brynaeron. His health deteriorated, but as long as he had the diaries to keep him amused he remained in excellent spirits. To my great delight, he renewed his old friendship with Billy Thrice. I drove him down to Green House several times, and listened as the two old fellows reminisced and laughed, and told tales about the characters of the town which I shall refrain from repeating. When Billy died three months ago, one of his carers told me that he was quite contented, and that his last words had been: "A good old life I have had, Rosie. And thank God I have paid my debts."

There are two further things that I omitted to mention in the foregoing pages. The first thing concerns the young woman with whom he had a passionate affair during the Second World War. He never did tell me her surname, but he told me last Christmas that her Christian name had been Martha. And the second thing to report is that Abraham left me four things in his will -- an old and very arthritic sheepdog called Megs, and the last three volumes of Mistress Martha's diary.

✿✿✿✿✿✿✿✿✿✿✿✿✿

The Death and Life of Mr Jenkins

Notes

1. The Ancient Borough of Newport, which features strongly in all of the stories, has a medieval charter and in the period 1778-1855 (the lifetime of Mistress Martha) it had a peculiar system of administration arising from its position at the centre of the Marcher Lordship of Cemais. The Mayor was appointed annually by the Lord Marcher. Criminal cases were dealt with by the Petty Sessions and Assize Courts, while civil cases were heard by the Court Leet, Court Baron and View of Frankpledge. The commoners also enjoyed certain privileges and protected them aggressively. In some instances the Mayor and the burgesses had more authority than the squires and magistrates, and down through the centuries there were many power struggles leading to violence, murder and anarchy in the town.

2. The Society of Sea Serjeants really did exist. It portrayed itself as a social and sociable club for gentlemen and their families, but it was also a "mutual support" organization which promoted the interests of the local squires through price fixing, trade deals and political pressure behind the scenes. Because it was always a "secret society" like the Freemasons, it was viewed with suspicion by non-members. It is reasonable to assume that at least some of its activities were corrupt and that it encouraged certain types of criminal activity.

MARTHA MORGAN'S STORY

EXTRACTS FROM THE PAGES OF HER DIARIES FOR 1845-55, TRANSLATED FROM THE DIMETIAN WELSH DIALECT BY ABRAHAM JENKINS

2. Older if not Wiser

17th May 1845

"Dammo, Mistress Martha *bach,* hardly recognized you, I didn't, with your hair all gone white!" So said Master Elijah Collins, ninety-five years old and therefore old enough to remember the time when I was young, black-haired and full of the joys and miseries of spring. We met by chance outside the Royal Oak, where Elijah still enjoys his Thursday jar of ale just as he did with Grandpa Isaac half a century ago.

"Why, Master Collins, how good it is to see you!" said I. "And looking as sprightly as ever, with a healthy complexion and a gleam in your eye. I perceive that you have been arguing again."

"Huh! Been giving those fat swine from the Society of Sea Serjeants a piece of my mind. They meet in the upstairs room every Thursday afternoon, in theory to discuss foreign trade but in reality to scratch each other's backs. "

"But squires and merchants have always scratched each other's backs, Elijah. No point in getting upset about it."

"I'm not so sure, Mistress. There's trouble brewing in Ireland by the sound of it, and the whole lot of them think they are well placed to turn a tidy profit -- no doubt carried on the backs of some miserable starving Irish peasants. Anyway, must get back home for my afternoon nap. Good day to you, Mistress. And take care."

He doffed his hat, and off he went along East Street. Take care? Now why should he say that to me? I furrowed my brow and shrugged my shoulders, and carried on with my errands in town.

Older if not Wiser

When I had completed my shopping, and had exchanged pleasantries with those townspeople who were out and about on a fine May morning, I hitched up my skirts and strode homewards past the church and castle and up the narrow rutted lane of Greystones Hill. As I walked, I realised that I was puffing and panting more than in the old days, and pondered on the fact that I was beginning to get old. But I still enjoyed the exercise and the fresh air, and I consoled myself with the thought that many other ladies of mature years chose not to walk anywhere, and that some of them hardly had the energy to get out from under their linen sheets and woollen blankets until the day was half gone. And yet here was I with twenty-five pounds of groceries in the basket upon my hip, a good honest sweat upon my brow, and a world about me that was bursting with colour, suffused with fragrance and ringing with the music of birds and insects. Life was truly not too bad.

"Good day to you, Mistress. And take care........." Those words of Elijah Collins stalked me as I struggled up to the top of the hill and saw the ramshackle Rising Sun Inn ahead of me. I could not remember the old fellow ever saying that to me before, even at the height of my battles with treasure-hunters and predatory squires or during my somewhat irresponsible activities with the Rebecca Rioters last year. Did he know something that was hidden from me? Did I have some unknown enemy lurking in the shadows of the back streets of Newport, or among the ranks of the squires and merchants who ran the town? I thought I was on good terms with everybody, but I knew that some squires were not amused by the reforms forced upon the turnpike trusts following the Rebecca Riots and that some of them might hold me personally responsible for a decline in their fortunes. Then again, had I not personally tried to mediate between the squires and the rioters, and had I not argued over and again for a peaceful and political solution to the problems faced by the suffering farmers and labourers of this area? The squires had got their peaceful solution, duly delivered by Parliament. Surely nobody actually **believed** the rumours of me being involved in one of the riots myself, even if such rumours were true? Had somebody who knew the truth of the matter been whispering in dark corners about the nocturnal activities of that subversive lady called Martha Morgan of Plas Ingli? I could not believe that -- very few people knew the truth about me and the rioters, and those who did were mostly family and friends, and models of discretion.

Older if not Wiser

With these thoughts buzzing around like bumble bees in my brain, I reached the Plas Ingli lane and turned up towards the common. There to the right was the bluestone summit of Carningli, my mountain and my cathedral, place of secret angels and guardian ravens, place of memories gathered over almost fifty years since my arrival from Brawdy in 1796. How long ago that seemed! Then I had been young and in love, pregnant and fearing the ordeal of a hasty marriage; now I was a widow, a mother and a grandmother, exchanging love and respect with a veritable flock of young people. Then I had harboured dark thoughts about taking my own life and had indeed set about the planning of the evil act; now I was as content as any old woman has a right to be, with melancholia banished for good and with a somewhat more balanced manner of looking at the world about me.

And today was my birthday. Later on, at four o'clock in the afternoon, my guests would arrive and I would be enveloped in laughter and chatter. Bessie, Liza and her daughter Gwenno, respectively housekeeper, lady's maid and housemaid, would at this moment be preparing tasty things in the scullery and kitchen, and I pondered on the good fortune that had brought them into my house and into my life. We have shared a great deal of happiness together, I thought, for they are truly much more to me than servants. I love all three of them dearly, and I know that they love me. They have shown it over and again, and I thank God for it. Bonds such as those which hold us are as strong as they are rare. How could it be otherwise, I thought, given the events of the past year or so?

I shivered at the recollection of the afternoon of last year's *Cnapan* contest when the four of us had faced violation and death at the hands of four evil men who were on the run from the forces of law and order. Together, we had contrived to escape from that appalling situation, leaving one man dead on the kitchen doorstep and another spreadeagled lifeless and covered in blood and gore on the very table that was now being used for the preparation of fruit tarts and currant buns. Even now, the thought of it caused my blood to freeze in my veins. Surely we should have gone out of our minds had it not been for our ties of loyalty and comradeship, for as each one of us recoiled in terror at the recollections of that day there were three others who tried to remain strong and resolute and to keep a tenuous hold on sanity. For months afterwards we all suffered from nightmares and a fear of dark and strange places, and I fought off my demons on many difficult days by retreating to my secret cave on the mountain, by curling up like a small baby on my bed of moss, and by letting my tears flow. My whole being must have been affected more than I myself appreciated, for over the course of nine months my hair turned from coal black to snow white. Bessie and Liza needed love and understanding too, and there were many days on which they could not work and could hardly communicate with friends and family.

Gwenno, the youngest and prettiest of us involved in that terrible day, suffered most of all, and in spite of the loving care of her husband Gomer she has become timid and frightened, and I have to handle her with great delicacy when she is here in the house or dairy for three days each week. She is also with child, and currently afflicted by bouts of the morning sickness, so I do not get a great deal of work from her in exchange for my shillings. But Gomer makes up for that by doing the work of two men when he is here for his three days, and I cannot complain.

"Why, you are very pensive this morning, Mistress!" said Bessie, standing at the kitchen door and brushing flour off her apron. "I declare that you have walked all the way up the lane and into the yard without noticing that there are at least a dozen red kites above the mountain today, and that the world has transformed itself into a boudoir of bluebells."

I came to my senses in a moment and had to laugh. "My dear Bessie," I said, "I always said that you should become a poet when you retire. But retirement is out of the question, since I need you here to keep me under control. Forgive me, but my mind was far away. No -- that is a lie. It was right here, in this dear old kitchen. Now then, how are the preparations?"

"Almost ready. Have you got the crabs from Shemi Shellfish and the sweetmeats from the new shop beneath the castle?"

I confirmed that I had in my wicker basket everything that had been on my shopping-list, and without further ado I handed them over to the experts. I gobbled down a quick lunch of bread and butter, cheese and fruit cordial. Will and Gomer wandered in from the fields, and as we ate we talked briefly of weather, lambs, hay meadows and cattle prices. Then I rolled up my sleeves and embarked upon my next task for the day, which was to whip up the three pints of fresh cream required for the delectation

Older if not Wiser

of my grandchildren. In the dairy of a grand estate or a well-ordered gentry house there would be a full-time dairymaid for such arduous work, but times are tight and I cannot afford one. In any case I quite enjoy working in the cool of the dairy, surrounded by cold wet slate slabs and with the whiff of the morning's fresh milk in my nostrils. I have always worked while the Mistresses of other estates have lounged and embroidered. Activity suits me, and without it I should surely have become a toothless old crone long since.

Now it is late at night, and I am alone at my little desk, looking out through the open window of my dressing room across a silent and sleeping *cwm* which is illuminated by the light of a half-moon. The air is warm and fragrant. There are just a few lights in the valley, and I can make out faint wisps of smoke from Brithdir and Waun Isaf and Plain Dealings, swirling upwards towards the stars. The tawny owls are busy in Gelli Wood. The Penrhiw sheepdog is barking, which probably means that the old dog fox which lives among the rocks at the foot of the southern mountain slope is prowling around the chicken house. Otherwise, everything is serene, and I can indulge in a new communication with my diary, after a lapse of about nine months. I have to say that I enjoy scratching away with my quill pen just as much as I did when I first came to the Plas. They have new iron pens nowadays, but I am not greatly attracted by them, and much prefer to use something white and beautiful that once aspired to flight and freedom.

We have had a truly splendid celebration, which leads me to face my sixty-eighth year with equanimity and even enthusiasm. Most of my family came. Brynach and his children Rose and David; Betsi and her husband Ioan and son Benjamin; then my dear friends Shemi Jenkins the Wizard and Sian his cheery wife; my head man Will and his wife Tegwen and little daughter Bronwen; Gomer, the son of Shemi and Sian, and his wife Gwenno; and finally my old friend Patty and her husband Jake from the Parrog. My servants Bessie and Liza were of course here already. And finally my beloved Daisy, to whom I refer as my prodigal daughter, returned from town just in time for the party, bearing a most beautiful red silk dress imported specially from Messrs Simpkins of Bond Street in London -- my present from the whole family. I was moved to tears, and they insisted that I should go to my dressing room and put it on immediately. Of course I obeyed instructions, and when I slipped into it I have to admit that I experienced more than a shiver of pleasure. Liza helped me to put up my hair and to choose a rouge colour for my cheeks that matched the dress. When I swept downstairs again afterwards the assembled company cheered and laughed, and I felt like a queen. I thought the dress a little too daring and a little too red for an old lady like me, but they all flattered me and said that my bosom was still firm and my waist still slim, and Shemi said that I looked more alluring than many youngsters of his acquaintance who were one-third my age. At that, Sian boxed his ears, and I blushed, and they all thought that highly entertaining.

"Mother dear," laughed Daisy, "I think I could organize a new career for you in London as a courtesan. I have some excellent contacts.........."

"And I could give you some lessons, for a small fee," grinned Patty, reminding me that she had once, long ago, been forced to work as a prostitute on the Parrog.

"No thank you, my dear friends. It is my intention to retire to the country very shortly. In any case, I am too old to appear in the company of dukes and princes, rakes and rogues."

"Far from it, Mother. Some of them are even older than you, and would give their fortune for a feisty widow in a red dress!"

And so the silly conversation went on, a little too close to the knuckle -- or so I thought -- for my young granddaughter Rose. We exchanged glances, and she gave me a big wink, and the pair of us had a fit of the giggles.

We all ate an early supper in the dining room, which we use too seldom. Daisy insisted that we should use our best silver cutlery, bone china and lead crystal glasses, and Will (who is in charge of the Plas cellar) found some quite splendid wines which must have arrived one dark night when I had been looking in some other direction. We ate prime baked ham, potatoes, carrots and sweet chutneys, followed by sugared fruits and fresh cream, and then *bara brith*, Welsh griddle cakes and currant buns. I enjoyed myself so much that immediately afterwards I had to obtain relief by changing out of my new dress, which was too tight for overeating. But I needed to change into my walking clothes anyway, for we followed the meal with a stiff walk upon the common during the cool and quiet of the May evening. In doing that, we were following a tradition established by my dear friend Joseph Harries the Wizard, who came to the Plas every year for my birthday and who led little groups of overindulged guests far and wide over Carningli and Mynydd Melyn, year after year, looking at birds' nests, flowers and frogs and talking of clouds and rocks and all manner of natural mysteries. How I miss that dear kind man to this day! He was the one who taught me, above all else, to know myself and to be myself, and I still feel that he knew me -- the real me -- better than my husband David or my beloved Owain whom I longed to marry but never did. It is almost twenty years since Joseph died, taking with him a piece of my heart into the stony ground of Jabes Churchyard. I had known him for thirty years.

What a strange mood I am in today! I have experienced joy and suffered the terrors of recollection, and I have been uplifted by nature and by the love of family and servants and friends. Then I have been puzzled by simple words and little hints, and by a strange mixing of past, present and future. My puzzlement was compounded this evening, when the long shadows of the night were filling the valleys and spreading up the hillsides and when my guests were taking their leave. The last to leave were Shemi and Sian. Shemi, who knows everything, gave me a warm embrace and looked me in the eyes with a greater tenderness than usual. "Good night, Martha," he smiled. "Thank you for a wonderful celebration among the best of friends. Sleep well. And just you take care."

ΩΩΩΩΩΩΩΩΩΩΩ

25th May 1845

I am unsure why I have picked up my quill again, but the very act of embarking on a new diary causes a flutter of apprehension in my heart, for I have noted that in the past the urge to write has always been followed shortly thereafter by some dramatic or even tragic event. Conversely, there have been times in my life when I have not been at all moved to sit at my desk with inkpot and quill at the ready, and with blank pages before me. Those have been for the most part the times of childbearing or

Older if not Wiser

of preoccupations with family and estate matters. Sometimes I have been too busy, and sometimes too happy, and sometimes too tired to write anything at all. Once upon a time, when Brynach was very young and when I had nightmares about a mysterious figure called The Nightwalker, I wrote nothing at all for years on end; and on other occasions I wrote nothing because I was afflicted by a sort of melancholia which might have landed me in a lunatic asylum had it not been for the love of my family and the ministrations of my beloved friend Joseph Harries. Each time they pulled me back from the black abyss into which I had descended, and taught me afresh how to listen to the song thrush on an April morning, how to feast my eyes on the magical colours of a springtime hedgerow, and how to breathe in the scents of new-mown hay, rambling honeysuckle and golden furze.

Is the fluttering in my heart caused by a premonition of things to come? I know that I have special powers, by no means as powerful as those gifted to wizards like Joseph Harries and Shemi Jenkins, but strong enough nonetheless to lead me to see battles in the sky and phantom funerals and other strange things. Such phenomena have terrified me almost out of my wits in the past. Indeed, when I look back I cannot resist a wry smile when I see myself as a young woman of twenty or thirty reacting with histrionics and hysteria and wild speculations to things that were, in some cases at least, more imagined than real.

That is not to say that I have not experienced real tragedy. I have had to cope with the murder of my beloved husband David and with the problems of bringing up a young family all alone; I have seen the premature death of that sweet, kind gentleman called Owain Laugharne whom I should have wed; and I have seen another gentleman blow his brains out because of his love for me which went unrequited. Other men have loved me, including one called Moses Lloyd who was so consumed by a murderous passion that he would have possessed me and then killed me had I not killed him in the process of saving myself. Then there was John Fenton the regency reprobate, and Iestyn Price the suffering hero, and Joseph Harries himself, and Daniel O'Connell the avenging angel, and Hugh Williams the solicitor. All of them except for Hugh Williams are dead, and I am left behind to mourn -- and in some cases, to celebrate -- their passing. I have almost lost count of the number of evil men I have seen to the gallows or to early graves. The latest villain was Squire John

46

Older if not Wiser

Owen, executed just one month ago for the murder of two men who did him no harm. Every one of these monsters had taken life without regard for the consequences of their actions; every one of them had been given the opportunity of a just defence before a court made up of good men and true; and every one of them had then paid the terrible price set by the law of the land. In truth, whole episodes of my life have been made up of the stuff of nightmares. But I am older and calmer now, and more in control of my emotions. I have promised myself that I will never again plunge into melancholia and that I will at least seek to cope with the surprises and the pain that go with a life lived to the full.

In seeking to understand the workings of Cruel Fate, and in some degree to minimise their effects, I have been to see old Elijah Collins at Llysmeddyg. When I turned up at his tidy house on the edge of town and got no response to my knockings on the front door, I let myself in as I had done many times before. I found him fast asleep in a comfortable chair in the back yard, with a big straw hat tilted over his face to protect him from the sun. I coughed politely and got no response, and then coughed more loudly, and at last he stirred.

"Ah, it's you, Mistress Martha!" he said. "Forgive me. Most ungentlemanly to be snoozing in such a fashion at the time of a visit from a fine lady. Mary has gone off to do some shopping, I do believe. You let yourself in? Good, good. I have been expecting you."

"Oh? How can that be?"

"Well, you have a nose for trouble, and a good brain behind those sharp eyes of yours, so I thought you might have read something into our brief conversation of some days since."

I laughed. "You are quite correct, Master Collins. Call it female inquisitiveness rather than female intuition. But in putting my name together with the Society of Sea Serjeants and with troubles in Ireland, am I adding three and three together to make ten?"

"Sit you down, Mistress," said the old fellow. "Now that I am almost awake I will stir myself and get you a mug of cider, and while I am about it I will get one for myself as well."

So I sat down and waited in the spring sunshine, and in due course he returned with our drinks. We wished each other the best of health, and then he reported on his concerns. "I do not have much to go on," he said, "but you know that trouble is brewing in Ireland?"

Older if not Wiser

"I thought that trouble was always brewing in Ireland, sir."

"Quite so. Well, this time it is brewing rather more vigourously and I have it on good authority that the trouble will be serious. My grandson William was over there two months back, and he was amazed that there has not already been a revolution like that which caused royal heads to roll in France many years ago. Too many paupers, too much rain, and not enough land to feed the mouths of the hungry."

"But it has always been so, Master Collins. I remember Grandpa Isaac, your old friend, explaining the Irish problem to me in similar terms at least thirty years since."

"We discussed it often. But the real problem is that nothing over there has changed, while the rest of the world has moved on. The poor people who live on the land have no security of tenure, not enough land for subsistence, no cash for buying the necessities of life, and no self-respect. Even the labouring classes need self-respect, would you not agree, Mistress Martha?"

"I have always thought so, sir, and have always sought to give my labourers opportunities for self-improvement."

"You are well known for it, Martha, and it does you credit. But did you know that in Ireland the idiotic laws made by our government of imbeciles effectively treat those who belong to good families and the established church as human beings, and everybody else as animals? Those who are Papists -- and that includes the whole mass of paupers and labourers -- cannot find education, cannot enter a profession, cannot engage in trade, cannot buy a good horse, cannot live in a town, cannot worship in freedom, cannot buy land, and so forth and so forth. I ask you, Mistress, as a reasonable person, how can all of that be justified in any enlightened and liberated society? I would hazard a guess that the slaves of the cotton plantations are better off........"

He was so upset by this recitation of evils that his voice faded away, and he shook his head in despair. "What you say is truly appalling, Master Collins, and I thank you for your explanation," said I. "I have read very similar things in the pages of my newspapers. But pray do not get too upset. I suppose there are limits to what we can do in West Wales, since we are physically far removed from the problems and indeed have difficulties of our own. Furthermore, neither you nor I have any means of exerting pressure on those who govern us."

Older if not Wiser

Master Collins smiled. "Oh, by all accounts you did not do too badly, Martha, in helping to draw the Rebecca Riots to a successful conclusion. I will not pry into your methods, but whatever they were they will probably not work for two great causes in rapid succession. No -- it has been my hope for years that merchants such as I might play a fuller role in civil life and in alleviating poverty. I fear that I am now too old to do much myself, or to exert great influence over others."

"Does this bring us, sir, to the Society of Sea Serjeants?"

"It does. Isaac was a member for years, until he resigned over some grand matter of principle. I am still a member, although at its meetings I feel increasingly out of place. It started off as a mutual benefit society for small squires and large merchants, with subscriptions and savings used for the support of those who fell upon hard times. It never was very secretive, and we used to hold many jolly social events each year, with wives and families welcome to attend. But in recent years it has become more of a secret society like the Masonic Lodge, and some of the younger members have even brought in silly rituals and passwords in order to protect it from outsiders. Utterly childish I call it, since we all know who the members are anyway. There are now little groups within the society, and that is an ominous development. They work together to protect trade and to prevent competition, like the corn buying rings of the bad old days. Those rings distorted the market and caused great local distress, Martha, as you may remember. It happened again not so long ago, when the Rebecca Rioters were abroad, and several corn warehouses went up in flames as a result. One of them was right here on the Parrog."

I frowned, and Master Collins divined that I was trying to make a connection between the Society of Sea Serjeants and the politics of Ireland. He laughed and continued. "The connection is quite simple, Martha. The prediction is that there will be either revolution or famine in Ireland, and possibly both. I would certainly not bet against it. There will be a huge demand for food, either to feed the starving, or to feed the army, or both. Fishguard, Newport and Cardigan -- our three local ports -- are all involved in the Irish trade, and all three are well placed to supply Southern Ireland. To put it simply, the men who belong to my cosy little society are merchants and landowners who control the local production and trade in foodstuffs. They also own shares in many of the local trading ships, just as you and I do. I know it as a fact that they plan to work together to hold up prices, to store barley and wheat for as long as possible, and to release supplies only when vast profits are there to be made. They assume that at some stage the government will intervene, and that there will be mass purchases by the state with heavy subsidies. When the price is right and the time is right, but not before, they will ship over thousands of tons of grain to Waterford, Cork and other places on the south coast."

I was horrified by these revelations, and asked: "But my dear Master Collins, what will be the consequence of this manipulation of the market? If it happens elsewhere, and merchants across the kingdom play these silly games, will not the price of delays in the provision of food be measured in human lives?"

"You are perfectly correct, Martha. If hardship strikes that beleaguered land, I imagine that every week's delay in grain shipments will lead thousands more to their graves. Do not ask me to calculate numbers. Maybe a hundred thousand, or five hundred thousand, or a million......?"

The thought was so appalling that I could say nothing. Master Collins was also silent for a while. Then I said: "Master Collins, who are these men?"

"You know them all, Martha. Who is building a new large corn warehouse on the Parrog at the moment?"

"Why, the Lord Marcher, so I believe, with some participation from Jacob Harry and William Howell?"

He nodded. "And who are the squires putting land down to wheat this spring?"

"Fools, all of them, according to my men Will and Gomer, who know that wheat is not a good crop for these parts. But Mefin Owen of Gelli Fawr has put in fifty acres of wheat, and Huws Bayvil even more, and it is rumoured that Watkins Ffynnonddofn and Rector Thomas are also involved. It is in my view more likely that they will be bankrupted than that they will make a fortune."

"That may be, Martha. But whatever happens to them, just you keep your eyes open."

"Where do I come into this, sir? I see no connection at all between these greedy men and me and the Plas. I do not even own any land. Brynach owns the Plas Ingli estate and the Llanychaer estate, and makes all the key decisions. He lets me manage the Plas and supervise the tenant farmers simply because he knows that I need something to keep me occupied. If I should fall ill, Brynach would probably get in a steward and I would greatly enjoy my old age sitting in the sun with no responsibilities, just like you."

Master Collins gave a great guffaw, and slapped his knees. "My dear Mistress Martha," he laughed, "I do not see it happening. You are quite indestructible! Why, you have used up at least ten of your cat's lives already, with no apparent ill effects apart from a most appealing change of hair colour." Then he became serious, and said: "These men have mentioned your name in my hearing, Martha. They fear your resolve and your principles, and your ability to mine a deep seam of sympathy and support from the local populace. They know that if there is resistance to their plans, you are likely to be at the heart of it."

"But I have long since given up on involvement in controversial matters, sir."

"I think I have heard you saying that before, Martha. And remember that these men have long memories. Mefin Owen saw his father go to the gallows because you fought for justice, and don't you forget that William Howell is a bastard who carries in his veins the same bitter blood as the monster John Howell. I need not remind you that he was another of your enemies who was strung up from the gallows tree. These men blame you for their family misfortunes, although it would be more logical for them to blame their evil ancestors for retribution called down upon their own heads. And you have done no favours to Madoc Huws or Rector Llewelyn Thomas either, by thwarting various of their foolish moneymaking ventures. No, Martha, I know enough about the minds of men to urge you to be careful, and to avoid anything that might give them an opportunity to attack you. Just now the dogs are sleeping. Let them lie."

Then Mary came back with her shopping, and I took the opportunity to thank the old gentleman for his courtesy and his advice and to set out for home. On the way, I found myself pondering deeply once again, and -- strange to relate -- more worried about his wellbeing than mine.

ΩΩΩΩΩΩΩΩΩΩΩ

Older if not Wiser

28th May 1845

Since my conversation with Master Collins I have been thinking at length about the plight of the downtrodden people across the water and consequently neglecting my own affairs. They can wait a while, and I have found good reason, in pondering the misfortunes of others, to count my blessings.

I do not deny that real tribulations have been heaped upon me in past years and that they have been terrible in their intensity, but they have been mercifully short-lived, and I know from looking around me that they have been as nothing compared to the inexorable and never-ending sufferings of paupers and vagrants, landless labourers and those who are diseased and wasted. Then beyond my own horizon I know from my newspapers that there are prisoners and slaves, and those who struggle but to starve in lands afflicted by famine, and those who die on the fields of battle to support the ambitions of madmen who have lost all sense of Christian virtue and who lust after wealth or power.

I am one of the lucky few. I have a modest income and a tidy fortune, and as a sort of insurance against future disaster I even have a treasure hidden beneath the turf ten yards from the wall of the Plas, in a location known only to me. I have one son and two daughters still on this good earth, and living close enough for me to see them whenever I need their company or they need mine. Then there are my eight grandchildren -- three fine young men born to Betsi and Ioan, three born out of wedlock to my sweet and prodigal daughter Daisy, and then Rose and David born to Brynach and his lovely wife Anne, who died in childbirth. That is just the start of it. Bessie and Liza are truly members of my family, as are Will and Gomer and Gwenno who come and go most days, and Shemi and Sian who both lived beneath this roof for more years than I care to remember before their marriage and their move to Werndew. And Patty and Jake, who have made their way in the world, and a modest fortune to boot, through hard work and astuteness in the tough seaside community of Parrog. The net spreads wider and wider, tightly knotted by shared experiences, and strong enough to trawl the depths and to surface over and again, only slightly harmed. We are here and there for each other, and we exist in a peculiar world of our own making in which all of us have long since lost count of debts incurred and debts repaid. That, as I often remind

Older if not Wiser

myself, is a sign of real friendship.

So the sun still sails high above the scudding clouds of a breezy May day, and tonight its place will be taken by a silver moon which is just on the wane. Every morning when I open the shutters and slide down the sash of my bedroom window I am greeted by a full-throated dawn chorus which seems to come from every bush and tree between Carningli and Carnedd Meibion Owen. On calm days the *cwm* is filled at sunrise with wraiths of mist which perform ethereal dances before fading away to reveal waking cottages, and the greenery of Tycanol Wood, and fields full of maternal ewes and new-born lambs belonging to Cilgwyn Mawr, Ysgarwen and Fachongle Uchaf. The great sheet of bluebells which spreads across the paddock in front of the Plas is at its best, painted with a purple-blue colour which can never be recreated by an artist and which is so intense that it almost pains the eyes. And then there is the scent, which they tell me can be picked up across the *cwm* when the wind is in the north. The hedgerows are full of magic too, with celandines and buttercups, violets and oxeye daisies, red campions and foxgloves and cow parsley all jostling for prominence and attention before the heavy grasses, docks and nettles of high summer overwhelm them.

And so the land endures. When I am dead and gone the old mountain which stands proud between the Plas and the sea will still glow silver in the light of the sunrise and gold in the rays of the setting sun. The crusty lichens which cover the bare rocky summits and the tumbled boulders will still enhance the muted greys and blues with daubs and splashes of orange and red, white and green and even a colour more black than soot. The ravens will be there, I dare say, until the end of time as they have survived since the beginning of time -- for I can truly not imagine the mountain without them. When I was a child I was told by my father that ravens are much maligned by the English, who think them to be harbingers of doom; but I know, as all Celtic people know, that these great birds are noble creatures who have seen everything and know everything. Indeed, since the ravens inhabit a place which has the English name of Angel Mountain, they might indeed be the black angels who have been chosen by God to guard its purity.

And the ephemeral world imagined, created and destroyed by man as the generations march across the landscape? As I grow older I see change on all sides, and I fear that much of it is beyond my comprehension.

Older if not Wiser

The world has become a harsher place with old certainties replaced by doubts and conflicts, and men replaced by machines. But I will move with the times where I can, while holding to the old values of love, loyalty and compassion, and while burying my roots ever deeper into the rocky soil of this beloved land.

This land, this place! Already I am so much a part of it, and it is so much a part of me, that when I think of it a thrill permeates my whole body. With the passing of the years this union of person and place has almost taken the place of sexual desire, and has given me a sort of contentment which is both sensual and spiritual. Perhaps I have slipped into this way of thinking and feeling because I do not have a good man at my side and because I have to cope with loneliness, but I declare that I do not feel lonely or deprived in any way, and in my present mood of optimism I have to admit to a life of contentment and fulfilment.

So whatever life may throw at me in my declining years, I will not complain. I will try to accept tribulation with fortitude, and try to find the sunlight which silvers the edges of black clouds. I will be faithful to my friends and give all the love that is in me to my family and to whomsoever may need it. But I will also remain true to my principles and fight injustice and intolerance where I encounter it. And I will never, never apologize for my beliefs or my actions if, to my way of seeing things, they have sprung from a reservoir of good intentions and if they do no harm to man or beast.

ΩΩΩΩΩΩΩΩΩΩΩ

10th June 1845

The last fortnight has been like a truce before a war or a period of calm such as one finds at the eye of a storm. I have experienced wars before, and I fear that another one may be upon me.

Just at the time when I should be devoting all my energies to the planning of the hay harvest, I have been distracted and even terrified by powerful premonitions on three successive nights. I have not shared them

Older if not Wiser

with anybody, for the sharing of dark secrets about the future inevitably does more harm than good. In any case one cannot shift Cruel Fate once he has decided to have his way, and if he has lives to claim it is better that his victims should be innocent rather than terrified.

On each occasion, at around two o'clock, with the night at its blackest and with hardly a sliver of new moon to illuminate land or sky, I have had the same dream. In it, I have been standing as an observer, trapped and uninvolved on some strange riverside quay with people wandering about as if in a trance. I do not recall that I recognized any of them, or the location. Tied up at the quayside was a fine three-masted sailing ship, making ready to set sail for some foreign port. I knew that, because no cargo was being unloaded, and because large quantities of provisions were being taken on board. As I watched, a funeral party arrived on the quayside, with a hearse at its head. The coffin was taken down and placed on the quayside, as if it was intended for transportation by the ship. But it was not taken on board, and after the briefest of funeral ceremonials the mourners simply paid their last respects and left it there on the ground while they walked away. Then after a while the same thing happened again. Another funeral party came, and another coffin was laid on the ground at the quayside. Again there was a short ceremony, and the mourners paid their respects, and left without taking the coffin on board. Then at last various sailors and officers went on board the ship and made ready for the sea. The gangplanks were hauled up, and the heavy ropes were cast off, and with a minimum of sail set the vessel drifted slowly from the quayside and out into the channel where it caught the wind. Nobody was left on shore to wave farewell, and I thought that very strange indeed. From my vantage point on the quayside I heard the shouted orders from the mate to the crewmen echoing across the water, and soon all the sail was unfurled. The ship gathered speed and then was lost to sight as it went round a bend in the wide river, leaving me to contemplate the two coffins. I approached them, perhaps with a view to finding out which unfortunate souls were contained within them, but before I could read the lettering on the lids I awoke with a start, soaked with perspiration and with a pounding heart.

Three times. An identical dream each time, and most recently last night. I tried to hide my confusion and my distress this morning when I went down to breakfast, but Bessie reads my mind almost as well as she reads an open book, and said: "Good morning, Mistress! If I may say so, you look more bothered and more tired than is appropriate on a fine morning such as this. Did you not sleep well?"

"No, Bessie, I did not. And nor did I on on the night before, and on the night before that. Silly nightmares. I always feel fretful before the hay harvest, lest the rain comes at the last minute and lest all is lost. Probably I am beginning to feel my age, worrying more than I should about matters beyond my control."

"There are no worries on the weather front, Mistress. Shemi told me yesterday that we would get the harvest in before the rain arrives, and he is never wrong. Just you relax, and get a good breakfast inside you before the Irish arrive, looking for work. I hear that sixty of them landed at Fishguard yesterday."

So breakfast, and the practicalities of the hay harvest, banished my dark thoughts and carried me through the day. But now, as I sit in the quietness of my own room late at night, with just a murmur of conversation downstairs from the servants in the kitchen, my mind has turned again to the dream and its meaning. Two coffins and a sailing ship. Near or far? Family or friends? My ship, or one belonging to some other? And are these images burned into my brain related in some way to my recent conversation with Elijah Collins? I dare say that I will drift into sleep after setting down my quill pen for the night, no closer to solving the mysteries which have been set before me.

ΩΩΩΩΩΩΩΩΩΩΩ

29th June 1845

We have had two weeks of strange weather, unseasonably grey and cool, but apart from a few drizzly spells it has kept dry, and the hay harvest is in. The Irish came as usual, although I was disappointed to see no sign of the O'Connell family who have been turning up at the Plas for the hay harvest for as long as I can remember. I gave work to one family of seven who had travelled all the way from Galway, and not surprisingly they

Older if not Wiser

knew nothing of the O'Connells, who are resident in the Wexford district. They tried hard enough, poor things, but they were skin and bone when they came, and I discovered too late that the father and his two sons were useless with scythes in their hands and not much better with hay-rakes or pitchforks. They appeared to be short on both skill and energy, but I had no heart to send them packing, in spite of noisy grumbles from Will and Gomer. Not for the first time, I found myself transformed from harsh employer to philanthropist, and I had to comfort myself with the thought that all the members of the family, including three little children, were a little wealthier and a little plumper when they went on their way.

With six of my tenants and labourers scything, and with twelve others turning and raking we managed well enough, and we were all grateful that we did not have to contend with the white-hot weather which has been so burdensome to us in past harvests. And I have bought a mechanical turning device which is pulled behind a horse, and also a horse-drawn hay rake which enables us to gather the turned and dried hay into neat rows ready for gathering and pitching onto the gambo. Will grumbles that "one day, Mistress, machines will do away with people altogether", but Gomer is mightily impressed with our new acquisitions and is now urging me to search in the agricultural catalogues for machines which will cut hay efficiently and pitch it onto wagons and hay-ricks. One day I will conduct such a search, but not yet, for machines can only be acquired from ready cash, and that is one thing that we West Wales landowners are short of. Our tenants traditionally pay a proportion of their rents in the form of labour and provisions, and if we were all to demand cash instead of "in kind" payments the whole system of mutual benefits and services which supports the farming economy would collapse. Among the tenants of our estate, where would Jethro Griffiths find the £70 needed to pay his rent for Dolrannog Isaf, or Gomer Jenkins the £50 needed for Penrhiw, or Gwyn Williams the £65 needed for Gelli? Strictly the estate belongs to Brynach, but because he lives more than six miles away at Plas Llanychaer, and because he has enough to worry about on that rambling and run-down estate, he leaves all matters to do with nearby tenancies and tied cottages and so forth in my hands, but I know that he shares my view that a happy band of tenants and workers is worth more than a few pounds saved on a hayfield.

The memory of that strange premonition (if such it be) has faded somewhat, to my great relief.   Nobody has died, and nobody in my immediate circle of family and friends is ill, to the best of my knowledge, so I simply have to get on with life.   That dream ship does cause me some concern, and I wonder whether I have received a signal that one will shortly be lost.   I own a majority of shares on one vessel, the *Mary Jane*, and one-fifth shares in three others, and so, as a precaution, I have made discreet enquiries as to whether there are any other local squires who might be interested in acquiring my shares.   However, cash is so tight that not one of the good families in the neighbourhood is buying shares in vessels just now, and if I try to sell them to one of the merchants on the Parrog, or one of the traders in town, the word will pretty soon be about the place that Mistress Morgan of the Plas is in dire financial trouble, and is desperate to raise cash.   That sort of speculation has too often, to my certain knowledge, led to the decline and fall of a tidy little estate, and I will not let it happen to ours.   So all I can do for the moment is pray for the safe return of all four vessels which are out and about on the high seas fetching and delivering cargoes at the discretion of their masters.   When they do return to the Parrog with their holds full of fabrics and utensils, salt and sugar, hats and umbrellas, citrus fruits and timber, iron goods and wine, and all manner of other luxuries and essentials, I have to hope that my returns will come as they have done before.

ΩΩΩΩΩΩΩΩΩΩΩ

2nd July 1845

With the turning of the month we have seen the arrival of the first big wave of summer heat.   As I write, I am sitting in the afternoon shade of my favourite apple tree, on a wooden bench made for me many years ago by Shemi from the branches of a fallen oak.   I have a long drink of fruit cordial at my side, and I have on my lightest cotton dress, so I am as comfortable as one can be on such a day; but it is still unbearably hot, and hard work is out of the question even for the labourers who are supposed to be clearing the long ditch which drains the bottom part of the common.

Older if not Wiser

The cattle are desperate for water, and the sheep -- which are all sheared long since -- are huddled into every patch of shade they can find. Even the lambs, three months old and normally up to all sorts of mischief at this age, are too tired to clamber onto stone walls or to seek out unrepaired gaps in hurdles and fences. A strange sort of silence has settled across the landscape, which quivers in the heat haze. The sky is as wide and azure as a trackless ocean, and it is occupied solely by the flaming orb of the sun. It does not happen often in Pembrokeshire that there is not a cloud or a bird to be seen, but today is such a day. I should be impressed, but I fear that I am not, for this is not good farming weather. I want sun like this in August, when the corn is tall and the ears are full -- but not now.

I will cheer myself up by writing of a most interesting gentleman whose acquaintance I have made within the past nine months. We first met under the strangest of circumstances, in late October of last year. Daisy was feeling miserable, and Bessie was complaining about the quality of the main crop potatoes. I recall that it was a breezy autumnal day, and that after a difficult morning spent in the kitchen in the company of two irritable females, I needed some fresh air. I did not feel too bright myself. I decided upon a walk on the mountain, and having dressed up warmly and having pulled on my most comfortable boots, off I went. As I have done a thousand times before, I followed the water pipe from the house up to Ffynnon Brynach, my sacred spring, and there I anointed myself and sought to wash away some of my own irritability. Feeling better, I strode onwards and upwards, and soon I was among the countless tumbled boulders which make up a steep apron beneath the summit crags. I pondered on whether I should go to my cave and enjoy its dark and comfortable silence for a while, but I thought better of it and decided to climb to the summit instead. So up I climbed, with my old joints creaking more than a little. But my elation quickly banished my discomfort, and as the view opened up the air was so clear that I could see the Wicklow Hills of Ireland and the great summits of North Wales. My mood was transformed, and I suppose that when I reached the summit I was singing a little song to myself and gazing into the distance rather than paying attention to what was beneath my feet.

Imagine my surprise when I literally stumbled upon a gentleman who was sitting stock still on the grassy patch adjacent to the highest rock. I think he might have had his eyes closed and his hands resting easily in his lap until I disturbed him so rudely, but I lost my balance and my composure and fell over him before ending up sprawled on the grass in a most undignified fashion.

"Oh my dear lady," said he, sounding very flustered. "Please forgive me. I had no idea that people were likely to pass this way, and I was in the midst of a deep contemplation.........."

"No no, my fault entirely," I spluttered, spitting bits of grass out of my mouth. "I really must look where I am going in future."

The gentleman leapt to his feet and helped me up, muttering more apologies and then seeking to brush the grass and the mud off my dress. Then he realised that placing hands upon a total stranger was a considerable impertinence on his part, and he pulled his hands away as if he had touched a fiery furnace, and became even more flustered. "Oh dear me!" he gasped. "I do apologise. Quite unforgivable. Very unfortunate. Most unfortunate indeed!"

Then our eyes met, and no further words were necessary, for we both realised in an instant that our encounter was pure farce and that the rules of etiquette were for a moment entirely irrelevant. I could not resist giggling, and neither could he, and soon the pair of us were roaring with uncontrollable laughter there on the highest peak of the mountain and no doubt disturbing the resident angels in the process. He had to sit down on a rock in order to regain his composure, and so did I. At last he offered me a red kerchief with which to wipe away my tears, and the rules of good behaviour were re-established.

"Now then, Madam," he grinned. "Here we are, rolling about with gay abandon on the top of a holy mountain in broad daylight, and we have not been introduced. Pray tell me, with whom do I have the pleasure.......?"

I decided that I liked the sound of his voice, which was light and cultured. "Martha Morgan of Plas Ingli, sir," I replied. "If you look on the south side of the mountain you will see my blessed home, whitewashed and shining in the sun. It is the highest house on the mountainside, hard up against the edge of the common."

"Of course! It is a great pleasure to meet you, Mistress Martha. Your reputation has gone before you, and I have to say that you are every bit as handsome as I have been led to believe, even with mud upon your left cheek and a piece of grass sticking to your right ear."

Older if not Wiser

"Sir, you are very forward and very impertinent. I will let your compliments and your insults pass, since you too might look passably handsome were it not for the mud on your trousers and the holes in your shoes. And your name, if you please?"

"Amos Jones from Radnor. I am a minister of religion, and I am here to preach to the unconverted."

"What, here on top of Carningli?"

"No no, Madam. I arrived this morning in town, having ridden over from Narberth. I fear that my scruffy trousers and unsatisfactory shoes are the result of three falls from my horse on this very morning. I will not show you my bruises. That creature has the devil in him, but I will lead him into the pathway of righteousness, just you wait and see. Where was I? Oh yes, I was about to say that after finding a simple lodging house I walked around the town, and got talking with various kind townsfolk. They told me about the Bowens of Llwyngwair, and the Morgans of Plas Ingli, and the Owens of Gelli Fawr, and various other old families, and they also told me how to find the path up onto the mountain. So I decided upon a period of prayer prior to starting my preaching activities. After taking a light lunch I climbed up from the town, and I fear that you stumbled upon me when I was quite lost either in confession or supplication -- I forget which."

"You have my admiration, sir. You sound like a very determined and committed Christian gentleman. But why have you come to Newport, when the whole world is full of heathens waiting to be saved?"

"Several reasons, Mistress Martha. May I call you that.....?" I nodded and smiled. "Good, good. You are very kind. Well, if truth be told, I have done a good deal of the world already, having been on the road, walking and riding, for around thirty years. Only the Lord knows how many sermons I have preached during that time, how many times I have been sent packing by drunken rabbles, and how many times I have slept in hedges under the stars. But the rewards are incalculable, Mistress, for in my time I have been an instrument of the Lord in saving many lost souls."

"Very creditable, sir. But why Newport? And why now?"

"I am not entirely sure. I think that I am here because of some sort of divine guidance. Three weeks since, when I was preaching not far from Swansea, I got talking to a fellow about the Sermon on the Mount, as one does. We chatted about mountains as sacred places, and for some reason he

Older if not Wiser

told me about a little mountain called Carningli near Newport. I knew instantly that it was my destiny to visit it as a pilgrim........."

"That sounds very mystical, Master Jones. Are you a believer in destiny, and guidance, and such things?"

He did not reply, but looked me in the eye, and continued with his explanation. "And this same fellow also told me about the terrible Mistress of Plas Ingli who was drawn to sin as a white butterfly is drawn to a cabbage, and who was certainly beyond redemption. Now **that** was a challenge too great for any preacher to pass over."

At this, I felt my cheeks burning, and I dare say my eyes were blazing too. "Sir, I take the gravest exception to that remark. I will have you know.........."

And too late, I realized that the impudent fellow was teasing me, and that his eyes were sparkling with laughter. "Aha, Mistress Martha!" he chortled. "I see that you are even more beautiful when you are angry. If God wills it that we should meet again, I trust that I will see you angry again, to remind me of this moment." Then he held his hands up as if in surrender, and became serious. "I am sorry. They tell me that I am too frivolous to be a preacher, and I apologize without reservation for my lack of respect. I have no right to speak to you as I might speak to the oldest and dearest of my friends. Will you forgive me?"

What option did I have? So I gave him as fierce a gaze as I could manage, and swallowed hard, and nodded. This Master Jones was either as mad as a March hare, or as sane as a saint -- I could not decide which.

"You are very kind. To be honest, Mistress, I have to say that the reports which I have received about you from both near and far are so glowing that it would be indelicate to repeat them. Already I can confirm what I have heard about your appearance, your sense of humour, and your spirit. That, I dare say, is enough to be going on with."

"Quite so. I have had quite enough embarrassment for one day, thank you very much. Now sir, I want to hear about you. You were telling me about your strange calling to Newport."

"Ah yes. It was perhaps not so strange. My father Edmund Jones was also a pastor. He was a wonderful man, a devoted father and a great student of the spirit world. He travelled far and wide across Wales as an itinerant preacher, and was greatly attracted to this place which he referred to as "The Land of Mystery and Enchantment." He came here

Older if not Wiser

several times and told me stories about Pwyll Prince of Dyfed and Manawyddan the Wizard. He said that in the old Welsh books there were frequent references to this district, and to the adjacent coasts of Cardigan Bay, as the place where the *Tylwyth Teg* might be found. And he said that not far away is the entrance to the Otherworld, in which the heroes, the gods and the wizards of the Celtic world might be seen by those who have eyes to see. When I heard about Newport and Carningli from this old fellow in Swansea, who heard it from another fellow from these parts who was terribly deformed in some military campaign, I made a sort of connection in my head............."

"Iestyn Price?" I whispered.

"Pardon? Are you all right, Mistress? You are suddenly pale, as if you have seen a ghost."

I nodded. "Yes, yes, I am all right. But his name was Iestyn Price?"

"The old fellow was called Tom, as I recall. He never mentioned the name of the soldier, but I gathered that he worked in the furnaces and had a son in these parts, whom he periodically visited."

I had been standing, but now I had to sit down. I must have looked terrible, for Master Jones became concerned for me. He did not dare, after his previous indiscretions, to put his arm around me and comfort me, so he did the next best thing. He took off his stained and battered jacket, and put it over my shoulders. Then he stood back, and looked embarrassed.

At last I managed a weak smile. "I am sorry, Master Jones. I too have made a sort of connection. One day I will tell you about it. Pray continue."

"There is not much more to tell. I headed for Newport on that monster of a horse, who will end up as sausage meat if he does not mend his ways, and do you know what? I passed through Brynberian yesterday, over beyond those mighty rocks they call Carnedd Meibion Owen. You know it? Yes, I dare say you do. They have a fine new Independent chapel there, and when I came upon it I asked if I might go inside to pray. By all means, they said, and when I emerged refreshed some thirty minutes later I talked to some of the elders and deacons who had miraculously appeared from nowhere. I told them of my preaching mission, and they told me that theirs was a Chapel with a strong congregation but no minister! Now Mistress, would you not agree with me that that was as true a call from the Holy Spirit as you are ever likely to see? It is arranged that I will meet these respectable gentlemen again on the day after tomorrow, and if it is the wish of the Good Lord I may, before long, have a church of my own and a roof over my head! Is that not a sort of miracle, Mistress?"

I had to laugh at his innocent enthusiasm, and his faith, but most of all I had to share his laughter and his pleasure. So we talked and talked of this and that, and quite lost track of time, until suddenly I realized that it was almost dark. "Oh my goodness!" I exclaimed. "It must be almost six o'clock. If I leave it a moment longer they will be sending out a search party from the Plas. I must go. Will you come with me and join the disreputable Morgans of Plas Ingli for a simple supper?"

"Thank you, Mistress, but I must decline. I am not dressed for a social visit, as you have reminded me. In any case, I promised that I would be back at my lodgings in time for supper at seven, and I will surely be late. I fear that I must descend on the north side of the mountain while you descend on the south. Will you be quite safe on your own?"

"I know every inch of Carningli, sir. And I have the angels and a full moon to guide me. The northern path is a good one, once you have descended through the boulders, and there is still just enough daylight for you to make it out. Lower down the moon will help you. Take care, and I trust that we shall meet again."

"May I call and see you, Mistress, when I have sorted matters out with the Brynberian elders and deacons?"

"Of course. Send me a day's warning, and I will ensure that we get something out of the larder fit for a travelling preacher who has not had a decent meal for six months."

He smiled, and kissed my hand, and then gave a deep sweeping bow the like of which I had not seen for many years. Then he disappeared between the rocky outcrops which flanked the northern track, and headed for his lodging house supper. I sat for a while and watched him descend, leaping with surprising agility from one rock to another. I found myself strangely perturbed by the thought that he might slip and hurt himself, or even fall and lose consciousness, and freeze to death on this cold October night. But I laughed off such silly concerns, jumped to my feet and hurried home as fast as my legs would carry me.

I still experience a sort of thrill, even now, at the recollection of that first strange meeting with the eccentric Amos Jones nine months ago. Now I will stop, for the sun is sliding towards the western ocean and I can hear

Older if not Wiser

Will calling the cows home for milking. That means that it is fifteen minutes past four. I will continue with my narrative tomorrow, if it is not too hot for me to hold a quill pen and move my wrist.

ΩΩΩΩΩΩΩΩΩΩΩ

3rd July 1845

When I got back to the Plas on that October evening it was very dark, and Bessie and Daisy were beginning to worry about me. Daisy scolded me as I might have scolded her forty years ago. "Mother *bach*," she said. "You have been on the mountain again in the pitch blackness, have you not? I have told you before, and I will tell you again, that you are much too old for such adventures. And just look at that dress! Covered with grass and mud, and dirt on your face too!"

Bessie had seen it all before, and she saw from the smug expression on my glowing face that there was nothing at all wrong with me, and that I had been enjoying myself. "Don't fret, Daisy," she said. "You just let your old mother be. She has been having fun -- can you not see that? In fact, I would go further, and hazard a guess that she has been up to no good."

"What an outrageous suggestion, Bessie!" said I with as much ferocity as I could muster. "Well, since you ask, I have indeed been up on the mountain. And while I was up there, enjoying the view, it was my misfortune to fall over a minister of religion who was saying his prayers."

At this, both Daisy and Bessie fell about the place with hysterical laughter, and it was as much as I could do to calm them down. "It is perfectly true, I tell you!" I protested to the disbelieving heathens who live beneath my roof. "To lie would be a sin, and I have given up sinning."

At last they calmed down enough to take my narrative seriously, and over supper, with Will also in residence for the evening, I told them everything. They were greatly entertained, and when I told them that Amos Jones the preacher was the son of another preacher named Edmund Jones, Bessie exclaimed: "Well well, I see the connection now, Mistress. A reverend gentleman called Edmund Jones came here long ago, when I was newly started at the Plas as a housemaid. That would have been before your time. He preached in the open air down at Trefelin ford, and I recall that he visited the Plas and blessed the new house which was then being built to replace the old one lost in that terrible fire. Grandma Jane and Grandpa Isaac said that his blessing gave them great strength at a time when lesser mortals might not have coped."

"That would have been fifty years ago, Bessie. You are blessed by a good memory. But what a strange coincidence! Do you remember what Jones the Father looked like?"

"Yes -- quite good looking, as I recall, with sandy hair, and a weatherbeaten face, and a slight build. And very piercing light blue eyes -- I remember them clearly. But he was the world's worst preacher, and while I dare say it is the calling of itinerant evangelists to inject their congregations with good doses of the Holy Spirit, I recall that when I heard him at Trefelin ford I was more inclined to fall asleep than to scream in ecstasy."

We all laughed, and Will asked "Why then, Bessie *bach*, if his preaching was so forgettable, do you remember him and his visit at all?"

"Partly because of the impression he made at the Plas, and partly, I think, because of his name and his reputation. He was not called Jones the Father at all, but Jones the Prophet."

"How intriguing!" said I. "Master Amos said that his father was a great student of the supernatural. Now it appears that he was a prophet too.........."

"And a writer, Mistress. I recall that when he came to the Plas he met Master Harries the Wizard, and they conversed for a very long time. I do believe that he gave the wizard a book which he had written himself."

"More and more extraordinary, Bessie. I am sure I have seen that book and even handled it. It was in Joseph's library when he died, and it came back here to the Plas when I emptied Werndew and embarked upon the rebuilding of the cottage. Together with Joseph's wands and robes and collections of herbs and medicines, it sat in one of the upstairs cupboards for several years, until I gave everything to Shemi when he started his career in wizardry. I do believe that I even thumbed through its pages. It looked interesting, and was all about ghosts and spirits and demons, although I remember that it had the world's longest title which started with the

Older if not Wiser

words *A Relation of Apparitions of Spirits* or some such thing."

"Enough of fathers, Mother," said Daisy. "How about the son? It is obvious that you liked him more than a little. Is he handsome?"

"Not especially.   He has an open and friendly face, with high cheekbones and very blue eyes, which I presume to be inherited from his prophetic father.   And sandy hair which he cuts short.   But of course his nose is too small and his ears are too big for him to be really striking."

At this, Bessie hooted with laughter.   "Of course, Mistress, it would never do for him to be **too** perfect! I perceive that you already have a soft spot for him. Is he old enough to be interesting?"

Trying hard not to blush, I replied: "Maybe in his middle fifties? It is hard to tell.   What with his long years on the road, he may be younger than he looks."

"And a thought from me, Mistress, if I may be so bold," said Will, demonstrating a singular awareness of female susceptibilities and a singular concern for womankind. "Are you sure that this encounter on the mountain top was not carefully planned by Master Jones?   From your description of events, I might, if I was a cynical fellow, see an ancient male strategy being played out before our very eyes."

"No, never, Will," I protested. "I am far too old and battered to be seduced. In any case I am sure that Master Jones was genuinely at prayer when I stumbled across him, and equally sure that he had not the slightest expectation that anybody would come to the top of the mountain during his devotions. Indeed, he was there because he wanted perfect peace and no interruptions.   Fate may have planned our encounter, but I am sure that that religious gentleman did no planning at all."

"Hum hum," said Will, puffing on his clay pipe. "I hope that you are right, and that he is simply a lonely fellow in need of friends. Meet him, will we?"

"That is my hope and my expectation. I dare say I will get a note from him when he has completed his business with the Brynberian deacons and when he has preached a few sermons for the consideration of the elders."

"Let us hope, Mistress, that they are better than his father's," said Bessie, "or he will pretty soon be sent packing by those who are thirsty for righteousness."

Our conversation was at an end. Bessie cleared away the dishes and

67

started on the washing-up in the scullery. Will settled down with his pipe and his newspaper in the settle by the fireside which used to be occupied by Grandpa Isaac. Daisy took up her sampler and resumed work on it with exaggerated intensity. I pretended not to notice, and picked up where I had left off on the knitting of a pair of socks for my grandson Owain. I could see from the corner of my eye that Daisy was looking at me intently, and when at last I glanced in her direction she gave me the slightest of winks, and I blushed like a fourteen-year-old.

ΩΩΩΩΩΩΩΩΩΩΩ

15th July 1845

My most recent diary entries have referred to events which took place back in the autumn of last year. Since then I have received many social visits from Master Amos Jones. I have more to say about our developing relationship, but not now, for I have been plunged into yet another family crisis. I know now whose corpse was contained in the first coffin to be delivered to the quayside which I observed in my dream. My brother Morys died ten days since after a short illness of which I had been unaware, so I have spent most of the time since my last diary entry in the big house at Brawdy, doing what I could to help his wife Nansi and the rest of his family left behind on this troubled earth.

I rushed to Brawdy as soon as I received the news, leaving Daisy in charge of the Plas. Nansi, with whom I have developed a firm and loving friendship over the years, surprised everybody by the manner in which she simply fell to pieces on the realisation that she was now alone. I was surprised more than most, for all of my early memories of her are of a strong and resolute woman who betrayed her emotions hardly at all and who was capable of coping with everything. Indeed, I remember being thoroughly envious of her calm competence. But when I arrived I found that Nansi would not leave the side of her dead husband and that she would not even accept that he was dead. She did not cry, but looked around her with wild and terrible eyes, as if pleading with her nearest

Older if not Wiser

and dearest to tell her that Morys was simply fast asleep. Her daughter Jane told me that she had stopped eating and that she had not slept a wink since the death had occurred in mid-afternoon two days earlier. Jane was distraught, because in addition to trying to cope with her own grief she was desperately worried that her mother was now willing herself into a premature grave. Thank God that her sons Edward and Robert were both there, and that they were old and sensible enough to get on with funeral arrangements and with the running of the estate. Edward, as the older of the two, was now in any case the Squire of Brawdy, so he had to accept responsibility for everything.

At last we had to pull Nansi away from the corpse so that the undertaker could do his work; and during the *Gwylnos*, when Morys lay in his open coffin in the parlour so that all the neighbours and friends could come and pay their last respects, poor Nansi would not move out of the bedroom. The funeral was one of the biggest seen in the parish for many years. Nansi refused to attend at the church or the burial in Brawdy Churchyard, and in order to give some relief to the three children and their families I stayed with her at home. That was not easy, for Morys was my beloved brother with whom I had always had a gentle and easy relationship. I was not able to say my last farewells to him until a couple of days later, when the others had recovered from their own ordeals and had waved off the friends and relatives who had travelled from far afield. Then, when Jane and the others felt able to take over the duty of looking after Nansi, I was able to go to the churchyard all alone and shed tears on his grave.

Dear kind Morys! To me he had always been the perfect older brother, ready to scold me when I was young and foolish, to warn me about the consequences of my wilful behaviour (for I was indeed a disobedient and rebellious child), and to pick me up when I fell. He had even gathered me up when I fell from grace, in the days when he had been the rector of a small parish in Carmarthenshire, by performing a marriage ceremony under license for David and myself in conditions of great secrecy when I discovered that I was with child. That was almost fifty years ago. It seemed even longer, when I reflected on the tumultuous happenings of the years between then and now. Not long after that secret marriage ceremony (and perhaps because of it) he left the church and became a Baptist minister instead, looking after a little flock in Haverfordwest until, on the

69

Older if not Wiser

death of my father in 1817, he inherited the Brawdy estate. After that, he had devoted his life to the estate and to his family, and to looking after our mother Betsi who died only four years ago at a very ripe old age. Now he was gone, leaving just us three girls -- Elen, Catrin and myself -- with our fond memories of childhood days around the Brawdy estate, in the deep wooded valleys of Rhyndaston and Brandy Brook, and on the great cliffs of St Bride's Bay. Elen was in America, out of sight but not out of touch, but it was a blessing that Catrin and I were together around the time of the funeral, and we talked at great length, day after day.

With her parents long since dead and buried, and with no brothers or sisters of her own, it now emerged that poor Nansi had precious few close friends, for she had devoted herself to her own husband and children to such an extent that she had hardly ever, over the course of almost thirty years, ventured beyond the main gatehouse of the Brawdy estate. That was surprising, since she had previously been a minister's wife enjoying a multitude of contacts with people from all walks of life. In her time in Haverfordwest she had even ministered to the needs of the poor souls incarcerated in the filthy gaol not more than two hundred yards from the door of the manse. She had been a perfect companion for Morys, a model mother, and a veritable angel of mercy. So why had she turned inwards upon herself? Catrin and I speculated endlessly about this, as did her children and their spouses, but I suppose the truth will never be known.

At any rate, I decided yesterday that I could not stay at Brawdy any longer, and that Edward and his wife Susan needed to take responsibility for Nansi's welfare. They accepted that themselves, while complaining that they would never be able to communicate with her as I did. Before I left, I spent a couple of hours with Nansi in her bedroom. She seemed to have shrivelled up to half her former size, for she had eaten hardly anything since Morys's death, and her skin was the colour and texture of ancient parchment. I decided that I had given her enough sympathy and understanding, so now I gave her a good talking to instead. I told her that she was not the first or the last woman on this earth to lose a beloved husband, and in case she had forgotten the details I reminded her of my own dear men, David and then Owain, who had gone before me to their graves. I also reminded her that she had lost no child of her own, whereas I had lost both Dewi and Sara in the prime of life. In talking like this I dare say I was being rather crass and cruel, but in truth I was angered by

Older if not Wiser

her whimpering and moaning, her obsession with grief, and her apparent determination to die. Then I reminded her that she was behaving like a selfish old woman, intent upon causing the grief of her own offspring to be compounded by yet more grief when she soon went to her grave. At that, some spirit came back into her eyes, and she whispered: "Surely, Martha, that is not what you and the others think?" I told her that indeed it was, and that it was high time she thought of others rather than herself. Then I asked her what Morys would have wanted from her in the way of behaviour. Would he be proud of her demeanour should he be looking down at her, this very moment, from his assured place in Heaven? He would most certainly not! Indeed, he might well be thoroughly ashamed that such a fine woman, with a loving family and so much to live for, should have transformed herself into such a snivelling wretch, hanging on within an inch of death. "Die if you like, Nansi," said I. "But do not expect me to come to your funeral. I only attend the funerals of those whom I respect, and those who have good deaths. I fear that you have lost my respect, and that you are intent upon a bad, bad death."

Then I got up, and I saw that she was shivering with emotion. I kissed her on her cheek, and held her hands in mine, and pulled her to her feet. And so she wept, for a very long time, with my arms about her and with her head buried on my shoulder. Edward and the others, who had been downstairs, heard the commotion and came rushing up to the bedroom, but I saw them as they entered, and ushered them away again with my eyes and a little movement of my head.

When Nansi was done with weeping, I wiped away her tears and helped her to change her dress. We did not exchange a single word. At last she managed a weak smile. "Martha, are my eyes very red?" she asked.

"Of course they are, Nansi, and that is as it should be. Edward and the others will not think you any less beautiful for it. Now then, let us go downstairs and see whether there is something on the kitchen table for lunch. You may eat a little and drink a little, and then a little more for supper. By the time you come to visit me at the Plas in three weeks' time, I expect you to have grown back into that pretty blue cotton dress of yours which is currently three sizes too big. I will invite Catrin too. Will you promise to come, and will you wear that dress?"

"How can I, Martha? I will still be in full mourning."

Older if not Wiser

"No no, by then half mourning will do. Wear your black crepe veil and cape, and I promise you that you will not be criticised."

She smiled, and nodded, and the two of us went down to the kitchen hand in hand.

Now that I am back at home in the Plas, I have to admit to being greatly relieved. Nansi will be all right, with the loving care of Edward and Susan and her grandchildren and servants. But, on looking back, I shiver at the thought of the blunt and brutal approach which I used to bring the poor lost soul back into the real world, and feel certain that such methods do not even exist in the manuals of those who counsel the grieving and bring healing to the sick. Morys, who was in his time famous as a soother of troubled breasts, would certainly not have approved. Not for the first time, I think that I have got away with something which might have had a quite different outcome. Well, life must go on, as the old people say, and I will look forward to a rewarding few days sometime next month in the company of Nansi and Catrin.

ΩΩΩΩΩΩΩΩΩΩΩ

20th July 1845

I was quite exhausted when I returned to the Plas after the emotional turmoil of Brawdy, and took several days to get my strength back. But Daisy and the others had managed perfectly well in my absence, and I had to remind myself that I had been away in the past, sometimes for prolonged periods, without the estate collapsing or disappearing. This realization brought to mind a little episode when I was very young and full of my own self-importance. My father had taken me for a walk past Brawdy Churchyard (where he, and my mother and my dear brother now lie) and he had pointed in over the old stone wall and said: "Now then, Martha, I want you to remember this whenever you think that others cannot cope without you. That place over there is occupied entirely by indispensable people."

So on the basis that we come and we go without the world taking any

Older if not Wiser

of our arrivals and departures too seriously, I shall continue to describe my disjointed relationship with Master Amos Jones. After that first meeting on the mountain top he did write to me after a few days to explain that everything was now arranged with the deacons at Brynberian Chapel and that he would shortly be taking up a position as pastor on a trial basis, to see whether he and his congregation liked each other. He would receive no payment, but would be given free lodgings and food in the home of a faithful chapel family, and furthermore he would be free to travel and to preach to the unconverted for two weeks out of every four, and even to visit his wife.

I cannot explain why, but that last piece of news in his note caused my heart to miss a beat. It had not even occurred to me that he might be married, and indeed I had assumed that the life of an itinerant preacher was entirely unsuitable for a married or family man, and that therefore he must be a bachelor. He had not mentioned a wife or family during our conversation on the mountain top, and indeed I had omitted to ask him about his personal circumstances, so interested had he been in finding out all about me and something about the Plas.

I wrote back to the preacher at Capel Brynberian to invite him to join us for supper on the following Wednesday, and after sending Will off to deliver my letter I passed on my latest discoveries to Daisy and Bessie. "So he is clearly set to stay for a while, if not longer, Mistress," said Bessie. "That should make life interesting. And a happily married gentleman, is he?"

"Married, yes. As to the happiness, I cannot hazard a guess. But if I was to be married to a travelling preacher, I imagine that I would not be the happiest person in this world -- unless, of course, he was to be so mad or cruel that I would be glad to have him out of the house and out of my bed."

"Now then, Mother," sniggered Daisy. "No talk of marriage beds, if you please. Let us speculate that Mistress Jones is a mighty rock upon which a loving marriage is based, and that she sacrifices her own interests and happiness for her husband's high and sacred calling."

So we left it at that, and when I sat in the quiet of my own room several hours later at bedtime, I tried to analyse my own initial response to the news that the minister was married. Surely I cannot have harboured any hopes of a deeper friendship with an eccentric fellow whom I had met under the strangest of circumstances only a few days before? I

Older if not Wiser

knew hardly anything about him, and as Will had suggested, he might indeed have been an opportunist or even a charlatan. Was I really so lonely in this awkward time between middle age and old age that I allowed my heart to miss a beat simply because an attractive man looked me in the eye and paid me a few outrageous compliments? I thought that Master Jones was much younger than me, with the social status of a travelling nonconformist preacher, somewhere below the status of a clerk or a curate and somewhere above that of a tenant farmer. In reality, from the look of his clothes and shoes I surmised that he was probably destitute, and therefore on a par with those who inhabit the Cardigan and Narberth Workhouses. He was probably kept alive by the charitable donations of well-wishers. He and I appeared to be socially incompatible. And yet he was well educated, well-spoken, and even happy. And although I considered his commitment to religion and evangelizing misplaced, I could not deny that he seemed enthusiastic and contented. I have always liked to see enthusiasm in a man, and on thinking about this I recalled that one of the dearest friends of my life had been Joseph Harries, wizard and *dyn hysbys*, healer, herbalist and apothecary, solver of mysteries and scourge of criminals, and enthusiasm personified. He and I had been from opposite ends of the social spectrum and yet we had shared a deep and enduring friendship. In some ways Master Amos Jones reminded me of Joseph, with his sharp eyes and his ready wit. Enough, enough. Master Jones was married, and that was the end of it.

On the Wednesday he did come, and to their credit Bessie and Daisy prepared a feast fit for a king. We ate a spicy tomato soup and crusty rolls to start with, followed by sewin caught to order by a nameless friend of Will's, followed by veal cutlets and five vegetables, and rounded off with blackberry pie and fresh cream, caraway seed cake and crystallised fruits. As ever, with the inestimable Will becoming ever more astute at spending my money, we drank excellent wines during the meal and fine China tea afterwards.

Eight of us sat down to dinner together -- Daisy, Master Jones and myself, and then Bessie, Will and his wife Tegwen and Liza and her husband Tomos. My servants do not get many treats in life, and I thought it would be a pleasant thing for them to dress up for a change and to feast in the Plas Ingli dining room, with no expense spared, in the company of a visiting evangelist. The evening was a great success, although it started

74

Older if not Wiser

off awkwardly when the preacher arrived too early, having miscalculated the distance between Brynberian and the Plas. He looked rather like a poorly dressed scarecrow, having borrowed blue breeches, a yellow waistcoat and a red jacket from the kindly Master George Ifans with whom he was lodging at Tregwynt. Daisy could scarcely contain herself, and she said afterwards that his attire would have been well suited to an afternoon out on Mynydd Preseli with the Cemais Hunt, but her sniggers were soon banished by the unselfconscious charm of our guest, who melted hearts as easily as he chatted to all and sundry. He explained to us in the parlour before the meal that he did have feelings of guilt about enjoying good food, good wine and good company when so many of his flock were starving, but we argued that conviviality was not a sin included in the Ten Commandments and he accepted the points we made as "persuasive but not conclusive". Just this once, he said, out of deference to the Mistress of the house, he would endeavour to enjoy himself. He made no attempt to hide his calling or his heartfelt beliefs, and indeed thoroughly enjoyed a deep theological argument with Daisy over the fish course while the rest of us listened in wonderment.

We all ate too much and drank too much, and I am ashamed to admit that at around three in the morning the strains of several of the wonderful hymns of Charles Wesley and Williams Pantycelyn echoed around the *cwm*, lustily destroyed by eight of us who should all have known better. My excuse is that Master Jones knew no other songs, and that the rest of us had to defer to our guest. At the end of it all, it was clear that Master Jones could not find his own way back to Brynberian. I was about to insist that he should settle down in our spare room for the night, but Daisy, who has forgotten more about scandal than I will ever know, jumped in first and asked if Will and Tegwen might be able to put him up for what was left of the night in their cottage. Of course they readily agreed, and when we had all said our farewells, they went off unsteadily into the darkness, guided by instinct and a swaying lantern.

Next morning Master Jones called in, looking somewhat the worse for wear, to thank me for my generous hospitality and to apologize for his lack of self-restraint. I told him that he had nothing to apologize for, and that we had greatly enjoyed his company. Frivolously I suggested that if he had to make his peace with God he could do it by preaching a sermon on abstinence to the devout people of Brynberian on the following Sunday. He

Older if not Wiser

grinned and said "Now that sounds like good advice, Mistress Martha! I shall take it!" And he bowed and jumped onto his obstinate horse, and after a few minutes of cajoling went slowly on his way.

When he had gone, we three women got back to the task of tidying up the house and washing the glasses, dishes, and cutlery. Of course we had to discuss our guest, and I was greatly relieved when both Bessie and Daisy pronounced that there was not an ounce of deceit in Master Jones, and that he was as honest and as innocent as the day he was born. What else had we discovered about him? Daisy said she had discovered that the preacher has a fierce antagonism to the theology of Master Calvin, and predicted that that might lead him into trouble with certain of the Brynberian elders. Bessie said that she had noticed that he had not spoken of his wife once during the entire evening, or mentioned any offspring, and that she was convinced that the marriage was childless and unhappy. And I pondered deeply, and said nothing at all.

ΩΩΩΩΩΩΩΩΩΩ

3. Secrets and Lies

21st July 1845

Today it is Sunday, and my favourite granddaughter Rose, as pretty as a child yet blooming into womanhood, has been to see me. We talked about young gentlemen, and clothes and music, and much else besides. Then the conversation turned to diaries, and when she told me about hers I revealed that I too had been scribbling away for many years. I showed her my current volume, and although she is a fluent Welsh speaker and reader she was quite amazed that she could not understand a word of my writing.

I did not tell Rose just how much I have bared my soul in past volumes, or what I have done with them. One diary rests in a tin chest almost directly over my head as I sit here at my dressing table on this calm May night. It is tucked into the angle between joists and rafters in the darkness of the attic, and will stay there, I trust, until this dear house becomes old and ruinous as it surely will. Another, describing the most exciting and brutal time of my life, is nestled innocuously between two of Master Shakespeare's plays in the library of Plas Pontfaen, the childhood home of Owain Laugharne to whom I was betrothed. Another has gone to my son Brynach at Plas Llanychaer for safekeeping, in exchange for an oath on his part that he would keep it hidden for at least fifty years after my death. And the most recent has been entrusted to my friend Tom Foster, a young man of prodigious talents who is a reporter on *The Times* newspaper and who proved both his friendship and his discretion in full measure during the turbulent years of the Rebecca Riots. I do not greatly care what happens down the years to my little volumes, so long as they remain hidden for as long as I live and for the time that needs to elapse so as to avoid the embarrassment of my children and grandchildren and any others who might have known me.

There are developments to report. I have received two letters. One came from Brawdy, and was written by Nansi. It was calm and collected, and confirmed in my mind that she is on the way to a good recovery from the despair which afflicted her following Morys's death. She said that she would come to see me in the middle of next month, and would do her best to expand to the point where she could fill that pretty blue dress of hers. That was good news, and I immediately replied with a suggested date for her arrival at the Plas, and wrote to invite Catrin to come at the same time. We will not exactly have fun together, for it is still too soon after Morys's death, but I hope that we will be able to share -- and maybe laugh about -- memories of a beloved brother and husband. It will be the middle of the corn harvest, and the Plas will not exactly be a place of serenity, but the hubbub will do Nansi good. I might even encourage her to help out on the cornfield, if she is not too obsessed with mourning etiquette.

My other letter was from sister Elen in America, very newsy and cheerful and describing the delights of a New York summer. It was difficult for me to read, because she had written it shortly after midsummer, of course without any knowledge of either the illness or death of Morys. She could not have received any of the letters written by Catrin, Edward or myself on behalf of the Brawdy family, and I was saddened and angered by the thought that our letters had probably crossed in the middle of the great Atlantic Ocean as they had done on previous occasions of family bereavement. When she finally received our sad letters, I imagined that she would be mortified to think of us here in Wales reading her flippant and frivolous remarks at a time when we should all have been grieving together, as a family. Such is the penalty -- one of the penalties -- of migration to a faraway land.

ΩΩΩΩΩΩΩΩΩΩΩ

27th July 1845

I have omitted to report that over the past few months we have all learned a great deal more about Master Amos Jones. He is still the temporary pastor of Capel Brynberian, and he still has his lodgings at the little farm of Tregwynt when he chooses to use them. He stayed in the neighbourhood until mid-December of last year, and then off he went on that rebellious horse of his towards Radnor, in order to spend Christmas with his wife. Before he went, the deacons offered him a cottage within a

Secrets and Lies

stone's throw of the chapel if his position should be confirmed at the end of his year of probation, and the expectation was that his wife would then wish to join him here; but he did not appear very convinced about that, and explained away the situation by saying that Mistress Jones might well prefer to stay in Radnor where she is among friends and is not far from the rest of her family. So the matter of his accommodation is at present unresolved.

Since the beginning of this year Master Jones has been away for much of the time, preaching all over Wales. He has become one of the best-known of the travelling preachers, and indeed he has been at least partly responsible for a great spiritual awakening in West Wales in particular, for his sermons have attracted vast congregations. I have heard him on three occasions, and on each of them I was greatly impressed by his erudition, his knowledge of the scriptures, and his *hwyl*. At Crymych in the month of March he preached to a crowd of at least a thousand on the slopes of Frenni Fawr, and there were scenes of raw emotion during which a hundred or more publicly bewailed their sinfulness and committed themselves to the service of the Lord. Something similar, with only slightly fewer people in attendance, happened at Puncheston in February on a dark and bitterly cold day when all sensible folk might have been expected to stay at home by the fire. And then I heard him again at Eglwyswrw in April, when he preached with great power.

During my time at the Plas I have seen these awakenings or revivals on several occasions before, at intervals of maybe fifteen or twenty years. It is a simple matter to put them down to the miraculous workings of the Holy Spirit, but I suspect that there is more to it than that, and that each awakening can be attributed to the zeal and superhuman energy of a charismatic preacher who is in the right place at the right time. Master Jones is certainly such a preacher, who happens to have moved into this area at a time when many of the churches and chapels were at a low ebb, with small and dispirited congregations and with growing concerns about drunkenness and other sinful behaviour across the community. I have spoken many times to Master Jones, on his visits to the Plas, about the manner in which he can manipulate a crowd and about reactions among his listeners that I would call emotional or even hysterical; but he laughs in that disarming way of his and claims that he is but a vessel used by the Lord to bring salvation to the wicked and balm to the suffering. I remember

Secrets and Lies

his words during one conversation. "Yes, Martha," he had said, "I freely acknowledge my role in working up a crowd to a pitch of excitement. That is where my skill as a preacher comes in. It is a gift which my father never had, and I have to assume it to be a gift given by God. I take a pride in it, as a great actor or musician does when he has moved his listeners to tears. Then you might ask yourself -- as I do every time I am on my knees before God -- whether my preaching brings benefit or harm. Benefit every time, Martha. If I can bring men and women to face up to their weaknesses, and to be kinder to each other, be it for a day or a year or a lifetime, and to seek personal salvation, and to enjoy fellowship rather than loneliness, then I will have done something with my life."

I am still trying to understand Master Jones's personal creed and system of beliefs, and I wish I had listened with greater attention to the dull sermons of my young days. If I had, I might now have a greater understanding of matters theological and appreciate why it is that Rector Llewelyn Thomas denounces my friend as a heretic and why even some of the elders of Brynberian are mumbling about his "distinctly unorthodox views." Well, I thought Independents were supposed to hold unorthodox views -- if they did not they would presumably still be faithful attenders of Brynberian Parish Church. One thing I have noticed is that Master Jones talks a lot about spirits and appears perfectly comfortable while chatting about ghosts and goblins, demons and familiars, spells and charms. While other religious gentlemen roundly condemn everything to do with the world of the supernatural, Master Jones sees no incompatibility at all between his Christian beliefs and the old beliefs said to have come from pre-Biblical days. He sees the strange phenomena which terrify normal mortals simply as the manifestations of unhappy spirits who need to be spoken to, calmed and put at their ease if they are to go away and stay away in the spirit world. In all of this, Master Jones seems to have a creed closer to that of wizards like Joseph Harries and Shemi Jenkins than to that of the Bishop of St Davids. He is altogether a very interesting fellow.

He is also a prophet, like his father. I have not yet pressed him on his premonitions or reading of omens, but I have it on good authority from Bessie that three months ago he sent a message to some place near Aberaeron where he was due to preach on a certain date, stating that he could not come because of torrential rain and damage to the only bridge over the river. His friends in that neighbourhood were greatly offended, since the weather was perfectly fine and since the bridge was in good order. But sure enough, early on the day of his preaching engagement the heavens opened, the river level rose by five feet, and the bridge was swept away. I have heard other stories too, in similar vein, and indeed so widespread are the rumours of his prophetic abilities that he has now been labelled "Jones Minor Prophet". This distinguishes him from his father, who is still widely remembered in these parts and who is now accorded the posthumous title of "Jones Major Prophet."

The new title is apt in another way too, since Amos was of course one of the minor prophets who has his own tidy little book in the Bible. I must settle down to read it, for it may give me further insights into the priorities and beliefs of the dear man for whom I am developing a considerable admiration. I am sure that his father, the late lamented Reverend Edmund Jones, will have prayed long and hard, and hopefully received guidance from on high, before choosing the right name for the little baby whom he held in his arms at the baptismal font.

ΩΩΩΩΩΩΩΩΩΩΩ

22nd August 1845

I have been so preoccupied with the corn harvest, and with the visit of Nansi and Catrin, that I have hardly had time to address an issue which is making me very confused.

Right in the middle of the wheat harvest, when Nansi and Catrin were still here and my hands were full with social duties and the organizing of harvesters, Brynach turned up in the Llanychaer carriage without warning, accompanied by Rose and David. It was mid-morning. Of course a part of me was delighted to see them, and I did my best to hide my slight irritation at my son's lack of consideration. I invited them to settle down for a meal so that we could all talk together. But Brynach would not stop, and asked if Rose and David might stay for a night or two while he rushed straight on to Carmarthen on some urgent business. "You

Secrets and Lies

know that the children are always welcome at the Plas," said I. "But is your business so urgent that you cannot even come in for a bite to eat, and chat with your aunts for an hour or so?"

"I am very sorry, Mother," replied Brynach, "but this matter has to be attended to this very evening, and I may already be too late. Please forgive me, all of you. I will be back tomorrow, or on Wednesday at the latest." And with that he unloaded the children's baggage, gave each of us a quick embrace, and jumped back into the carriage. His man cracked the whip, and horses and vehicle went careering off down the driveway towards the Cilgwyn Road, scattering chickens as it went.

When the dust had settled and I had recovered from my astonishment, I looked at the children. They appeared to be as confused as I, but they were not upset so far as I could ascertain, and they ran immediately upstairs to the room in which they had slept on many previous occasions, next to Daisy's bedroom.

There were twenty harvesters to feed, and carting and rick building to supervise, so for some hours I had no time to ponder on the strange circumstances surrounding this unexpected visit. But at last, when eleven-year-old David was playing in the rickyard with some of the other children from the tenants' farms and labourers' cottages, I managed to talk to Rose, who is fourteen and old enough to know what is going on. "Now then Rose," said I. "You are very close to your father. What is all this about?"

A shadow came over her face, and she replied: "I wish I knew, Grandma. But Papa has not been himself lately. With the harvest in full swing, he has shown very little interest in it, and has passed all of the decisions over to his head man Albert. He explained that as a matter of delegating responsibility and rewarding long service. Albert was of course very flattered, and will manage perfectly well. But........."

"Well, dear child?"

"....... there are other things I do not understand, Grandma. He has been coming and going very often over the past month or two, although never staying away overnight, and writing a lot of letters, and receiving many visitors."

"What sort of visitors, Rose?"

"I am not sure. Papa has been very secretive, but I think that one or two of them might have been attorneys, for they carried with them very big bags and bundles of papers."

"Did they look sad or happy, in your estimation?"

"I thought it was the business of attorneys always to look sad, Grandma."

I laughed, and suddenly I came to a realisation as to what this might all be about. So I asked: "Have the visitors included any fine ladies?"

"Well yes, now that you come to mention it. Three at least, with their fathers to look after them. Each of them was very pretty, and I thought their clothes quite beautiful."

"And did one of them seem to make your Papa particularly happy when you saw them together?"

"I cannot be sure. There was one who was very jolly, and who made him laugh a lot. I think she was called Lisbet, and she and her father came all the way from near Carmarthen. I forget the name of their estate."

"So there we have it, Rose! I do believe that your father might be in love, and is planning to be married! He always was very secretive, and very good at hiding his emotions. But men behave in strange ways that we women will never fully understand. Sometimes, when they should laugh and smile, they appear listless and forlorn instead. But you are old enough to know that since the death of your dear mother eight years ago, your Papa must have been very lonely indeed in spite of having you and David for company. A man needs a wife, and a fine estate needs a Mistress. Has your Papa never talked to you about such things?"

"Yes, now and then. But would he not seek a blessing from David and me if he is planning to get married?"

"Of course. And if marriage is the business in hand, I am sure that he will make no commitments until you and your brother are in full agreement. With a bit of luck, he might even seek the blessing of his old mother."

Then Rose noticed the tear in my eye, and came and put her arms around me. "Now then, Grandma, don't you fret. My father loves you more than anything in the world, and would never do anything that might upset you. Perhaps he wants to put everything in place before raising your hopes of a new marriage in the family, and then dashing them again?"

"You may be right, child. Marriage these days is a complicated business, which is probably why you have seen attorneys coming and going.

I never did understand marriage settlements, but I dare say they are essential if one party to a marriage is not to marry too far up and the other too far down."

"So do you think, Grandma, that Papa has gone rushing off to Carmarthen in order to arrange a settlement?"

"Let us hope so, Rose. Perhaps the forlorn look on your father's face this morning was the look of a man both apprehensive and in love, and let us pray that he has a broad smile on his face when he returns. We both want him to be happy, do we not?"

And my granddaughter nodded and laughed, and we embraced. Then I had to return to the small matter of the harvest, and we two had no time for further confidences.

As I write this late at night, with the harvest moon sailing high overhead, I trust that Brynach is making sound decisions during his absence. He is a good man, and quite old enough to take responsibility for his own life, but I still feel a little upset that he has not sought my advice or my blessing in what might be by some distance the most important decision of his life.

ΩΩΩΩΩΩΩΩΩΩΩΩ

23rd August 1845

Brynach has still not returned, but mine is not to reason why, and in any case we have been celebrating harvest home. With Catrin and Nansi still here, and with the extra hands of Rose and David, the wheat harvest has gone along with great gusto, blessed by bright weather and a good drying wind. It is a small harvest anyway compared with the barley harvest, with only two fields to be cut, gathered, stooked and carted. We have managed without the Irish in the wheat fields this year, but they have not gone short of work, since I sent them off to Gelli Fawr, Ffynnonddofn and Bayvil in the certain knowledge that there were at least thirty wheat fields to be harvested and that labour would be in short supply. They needed the work, poor things, but I had mixed feelings about sending

Secrets and Lies

them to provide sweated and underpaid labour for three squires whose sole intention is to pull in a good harvest and then hold it until the number of deaths from starvation or conflict in Ireland is so great that the Government will pay well over the odds for any shipments of grain that they can get from the ports of West Wales.

As ever, we rounded off the harvest with traditional high spirits. This morning the last few stalks of standing wheat in the middle of Parc Haidd were assaulted by flying and whirling sickles thrown by the men from ten yards away, and I thank God (as I do every year) that nobody was decapitated. Gomer was the one who managed to slice off the last stalks, and he was roundly cheered and chased by all the lasses who happened to be in the vicinity. He did not flee all that energetically, which was understandable given that he had been slaving with a sickle under the hot sun for three days, and was kissed by all those who could get at him before he was rescued by his wife Gwenno. She took the horseplay in the spirit in which it was intended, and now that her bouts of morning sickness have come to an end, it was good to see her with tears of mirth rolling down her pretty cheeks.

This afternoon I rang the Plas Ingli bell, as it has been rung every year since the Morgans came to this place, to call in the gleaners. They came as ever, women and small children, from all of the cottages and hovels on the estate, watched over by Will in order to ensure that there were no interlopers in their midst. I know that there are others in the woods down by the river, and in hovels on the common, who are desperate for a basketful of wheat ears and bits of straw, but my charity can only extend so far. And this evening, with the wheat rick thatched and ready, we have feasted and danced in the barn, with music from my old harp and from Gwyn Williams's tin whistle. All the tenants were there, enjoying my hospitality as a reward for their labours, although in truth I was under no obligation in that regard since the provision of labour is required in lieu of cash under all of our tenancy agreements. We provided at least fifty people with food and drink and, as ever, Bessie was the one who worked miracles and received the cheers of the assembled company at the end of the meal. Every year she grumbles that the larder will be emptied as a result of my largesse, but every year she seems to fill it again, from our own good little garden and from elsewhere, just in time for the next feast in the calendar. Of course this way of life cannot go on for ever, now that men and

Secrets and Lies

women are moving off the land and into the cities and now that machines are being bought by all of the progressive squires. But I am old, and have no great liking for progress that costs lives, and so I will continue to look after my cheerful flock for as long as there is red blood in my veins.

After the feast, it gave me great pleasure as I plucked away on my harp-strings to notice that Rose was the belle of the ball (or rather, the belle of the *twmpath*), with her rosy cheeks and black hair and the slim waist and small firm breasts of one who will shortly be turning the heads of young gentlemen and sending servant boys mad with passion. She will need to be protected, I thought, rather better than I was protected at her age. And I was glad to see Catrin dancing and Nansi smiling and laughing. I could not convince her to abandon her black taffeta for the evening, but in retrospect that might have been a gesture too far for a gentlewoman who is still in half mourning.

I did one further thing this evening. Now that Gomer and Gwenno are established at Penrhiw as tenants following the death of Waldo Tucker, and now that they will shortly have a small baby to deal with, I dare say I will not get my six days a week of labour out of them for much longer. I will be short of servants, and neither Bessie nor Liza is as fit and healthy as I would like. So I have taken on Will's son Gerallt as a cowman and his daughter Myfanwy as a dairymaid. He is twenty-one years old and she is sixteen, and I have observed them both closely enough during both the hay harvest and the corn harvest to know that they are fit, strong, honest and intelligent. Up until now they have been labouring here, there and everywhere for a few days at a time, and although I should strictly not take them on until All Saint's Day I am not minded to wait. I have an intuition that I need them now. When I told Will he became very emotional, and gave me an embrace so warm that he scratched my face with his stubble. So now the third generation of Owens will be in service at the Plas, and that is something for me to celebrate in memory of the redoubtable Mrs Owen (Will's mother), who kept me in my place when I first arrived at the Plas as a slip of a girl in 1796.

The new servants will move in tomorrow with their meagre possessions. Gerallt will have the room once occupied by Billy and Will, and Myfanwy will settle into the little room under the stairs, next door to Bessie. They will have privacy, which is more than they ever had when they lived with their parents Will and Tegwen.

Secrets and Lies

Now it is late at night, and I have packed Rose and David off to bed. I too am exhausted, and will sleep the sleep of the just. Catrin and Nansi have also retired. Music and laughter are still echoing around the yard, and I dare say that, under the less than watchful eyes of Will and Gomer, dancing and other sports will go on until the early hours on the threshing floor and in the hay piled up against the west wall of the barn.

ΩΩΩΩΩΩΩΩΩΩΩΩ

24th August 1845

Today has been a day of thunderstorms and torrential rain, and of comings and goings. Catrin's son John came this morning in the Castlebythe covered carriage, and after affectionate farewells he drove his mother and his Aunt Nansi away into the deluge. Nansi will stay tonight at Castlebythe, and will be collected from there by her son Edward some time tomorrow. We have had a most agreeable time together, we three women, and I am sure that my visitors have enjoyed themselves in spite of a multitude of distractions.

In the middle of the morning, between spells of rain, Will brought up Gerallt and Myfanwy on the gambo, with their things. They settled into their rooms, and I had to devote some time to informing them as to my requirements and their daily duties. They did not need very much training, for they know the Plas well and have worked here often before, as small children on stone picking and bird scaring duties, and as older children at harvest time and ploughing time. They have both helped in the past during the Christmas festivities, and I dare say that their father has told them almost everything they need to know about my likes, dislikes and expectations.

And then this afternoon Jones Minor Prophet turned up without warning and looking very bedraggled, having been thrown from that terrible horse of his three times between Brynberian and the Plas. This time neither he nor I could blame the creature, for great flashes of sheet lightning and crashes of thunder are liable to cause even the most placid of

Secrets and Lies

mounts to panic, and I thought it a miracle that the creature had not flung off its rider and bolted to the other side of Mynydd Preseli in such conditions. Will calmed the horse down and found a stable space for it, and we took Master Jones in and found him some dry clothes in a chest in one of the servants' rooms. They were meant for a man twice his size, but he put them on anyway and emerged into the kitchen looking perfectly incongruous, with a heavy striped flannel shirt, baggy corduroy trousers and a woollen jacket from which all the buttons were missing. The last person to wear them was probably Shemi, shortly before he left the Plas to train as a wizard.

We all hooted with laughter, and to his credit Amos was entirely unconcerned, and gave us all a cheerful grin. That, I thought, was probably down to long years of practice in putting up with jeers and laughter on his preaching expeditions. I think he enjoyed being fussed over by Bessie, Liza and myself. Even Rose turned up and started clucking over him like an old hen. Between us we gave the poor fellow a hot mug of milk, since he was still shivering from his soaking. "Thank you, ladies. You are very kind," said he. "It is good to know that there is a home from home here at the Plas on occasions such as this, and that there are angels to minister to my needs."

There was more to that comment than met the eye. So I said: "Oh? Is this occasion a difficult one then, Master Jones?"

"Yes and no, Mistress Martha." He looked round apologetically, and decided that four females was more than he could cope with at one time. "Would it be possible, do you think, for us to chat for a moment in private, perhaps in your parlour?"

"Of course. Just this once I will allow it, although I should strictly be protected by a chaperone while in the presence of such an elegant gentleman. Please excuse us, ladies."

Once Master Jones and I were seated in the parlour he explained the purpose of his visit. He said that he wanted to say farewell, since he would be leaving for a long preaching journey across the length and breadth of Wales. As he said that, he saw the shadow on my face, and laughed. "I am flattered to see disappointment in your countenance, Martha," he said. "But I must follow my calling. I am getting to love both this place and my flock of good Christian people at Capel Brynberian, and I am pleased to be able to tell you that the deacons have today confirmed

Secrets and Lies

my appointment. They want me to start with my pastoral duties in the middle of November, and that is something that I look forward to."

"Oh, I am so pleased for you, Amos! That means that you can start to lead a normal life again!"

"Thank you, Martha. I am not sure what a normal life is, since I have spent so much of mine on the road with nothing in my head but sermons and prayers and nothing in my bag but a few scraps of food."

"Well, you deserve a little comfort after all the years of your life given to God, and after all the suffering you have endured. Think of your health for a change."

"Oh, indeed I shall," said he, standing up and striding around the room. "I shall not give up preaching in the open air, but once I am settled it will be more difficult for me to get away. So, with the permission of the deacons, I will now make one last grand tour, riding on the wave of the current great revival, and preaching at least fifty sermons. I hope and pray that I will be a conduit for the Holy Spirit and bring salvation to thousands of lost souls."

At this, I had to laugh. "Oh Amos," I spluttered, "you are truly a saint! How I wish I had your capacity for rising above personal problems and difficulties and seeing a grander and more noble picture!"

"No no, Martha, there you are wrong. I am very much aware of ..... personal things........." He spoke very quickly, and then checked himself. Our eyes met. Then he turned his back on me, as if he could not bear to look at me any longer, and he said: "I do not expect you to understand what it is that drives me, Martha. Suffice to say that it is important, for more than one reason, for me to get away to distant parts for a while." His voice was thick with emotion, and I knew not how to react. My heart was suddenly pounding so loudly that I was sure he would hear it. Time passed, and in truth I have no idea whether it might have been measured in seconds or centuries. But at last he turned round to face me. There was a firm set to his jaw, and his blue eyes were icy cold. Then they melted, and he managed a weak smile, glanced out through the window, and said: "I see that the rain has eased off. I must be on my way, since I preach in Cardigan this very evening at seven o'clock. Goodbye, Martha."

I was still sitting in my favourite chair by the fireplace, which was just as well. Had I been standing, I fear that my legs might have given way beneath me.

Secrets and Lies

"Goodbye, Amos. Take care, and come back safe and sound." That was all I could say. I held out my hand, and he kissed it before giving a deep bow and striding out of the room. I sat there for a long time, listening while he bade farewell to the others in the kitchen and gathered up his things. I heard snatches of conversation. "These clothes?" "Just you keep them till you return....." "Are you sure, Bessie?" "Mistress Martha would wish it......."

Then I heard the sound of hooves on gravel, and I looked out of the window to see Jones Minor Prophet riding away down the drive, reasonably well protected against the weather by an old oilskin that used to belong to my servant Billy. Two bundles containing most of his worldly possessions were slung across the horse's rump behind the saddle. As I watched he stopped and turned for a moment. He probably saw me standing in the parlour window, but he did not wave, and neither did I. Within a few minutes he was out of sight, and there was nothing to see but black thunder clouds piling up over Mynydd Preseli and gathering their resources for the next assault on our senses. Then a fork of lightning ripped open the sky above Carnedd Meibion Owen, followed after a second or two by a great bass drum-roll of thunder and by the heavy splattering of raindrops which signalled the start of the next deluge. Poor Amos, I thought, poor Amos, to be out on such an afternoon..........

"Mistress, that was not very like you, to just sit here while your guest went on his way," said Bessie, sweeping into the parlour with a duster in her hand. "Is it not your custom to wave farewell from the kitchen doorstep?"

"Indeed it is, Bessie. But today I feel a little fatigued. In any case, I said my farewell to Master Jones here in the parlour."

She came and stood before me and lifted my chin with her forefinger, as one might with a small child who has been sulking. She looked me in the eye and gave a smile and a little shake of her head before continuing with her dusting. Then she said: "Just you take care, Mistress."

At that, I exploded. "Whatever do you mean, Bessie? Why does everybody advise me to take care these days? I take care all the time! Indeed, I am one of the most careful people I know! And I can look after myself perfectly well, thank you very much, without any help from you........"

Secrets and Lies

My beloved housekeeper and guardian angel was not really dusting in the first place, but she stopped it anyway and came and sat beside me. She put her arm around my shoulder. "I am sorry, Mistress, for my impertinence. But I love you very much, and I will not hold my tongue when there are things that should be said. You know, I suppose, that Jones Minor Prophet is in love with you?"

"Nonsense, Bessie! He is a happily married man, you know that. And in any case, how have you come to that conclusion?"

"Observations, Mistress. I have been watching men all my life, and when they are in love they look like puppy dogs. On more than one occasion recently Master Jones has looked just like our youngest terrier who has fetched a stick and earned a lump of sugar."

I had to laugh. "Bessie, you are priceless! Men are a good deal more complicated than puppies."

"Don't be so sure, Mistress. At any rate, I have been watching Master Jones on his last few visits. He is not a happily married man, of that I am convinced. He loves your company, and that is reciprocated. But his heart is in turmoil just now, and I think his instinct for loyalty to his wife is slipping away, and is being replaced by a passion he has never known before. He has certainly seen a good deal of the world. But in some ways he is a very naive fellow -- would you not agree?"

After thinking for a while I had to nod. Then after a long silence Bessie said: "And your own feelings for him, Mistress?"

I thought long and hard, for I had never confronted this issue before. Then I said feebly: "But I am much older than he is, Bessie. How can a respectable fellow like him feel any passion for a woman who is from a different class and who is in any case already wrinkled and white-haired?"

"Stranger things have happened, Mistress. Do not forget that you are still very beautiful, and well capable of turning heads in the street. And you are intelligent enough and mature enough to be very interesting indeed. Back to my question, which you have avoided. What are your feelings for him?"

She held my hands in hers, as a multitude of images, emotions and recollections rushed through my heart and my head. Then, thank God, before I could fashion a reply that was reasonably honest, there was a clattering of hooves which became audible over the sound of the driving

Secrets and Lies

rain outside. My attention was diverted, and so was Bessie's.

We both sprang to our feet and ran through to the kitchen. We opened the door to see that Will had come out from the barn to help a mysterious rider to dismount from his exhausted steed. He took the horse, and the rider came over to the kitchen door with water streaming off his hat, cape and oilskins. I did not recognize him. "Mistress Martha Morgan?" he asked.

"Yes, that is my name."

"A message for you, Mistress. From Carmarthen, from Master Brynach Morgan."

My heart missed a beat as the fellow took a waterproof bag from under his cape, opened it and handed over a sealed message. We invited the messenger inside and while Bessie and the others helped him off with his sodden outer garments, and got him something hot to drink, I went back into the parlour with my heart beating wildly. I need not have been so worried, for this is what the message said:

Blue Boar Inn
Lammas Street, Carmarthen   Wednesday 24th August 1845

Dearest Mother
Do not worry, for I am quite well. I am aware that I promised to return to the Plas with my business concluded by today, but I fear that things are taking a little longer than expected.

I knew that you would be concerned, and that is why I am sending this by special messenger so that you will receive it before the day is out.

It is now my intention to return on Friday the 26th day of the month, and I trust that I will have a favourable outcome to report which will make you very happy.

Tell Rose and David of my message, if you will, and send them all my love and kisses. I love you all,

Your son
Brynach

When I had read the letter I had a moment of concern that it had been written in the Blue Boar Inn rather than in some fine gentry house in the Carmarthenshire countryside, but there was probably a simple explanation for that, and I decided that I should react with relief and happiness to Brynach's words, as he had intended. I called David and Rose down from their room and read the letter out loud to them. "There now," I said. "Your father appears contented, and confident that his business will soon be concluded. It was kind of him to send us a message through the storm, was it not?"

"Yes, Grandma," said the two young people in unison.

"Are you happy enough to stay here at the Plas until Friday?"

"Of course, Grandma," said Rose. "I like it here better than at Plas Llanychaer anyway, since ours is such a big dark old house."

"Can we please go back up to our room and carry on with our paintings now?" said David.

I smiled and nodded, and off they went up the stairs, carrying my grandmotherly love with them. They are truly fine young people, both of them, and I hold nothing against them other than the fact that they are growing up too fast. I wish them all the happiness in the world, including a new mother. Let us hope that Brynach will oblige in that regard.

ΩΩΩΩΩΩΩΩΩΩΩ

25th August 1845

Time has been hanging heavy today, as Brynach seeks to complete one mission in Carmarthen and as Amos rides north on another. I miss them both, and I wish that I knew more about what they are fleeing from and searching for.

I feel hemmed in and even trapped, and I suppose that that has something to do with the weather, for the thundery showers have continued all day and we have had so much August rain that streams of muddy water are pouring out through all of the field gates, and little lakes are being ponded up on the upslope sides of hedges and stone walls. The river down at Cilgwyn Ford is in full flood, and that is something almost unheard of in the month of August. God help those who have not

Secrets and Lies

finished their wheat harvests. Patty came up from the Parrog this morning to fetch some butter and cream, and reported on the news that Huws Bayvil has seen ten fields of wheat flattened and destroyed, and that another eight fields are destroyed at Gelli Fawr. I cannot rejoice in the misfortune of others, but when Will heard the news he said "Those bastards Huws and Owen had it coming to them. I know for a fact that both of their head men advised against putting in too much spring wheat. In this area, Mistress, the weather always breaks before the end of the month, it does, before the ears are plump. We got away with it here, Mistress, because our fields are dry and face south. Bayvil has too much wind, and Gelli Fawr faces north and has cold, cold soil. They should have known better. Silly buggers." And he puffed on his pipe and looked very contented.

"Don't you be too hard on them, Will," I said. "We have had our harvest failures too -- don't you forget that. And too recently for comfort. The summer of '38 was truly terrible, and that of '41 not much better. We almost starved on both occasions, and many others did. More than once we have had to abandon Christmas because of an empty larder. We live on a knife edge, all of us, and sometimes the slightest misjudgement can transform a bountiful harvest into a disaster."

"Ah, diversity is the secret, Mistress, and you know that better than most of these modern squires with their fancy ideas and their educated stewards. If I may say so, you are the best squire in the district. You had sound teachers in Grandpa Isaac and good old Billy. Stands to reason, it does. Something from cattle, something from sheep, something from corn and then you can sleep. That's an old saying that I just made up, Mistress. Not bad, don't you think?" And he chortled to himself, and looked contented again, while his offspring Myfanwy and Gerallt looked embarrassed.

This afternoon, with the weather too bad to be out and about in the fields, I had a visit from Betsi and Ioan, who had heard from one of their servants at Brithdir that Rose and David were at the Plas, and that Brynach had gone to Carmarthen. The two of them joined Daisy and myself in the parlour for a light afternoon tea. I showed them Brynach's letter and shared with them my thoughts on the purpose of his mission, and I enquired whether they were any better informed than I about the young heiresses whom he now seemed to be pursuing. They all looked

Secrets and Lies

perplexed, and claimed to be quite in the dark, but Ioan said very little, and I suspected that he might know more than any of us women. I pressed him, perhaps a little unkindly, to give us his interpretation of the comings and goings at Plas Llanychaer and of the visit to Carmarthen. But he simply shrugged and said: "I am certainly not party to Brynach's plans, Martha, even though we meet often and talk man to man about estate matters. I may know a little more than you, but he asked me to hold my tongue and to allow him the privilege of putting you more fully in the picture when the time is right. I must not betray his trust, nor would you expect me to."

And having demonstrated how little he knows of the female mind, my dear son-in-law, for whom I have previously had the greatest respect, tucked into another slice of currant cake with a serene smile on his face, leaving us three women to stew in our own juice. There was a strained silence; at last all four of us burst into laughter simultaneously, and I had to accept gracefully that Ioan knows the female mind quite well enough. In due course Betsi and Ioan returned to Brithdir, and Daisy went with them, leaving me alone with the servants.

This evening, after supper, I was in no mood for sitting up late. So I retired at the same time as Rose and David, chatted to them for a little while in their bedroom, and then bade them goodnight. As I walked along the passage I saw that the thunder clouds were drifting away and that the landscape was intermittently illuminated by the light of the full moon. The air felt fresher too, as it often does after a period of rain. I settled into my dressing room, pulled the shutters back as far as they would go, and allowed the silver light to flood in. On an urge I blew out my candles and sat quietly in the mellow darkness, allowing my eyes to adjust to the light of moon and stars. I felt surprisingly at ease with the world, given my recent irritations and my maternal worries about Brynach. And then my mind drifted to Amos Jones and to the events of yesterday. What a strange scene that must have been in the parlour, for anybody outside and looking in! Me sitting by the fireplace, dressed in my normal daytime attire, doing my best to appear unflustered, and Jones Minor Prophet also seeking to control his emotions, and trying not to say too much, while dressed in Shemi's old farmyard clothes which made him look -- not for the first time -- more like a scarecrow than a respectable minister of religion. Dear Amos! Was there anybody in the whole wide world less concerned about

Secrets and Lies

appearances? And could it possibly be true that he loves me?

And then another urge came over me, and I tiptoed to the bedroom door which opens onto the passage, and locked it from the inside. I went across to my full-length bedroom mirror and stood before it in a pool of moonlight. Could it really be true that I was still beautiful, and still desirable halfway through my sixty-eighth year? I looked myself over, as I had done many times as a young woman, before and after my marriage to David, and I think I saw the same person. My face was lined, certainly, but my eyes were still bright, and I thought my nose and my lips perfectly passable. But that thin white hair which had once been thick and black? Then I decided to take out, ever so slowly, the pins and clips that held it up without ever taking my eyes off the mirror. At last it all tumbled down over my shoulders, and a shiver passed through me as I realized that it was still beautiful and something to be proud of. A gentle warmth permeated my whole body, and I decided to continue with my little game. I even glanced at the door to reassure myself that it was still locked, and that nobody was going to burst in and take me unawares.

Feeling more than a little guilty but also excited, I took off my slippers and stockings, and stretched out one leg and then the other into the pool of moonbeams. Owain thought my legs very pretty, and I thought them still shapely. I let my shawl slip off my shoulders and slide to the floor. Then I slowly undid the buttons on my satin jacket, eased my arms out and let it drop. Next, my blue silk dress which had rather more buttons and bows at the back than I would have liked, and which Liza helps me to get into on most afternoons at about five when the day's work is done. I had a considerable struggle with it, and at first cursed beneath my breath, but then I found it amusing and giggled quietly instead, and turned my disrobing into a seductive performance designed strictly for my own pleasure. At last I wriggled free, and having pulled my arms through the sleeves I let it fall off my breasts and then off my hips and then finally onto the floor.

I stepped out of the encircling garment and put it onto the chair at my bedside. Then I continued with my task before the mirror, removing my three petticoats one after another, ever so slowly and savouring every moment, and then loosening my stays and throwing them aside. Finally I removed my chemise and my undergarment and stood naked in the silver moonlight of the warm August evening. I turned this way and that with

Secrets and Lies

my eyes fixed on the glass, and pulled in my stomach and thrust out my breasts just as I had done as a young woman. I brought up my arms and clasped my hands behind my head, which I believed, many years ago, to work wonders on my profile. And now, as then, I felt that I was aglow with a quiet sort of passion which reminded me that I still had red blood in my veins and the feelings and instincts of a woman. My breasts were still acceptably full and firm, and my waist still reasonably slim in spite of a few rolls of flesh that I could have done without. My bottom was a little flatter than it had been in my youth, and I did not really like the look of my thighs, but I thought that on a dark night I might pass for a forty-year-old, so long as the observer was not too knowledgeable. How knowledgeable was Amos Jones, I wondered? Would he, if he were ever to see them, like the look of my breasts and my hips? Would he like the taste of my lips and the touch of my nipples against his breast? Did he have gentle hands? And what would it feel like to lie with him, and to play with him, and to feel him inside me, and to rise together to a high peak of passion? Was all of this possible? Could it ever, in a perfect world, be as I imagined?

I slipped beneath the cool sheets of my bed, running my hands over my own body, and let my imagination run away with me as I abandoned all of my inhibitions. Ecstasy flooded through me as my breathing quickened and my heart thundered. I did not want to let go of the moment, and held onto it for as long as I dared. At last I became calm again, and breathed slowly and deeply as I tried to regain my composure. For a while guilt took over from pleasure, but then I sent that impostor packing, and thought "This is my body and my temple. If I cannot worship it myself, where is my self-worth? And if others choose to worship it too, so be it. I am old and have little enough excitement, and I will not complain..........."

That was an hour ago. Suddenly I felt frightened, and cold. I got up out of bed and put on my night-dress and dressing gown. The moon had moved on, and the room was now dark. I struck a Lucifer match and lit a few candles, and then set about clearing up the garments which littered my bedroom floor. Now everything is put tidily away, and when Liza comes in first thing in the morning with her cheery greeting and an announcement about the weather, she will know nothing of my juvenile fantasies.

So I sit here as a curlew calls somewhere overhead and as the owls chatter in the chestnut tree at the far end of the orchard. Now I have put

everything down, for better or worse. Am I in love with Amos Jones? I truly
do not know my own heart and I do not know what I want. Love in the right
circumstances is the most wonderful thing in the world, but if there are
obstacles in the way, as there surely are in the case of Amos Jones, love
causes nothing but trouble. Now I will go to bed again and try to sleep. And
if I dream of Amos Jones, may God forgive me.

ΩΩΩΩΩΩΩΩΩΩΩ

26th August 1845

The estate has collapsed, and my dreams are in tatters. This dear place on
the flank of my beloved mountain is in the process of passing over to some
vile family which knows nothing of the tears, blood and sweat that have
gone into the fashioning of buildings, fields, lanes and ditches over
centuries. The Morgans created this place where once there were bogs and
barren expanses of boulders, furze and bracken, and it is mine to hold in
trust for future generations holding that name. It is my duty to remember
and record its history, its traditions, its virtues and its vices, and according
to the law it is mine to hold until the day that I go to my grave. Or so I
have assumed, innocent and trusting creature that I am..........
Is it not my fate and my mission to look after those whom I love, who
live and work on this land? Have I not declared over and again that I will
never leave the Plas, and indeed **can** never leave this place, since it
nourishes my soul and since I would starve and die were I to be condemned
to live anywhere else?
This beloved house is not simply a piece of property to be evaluated
by attorneys and bought and sold with cold detachment. It is my house and
my home. It belongs in equal measure to those who dwell with me beneath
its roof -- Daisy and Bessie, who are the past, and Gerallt and Myfanwy,
who are the future. Where will I go, and where will they go, if we are to
be evicted by some horrid new squire? Who will look after my tenants at
Penrhiw, Dolrannog and Gelli? How will the new master of the estate
know how rents are to be paid, and who pays with eggs, and who pays

Secrets and Lies

with geese, and who pays with labour in that month or this month? How will he know which horse panics at the sight of a goose and which cows give the creamiest milk? How will he know where the best blackberries are to be found, and which field has the best mushrooms? The estate will be destroyed, utterly destroyed.

And he (for it will be a man) will not know the happenings that have made this house what it is. It is a place founded on love and trust, but he will not know that, or even care. He will not see the spirits of Grandpa and Grandma in their settles on either side of the *simnai fawr*; he will not see Joseph Harries running round the kitchen table and giving piggyback rides to my small children; he will not see the Christmas feasts and the visits of the *Mari Lwyd*, the *Ceffyl Pren* and others who have brought the past into the present; he will not see David, drunk and dirty, in his bathtub at the end of some famous *Cnapan* victory. The joys, the tragedies, the disputes and the dramas which have been enacted between these walls will mean nothing to him.

The loss of this place will be almost more difficult to bear than the loss of a beloved husband or child. I have borne such loss since my arrival here, and more than once. But grief at such times is mitigated to some degree by the love and support of those who remain, and by the knowledge that the land endures and that the Plas still stands proud and white on the mountainside as a beacon of hope for the future. But if the house is gone? What then......?

My whole body is shaking with emotion, and I cannot find the right words to express the turbulence I feel in my breast. Anger, fear, grief, resentment, frustration, recrimination. Empty words, and utterly inadequate.

Tonight -- and this has happened only once or twice before since I started this diary of mine many years ago -- I fear that I am too upset to continue. I cannot weep and write at the same time.

ΩΩΩΩΩΩΩΩΩΩΩ

Secrets and Lies

1st September 1845

A week has passed, and I have recovered my composure sufficiently to continue with my alarming narrative.

As soon as Brynach arrived back from Carmarthen in the Llanychaer carriage I knew that he was the bringer of bad tidings. Rose and David rushed out to meet him, and he embraced each of them warmly enough, but there was a stiffness in his manner, and when I glimpsed his face I saw that his manly good looks had been transformed into the looks of a man twice his age. He was unshaven, his jaw was tense, and his eyes were sunken and almost lifeless.

"Father, do you have a new wife to tell us about?" asked David, with his eyes gleaming.

"I fear not, son," replied Brynach. "Let us go inside. I will tell you everything later on, but first you must bear with me, for I must talk to your grandmother."

He kissed me on the cheek, but could hardly look at me. He took me by the hand and without saying a word led me through the kitchen and along the passage to the parlour. We went inside, and he closed the door.

"Sit down, Mother, please," he said. Then he strode back and fore for what seemed like an age, rehearsing in his mind once again the things he needed to say, although I dare say he had done that already, a thousand times over, during the long journey from Carmarthen. I sat in my favourite chair, petrified.

"Mother, this is the most difficult moment of my life," he said at last, still striding and still unable to look me in the eye. "Doubly difficult because of who you are, and because of what you have done for me, and because I love you so much."

I still did not know what this was all about, but I felt the tears trickling down my cheeks, and I said feebly: "Brynach, *cariad*, I understand all of that. Now kindly stop all that wandering about, and come and sit by me and put your arm around me. Then you can say what you have to say."

He did as instructed, and finally caught my eye with a look of such terrible despair that I could hardly credit it. "Mother," he said, "I fear that the estate has collapsed, and that everything must be sold."

I was dumbstruck, but eventually I managed to whisper: "But how

Secrets and Lies

can that be, *cariad*? Whenever we have spoken on estate matters, you have assured me that both the Llanychaer and Plas Ingli estates have been in good heart."

"True, Mother. Your management of the Plas and its tenant farms has been exemplary, but Plas Llanychaer was always a more difficult estate to deal with. When I inherited it from old Squire Price thirteen years ago it was in a ramshackle state, and I soon discovered that not enough was coming in to pay for its upkeep. As you know, I sold two tenant farms five years since, after successive harvest failures had brought many of us to the edge of bankruptcy. For a while that kept me solvent, but in the last three years I have had many sleepless nights as the bills have mounted up on my desk........"

"But if you have had problems, Brynach, why have you not shared them with me, or with your sisters? And surely Ioan, who is your best friend, might have helped with advice or money?"

He shook his head. "I did confide in Ioan, but you know as well as I do, Mother, that he has no money to spare, having been bankrupt himself when the Cenarth estate collapsed. He helped me with support and advice, and we went through my books together with a view to effecting certain savings, but that was really all he could do for me. He swore to me that he would not tell you anything."

"He was as good as his word, Brynach. But I could have helped. I may have nothing under the bed or in the bank, but I do have a little cash put away in case it should ever be needed. I could get it now, if things are desperate......"

"Too late, and probably far too little, Mother. You have balanced the books at the Plas, no more and no less. And in doing that you have achieved miracles. I saw no point in dumping my burdens onto your shoulders, when you had quite enough to worry about while those Rebecca Rioters were abroad. And after your nightmare in the kitchen of this dear place, in the spring of last year, do you really think that I could have come to you and said "Mother, I fear that the estate is in grave danger"? No, and no again. I would have been a monster, had I even suggested that I had problems."

I nodded reluctantly. "Thank you, *cariad*," I said, kissing his cheek. "I understand what you say. So what did you do?"

"I took advice from Wilkins Legal in Newport and Morris Legal in

Secrets and Lies

Fishguard, who has always looked after Llanychaer, and they both advised that the future lies not in land, but in coal and the other great industries that are shaping the new world."

"Coal and great industries, Brynach? Fortunes to be made, but also fortunes to be lost."

"As I now know to my cost, mother. I got to talking to some of the other young squires in this area -- Joshua Lloyd Cwmgloyn, Alwyn Gittins Tredrissi, and others -- and I discovered that they were also in deep trouble. They were excited by the good new coal mines in South Pembrokeshire, and we decided to form a consortium and to invest heavily in one of them, together with a Squire Hugh Owen from those parts."

"One of the Owens of Gelli Fawr?"

"Not related at all, as far as I can gather. But he was recommended to us as a sound businessman and a hard taskmaster who had the happy knack of making money. Together, in conditions of great secrecy, we invested in a great expansion of a productive pit, backed up by the best surveys that money could buy."

"And how did you raise the money if the Llanychaer estate was in such trouble and you had no cash reserves?"

"Borrowings against the estate."

"And the name of the colliery, Brynach?"

"The Garden Pit, at Landshipping."

"Oh no!" I moaned. "You need tell me no more, son. I remember reading about it in the *Welshman*, early last year if I am not mistaken. A terrible, tragic occurrence. Were not the workings out under the Cleddau River, too close to the river bed, and did not the water break in under the weight of a spring tide with fearsome loss of life among the poor workers?"

"Your memory is too good, Mother. It was the worst disaster in living memory to strike the coal business in the county. God only knows how many were killed -- the Official Inquiry said forty, but the locals in those parts swear that the real figure was closer to eighty. Throughout the last eighteen months you might or might not have noticed that I have been coming and going a great deal, helping with the aftermath, trying to help the bereaved families, and dealing with the government inspectors and the Inquiry. It has been a thoroughly dispiriting business, Mother, made worse by the fact that Hugh Owen has proved to be a man who drives his workers like a slave owner, who has no regard for safety, and who cuts costs at every possible juncture. Garden Pit was a disaster destined to happen."

Again I could do no more than whisper. "Oh, my poor son. I knew nothing of all this. If I had, I could surely have helped you in some way......"

"I doubt it, Mother. And let us not forget that my problems were and are nothing as compared to those of forty or more families at Landshipping who have lost fathers, mothers and even small children in the black flooded tomb that was supposed to make my fortune."

There was a long silence, and then Brynach breathed deeply and continued. "You need to know the extent of this disaster, Mother. I owe £20,000 including interest, and my creditors are calling in their money tomorrow. I have to attend at the office of Morris Legal at ten in the morning."

"Oh my God. That is a huge sum, Brynach. I had guessed it to be only half as much."

"What is done is done. The only way that I can now avoid litigation and possibly prison is by selling the estate. If I am lucky, my creditors will take the estate in exchange for the debt."

"And your confederates? What will happen to them?"

"All ruined, Mother. Five of the estates in this district will be on the market, as of tomorrow."

Then I recalled my conversation with Rose, and my speculation about young heiresses, and marriage settlements and so forth. So I said weakly: "And the young ladies who have visited Plas Llanychaer over recent months?"

"I might as well be honest. They represented my last chance. The only means open to me for the saving of the estate, after the Garden Pit disaster, was marriage to a wealthy heiress. Morris Legal, who was to some degree responsible for my misfortunes, having given me very unsound advice, tried his best to repair the damage. He has an encyclopaedic knowledge of the families of West Wales, their fortunes and their connections. He advised me to think first of the grand estates of Carmarthenshire, where there appear to be more eligible daughters per square mile than elsewhere in the land. He arranged various introductions, and I made visits to St Clears, Laugharne, Ferryside and various other places during the social season. One or two of those visits were quite productive, and resulted in return visits to Llanychaer."

"And so?"

"Horrible, silly, shallow girls, most of them, Mother. Some of them I could not abide, but there was one, Lisbet Preece of Henllan, whom I met several times and whom I thought very beautiful and very jolly." He paused, and looked into the distance, focussing on nothing in particular.

"Do you love her, and does she love you?"

"I think so, Mother. But her father, Squire Gilbert Preece, has three other daughters as well, and while he is keen to marry them off he is not so keen to let go of a substantial part of his fortune in the process."

"That does not seem to be a very sensible strategy, son. Does he prefer to hold onto them until they are worth nothing on the open market?"

At that, Brynach laughed, which was the first blessing of a miserable day. "No no, Mother," said he. "I do Squire Preece an injustice. The real hindrance to a marriage between Lisbet and me was the Llanychaer estate itself. When Squire Preece and his attorney came to inspect it, they were not impressed. And when I showed them my books, and they discovered the full extent of my debts, they were horrified."

"But Brynach, you own Plas Ingli as well, and its tenanted farms. Put together, the two estates must be a very attractive proposition for a father wishing to be rid of a daughter."

"There you are wrong, Mother. You have a life interest in the Plas Ingli estate, which means it cannot easily be split up or disposed of. It is yours to enjoy until the day you die."

"Would it help, son, if I was to die in my sleep tonight?"

"Not a great deal, Mother. It is already too late."

"But if I choose to revoke the settlement which we made some years back, and if you and I go to Morris Legal and demand that the document be torn up and thrown in the fire, what then? Would you not have instant access to the Plas, and be able to sell it to any willing buyer? Alternatively, would it not be counted as a great asset in negotiations about a marriage? Even if you have to sell the Plas, you could pay some of your creditors, marry your Lisbet, and then use her dowry to repay the rest of your debts."

Brynach looked perplexed, and thought long and hard before saying: "I really do not know the answers to your questions, Mother. I am not

Secrets and Lies

trained in the law."

"Will you seek the advice of Master Morris when you see him tomorrow?"

"Well, if you insist .... but I cannot and will not ask you to make this sacrifice, Mother. I know that if you leave the Plas, you will surely die within weeks or months."

I held his hand in mine, and kissed it. "The estate is more important than any of its inhabitants, Brynach. And you have Rose and David to think of. I urge you to save the estate for them and out of respect for the Morgans who have gone before us. Look on the bright side -- if you marry Lisbet and your debts are cancelled, the Plas will still be in the family, and I can stay for as long as you choose to tolerate me. And if you have to sell the Plas, maybe the new Master will be kind enough to let me stay, or at least give me a roof over my head somewhere or other."

Brynach shook his head and was about to say something, but at this point there was a polite knock on the parlour door, and Rose popped her head into the room. "Excuse me, Grandma and Papa, but David and I have waited a very long time, and we wonder if we might hear the news from Carmarthen?" Brynach and I realized at once that we had talked for a very long time, and that it had not been fair on the children. My son jumped to his feet, then bent over and gave me a kiss on the cheek.

"Please, Mother," he said, "say nothing to anybody else about our conversation until I have been to Fishguard tomorrow morning. I will come to see you in the afternoon, by which time our fates will be sealed. I must go back to Llanychaer now, and I will take the children with me and tell them what they need to know."

He put his arm around his daughter, and the two of them went to collect David in the kitchen. Their bags were already packed, and a few minutes later the Llanychaer carriage rattled out of the yard and along the drive, escaping from one gloomy place and heading for another.

So it was that I went to my room on that night without eating or drinking, and without exchanging a word with anybody else. I tried to record the events of the day, but could not. And I cried myself to sleep, convinced that the world was about to come to an end.

Secrets and Lies

2nd September 1845

Not for the first time, my prognostications of doom proved to be ill-founded. When Liza woke me up on the following morning she saw my distress and tried her best to cheer me up, but I fear that my mood was as black as a thundercloud, and I was not very civil to her. She chatted about this and that, and hinted that Daisy and the servants had been talking late into the night in the kitchen and were keen to know what was going on; but no matter how much she tried to squeeze little snippets of information out of me, I would not betray Brynach. I managed to eat a small breakfast, and when Daisy tried to interrogate me, I fear that I snapped at her and made her quite upset.

I spent the morning walking around the estate, fearing that this might be my last opportunity to enjoy the sights and sounds and scents which were as familiar to me as my own body. I omitted to respond when Bessie rang the lunch bell, and kept on walking alongside the stone wall that separates the top fields from the common, from where I could obtain a good view of the driveway. Every minute felt like an hour, and at last I saw and heard Brynach as he approached on his black hunter. I rushed back down to the yard, and arrived just as he was dismounting. Gerallt took his horse while I gave him an embrace which almost took his breath away. "*Cariad,*" I said, holding back my tears, "thank God you are here at last! I have almost been out of my mind with all this waiting!"

Then he gave me a little smile of reassurance, which lifted my spirits by a few inches. "You always did worry too much, Mother," he said. "Now then, another discussion in the parlour, if you please."

"I want Daisy to be with us, Brynach."

"Of course," said he without hesitation. "Where is she?"

Daisy emerged from the kitchen, where she had been helping Bessie in the manufacture of pastry on the kitchen table. Brynach went up to her and embraced her warmly. "Please forgive me, sister, for my discourtesy of yesterday," he said, holding her hands in his. "I was not myself, as you might have gathered. Today I am somewhat more in control of my emotions. Shall we three retire? And Bessie, is there a chance of some tea, and a plate of those miraculous griddle cakes, in thirty minutes?"

"Anything for you, young Master, as ever," said Bessie with a cheeky grin.

Secrets and Lies

With the atmosphere already a deal lighter than on the previous day, we settled into the parlour. First of all, we brought Daisy up to date with the matters already described, although in truth I was desperate to know the outcome of the morning's meeting in Fishguard. Then Brynach said: "And so we come to the conclusion of these matters. First, my visit to Carmarthen which was longer and more difficult than I had anticipated. I dare say, Mother, that you have speculated about that?"

"Indeed I have, son."

"Well, it was a last-ditch attempt on my part to find a wife and save the estate. There was a grand ball in the Regency Rooms, as there is every year at the end of the harvest. I contrived to get myself invited, with the assistance of my attorney and an old friend of his, namely the solicitor Hugh Williams. He has very good connections. He has a very soft spot for you, Mother -- you know that?"

"I am aware of it, Brynach," said I, trying not to blush at the recollection of a certain past indiscretion. "As you will recall, he and I worked well together at the time of the Rebecca Riots."

"At any rate, he was a pillar of strength in Carmarthen, making introductions, arranging meetings with squires and their attorneys, and so forth. The ball was a disaster, and I wish I had not gone. Lisbet was there, and she and I could not keep our eyes off each other. I met various other heiresses, and danced with some of them, but I could not concentrate on the matter in hand, and thought all of them plain and dull by comparison with Miss Preece. I managed to snatch a conversation with her, and then she told me, with pain in her eyes, that she is engaged to be married to the oldest son of the Llys-gwynt estate near Llandeilo......."

"Oh, you poor thing," said Daisy, putting her arm around Brynach's shoulder and kissing his cheek. "Her father's doing, obviously. But could she not have resisted his wishes?"

"Of course not, Daisy. He was set against me from the start, and had greater ambitions for her." He paused and swallowed hard, and I could see the pain in his eyes. Then he pulled himself together and continued. "Master Williams tried to rescue something from this disaster, and insisted that I should stay for another two days while he sought to find me a wife. Morris Legal even travelled from Fishguard with all the estate maps and books. We visited four more estates in the vicinity of the town, and had meetings, meetings and more meetings. More young heiresses, more fathers and mothers, more attorneys, more smiling and bowing and scraping. And always, when squires and their attorneys examined the books and discovered the extent of my debts and the entailment of the Plas Ingli estate, they shook their heads and shook my hand and said farewell. Master Williams even offered me a personal loan free of interest. He is a good man, and meant well, but I could not take it. What is the use of taking one loan just to pay off another? In the end, I was quite exhausted, and had to come home."

There was a long pause as my poor son relived those horrible days and hours in Carmarthen. Then Bessie knocked on the door, and she and Myfanwy discreetly brought in tea and cakes, left them on the little table by the fireplace, and retired. As Daisy poured out the tea, I said: "Now we are almost up to date, Brynach. And this morning? What happened in Fishguard?"

"Something bad and something good to report, Mother. The bad news first. The estate is indeed lost, and documents are now signed which pass the whole of the estate across to a new owner."

I moaned, and so did Daisy. I suppose I was expecting that news, and when it came I received it with little emotion. I felt no black despair, but simply a sort of emptiness in my breast. All I could say was: "From a good old family, I hope?"

"No, Mother. He is one Wilmot Gwynne from Swansea. He made his money from copper and coal. When he was a young man, he was befriended by my father Iestyn while the two of them were working on the coal tramway near Llandore. He admired his courage, and developed a great affection for him. Now he has damaged lungs, and is not in the best of health. Six months since, he came to visit me, having often wondered what this place Llanychaer looked like. He was looking for a West Wales estate -- I was not inclined to help him at the time, since I was determined to find my own salvation. But Wilkins Legal kept in touch with him, and unbeknown to me, while I was pursuing young ladies in Carmarthen he travelled to Swansea for further discussions. Much to my surprise, he was in Fishguard this morning, sitting in one room of Master Morris's office while I met with my creditors in another."

"Has your attorney betrayed you, Brynach?"

"Far from it, Mother. His behaviour has been exemplary, and we all have a good deal to thank him for. The squires who assumed that they

Secrets and Lies

would by now be in possession of the Llanychaer and Plas Ingli estates have gone home with scowls on their faces but with £20,000 in their pockets. Master Gwynne has paid £22,000 for the estate, and all the papers are signed by the pair of us and witnessed by Master Robert Morris and his clerk."

So it was done already. Llanychaer I had never had any great attachment for, and its loss was a personal one for Brynach. But Plas Ingli? This beloved old estate had passed out of the hands of the Morgan family without any great commotion in the sky, without any earthquake, and without even any disturbance in the routines of the household or farm. As we sat here in the parlour, quietly drinking tea and discussing the end of my world, Bessie and Myfanwy were working in the dairy, Liza was cleaning the rooms upstairs, and Will and Gerallt were working in the garden. Why were there no thunderclaps or trumpet fanfares? Did nobody care? Did nobody care?

I felt tears rolling down my cheeks, and I managed to ask: "So that was the good news, Brynach?"

Daisy came and put a consoling arm around my shoulder as he replied. "No, Mother *bach*, that was still the bad news. The good news is that Wilmot Gwynne is a true gentleman, even though he does not come from a good family and even though he has made his fortune through honest toil. When he was told of the full circumstances surrounding my two estates, he immediately said that he would respect our agreement by which you may remain in residence for the rest of your life."

"Can that really be true," I whispered, wiping tears away from my cheeks. "Why should he wish to tie his hands in this way?"

"I suspect, Mother, that it is out of respect for you, and that he knows something of your attachment for the place."

"But he knows nothing of me, Brynach. I certainly know nothing of him. Have you been arguing my case with him?"

Brynach laughed. "It was not necessary, Mother dear," he said. "Do not forget that Wilmot Gwynne was an old friend of my father Iestyn. He knew about me back in the old days in Swansea, and he certainly knew a great deal about you. Father must have spoken about you often, and in very glowing terms. This morning, after shaking hands on our deal, Master Gwynne and I went to the Royal Oak to share some lunch, and we got on splendidly. He said that he was quite convinced that Father was in love

109

with you. Did you know that?"

I nodded, and felt the tears on my cheeks again. "I am sorry, Brynach and Daisy," I sniffled. "I am very emotional today. There is just too much going on in my head and my heart."

"We understand that fully, Mother dear," said Daisy. "Just you take your time. When you are ready, Brynach can continue. I imagine that there is little more to tell anyway."

For a minute or two I composed myself, and Daisy poured me another cup of tea. At last I said in a rather feeble voice: "But what of Penrhiw and the other estate farms, Brynach? We must look after Gomer and Gwenno, and the others........"

"They are safe, Mother. Wilmot has said that his main interest is Llanychaer, and that he thinks Plas Ingli to be too far from Fishguard for easy management. He does not want to employ a steward. He promised me that he will respect the existing tenancy agreements here, and I trust his word. You will continue to run the Plas Ingli estate exactly as you have, except that in future he would like to be informed of any changes in wages or rentals in case they affect the balancing of the books."

"But what of you and the children, Brynach? Will you come back to the Plas? You know that you will be welcome here. You can run the estate again, if you wish, now that I am feeling my age........"

"No, Mother. I will not do that. But there is no need for any hasty action. Master Gwynne and his wife cannot move to Llanychaer until after Christmas. They have properties in Swansea to sell, and business affairs to sort out. They want to employ all of my servants, and they are also happy for me to stay and keep the estate ticking over until they move in. That means that I have four months in which to make plans for my future."

"And what of the children? This must have come as a great shock for Rose and little David. How do they feel?"

"Less upset that you might have imagined, Mother. Rose has never liked Llanychaer, and has always said that she prefers Plas Ingli. And little David thinks that the prospect of moving somewhere else is terribly exciting."

So that was the detail of our discussion. Things are certainly bad, but they could have been a great deal worse. The Plas is still mine to have and to hold, even though it is now owned by a stranger. So I can live out my life in reasonable comfort. Master Gwynne and his wife will come and visit us some time in the next week or two, so I gather, and I await that visit with some trepidation. My main concerns are for the children and especially for Brynach, who has lost his estate, his reputation, and his sense of self-worth. I also fear that he is still in love with Lisbet Preece, a sweet lady who has been cruelly snatched away from him and betrothed to somebody else. He is putting a very brave face on things, but I suspect that over the coming days and weeks, as he comes to terms with his new situation, he may have to deal with deep, deep despair. I **think** that he is strong, but I am not sure of it. We have been unable to rescue him financially, but I hope and pray that between us Daisy, Betsi, Ioan and I can keep him afloat emotionally, by giving him all the love that is in us.

$$\Omega\Omega\Omega\Omega\Omega\Omega\Omega\Omega\Omega\Omega\Omega\Omega$$

3rd September 1845

This morning I was so exhausted that when Liza tried to get me up I pleaded with her to let me be. Having opened the shutters, it is to her credit that she closed them again, and allowed me to sleep on in the warm darkness of my room, oblivious to all the sounds of the farmyard, until I heard the clanging of the lunch bell. Then I staggered downstairs in my dressing-gown, no doubt looking like one of the witches of Macbeth, to find that the world had not ended, and that Daisy and the servants were getting on with life as they had done yesterday, and the day before that, and back to time immemorial. Bessie and Will and the others knew a little about the collapse of the estate, of course, and appreciated why I was tired and upset, but they all behaved as angels would have done, and fussed over me as if I was a delicate invalid who needed to be kept alive by hook or by crook. I dare say that Bessie would have buttered my bread for me and put it into my mouth for me, had I requested it, but at last I had to laugh, and soon the kitchen was alive with a great hubbub of conversation as all of my servants asked about the details of what had happened to Brynach and the two estates. Were their jobs safe? What about the rents? Would we still be able to buy a new bull this autumn?

Secrets and Lies

What about Gomer and Gwenno? How much barley would we sell, and when? How many labourers would the new Master need? And so on ....
   After lunch I decided that I needed fresh air. So I put on my day dress and walking boots and set off for the mountain. As ever, the effect on my spirit was nothing short of miraculous. I anointed myself at Ffynnon Brynach, and drank some of the crystal clear and sacred water from my cupped hands. The skylarks were still fluttering high in the sky and singing as they had done in April. The sun was still high and warm, as befits a day at the onset of the blackberry season, and the thick blanket of bracken that surrounds the mountain moved to a gentle rhythm in tune with the zephyrs that came in from the west. As I walked through it I imagined that I was a mermaid gliding through waving forests of kelp far out in the bay. Then I was up amongst the boulders and the crags, with the familiar south face of the mountain towering above me. Summit or cave today? I decided on my cave, for a visit to the summit would have brought memories of Jones Minor Prophet into my head, and I knew that I was in no fit state to deal with them. So I turned left off the sheep-track and followed my familiar route through crags and narrow crevices towards the cave entrance. I went beneath one massive boulder almost as large as a cottage, and around the precarious edge of another, and then along the little track known only to me and a few sheep. I noticed the old raven perched on a crag halfway between me and the summit of the mountain; he had his mate and two young ones with him, and as ever he was completely unperturbed by my presence. There was the cave entrance, quite hidden from any who did not know it, flanked by little clusters of dry grasses and ferns and marked by the rowan tree which would soon be drooping beneath the weight of bright red berries. I slipped between the flanking pillars of blue rock, and then I was inside my beloved sanctuary, the place in which I felt truly at peace.
   My eyes soon adjusted to the darkness, and I made my way to the back of the cave where I had my little bed of dried mosses, grasses and ferns. There was my sheepskin, draped over a rock near the entrance, just where I had left it. There on a dry ledge were the candles and matches which I had brought up a year or so ago and which I used to illuminate the interior when it was cold and dark outside. But today there were rays of sunshine filtering through crevices in the rock, and there was quite enough light inside for me to see by. As I had done many many times before, I sat

Secrets and Lies

quietly on my mossy bed, closed my eyes and breathed deeply. Surrounded by the maternal warmth of the mountain, my cares and my troubles faded away in my mind's eye until they were lost in the hazy distance.

I must have fallen asleep, for I was awakened by the Plas Ingli dinner bell. "Oh dear, Bessie will be angry with me again!" I thought, and in fear that I might miss my dinner I shook myself down, gathered up my skirts and petticoats, and went out again into the daylight. The evening was warm and mellow, and the breeze had entirely faded away. The ravens had left their watching crag and they were now high above the summit, wheeling around and observing their territory from a height of maybe three thousand feet. Thirty minutes later I was back at the Plas, taking my place at the kitchen table, only a little late for my meal, but nonetheless having to put up with the reproachful looks from Bessie that she normally reserves for small children.

In putting down my jottings for the day, I am reminded that thus far my dear daughter Daisy has been conspicuous by her absence from many of the events recounted. I must explain. I am still learning to know her again, because it is not much more than a year since she returned from a life of prodigality and debauchery in London. When she turned up at the Plas in June of last year it was one of the most wonderful moments of my life, for she had walked out of the Plas twenty-three years earlier, swearing that she would never return. She and I had always had a difficult relationship, I dare say because we were too much alike to live in harmony beneath the same roof. After a period of increasing friction, she took up an invitation to travel to London, where she was intent upon becoming a famous actress and enjoying a life of privilege and glamour. I am still not sure of what happened, and when, because she has chosen not to tell me, but I am sure that she got caught up in a range of liaisons with wealthy gentlemen and with at least one duke, and that she moved about perfectly easily at Court and among the royals. It became obvious to me last year, when she helped with the passage of the Turnpike Trusts Act, that she knew a great many Members of Parliament and knew too much about their personal habits for their peace of mind. She has three children born out of wedlock and with different fathers, but these gentlemen pay them good allowances, and they appear to want for nothing. Daisy loves them dearly, and writes to them frequently, and she promises that they will travel from London and visit us at the Plas before too long.

Secrets and Lies

When she arrived home without warning last year she had a pasty complexion and was greatly overweight. Her beauty was there somewhere, hidden beneath layers of rouge and talcum powder and lip colour. She was as confident and bouncy as ever, but deep inside I fear that she was gravely hurt, having been rejected by her latest patron and replaced by somebody younger and prettier. So she moved back to the Plas, threw away her ostrich feathers and dresses that would have made her look like a clown in West Wales society, and became once more a country woman. I am still astonished when I think of the ease with which she has made the transformation. She helps me to run the estate, and is very sharp with figures. She has a fine manner of speaking, and her English is now better than her Welsh. She has paid attention to her diet and she knows how to work hard. She rolls up her sleeves when she has to, and is perfectly unpretentious, and she has an earthy sense of humour which greatly appeals to the servants. Many a time have I had to raise my eyebrows and tut-tut like the grandmother that I am while she has been relating some scandalous tale about the Prince Regent or Master Peel or some other famous fellow.

She is now slim and fit again, and very beautiful given that she is 44 years old. I hope she will be happy, and that she will find a kind man with whom to share the rest of her life. Maybe she has seen quite enough of men -- I cannot tell. She certainly does not sit about and mope. She is determined to make her own way in the world, and so when she is not here at the Plas she is out and about giving lessons to genteel young ladies at various of the gentry houses of the district. She will not refer to herself as a governess, as she insists that would reduce her value. Sometimes she acts as a chaperone for heiresses who are attending balls or the races. Sometimes she stays for a week or more at the house of some young lady whose Mama and Papa are away on a social visit. She has been asked many times to take up a permanent position with one family or another, but has always declined because her first love is the Plas and because her first loyalty, she always says, is to her old and decrepit mother! She always was very insolent. Nonetheless, my Daisy is perfectly wonderful, and I think the world of her.

4. Crossing the Gulf

7th September 1845

I thought that I had finished with emotional crises, but now another one has come along and hit me with the force of a hurricane. This afternoon, after the arrival of the mail coach from Cardigan, a letter was delivered to the Plas. I saw at once that it had come across the sea from America, and that it was from my sister Elen. This is what it said:

Number 29
Fifth East Street
New York   *5th day of August 1845*

My Dearest Sister,

Today I received three letters from Wales -- one from you, one from Sister Catrin, and one from our nephew Edward at Brawdy. All with the same truly terrible news of the death of our beloved Morys. I was deeply saddened, and the more so because I had no idea that he was ill or that there was any concern for his health. I wept bitter tears, not only of grief for a wonderful brother and kind counsellor, but of fury because of the gulf of thousands of miles of grey and heaving ocean that separates me from the family and home which I love. After all these years I still long for the sights and sounds of our beloved Brawdy, and they pull at my heartstrings more strongly than ever at times such as this.

Now dearest Papa and Mama have gone, followed by our older brother -- and I have missed all three of their funerals and have had no chance to say farewell and to pay my last respects. Indeed, on each occasion I have not received the sad news until the funerals have been over and done with, and you have suffered and grieved in Wales without me. A curse upon this grey ocean that keeps us apart!

And I feel even greater remorse because I know that the last letter I wrote was as cheerful and frivolous a letter as I can remember in a long while -- full of funny news and inconsequential remarks, and bubbling with

115

Crossing the Gulf

the joys of life. That letter must have passed yours somewhere in the middle of the ocean, and you must have read it in the midst of your grief. How crass and how cruel, Martha! How can I forgive myself?

There is, I fear, more sad news, and I must tell it while I have the strength to do it. My sweet kind husband Tom is dead, having been struck by a coach and four in the street not far from our home.

When I read this I had to stop and read it again and again, as I felt the blood freeze in my veins. Another death in the family. The second death -- and within weeks of the first. So the events portrayed in my premonition were coming to pass. I cursed that dream, and cursed it again and again, and as before I felt that my foreknowledge had somehow precipitated the event. My rational being told me that this could not be so, but I was furious and upset in any case. Oh my poor Elen! Thousands of miles away, and having to bear the burden of widowhood without any of her family around her! I have wept a good deal lately, and now tears welled up into my eyes again. But I had to read on.

If there is any consolation to be derived from the event, it is that he died instantly and was spared the days or months of agony that others have to bear as they face death. The police brought his body home, and I dare say somebody will be charged with furious driving on the street, but that is of no concern to me. He is gone, and I am alone.

It is very hot here at this time of year, and it is the custom to hold funerals promptly. So with the help of the pastor of our church and various kind friends arrangements had to be put in hand straight away. The funeral was held last Friday, in the Welsh Presbyterian Church not far from our home, and dear Tom is now at rest in the churchyard.

I fear that neither Susanna nor George was able to attend the funeral, and indeed to this day I dare say they do not even know that their father is dead. Susanna is working as a governess for a wealthy family in New Orleans, and George has gone off with a wagon train, seeking his fortune in California. I have no idea where he is, and indeed I have no means of communicating with him until he writes and sends me an address.

Oh Martha, I feel so desolate and lonely! I have two servants who are very kind and caring, but this big house feels so cold and empty without Tom! Every time I turn from the passage into his study I expect to see him there. Every morning when I come down to breakfast I have to sit at that big table all alone. I have suddenly realised that there is no longer any laughter in the house, and no animated conversation, and no loving words or touches from my good man. And he WAS a good man, Martha. I have loved him with every ounce of my being, and he was everything to me. Oh God, what will I do without him?

I cannot continue. Write to me soon, if you will, and tell me some good news. God knows, I need cheering just now. When my emotions have calmed down, and if I can find the strength, I will write again before many days have passed.

A curse upon this ocean!

God bless you, Martha, and may He take good care of you and the rest of our beloved family.

Your loving sister

Elen.

What could I do, on reading this tragic epistle, other than weep? Truly, only the hardest of hearts could have remained unmoved by her words, and I am moved again now, to the extent that I will have to stop for the time being. I have read it at least ten times since it was delivered, and I do not know what to do. Indeed, is there anything I can do to lessen such misery, with that wretched ocean between us?

ΩΩΩΩΩΩΩΩΩΩΩ

9th September 1845

For two days I have mulled over Elen's letter and have tried to work out what to do. I have talked to both Betsi and Daisy, but they have not been a great deal of help. They knew Elen hardly at all when she surprised everybody almost forty years ago by suddenly taking a sailing ship from Bristol to New York, and although they have been informed by me, over the years, as to the little bits of family news contained in Elen's letters, she has remained a stranger to all of my family. They call her "our American aunt", but they have no idea what she looks like, how she speaks, or how she lives. Their cousins Susanna and George are just names to them, and I dare say that they will never meet. So I cannot be too surprised if they find it difficult if not impossible to understand the misery which has afflicted me since the receipt of that letter. Daisy is very kind, and puts my miserable mood down to the fact that I have received too much bad news lately, but I know only too well that there is more to it than that. There is **much** more to it than that........

This evening I excused myself early from the kitchen after supper, and I have spent three hours sitting silently at my desk, gazing out over the darkening *cwm* and listening to the evening chorus of little birds. And I have been thinking so much that my head aches. I have now made one of the most hazardous decisions of my life, and I hope and pray that it does not rebound on me and cause even more pain to myself and to those whom I dearly love.

Tomorrow it looks as if it will be a fine warm day once again. I will get up early, and take a light breakfast, and then I will walk over the mountain on that familiar and well-worn track which heads westwards. After three hours or so I will arrive at Plas Llanychaer. Brynach, foundling and adopted son, will be surprised and delighted to see me. I will walk with him in the old walled garden which holds the grave of his father Iestyn. And I will tell him everything.

ΩΩΩΩΩΩΩΩΩΩ

10th September 1845

For better or for worse, it is done. Now I have to wait for the consequences. I arrived at Llanychaer in mid-morning, to find Rose and David in the middle of their lessons, with their father nowhere to be seen. The children were delighted to see me, and tried to use me as an excuse to abandon their studies for the day, but I would have nothing to do with that idea, and sent them back to their tutor. One of the servants thought

Crossing the Gulf

that Brynach was inspecting the cattle in one of the lower fields, and offered to go and find him for me. I said that I would walk in the walled garden while I waited.

At last he arrived, looking flushed after his long trot back to the house. He expressed surprise and delight that I had walked all the way from the Plas to pay him a visit, and he embraced me warmly. He asked his housemaid to fetch some fruit cordial for me, and then we walked arm in arm through the pretty garden of fruit bushes, vegetable plots and flower borders.

"It is good to see you with some colour back in your cheeks, Brynach," I announced. "I have been more than a little worried about you. How are you coping with everything?"

"Well enough, Mother. I am gradually getting used to the idea of being a squatter in somebody else's house, and console myself that this disaster could have been a great deal worse."

"And how have your servants and tenants taken the news?"

"Surprisingly well. The older ones were perfectly aware that Plas Llanychaer was in trouble, and that it had been balancing on a knife-edge ever since the days of old Squire Price. They do not blame me for taking risks in the hope of saving it, and neither are they totally surprised that my efforts have come to nothing. They have all seen estates changing hands before, and although they are loyal and honest workers, I dare say they will adapt perfectly well to a new Master and a new way of doing things. They will meet their new Master and Mistress next week."

"And the children?"

"They are tougher than you might think, Mother. In some ways they are tougher than me. After all, when they were very small they had to cope with the loss of their mother, and so this crisis is very moderate by comparison......."

His voice tailed away, and I saw that he was very emotional. I squeezed his arm, and for a while we walked in silence. His servant girl came with long drinks, and for a while we sat on a garden bench in the shade. Then we walked on. We stopped to smell a cluster of very beautiful late summer roses, and I said: "Tell me, son, about your feelings for Lisbet Preece. Was it very hard for you when she told you that she was betrothed to somebody else."

"Very hard, Mother. At first, I thought she was just a suitable

Crossing the Gulf

heiress, and that marriage to her might be a sensible business proposition, but I fear that I allowed myself to become too involved. I have to say that I am very fond of her, to the extent that I think of her almost all of the time, and yet I rue the day that I met her."

"Poor Brynach. And poor Lisbet. I think I understand your feelings, and I am sure I understand hers. I have been there myself -- in love, and with the object of my desire dragged away to some dark place beyond my reach. There is little I can say, other than that the pain will gradually ease."

It was time to change the subject, and quickly. So I continued: "Now then. Enough of your problems, dear son. I have a sad duty to perform here today, relating to other problems far away, on the other side of the Atlantic Ocean."

"You mean Aunt Elen, in New York?"

I nodded, and took my sister's letter from my purse. "Brynach, I want you to read this."

He looked more than a little puzzled, but did as I asked. He read the letter as we walked along slowly in the sunshine. "Oh, the poor thing," he said at last. "What a truly appalling tragedy, and so soon after the death of Uncle Morys. And terrible for you too, Mother, so far away and unable to comfort her. Have you written with words of consolation?"

"I will do that tomorrow. But first I have something to tell you."

More by design than chance, the pair of us were at that moment at the far end of the walled garden, adjacent to a small slate headstone with the following words inscribed upon it: *Here lies Thomas Price, metalworker, late of Swansea. Died of his injuries, 2nd September 1822.*

"Do you remember, Brynach, the occasion many years ago -- I think it was at the time of your coming of age -- when we walked in this garden in the company of old Squire Price?" He nodded, and I continued. "When we arrived here, all you knew about your origins was that you were born out of wedlock and abandoned on the doorstep of the Plas on a cold April night as a very small baby. You knew, too, that I had taken you in and loved you as my own son, as indeed I do to this day, and will as long as I live. We came to this spot, and the Squire revealed to you that the man who is really buried here is his son Iestyn Price, your father. We also told you that the Nightwalker who had haunted the Plas during your childhood years was none other than Iestyn himself, unable to stop

Crossing the Gulf

himself from visiting intermittently and watching from a distance as you grew from being a small baby into a fine strong boy. You were, as I recall, considerably taken aback at the time......"

"So I was, Mother. So would any young fellow have been. I still cannot credit my father's bravery and his steadfastness, especially in the light of the terrible injuries which he suffered in the wars against the French, and which you have described to me more than once. We spoke of such things just the other day, did we not?"

"We did, Brynach........"

"And did we not conclude that my father loved you, Mother, albeit from a distance? That is, to my way of thinking, a happy circumstance coming out of a tragedy. Since I started life as a bastard and a foundling, it is at least some consolation to me to know that my natural father loved my adopted mother!" He smiled and put his arm around my shoulder as we stood in the sun looking at Iestyn's grave. This was not working out as I had hoped. Skating around on the edge of the thin ice was proving more dangerous than I had anticipated. It was time for the truth. So I turned to him and took his hands in mine, and said: "My dear Brynach, there is more. You know me as your adopted mother -- and indeed that is what I am. But I am also your aunt, for your natural mother is my sister Elen."

Brynach stared at me with wide eyes, and for a very long time he said nothing at all. I tried to read the signs in his face, but could not. I had to continue before my emotions got the better of me. "I admit to you now that I knew it all along -- or at least since the day when your father told me everything, very shortly before he died. I have lied to you, and lied again and again, in order to protect your happiness and your innocence. I did it because I vowed to Iestyn all those years ago that I would never tell you or any other soul -- but that vow has been a great burden to me, and has bent my back like a mighty wooden cross. I think that now -- after 23 years and in present circumstances -- he would have wished me to tell you."

Still Brynach said nothing. So I kept on talking. "I cannot explain what has moved me to tell you now, but my sister's heart-rending letter, and the lonely predicament that she now finds herself in, has set me to thinking that there is perhaps one thing that might lighten her burden of grief -- and that is a letter from the son she abandoned and fled from when she was a young woman."

At last Brynach found his tongue, although his face had the pallor of someone who has just seen a ghost. "But I still do not understand, Mother. Where was I born, and under what circumstances?"

"In Bath, as the result of a brief liaison between Iestyn and Elen. I doubt that they ever loved each other; they did not know each other long enough for that. As I understand it, they simply met at a ball, and drank too much, and found one another very attractive, and one thing led to another."

Then Brynach frowned, as men do when they think. "But Mother, you have exchanged letters with Aunt Elen ever since she went to America. You must have mentioned the foundling on your doorstep, and the date of my birth, and the family likeness between you and I. Has she never asked after me.......?"

"Very frequently, Brynach. She always was far more interested in you than in any of the others."

"But has she never declared openly to you, in all of those letters over the years, that she has suspected that I am her son? And the Nightwalker -- you must have written to her about his appearances at the Plas, and surely she must have put two and two together, and worked out that he was Iestyn, hiding his face from the world?"

"I agree with you, son. Now that I look back on it, every letter from me had a special meaning for her, because it brought news of her beloved first son. I think that brought her joy, and to some degree washed away her guilt. She had, after all, abandoned you, and fled from her responsibilities as a mother. You would have died within a day or two of your birth, had it not been for Iestyn."

"Oh Mother -- may I still call you that? -- I fear that I am very confused. I do not know whether to love her or hate her."

"Love her, Brynach. She needs your love, even if it comes from the other side of an ocean."

"But why, oh why did she never acknowledge me if she knew me to be her son?"

"Only she can answer that, *cariad*. She and I have carried on this little charade for years -- she perhaps from the very beginning of your life, and I since I learned the truth from your father just before he went to his grave. Elen was always very concerned about reputations and appearances; she moved in very formal circles. When she got to New York she married Tom Bradshaw, a very respectable American gentleman. My feeling is

Crossing the Gulf

that he would have been mortified had he ever discovered that she had been involved in an illicit affair and had given birth to a child before leaving England."

Brynach nodded and understood. I had told him everything he needed to know, so I concluded: "My dear son, Elen is now 72 years old, and you are 38. She has lived with her secret since the day you were born. Her husband Tom is now dead. She is a lonely old woman who has little contact with her two legitimate children and who has nothing else in her life to alleviate her grief. I leave it to you to decide what to do next."

We were still, after all this time, standing before Iestyn's grave. Now Brynach paced back and forth with his face muscles tense and his hands clasped behind his back. I feared that I had done him great harm. The intensity of his mood was very difficult for me to bear, and I found myself shaking with emotion. "Brynach," I whispered, on the edge of tears, "would it have been better if I had not told you any of this? I thought it my duty, out of respect for both you and Elen. Will you forgive me if I have done the wrong thing......?"

Suddenly he abandoned his introspection. He turned towards me, and smiled. Then he strode over and clasped me in his strong arms. "God bless you, Mother!" he exclaimed. "Of course you have not done the wrong thing. The truth can never be wrong. You have kept this secret for far too long, and have protected the happiness of both your sister and myself in the process. At least I now know who I am, and that gives me strength. I have real Morgan blood flowing in my veins, and that makes me feel six inches taller and ten years younger, after the recent events which have aged me more than a little. Leave it to me. I will think for a few days, and decide what to do."

"And am I still your mother?"

He roared with laughter, and picked me up and swung me round, as I had seen him do often with Rose as a little girl. "How could I ever forget it, Mother *bach*?" he sang out as I screamed and laughed. "No son was ever more proud of his mother, and no son ever bore his mother so much love. I promise it! I promise it!"

After all that swinging and twirling, I was so giddy that I would have fallen over had not my dear son caught me up in his arms and kissed me on both cheeks. Then I cried on his shoulder. And in spite of everything, my tears were tears of joy.

Crossing the Gulf

13th September 1845

The last three days have brought me blessed relief, for I was utterly drained of energy after the bad news that has tumbled in to the Plas over the past three weeks or so. My walk to Llanychaer was tiring too, even though Brynach brought me home in his chaise. I needed to sit in the orchard, in the shade of the apple trees, snoozing off and on, and listening to the comfortable sounds of the estate as I drifted in and out of consciousness. The weather allowed me to do exactly that, and Bessie and Liza protected me well from unwanted interruptions. Apparently the chimney sweep came, as did the chandler from Fishguard, three pedlars, the rag and bone man and the itinerant knife sharpener. Dai Darjeeling came, in theory to sell China tea but in reality to whisper sweet nothings to Bessie, whom he has loved since he was a stripling. Then yesterday, since I felt in the right mood, I took a tin bucket and collected five pounds of blackberries from the hedgerows without meeting a single soul.

There was one brief interruption today. Master Wilmot Gwynne and his wife appeared, quite unannounced, causing Bessie and Liza to grumble later on about "merchants who become squires without first learning the rules of good behaviour." When they turned up it was mid-afternoon, and I was fast asleep in my wicker chair under the pippin apple tree. Bessie woke me up by shaking my shoulder and whispering in my ear: "Mistress Martha! Wake up, if you please! The new Master and his wife are here!" And as I yawned and rubbed my eyes, there they were, standing in front of me. I never was very good at waking up quickly, and became quite flustered, but I managed a curtsy, and Master Gwynne roared with laughter.

"Mistress Martha, I presume? No need for that bowing and scraping business, if you please! Delighted to meet you. Yes indeed. I am Wilmot, and this is my lovely wife Delilah."

This was not a normal form of introduction, and this was clearly not a normal squire. I held out my hand, and he kissed it. Delilah and I exchanged smiles and little curtsies. "I do apologize, sir, for not being able to receive you properly," I said. "With such a lot happening in recent weeks, I have been taking the chance of a few moments of quiet, in order to recover my strength."

"Perfectly understood, madam. My wife and I have been worried about you, on the basis that the loss of a good old estate must be a great shock to the system. But let me assure you, Mistress Martha, that we have every confidence in you, and that nothing will change at the Plas. You just carry on as you are!"

"Sir, you are very kind, and I will do my best for you. Excuse me, for I am neglecting my duties. Some tea and currant cake, perhaps?" The faces of my new master and mistress glowed with anticipation, and I asked Bessie, who was still hovering in the vicinity, to oblige. Then I said: "Let me call Will and Gerallt to move that wooden bench over here into the shade, so that we can all sit together."

"No need at all, Mistress Martha. They are busy fellows. Leave it to me." And he strode across to the heavy wooden bench, picked it up as if it was made of brown paper, and placed it delicately in the shade, facing my wicker chair. Then he picked up my small garden table, carried it twenty yards, and placed it nearby, anticipating the arrival of a tray of tea and currant cake, cups and saucers and plates. I could not help noticing his hands, which were big and calloused.

This is a fellow after my own heart, I thought. He does not stand on ceremony. He is used to hard work, and will do things himself now rather than getting someone else to do them in twenty minutes.

I observed Master Gwynne carefully. He is short in stature and has a stocky build, a barrel chest and an ample stomach. His face is strong and open, and he has bushy eyebrows and side-whiskers. He has a smooth brow and he has laughter-lines at his temples and around his mouth. His eyes are intelligent and grey, and good-humoured. I think he is a little younger than me. As to his dress, on this first meeting he looked more like a yeoman farmer than a country gentleman, with buff-coloured cord breeches, a grey woollen waistcoat, and a well-worn black frock-coat with unfashionably small lapels. His linen shirt was crumpled, and his neck-cloth was too large, and badly tied. The poor fellow was perspiring profusely in the heat, and was obviously grateful to be able to settle down in the shade.

His wife Delilah would not have been a great temptation to Samson, for she is a very large lady, with an extraordinary bosom, a rolling stomach and a more than ample bottom, all of which were only just contained on the occasion of our meeting within a flimsy pink muslin dress, cut very low and with a high waist. That was a fashion that faded away,

Crossing the Gulf

even in West Wales, some twenty years since. I shuddered to think what a struggle her poor lady's maid must have to fit her into her stays each morning. But she appeared not at all discomfited, and looked a good deal cooler than either her husband or I. And she is very vivacious, with a good complexion, bright blue eyes, golden ringlets, and a pretty mouth. With her face framed by a wide-brimmed bleached straw bonnet, she might have passed for a thirty-year-old, had it not been for her appearance from the neck down. She uses copious amounts of rose water and other unidentifiable perfumes, and her fragrance goes before her.

Oh dear -- those remarks about my new Master and Mistress appear very catty. But they are truly not meant to be, for I liked them both at once. If these are the sort of people who come out of the trades and industries with hard-earned money to buy their way into failing estates, let us have more of them. They will shock many of my neighbours, for sure, and blow away cobwebs from dusty places, but if a new world has to be fashioned, let it be fashioned by calloused hands.

Bessie arrived with tea and slices of moist currant cake, freshly baked. Then she departed, and while my guests tucked in with gusto, we talked. We got on famously, and I discovered that they knew a great deal about me. It turned out that much of what they knew had come a long time ago from Iestyn, but they had clearly made investigations through their attorney, and it was also apparent that they had been talking to Brynach at length.

"A fine boy you have there, Mistress Martha," said Delilah. "Those brown eyes, and his olive skin and thick black hair........ if I had been twenty years younger, I might have become besotted by him at first sight!" And then she frowned and thought for a moment, and spurted out: "Mistress This and Mistress That -- I find it all very bothersome, since in Swansea, among those whom we respect, we do away with formalities and use first names right away. That is the modern way, you understand. We cannot go on with this "Mistress Martha" and "Mistress Delilah" business as if we are passing in the middle of Regent Street -- would you not agree? May I call you Martha, and will you call me Delilah and my husband Wilmot?"

I laughed. "Of course, Delilah. Let us agree to it. If we are to be friends, as I hope we are, then the fewer formalities and obstacles the better."

Crossing the Gulf

So we talked perfectly spontaneously on all manner of subjects. It turned out that my new friends knew virtually nothing about farming or the country, and that their determination to buy an estate came not only from the need to invest Wilmot's copper fortune but also from doctor's orders, for the poor man had breathing problems caused by a lifelong exposure to noxious fumes in the Swansea Valley. He had been told that he would die if he did not get out into the country within a year, and he was not minded to go against doctor's advice. He said he already felt better, after just a few days in Pembrokeshire. I heard about their children and grandchildren, and they heard about mine. So the conversation came back to Brynach. Of course they knew that he was Iestyn's son and that he had been born out of wedlock, but they had the greatest of respect for him. Wilmot made it clear that he and his wife had feelings of genuine sadness that their good fortune in the acquisition of the estate was based upon Brynach's misfortune.

"Martha, that was one of the reasons for this little visit," he said. "We wanted to tell you that we hold that young man in the highest esteem. He tried with might and main to save his estate, and took a gamble which might have worked if he had had better guidance and if the forces of nature had not turned a profitable business into a disaster. I have gambled with large sums of money over and again in making my modest fortune, and while I have lost occasionally the gods have smiled upon me in a way that I have sometimes not deserved. Yes indeed -- he is a good man who has kept his integrity. I will call on his advice frequently between now and Christmas, and I hope that things will turn out well for him."

Then Delilah, to her eternal credit, immediately perceived that this talk of Brynach was making me feel very emotional. She sprang to her feet. "Come now, Wilmot *bach*," she said. "We have taken up enough of Martha's valuable time, and she needs to continue with her snoozing." She gave me a wink that would have done credit to a Penclawdd cockle-woman. "We must be on our way if we are to reach Haverfordwest by dark. May we call again soon, Martha? Never mind Wilmot and all this farming business. There are so many things I want to talk to you about, woman to woman."

Wilmot rolled his eyes and shrugged his shoulders, and said: "Yes, Delilah my dearest. Thank you, Martha, for your hospitality and for your friendly response to our unannounced arrival. I expect we will be here again some time next month -- and I hope that then you might give me some information about animals and crops and suchlike. I will write to you before we come."

I said I would be delighted to receive them, and as we walked back to the yard I thanked them again for their great tolerance and understanding in the midst of what was -- for the Morgan family at least -- a most difficult time. Their carriage was waiting, and a few minutes later I waved it on its way.

As I watched my new friends depart, I could not resist smiling to myself. If misfortune has to come, I thought, it might as well be delivered in the hands of colourful and eccentric folk such as Wilmot and Delilah. They are rough and ready and mercifully free of pretensions. And they have the great virtue of sensitivity to the moods of others, which is more than can be said of most of the fine gentlemen of this district. I declare that North Pembrokeshire has just acquired two free thinkers, and that the district will take a long time to recover from the shock.

ΩΩΩΩΩΩΩΩΩΩΩ

20th September 1845

With almost four weeks having elapsed since the collapse of the estate, it is a secret no longer, and everybody in the community is in possession of some version or other of the story. Some people think that Brynach drank the profits of the estate away, and others that he put down £50,000 in bets at Newgale races, and lost the lot. Such is the way with gossip and dramatic events, and we have to put up with it. We have had many visitors and many letters of consolation, and amongst our neighbours and real friends who do know the truth of the matter we have had nothing but support and offers of help. Some of the local squires and merchants have taken pleasure in our misfortune, but I know who they are, and I am not surprised. In the immediate neighbourhood, there seems to be genuine pleasure that Master and Mistress Gwynne will allow me to stay at the

Crossing the Gulf

Plas until the end of my days.

Thinking of consolation, I have written a letter to Elen, crafting my words as carefully as possible so as to bring her comfort. That was not easy, given our new circumstances. I did not tell her of my long and difficult conversation with Brynach, because he has still not informed me as to his intentions. Once he tells me that he has written to her to say that he is in possession of the truth about his origins, and that he knows she is his natural mother, that will release me from my oath of secrecy and I can write to her in an appropriate fashion. And I hope that there will then be a loving and regular correspondence between mother and son as the years roll by and as they learn to know one another from a distance.

Neither have I made any mention to Elen of the collapse of the Llanychaer and Plas Ingli estates, nor of the fact that Brynach must now find somewhere new to live and even some new profession. There is no need to burden her with such knowledge for the time being, and again I will leave it to Brynach to choose the right moment for revelations.

And while I am recording my commitment to the keeping of secrets, I must also express my unease at keeping the link between Elen and Brynach hidden from my daughters Betsi and Daisy, and from my servants. Should I tell them, or should I not? On balance, for the time being I will hold my tongue, lest this should cause some difficulty for Brynach and his children. Rose, after all, is at a difficult age, and to have her father's origins discussed by all and sundry might be very upsetting for her. When all is said and done, Brynach is a bastard, and the fact that he is my adopted son and heir does not make the reality any easier to bear. Rose moves in a world of carefully protected young heiresses, within which good breeding and old families mean everything, and I could not bear it if she were to be harmed by spiteful gossip from those whom she has thus far trusted as her friends. No, I will keep quiet until Brynach tells me that I may speak.

ΩΩΩΩΩΩΩΩΩΩΩ

5. Troubled Waters

5th October 1845

Brynach informs me that he wrote a letter to Elen in New York over a week ago, telling her that he knows everything and seeking to open up a loving correspondence with her. I have not asked him about the details of his letter, for he is a very private person and it would not be appropriate in any case. The poor fellow will be on tenterhooks now for the next six or seven weeks, for that is the least time it can take for a fast ship to carry his letter to New York and for another fast ship to carry his mother's reply. If there are storms or other delays, single crossings can still take twice as long as expected.

    We have had a pleasant diversion at the Plas with the first visit of Daisy's three children to Wales. I have been dying to meet them for some time, and indeed their holiday was planned long since. Daisy offered to postpone matters, given our recent upheavals involving both home and estate, but I would not hear of it, and decided that we all needed some fresh company to take our minds off miserable matters. So they came to Newport on the Cardigan to Fishguard mail coach a couple of days since, and Will collected them from the Llwyngwair Arms in our carriage.

    Daisy of course greeted them as if they were heroes returning from the defeat of Master Bonaparte, which was understandable since she has not seen them for more than a year. I welcomed them to the Plas, and they met everybody else, and because it was a blustery and rainy day we all rushed inside to the warm kitchen. That caused the first of many entertaining incidents, when daughter Amy (who is a very prim and proper young lady) whispered to her mother: "But Mama, is this not the servants' entrance?"

    Daisy roared with laughter, and said: "Daughter, as far as we are concerned it is the only entrance, used by servants, tradesmen, kings and prime ministers. Dogs and pigs are not allowed to use it. If you want to use the front door it is round on the other side of the house, locked and barred. God knows where the key is, since it is only used for weddings and funerals." At this, Amy laughed nervously, and glanced about her like a

Troubled Waters

frightened chicken, and probably thought: "Oh my goodness, what have I let myself in for?"

But for all their naivety about country life, they are fine young people, all three. Amy is the oldest, every bit as beautiful as her mother was when she was 23 years old. She is quite petite, with a trim figure, a lovely complexion and big brown eyes. She works as a dress-designer in an exclusive London salon patronised by duchesses and other grand ladies. Indeed, her own dress sense is quite exquisite, and she insisted on changing into some delicate new garment at least four times every day. So protracted were these transformations that she seemed to have time for little else. In London, her changes are probably effected more speedily because she has lady's maids and shop assistants to help her, but I had to explain to her that we had but one lady's maid called Liza, and that her priority was to look after me when she was not making fires or washing floors or milking cows. Amy looked aghast at that terrible piece of news, not least because it is absolutely unheard of in the best of circles for a lady's maid to do any manual work, let alone manual work involving dirty farm animals.

Then there is John, who is 19 years old and has ambitions to be a barrister. He is still training in London, and expects to be called to the bar in a year or two. He is a dark and somewhat morose fellow, and in that, says Daisy, he takes after his father, who shall be nameless. But he is tall and good-looking, and no doubt he will catch himself a fine wife in due course. He has a good allowance from his father, and he has described for me with some pride the bachelor apartment which he occupies in Mayfair.

And finally there is William, sixteen years old, absolutely charming, and as different from the other two as gold is from glitter. He has tousled fair hair, bright eyes and a ready smile, and I declare myself as a battered old grandmother to be thoroughly in love with him. He dresses very informally, with loose linen shirts and woollen trousers and comfortable jackets, and appears quite unconcerned about his appearance. Daisy scolds him frequently about his attire and his manners, and he responds obediently for a few minutes; but then he is off again, chatting about this and that, asking about everything, and informing us of the great plans he has for the reformation of agriculture. He is currently at Eton, and will shortly go to Oxford, but he will certainly not be a doctor or a lawyer or a clergyman when he is let out into the world. He will be a countryman and an inventor or an engineer, and since he wants to make machines for doing almost anything, he will probably change the world. His father, as he is happy to tell us, is Sir Thomas Wilson, who owns mills and canals and mines in Lancashire, and who gives him a perfectly adequate allowance.

I was surprised to learn that the three children do not see a great deal of each other. During our conversations around the kitchen table and in the parlour it has already become apparent that they are learning as much about each other as they are about us and the Plas, and Daisy has confided in me that that is one of the reasons for bringing them here for this little holiday.

It is unfortunate that there are so few other young people around at the moment to meet the three new cousins. Rose and David have been to the Plas to meet them already, of course, and in spite of (or because of) the big difference in ages they got along splendidly. But only one of Betsi's children -- twenty-four-year-old Benjamin -- is in residence just now, and because he is working on the Brithdir estate every day he has little time for socializing. Indeed he has little inclination for it either, for he is a hardworking and serious young fellow who is determined to do well with the estate when he takes it over from his father Ioan. His brother Abel has gone off to join the army, and Owain is boarding in the Grammar School in Haverfordwest. The three visitors need some young company, and in the coming week we will take them to Castlebythe to meet some of Catrin's grandchildren, and then to Trecwn to meet the younger generation of the Stokes family. That will be good for me too, since I will have a chance to meet my dear friend Mary Jane, whom I see too seldom.

In the meantime, we are all doing our best to train the three visitors in the ways of the countryside, teaching them what pigs, sheep and cattle are for, teaching them that nobody spends their time lounging about if there are tasks to be done, and teaching them above all else that the rules of etiquette relating to country house visits have long since ceased to apply in this dear place called Plas Ingli.

ΩΩΩΩΩΩΩΩΩΩΩ

11th October 1845

Well, they have gone, and in truth I was sorry to see them go. In the end, we managed to entertain them, if not royally at least with some style. On several occasions John and William went shooting with Gomer and Gerallt on the estuary or in Tycanol Wood, and they came back with ducks, wood pigeons and woodcock for the larder. They also went fishing on the Nevern River with the kind permission of Squire Bowen of Llwyngwair, and came back with four splendid sewin and two salmon. Amy, Daisy and myself enjoyed many bracing walks on the common and along the coastal cliffs between Cwm-yr-Eglwys and Newport. We women enjoyed tea parties with various friends in Newport, and made a number of interesting trips by carriage to examine antiquities and natural wonders, of which there are very many in this district. We even attended a theatrical performance in Fishguard, and enjoyed three musical evenings in the parlour of the Plas. Thus I was able to demonstrate to my urban grandchildren that we do enjoy the civilized things of life here at the Plas, and that we are not all barbarians.

One of the high points of their stay was another visit from Master and Mistress Gwynne. When they arrived, looking as bucolic and eccentric as ever, I saw flickers of superiority and little sniggers of amusement from the three young people, and John and Amy set out to have some fun at their expense. But Wilmot and Delilah are nobody's fools, and before long the tables were turned right about as they showed that you do not have to be dressed in the highest of fashions or have an apartment in Mayfair to know what is going on in the world. At last I took pity on the young sophisticates and retired with Wilmot and Delilah to my study, where we needed to talk about estate accounts and agriculture.

After that, over a cup of tea, Wilmot and William found each other, and when William discovered that the new Master of the estate had made his money in copper and coal, and knew all about steam engines and locomotives and pumps and pistons, he was immediately elevated to the status of a hero. As the rest of us rolled our eyes and grinned, the pair of them wandered outside and strolled in the garden talking about machines for at least an hour. At last Delilah had to drag Wilmot away, and his parting words to me were: "Fine grandson you have there, Martha! That boy will go far, just you mark my words."

Troubled Waters

The other high point of the visit was John's attempt to seduce Myfanwy, who has just turned seventeen. I know not what goes on in London, but he is obviously used to having a magical effect upon young and susceptible females. We were amused from the very beginning by his antics, as he preened himself like a cockatoo, chatted to her intently, paid her little compliments, and worked out very carefully what time people went to bed and what might be the best route to her room. At any rate, at dead of night we were all awoken by an almighty crash, and some of us tumbled out of bed, thinking that a burglar was making off with the family silver. I arrived in the kitchen to find Gerallt with a shotgun in his hand, and Bessie lighting the candles. At last we saw a figure crouching in the shadows under the kitchen table. It groaned. "Come out, sir!" shouted Gerallt, pointing his weapon and sounding very fierce. "With your hands up, if you please, or I will blow your brains out." Whoever it was under the table forgot where he was, and tried to stand up, giving himself a mighty thump on the head and causing another pitiful groan. At last he emerged with his hands up -- my grandson John, dressed only in a nightshirt and nightcap. He looked as if he had been in a battle, for there was blood coming from the wound inflicted by the table, and his right eye was already swelling up. Then Myfanwy appeared from the passageway leading to the servants' rooms, dressed only in her nightgown. The flush on her cheeks made her even prettier than usual, and she carried a fine bunch of flowers. I recognized them as the very same ones which had on the previous evening graced our dining room table. "You forgot your flowers, sir!" said she, looking perfectly calm and collected. She flung them onto the floor at Master John's feet, turned on her heel, and went back to bed.

Poor John. I almost felt sorry for him. With his passion well and truly subsided, we had to sit him down and attend to his wounds. He did not say a lot, for it was obvious to all and sundry that he had not been very successful on his amorous expedition, and that he had discovered that we females who live beneath this roof are well capable of looking after ourselves. We have, after all, had plenty of practice.

At breakfast Myfanwy looked very pleased with herself, and John sported a beautiful black eye. To the credit of all concerned -- including my adventurous grandson -- we saw the funny side of things, and fell about with laughter, especially when he held his hands up in a gesture of surrender as Myfanwy served up his porridge oats.

In mid-morning Will and Gomer organized both the carriage and the light chaise for transporting our guests to Carmarthen. There were five passengers and their bags to be carried: the three young people in the chaise and Daisy and Betsi in the carriage. Amy has invited both of them to stay with her for a week or two, and while Betsi was at first reluctant to accept, Daisy,who is very persuasive, convinced her that they will have a wonderful time in the city, looking at shops, visiting famous places and spending more money than they can really afford. I encouraged them to go. The two sisters spend little enough time together, and they need to renew their bonds and to spend time in a new and exciting environment. So they will go to Carmarthen and take the new-fangled passenger train that gets to London in only five hours. That is truly amazing, and will be an adventure in itself.

Suddenly the place is as quiet as the grave, and I do not know what to do with myself.

ΩΩΩΩΩΩΩΩΩΩΩ

12th October 1845

I have lost my son Brynach and my grandson David. They are not dead, but they might as well be, for they are set upon travelling to America as soon as it can be arranged, and God only knows if they will ever return. In my innocence, I failed to anticipate that it would happen, and that makes me angry and compounds my anguish. Oh, how much more grieving do I have to do before I go to my grave?

Yet again I am shaking with emotion as I write. But I am determined not to weep, and I am determined not to despair, but to seek some good in the new situation.

It happened like this. Brynach came to see me this morning, having ridden over the common on his hunter. He greeted me warmly enough, and we exchanged pleasantries. He was surprised to learn that Betsi and Daisy had gone off to London with the exotic grandchildren, and laughed at the atmosphere of calm which now pervaded the Plas after the bustle of the past fortnight. "This is as it should be, Mother," he said. "All that noise, on my last visit with the children, gave me a headache. Do you enjoy getting back to normal?"

"Yes and no," said I. "It was fun to get to know those good young people, and I have to admit to feeling a little lonely now that they are gone -- especially since my two daughters have gone with them."

Then he frowned, and I knew that he had something serious to say to me. "Come and sit in the parlour with me, Mother," he said, and led me by the arm into my most comfortable chair. He closed the door, and then came and sat opposite me.

He said: "I have made a very big decision, Mother, and I want you to be the first to know about it. As you know, I have written to Aunt Elen in New York and told her what I know. But it may be weeks and weeks before I get any response, and I find the uncertainty and the waiting very wearing. It is less than three months to the end of the year, when I have to vacate Plas Llanychaer. I cannot make plans here, because I do not know whether she will acknowledge the fact that she is my mother. So I have decided to travel to America, to seek her out and to make a new life for myself."

I could hardly speak, and the image of a three-masted sailing ship and a quayside came into my mind. At last I said, so quietly that I could hardly hear myself: "But Brynach, this was never my intention when I told you about Elen and Iestyn. In fact, I did not even consider the possibility that you might leave this beloved place, in spite of everything that has happened. I have always held to the belief that some solution might be found......."

"I know, Mother, I know. But the more that I think about it, the more I know that I cannot stay. I have lost the respect of my peers, and people do not know what to say when they meet me in the street. I have no estate to run, and no servants to instruct. I have no tenants and labourers to care for. The only thing I know is how to manage a group of people, a big house and a few hundred acres of land. I have no money in the bank, and only a little under the bed. Whatever else I try to do, somebody else will instruct and pay me and will know that I am a failed gentleman. I cannot continue as a magistrate, and I have had to dispose of all my shares in the turnpike trusts. I am in a horrible trap from which there is no escape."

Troubled Waters

"I appreciate that, son. I have been in such a trap myself, in the early days of this estate after the fire which killed David's parents and siblings. Then we had lost the house and almost everything that was in it, but we still had the estate and we still had the respect of the community. I see all too clearly that your predicament is worse."

"I will not take charity, Mother, from you or anybody else. Please do not offer me anything, not even a single penny of your savings, for I will be forced to refuse you. I brought this tragedy down upon myself, and have caused untold suffering to you and many others. I will now make a new life for myself, and through my own honest toil in a new land I will make another fortune. I am determined to do it, and please, Mother, do not try to deter me."

What could I have said? Anything about the dangers of an ocean voyage, or the dangers of a horrid climate, or the presence of strange beasts or hostile Red Indians would have sounded feeble and self-serving, as if I was thinking of my own comfort and convenience rather than his future happiness. So I held my tongue, but I must have looked so pale and so desolate that my dear son came and put his arms around me and held me tight, as if consoling a small girl who has fallen and hurt her knee.

Of course I wept, and afterwards blew my nose and said "Please forgive me, Brynach. I am a feeble and silly old woman. I seem to have been weeping a good deal lately. I do not know why."

"I know perfectly well why, Mother dear. Because you have been living through hell. But I urge you to look at what is positive. I will not be happy here, and I feel totally convinced that I will find contentment across the ocean. Is that not what you want?"

"I suppose so, Brynach."

"And I will give myself five years. If I have not made my fortune, and a new life for myself, by then, I swear to you that I will return."

"Brynach, I will be dead by then, so that is not much consolation."

"Rubbish, Mother! Just look at you -- still elegant and beautiful, and still turning the heads of red-blooded gentlemen in the streets of Newport. You will live for ever!"

At that, I did manage a little smile. Then I said: "And what of the children?"

"I have told them of my plans. David is thrilled at the prospect of going to America, but Rose refuses to come. She says that she loves you and the Plas too much, and that she wants to stay here with you. In any case, she hates the water and she hates sailing ships. Will you allow her to come and live at the Plas?"

"Oh Brynach, what a question! You know that I would like nothing more. She is a wonderful and sensitive child, and I would like nothing better than to have her near me as I grow old. That, at least, would be a gift, and would give me some reason for staying alive."

He squeezed my arm and kissed my cheek. "Good, good. Then it is decided. I have made investigations, and I have discovered that next month, on a date still to be fixed, Benjamin Evans of Cardigan has arranged for a vessel to take 30 emigrants and other passengers from Cardigan to Liverpool, to join the larger sailing ship *George Washington* for its voyage to New York. He has reserved places for David and myself, and now that I have spoken to you and have obtained your consent.........."

"Have I given my consent, Brynach?"

"I thought you had, Mother dear."

"Perhaps I did. I am very confused."

"Good, I thought so. As I was saying, now that we are agreed I will confirm our passages, and put down our payment. We will pay £4/10/0 each for superior accommodation, for I gather that those travelling steerage have to go through hell between Liverpool and New York."

That was more or less the end of our conversation. I was so numb that I do not recall anything else that passed between us. All I do remember is that in taking his leave he was as animated and excited as a small boy who has hit a bull's eye with his first arrow shot.

How can I deny Brynach this adventure, after all that has happened to him? And little David too -- surely a life in a new world will give him new challenges, and make a fine man of him............

Now I will go to bed, seeking -- I fear not too successfully -- to fight off yet another bout of misery.

ΩΩΩΩΩΩΩΩΩΩΩ

Troubled Waters

13th October 1845

With Brynach at Plas Llanychaer beavering away at his plans, I have spent most of the day wandering about the place in a daze, and getting in the way of my servants. Bessie became very irritated with me, and eventually decided that she had better seek to understand my black mood.

"Now then, Mistress," she said, sounding like a fierce governess, "enough of this moping about, if you please. I cannot get anything done today because you are permanently in the way. Would you like to explain what is going on? Are you missing those London grandchildren of yours? Or missing Daisy and Betsi? Or has Master Brynach brought you more news?"

"The latter, I am afraid, Bessie."

"Is it a secret, Mistress, or do you want to share it with me and Liza?"

"I have to share it with somebody. Will the pair of you abandon your chores for a moment, and sit with me in the parlour? There we will not be disturbed, if Myfanwy can keep an eye on the kitchen."

So we three sat in that comfortable room that had heard it all before. I decided to tell them everything; about the fleeting and fateful liaison between Iestyn and Elen all those years ago; about Brynach's secret birth in Bath; about Elen's shameful flight to America; about Iestyn's rush to Newport to leave the little mite on the doorstep of Plas Ingli; and much else besides, concerning the Nightwalker and his pitiful vigil over his son as he grew up. The only thing I did not tell them was that I had learned much of this story from the Nightwalker during an encounter in my cave; for I am still the only one who knows that the cave exists.

Bessie and Liza knew some of this tale, but not all of the details. There was a special poignancy in it for Liza, who first came to the Plas as a wet nurse and who was in effect Brynach's mother for the first years of his life. It was poignant because she would not have been producing breast milk at the time had it not been for the birth of her own little son Twm, who died when he was fifteen in a tragic accident. As I spoke I saw from her face that recollections were flooding into her own mind and heart, and Bessie held her hand as she held back her tears.

"And when, Mistress, did you tell all of this to Brynach?" asked Bessie.

"About a month ago, at Plas Llanychaer."

Troubled Waters

"And his reaction when he discovered about his real mother?"

"He was very shocked," I reported, "and hardly knew what to say."

"So would I have been, Mistress," said Liza, "if such news had come to me after all these years, and so soon after the collapse of the estate. That would be a lot to cope with, all at one time."

Then, much to my surprise, Bessie berated me for keeping the secret of his birth from Brynach for all these years. I tried to explain to her that if I had told him the truth, and if he had then tried to contact his real mother in America, that might well have destroyed Elen's marriage. It was Tom's death, I explained, that had now changed the situation. Still Bessie would not let me be, and accused me of selfishness in wanting to keep Brynach to myself. "How many times have you lied to him over the years, Mistress," she asked, "when he has asked about his mother?"

"Over and again, Bessie. I admit it. But sometimes lies are for the best, and I wanted to give him certainty, security and love, and not a childhood filled with doubts and fears.........."

Now I felt beleaguered and hurt under the lash of Bessie's tongue, and I was close to tears myself when Liza came to my rescue. "Let Mistress Martha be, Bessie," she said calmly.. "Don't you forget that she has had a hard time of it herself recently, and has had to carry a great burden of secrets without a good husband to help her decide what to do. You know what it is like yourself to be a widow, and I thank the Good Lord in his heaven for the fact that I have my dear Tomos to talk to at dead of night when something or other keeps me awake."

Bessie relented, and apologized for her insensitivity, and we three old friends smiled and embraced. Then I gave them their second shock by telling them that Brynach had made the decision to go to America with David, to meet Elen and to make his fortune.

There was a long silence, broken only by the ticking of the mahogany clock on the wall. Liza spoke at last, and said: "I understand him perfectly, Mistress. I think I would have done the same."

Bessie concurred, and that made me angry. "Well, I think he is being very selfish in going off and leaving Rose behind," I blurted out. "And I think he is being cruel to abandon me and all the others who love him. After all, have we not, between us, given him everything that he has?"

Then Bessie wagged her finger at me, making me feel like a petulant little girl. "Mistress Martha!" she stormed. "That was a very cruel and self-centred thing to say, if you do not mind me saying so. Whose best interest are you thinking of? Yours or his? Of course you have given him everything. That is what mothers do. But now you must let him go. You cannot keep on clucking around him like a mother hen for ever, Mistress! He has lost his estate and his reputation, and from what you say he has also been disappointed in love. After everything he has been through, he needs to get away and spread his wings. And if he has to go to America to do that, so be it. Over there he will be a new man with no history to drag him down. His mother Elen went to New York because she was fleeing from her past; to some degree Master Brynach also has to flee, but in my view he is being very brave, and it takes a real man to leave comfort behind and seek his fortune..........."

Then Liza kicked me too, while I was down. She said, again in calm and measured tones: "And do not forget, Mistress, that he is taking a huge gamble. Apart from the physical risks of danger and suffering, there is a risk that he will fail again, and that his mother will still reject him, when finally he finds her. I agree with Bessie, Mistress. Let him go, as we all have to let our children go. Give him your blessing, and treat him as a hero."

After all that battering, I suppose I should have cried like a baby. Indeed I would have done, had I been twenty years younger. But I feel quite proud of myself in that I breathed deeply, calmed my troubled heart, and said at last: "Thank you, my dear friends. Of course you are right, as ever. I will let Brynach go, and brave little David too. But do you mind, once they are gone, if I love Rose even more than I do already?"

My two beloved handmaidens smiled, and Bessie said: "I think that would be perfectly acceptable, Mistress, until it is time to let her go too." And so we embraced, and went back into the real world of the kitchen, where Myfanwy was stirring *cawl* over the fire.

ΩΩΩΩΩΩΩΩΩΩΩ

Troubled Waters

24th October 1845

Daisy and Betsi returned today from their holiday, bubbling with high spirits. They have so much to tell me about London, and passenger trains, and great shops and fine clothes, and strange people, that I declare they will not be finished with the task by Christmas.

And as for my news about Brynach and David being set upon a great voyage to America, they did not seem particularly surprised. They had clearly talked about their little foundling brother at great length during their time away, and said that if he had not made that decision for himself, they would have advised him on exactly similar lines. They saw the shock in my face, and without any prompting from Liza or Bessie, Betsi said: "Let him go, Mother, and let him fly away to the far side of the world, to make his fortune and find a new wife. You have done all you can for him -- indeed, you have given him far more than any young man has a right to expect. And we have made decisions on your behalf, have we not, Daisy?"

"Indeed we have, sister," laughed Daisy. "We have decided, Mother *bach*, that from this point on you will forget about family and home and grow old disgracefully. And do not worry about the estate. It is not yours, but at least, thanks to Master Gwynne, it is yours to enjoy to the end of your days. What more do you really want?"

And Betsi piped up again, and did a silly little dance as she spoke. "Think of yourself for a change, Mother. Have fun. Wear that wild red dress of yours to church on a Sunday. Travel to see the antiquities of Greece. Take up rowing or trout fishing, or drive a locomotive engine -- that seems to be terribly exciting. You are still vivacious and beautiful. Adopt a noble cause. Fight for the emancipation of the fair sex. Find yourself a new husband, and roll in the clover with him........."

"Out of here, the pair of you!" I laughed, chasing them out of the kitchen. "My reputation is bad enough already, and you are setting out a programme of self-indulgence for me that would make Mary Magdalene blush! What will the deacons of Capel Brynberian think of all this involvement, excess and debauchery? If I achieve but a fraction of what you have planned, I will surely be condemned to Hell."

Well, those two terrible daughters of mine have certainly cheered me up, and in the face of such female solidarity on the matter of Brynach's great decision it would be churlish of me to think or talk any further about it. I must submit to a majority verdict. Tomorrow, Betsi and Daisy are planning to travel over to Llanychaer in the light chaise, and they will give their blessings to their brother. And in their present elated and mischievous mood they will help to lighten his mood too.

ΩΩΩΩΩΩΩΩΩΩΩΩ

26th October 1845

Brynach has had a message from Master Benjamin Evans to say that the tide in Cardigan will be exactly right for the departure of his sailing ship *Emily Jane* on the 6th day of November. One week after that the *George Washington* will sail from Liverpool to New York. That means that Brynach has less than two weeks to sort out his affairs, pack up his things, and say his farewells. He will be back and forth between Llanychaer and Plas Ingli, I dare say, but as the fateful day draws closer, he and the children will become increasingly nervous, and I will do my best to stay out of the way. They will all come to the Plas on 5th November to settle Rose in, and then be off to Cardigan on the following morning.

Looking further afield, I have been reading in the *Welshman* and the *Cambrian* of ominous events in Ireland, which will, I fear, have repercussions in West Wales. In many areas a strange disease which they call "the distemper" or "the blight" has been affecting the potato crop, turning the foliage above ground into a black and soggy mess and also leading to the rotting of the tubers below ground. We had something similar in West Wales a few years back, but since we do not grow a large quantity of potatoes and do not depend upon them for our survival, we cleaned the ground and rotated our crops in the years that followed, and the problem went away. According to reports from travellers across St George's Channel, the digging of the main crop has been under way this month, and the blight has appeared in virtually every Irish county. In some places one-third to one-half of the crop has been destroyed, and the potato fields which are normally coloured bright green are now black, with the normally healthy tubers reduced to stinking putrefaction. The smell in certain districts is so foul that the peasants cannot bear to dig up the rotten crop, so it is left in the ground to turn into slime and filth.

According to a letter in the *Welshman*, the prognostications of famine in Ireland are real enough, because the mass of Irish peasants eat nothing but potatoes and grow nothing else on their land. They do not even know how to bake bread or cook meat or fish. Many of them have less than an acre of land on which they have to produce enough potatoes to feed maybe a dozen people for a year, but in order to pay their £5 rent and prevent eviction from the agents who run the big estates, they sometimes have to sell part of their crop and go hungry. The energetic families like the O'Connells travel to England and Wales each summer for the harvest, and might then return with maybe £20 saved, just in time to dig the potato crop and eke out survival over the winter months. Those who have planned well might have a few pounds left by April or May for the purchase of a little oatmeal or buttermilk, but such planning is by no means common, and the writer of the letter bemoaned the lack of enterprise amongst the mass of cottagers, who seemed to be more content to leave their fate in the hands of a benevolent God than to work their way out of poverty. That made me angry, for how do you work your way out of poverty when you have no education, no cash, no assets, and no energy?

All of this came into sharp focus this very morning when I bumped into my friend Elijah Collins in the street. We went into Mistress Molly James's Tea House for a nice cup of tea and a biscuit or two, and when we had finished with exchanging essential news he admitted that he was once again less than pleased with certain of his confederates in the mercantile trade. Then, as we sat in the window of the tea house, we saw Squire John Collyer Tredafydd and Squire Rhys Edwards Trefach passing by, involved in animated conversation. Elijah tapped on the window to attract their attention, and they came inside and joined us. I had not seen either of them for a very long time, and as we spoke I was reminded that many years ago, when I was a young and desirable widow, Master Collyer had been intent upon wooing me. It had come to nothing, of course, but I liked him then and I like him now, even though he is old and suffers from a swelling of the joints. Master Edwards is the father of Brynach's lovely wife Anne, who died in childbirth, and the maternal grandfather of Rose and David, so we had to talk for a few minutes on matters of mutual

Troubled Waters

interest. He had heard of the impending departure of Brynach and David to America, and said that he had been delighted to have a visit from the family yesterday during which they told him everything, including the story of Iestyn and Elen. That had surprised him, he said, and he admitted that in the circumstances it was understandable that Brynach should go off across the sea to seek his fortune. He wished the voyagers well, and shared my delight that Rose would be staying behind; and I promised him that she and I would visit Trefach more often in the future.

Then the conversation turned back to trade, and to the Irish problem, with Elijah complaining that he has had another row with the men who seem to be taking over control of the local branch of the Society of Sea Serjeants. He said that some of them had lost great sums of money through the failure of the wheat harvest, and that there would be little wheat in storage this winter, but they had good supplies of barley in the warehouses and were anticipating good profits by playing the market. "Do you know, my dear friends," he asked, "that some of those squires said this morning in the Royal Oak that "things are looking good in Ireland"? Did you ever hear such callous and unfeeling talk from fellows who call themselves gentlemen? Why, they are no better than rat catchers or body snatchers!"

"Quite right you are, Elijah," said Master Collyer. "I have seen those fellows dancing on graves before, and they will do it again until somebody stops them."

"But holding grain is not a crime, gentlemen," said I. "We all do it, and sell when the price is high and threatens to fall."

"But we also apply some ethical standards, Mistress Martha," said Master Edwards. "All four of us around this table have let grain go at less than the top price when the government has appealed to the market on compassionate grounds, and when starvation is widespread. I can think of five or six such occasions during the last thirty years."

"And is this such a time?" I asked. "My newspaper tells me that with perhaps a third or a half of the Irish potato crop putrefied in the ground, the cottagers are discovering that even when clean tubers are clamped for the winter they are not immune from the blight, and rot in storage."

"Correct, Mistress Martha. And that is where opportunism raises its ugly head. The peasants are already selling their full potato harvests on the open market, for fear that they will rot if they are clamped. So there is a glut just now, which was portrayed in the latest copy of *The Times* as a sign that all is well. Nonsense! Nonsense! All is not well! The price of potatoes has plummeted, but what will happen if nothing is clamped? What would happen to us if we had nothing in our larders? I will bet my last golden sovereign, gentlemen, that by Christmas there will be starvation and deaths in Ireland........"

"And then," interjected Master Collyer, "the likes of Jacob Harry, Huws Bayvil and Owen Gelli Fawr will be rubbing their hands in glee, and waiting for the government feeding programme to be brought in. They see tidy fortunes ahead of them, just waiting to be gathered in."

"But have they not learned anything from the debacle of the wheat harvest?"

"It seems not, Mistress Martha. They are now closer to the edge of bankruptcy than they were before, and bitter and angry to boot. They probably blame God for their misfortunes, and probably ask God in their prayers to shift the burden from their shoulders onto those of the starving Irish."

It was time for me to walk home to the Plas, for as I looked through the tea house window I could see from the look of the sky to the west that rain was threatening.

"I must be going, gentlemen," said I, rising to my feet. As they stood also, with various creaks and groans, I offered each of them my hand in turn, gave a little curtsy, and took my leave.

As I went through the door Master Edwards, who knows me quite well, gave me a meaningful look and said: "Don't you get involved with Huws and Owen and that lot, Mistress Martha. And just you take care."

ΩΩΩΩΩΩΩΩΩΩΩ

1st November 1845

As the day of departure for the *Emily Jane* draws closer, I have been feeling lonely and wistful. Perhaps Liza's recent reminder of the joys of

Troubled Waters

marriage and companionship has become embedded in my mind, and perhaps as one grows older one comes to value the company of loved ones more than hitherto. But I have realised that I miss the company of Jones Minor Prophet. I have not heard anything from him since he left on his travels, and I suppose he is somewhere in North Wales just now, preaching to the heathen and sleeping in hedges. Would that I could be driven by such strong belief, and sustained by the conviction that my witness was the means of saving souls! Would that I could be as innocent and happy as he!

Yesterday was Hallowe'en, and in order to keep my mind off Brynach and the children I thought of Amos instead. I thought that might be an innocent enough occupation, but then I found it difficult to get him out of my head, and instead of being occupied I became preoccupied. And suddenly, late in the evening, I thought that I might take advantage of the fact that I was all alone in the house. Daisy is away for a couple of days and nights, looking after the three daughters of the Squire of Henllys while he and his wife attend a family funeral in Aberystwyth. Gerallt and Myfanwy had gone home to their parents, all of half a mile away, because they are due for a little holiday and since this is, after all, one of the feast days in the calendar. And for the same reason Bessie had gone down to the Parrog to visit Patty and Jake, just for one night, in order to get some fresh sea air into her lungs. They had all promised me that they would be back first thing this morning, as indeed they were, since All Saints Day (today) and All Souls Day (tomorrow) are reserved for sorting out the animals and for slaughtering those that will end up dried, salted or hung beneath the kitchen and scullery ceilings. That involves hard work for all of us.

So it was that I had brushed aside their concerns about my being in the house all alone and having to fend off ghosts and goblins on All Saints Eve, not to mention burglars, arsonists, murderers and the like. I had waved them all away and said I would thoroughly enjoy an evening in on my own for a change, the first time such a thing had happened for many a long day. And indeed I did have a very relaxing time, sitting by the crackling kitchen fire, knitting a little, reading a little, and snoozing off every now and then. I had looked out through the kitchen window a few times and seen that all was well with the world, with smudgy clouds drifting across the night sky and occasionally obliterating the face of a waning moon.

Troubled Waters

So, to my sudden inspiration. It was, of course, connected with Jones Minor Prophet. Hallowe'en, I thought -- one of the three nights in the year when spirits are abroad, and when divination might reveal something interesting. With respect to Amos, I did not know my own mind, let alone his, so I thought I might employ an old trick called *rhamanta* which I had tried when I was fifteen or sixteen years old, in an attempt to obtain guidance. There was a procedure that had to be strictly followed, but I thought I could remember it. I knew that the trick was strictly for virgins, but I thought that because I had been virginal for more than a year (since my foolish dalliance with Master Hugh Williams on a hot day last August) I might get away with a liberal interpretation of the rules. If it works, the trick is supposed to give a young lady -- or an old one -- the identity of her intended gentleman or future husband.

I have to admit that more than a shiver of excitement passed through my body once I had made my decision, and as I set about the designated preparations. It was about ten o'clock. First, I went outside into the yard to ensure that there were no lights coming up the yard towards the Plas, and to satisfy myself that I would not be disturbed. I filled a bucket with ice cold spring water from the water tank at the side of the dairy, and carried it inside. Then I threw on some logs and stoked up the fire to a merry blaze. I locked the kitchen door and the side door to the scullery, and closed the shutters on all of the downstairs windows. I sat for a while in front of the fire and tried to keep myself calm, but that was not easy, and I found that my heart was beating wildly. I breathed deeply and started on the divination.

First, I removed my shoes and stockings. Then I took off my jacket and scarf, and placed them on one of the kitchen benches. One by one, all my other garments followed, as did my stays. Throughout this process, I remained calm and demure, because great displays of seductive passion are not recommended. At last I stood in front of the fire with only my undergarment left. My face and breasts glowed in the warmth of the flames. Finally I slipped out of my last garment too, and stood there entirely naked. I let down my hair, and shook my head until my tresses fell down over my shoulders.

Then I started on the feast. Still quite naked, I opened the door to the downstairs passage, and placed lighted candles here and there to illuminate my activities. I took a tray and padded back and forth in my

148

Troubled Waters

bare feet several times between the dining room and the kitchen, bearing with me a single place setting of our finest silver cutlery, china and crystal goblets from our glass-fronted cabinets. I laid the table very beautifully, with the place setting near the kitchen door and facing towards the main passage door. Then I trotted about over the old slate slabs, and back and forth along the passage between kitchen and larder, until I had a tasty cold meal laid out on the long oak table. There were fillets of fish, patés, cold meats, cheeses and pickled onions, sauces and relishes, cold potatoes left over from the previous evening, and even some late tomatoes. Then there were four different breads, a silver platter of good salty butter, a whole currant cake, a plate of griddle cakes, a blackberry and apple pie, a silver jug of whipped cream, and finally a cut glass bowl filled with fudge and jellied fruits. To complete the temptation, I placed a lead crystal decanter of superior claret in the middle of the table, just within the reach of my anticipated guest.

Half past eleven, I thought, and all is going according to plan. I felt shivery after all this naked meandering in the cold dining room and in the even colder scullery, so I stood in front of the fire again until the glow of anticipation once again permeated my body. Then I remembered the toasted cheese sandwich! Oh my God! It is perfectly well known among virgins that the handsome young gentlemen of the spirit world like nothing better than a toasted cheese sandwich on the stroke of midnight. So I cut two thick slices of bread, and a solid slice of Bessie's best Cheddar cheese, and set about my task with the long-handled toasting fork before the fire. Soon the sandwich was sizzling merrily and smelling extremely tempting, but I am old enough to resist temptation, and I placed it on the guest's plate. Perfectly done, I thought, and quite irresistible.

Ten minutes to midnight, and I had still not washed my undergarment! So with a mounting sense of panic in my breast I ran outside and fetched a washtub from the washroom, which involved a good deal of unlocking and locking of doors and furtive glancing hither and thither in case there were uninvited guests about. They would surely have died of shock had they seen the Mistress of Plas Ingli prancing about naked in the moonlight on a cold autumn night. Safely back in my kitchen sanctuary, I poured the cold water into the washtub before the fire and then washed my most intimate piece of clothing in it. That made my hands very cold, but sacrifices have to be made and difficulties endured during great

Troubled Waters

enterprises. Then I wrung all of the water from it and draped it across a chair-back in front of the fire to dry.

Everything was ready, and just in time I slipped out of the kitchen into the passage, and closed the door behind me. The midnight chimes echoed around the house from the clock in the parlour. I waited in the passage, still without a stitch of clothing on my body, for what seemed like an eternity. I started to feel very cold, and my nose started to run. And then I heard little sounds from the kitchen. They got louder and louder. With mounting excitement I knew that somebody was there, walking around. Whoever it was, he had got inside through a door that was locked, or a window that was shuttered, or down a chimney that was full of smoke and flames. Then I heard the sound of the bench being moved, followed by silence, and a low mumble. Was somebody saying grace? I heard liquid being poured from the decanter into a crystal goblet, and the sounds of knives and cutlery in contact with bowls and plates. This continued for maybe ten minutes, and still I resisted the temptation to peep through the keyhole in order to identify my guest. When I did my peeping, I would see him for sure, for I had arranged everything at the far side of the table with exactly that objective in mind.

After another five minutes I was shivering so much that my teeth were starting to chatter, and I feared that my presence might be given away. I could wait no longer, and gingerly started to remove the key from the keyhole. As I did so, I was surprised by a very loud belch from the kitchen. Was that the sound of a satisfied man, or a monster? I feared it was the latter, for it is well known in these parts that when Betty Poppins tried *rhamanta* as a young woman, hoping to see Jack Evans Penlan, all she saw was a great black monster with a horrible face and red fangs and a long tail. And she remained a miserable spinster for the rest of her life.

Perspiring profusely in spite of the fact that I was freezing cold, I put my eye to the keyhole. There was Amos Jones Minor Prophet, looking replete and contented, and licking his lips. It could not have been anybody else. I felt terrified and relieved and excited, all at the same time, and did not know what I was supposed to do next. Was the divination complete, or was there more ceremonial that had gone out of my head because of old age? So I looked through the keyhole again. There was nobody there, and the place setting was exactly as I had left it.

I burst into the kitchen, and there was not the slightest sign that

Troubled Waters

anybody other than myself had been near the place. I sat in Grandpa Isaac's old settle at the side of the fire, and held my hands in front of me, palms towards the flames. My mind was racing and my heart was again beating wildly. What were the implications of what I had witnessed? I just did not know. I felt ravenously hungry, and thought it would be a terrible thing to let that toasted cheese sandwich go to waste. So I carried it across to the settle and tucked into it. Then I felt thirsty too, and realized that the superior claret in the decanter would certainly go off if it was left there until the morning. So I poured a nice gobletful for myself, and then possibly another, and then perhaps even a third. I do believe that I was still sitting by the fire as naked as the day I was born, but my memory is a little hazy as to the details of what happened next.

I must have cleared up reasonably well, which says something for my training in household management, for when I came down in my night-gown this morning at five o'clock, before any of the servants had returned from their little holidays, the kitchen was well cleared. My clothes were all gone, and were upstairs in their appointed wardrobe places. The china, glasses and cutlery were back more or less where they were supposed to be in the dining room, and the washtub and bucket were back in the scullery. There were a few things that needed to be washed up, and I dare say that there were a few crumbs and bits of cheese on the floor. I had apparently broken one plate during my feast, but I thought that a reasonable price to pay for an interesting evening's entertainment. I went back to bed with a sore head, and slept for several hours more.

When I finally came down in mid-morning, Bessie and Myfanwy were both pottering about in the kitchen. "Had a pleasant evening all by yourself, Mistress?" said my beloved housekeeper, without looking up.

"Yes thank you, Bessie. Very peaceful it was. I read a little, and knitted a little, and sat by the fire......"

"....... and had a bite to eat and a drop to drink, by the look of the larder?"

"Quite correct. I was moved to have a simple supper on my lap at the fireside. And I had a sudden urge to have a drop of claret with my meal. Very nice too, it was. We must get some more bottles of it from Williams Grape, next time he calls."

"Just so, Mistress," said Bessie, as she picked up an empty bottle from the kitchen floor and went out into the yard, humming a happy tune.

Troubled Waters

6th November 1845

I have let go, and they have flown away. Sailed away, rather, since the *Emily Jane* drifted downstream from Cardigan Quay on the ebb tide shortly after noon today.

I am done with weeping for today, and now that it is evening I am resolved to be stoical and to think of the wonderful new life opening up for Brynach and David. But I will not -- cannot -- write at length about the day because it is all still too raw.

The bare bones of it are as follows. Last night, Brynach and the children came to the Plas, having visited all of their friends throughout the area over the past few days and having said their tearful farewells at Llanychaer. Rose told me this afternoon that the departure from the estate was very emotional, since all the servants, tenants and labourers love Brynach greatly. My dear son had still not fully recovered his composure when he came here. We enjoyed a strange dinner at 7 o'clock, and were joined for the occasion by Betsi, Ioan and Benjamin from Brithdir. It was strange because we all tried to be jolly, and drank heartily, and indeed contrived to be almost hysterical at times, but the laughter was of the sort that is generally reserved for the *Gwylnos* before a funeral, for it was truly borne out of grief and self-defence.

After dinner all of the labourers and tenants and their families came to say farewell, and there were many toasts for the future happiness of the travellers, and more tears.

Brynach, Rose and David set off for Cardigan early, with all their worldly possessions packed around them, driven by Gerallt in the carriage. Brynach and his little son wanted to settle their things into the ship in peace and quiet, and they wanted to say their farewells to Rose without too many distractions. Then the rest of us followed in mid-morning, using whatever conveyances we could lay our hands on. The quayside was a veritable pandemonium, since there were 30 passengers embarking, and all of them had families and friends intent upon saying goodbye, some with tears, and some with stern resolve to hold emotions in check. Squire Edwards Trefach was there, together with daughters Amelia and Jane, to say farewell to his son-in-law and grandson. Patty and Jake from the Parrog were there, as were Shemi and Sian. All of our servants made the journey on carts and gambos, except for Myfanwy and Will, who had to stay behind to keep an eye on the Plas. And, in a gesture which I found very touching, Wilmot and Delilah turned up as well, having travelled specially from Swansea and having stayed in Cardigan overnight. They wept tears which were as genuine as those of all the others, for I truly believe they have grown very fond of Brynach and the children.

I will not describe my own farewells to my son and grandson, for the recollection is too painful. Then we were all ushered off the ship, and the gangplanks were pulled on board, and the lines were cast off, and the gulf between the old world and the new widened inch by inch until the ship was caught by the current and drifted out into mid-river, where the sails were unfurled. Soon the waving figures at the ship's rail became a blur, and then the *Emily Jane* was lost to sight around a bend in the river. I did not realize it at the time, but I see it now -- the scene was exactly as in my dream repeated three times in the month of June. Two coffins delivered by Cruel Fate, and now one sailing ship........

My sweet granddaughter Rose was remarkably brave, and although I was desperately worried for her she remained calm and collected throughout the ordeal, and shed hardly a tear. She is a truly remarkable young lady.

For a long time I could not move, but then, holding onto Betsi on one side and Daisy on the other, I got back into the carriage and we headed for home. Rose travelled with me, and held my hand. I know now, as I knew when the ship slipped away, that I will never see either Brynach or David again.

ΩΩΩΩΩΩΩΩΩΩ

6. Fire and Brimstone

13th November 1845

It is now a week since Brynach and David set off from Cardigan Quay in the *Emily Jane*, and today is the appointed day for the departure of the *George Washington* from Liverpool, outward bound for New York. As I sit and write on a stormy night with squally rain, they are probably tossing about somewhere in the Irish Sea, and I pray that they are not seasick.

I might have been miserable today, but my spirits have been lifted by the return of my friend Amos Jones Minor Prophet. He turned up on that monstrous horse of his in the middle of the afternoon, once again soaking wet and once again needing a change of clothes. I wanted to throw my arms around his neck and embrace him, and give him a welcoming kiss on the lips, but I thought better of it since there were too many spectators standing around. I curtseyed and offered him my hand, and he kissed that instead. He said: "Why, Mistress Martha! It is very good to see you again after all this time."

He looked terrible, with sunken cheeks, an unshaven chin and a face more lined than I remembered it, and I was sure he had lost weight. He had also picked up a chill, and was coughing and sniffling so much that I felt quite concerned for him. "That is a nasty chill you have there, Amos," I said. "Too much preaching on windy hilltops and riding about in the pouring rain, I dare say. Sir, you need to be pampered and nursed back to good health. Bessie, do you think you can manufacture for our guest one of those miraculous cures of yours, made of hot milk, whipped up egg, brandy and assorted secret herbal ingredients?" Bessie grinned and said "No sooner said than done, Mistress," and set to work while we found some old clothes for Amos and sent him to Gerallt's room to change. Then we sat him down on the settle by the *simnai fawr* in order to warm him up and dry him out. Rose and I sat opposite him, while my three female servants carried on with their kitchen chores with ears flapping.

It turned out that our preacher friend had travelled, as planned, all over Wales during the course of the last three months or so. He had been received with warmth and acclamation in some places and with hostility

Fire and Brimstone

and abuse in others; such is the way with itinerant evangelists. He had travelled up to forty miles a day on his horse, sometimes stopping on impulse to preach at the roadside or in market places, and sometimes turning up as planned at some chapel where a revival was in full swing. Over and again he had been moved on from towns and villages inhabited by fierce vicars and petty constables, on the pretext that he was conducting illegal open-air meetings or breaching the peace. Three times, he said, he had been sent packing while attempting to preach on a Sunday, having been accused by chapel deacons of "breaking the Sabbath." He found that terribly amusing, and roared with laughter in the telling of the tale. He had preached 53 sermons and attended too many prayer meetings to count. He had been given food and shelter almost everywhere by kind Christian folk, but sometimes, on his long journeys across the trackless wastes of mid-Wales or the mountains of the north, he had been forced to sleep in barns, abandoned hovels or even in caves. Many a night had he spent beneath the stars, he said, and indeed he liked doing it when the weather was good. He said that throughout his mission he had been sustained by the Holy Spirit and that he had been the instrument through which hundreds, if not thousands, of lost souls had found salvation.

While Amos spoke Rose listened with eyes full of wonderment and mouth agape, for she had not previously appreciated the extent of his commitment to the cause, or indeed the hardships which men such as he had to endure. So I laughed and said to Amos: "Stop now, Master Jones! My granddaughter is truly amazed by your narrative, and if you go on for much longer I fear that she will be greatly moved, and taken away by the Holy Spirit. I cannot allow that, for I need her here by my side. Now then, you drink up that magical mixture of Bessie's while I bring you up to date with happenings at the Plas. You know, I suppose, that the estate has collapsed, that Plas Llanychaer now stands empty, and that Brynach and David have gone off to America?"

Amos was about to take a sip of Bessie's reviving concoction, but he stopped and looked as if he had been struck by a bolt of lightning. "What?" he spluttered. "Please, Martha, tell me that you are joking.........."

"Indeed I am not, sir. Rose will confirm all of it for you, and indeed this is the reason why she is here with me today. Is it not true, *cariad*?"

Rose nodded, and so I told Amos almost everything, omitting only

Fire and Brimstone

some details of Brynach's loss of Lisbet Preece that I did not want either him or Rose to hear. When I had finished, he said not a word but came across to me, took my hand and patted it in sympathy, and did the same to Rose, and I thought that a very strange but moving little gesture. Then he said: "Oh dear, oh dear. This is all very difficult for you, my dear Martha, and for me too, since I now feel guilty that all of this has happened whilst I have been away and unable to give you support."

"There is no need for guilt on your part, Amos," said I. "You have your life to lead, and I have mine. We all have our moments of sunshine, and then other moments afflicted by dark shadow. And we have all looked after each other very well, have we not, ladies?" So Rose, Bessie, Liza and Myfanwy all confirmed that through female solidarity we had come through the crisis, and we all managed to laugh.

"And this Wilmot Gwynne, your new Master? You say he is from Swansea? Would he be the copper master who broke ranks with all the others, and paid good wages and kept his furnaces going during the great strike of 1838?"

"Oh? I know nothing of that, Amos. He has not mentioned it."

"I was preaching there during the strike. There was hardship such as they had never known, which caused many poor people to turn to God. Master Gwynne was a truly enlightened and radical employer, Martha, and he had to put up with the fury of many of his fellows. I never met him, but he was greatly praised and greatly vilified. He is a strong man, and if he is now to run the Llanychaer and Plas Ingli estates, I think you can be well pleased."

We talked for another hour or so, and then Amos jumped to his feet, and said: "I thank you, ladies, one and all, for your loving attention. I am restored by the beauty that surrounds me. I must now return to my lodgings at Brynberian, for I sent them a message some days since, telling them to expect me this very afternoon. Winter is upon us, and it is high time to abandon my travels in favour of a more sedentary life, preaching from the warm comfort of the Capel Brynberian pulpit and looking after my flock. Preacher becomes pastor, for the time being at least."

Soon he was gone down the Cilgwyn Road, on his way to his lodgings at Tregwynt on the outskirts of the village that will become his home. I am very pleased to see him back. There are too many women beneath this roof, and every now and then it is necessary to have a man to talk to.

Fire and Brimstone

In a strange little epilogue to the day's events, I was sitting with Rose in the parlour after supper, in the glow of a fire of oak logs. We were both reading quietly. Suddenly she looked up from her book and said: "Grandma, do you know something interesting?"

"Oh? What might that be, *cariad*?"

"Well, did you notice that Master Jones Prophet Minor called you "my dear Martha" when he was talking to you today?"

"Did he really?" said I, hoping that my blush would be hidden by the rosy glow of the firelight upon my face. "Think nothing of it, Rose. He probably refers to all the ladies of his acquaintance in similar fashion."

ΩΩΩΩΩΩΩΩΩΩΩΩ

18th November 1845

By way of reference to my previous diary entry, there is now one less woman beneath this roof, for my lady's maid Liza is seriously ill and the prognosis is not good. She fell ill with a strange fever three days since, and I tried to keep her here at the Plas so that I could nurse her and give her the best possible treatment. But her husband Tomos would not hear of it, and he insists that she should be at home at Pantry where he can give her all the loving attention that he promised her on the day they were married. They have a tidy and comfortable cottage, and at least she is warm and dry there. I send food down every day, and have told Havard Medical to give her the best attention without any regard to cost.

Gwenno, Liza's only surviving child, has moved in to nurse her, in spite of the fact that she is herself heavily pregnant just now, and I have told her that she need not worry about her duties at the Plas until her mother is well again. I hope and pray that she will recover, but the doctor, who is back and forth every day, tells me that she has contracted either typhus or typhoid fever -- as yet he cannot distinguish the one from the other, for the early symptoms are very similar. She suffers from delirium, headaches, and has a horrid rash and high fever. She is also vomiting, and cannot keep food or drink down. Master Havard is giving her all the best medications as recommended in the scientific journals, but he is desperately worried that she is not responding to treatment. Four other people in the neighbourhood have already died from the disease, and ten others are desperately sick. It seems to be very contagious.

My friend Shemi Jenkins Wizard has also been to see Liza on several occasions, and he and the medical doctor have, as good friends and professional colleagues, discussed diagnoses and treatments. Shemi has given her various herbal potions and has tried other healings that he will not discuss with me or anybody else; but still he is very depressed about the outcome. All we can do now is wait and pray.

ΩΩΩΩΩΩΩΩΩΩΩΩ

28th November 1845

Poor Liza has gone to her place with the angels, but it will always be a sadness to me that I did not know of her rapid decline in the last days of her life in time to give her comfort. She lost consciousness towards the end, and although I had asked to be kept informed if there was any change in her condition, Shemi and Amos were there with her, and they decided that it would have been too distressing for me to see her as she was, covered with dreadful sores and with her skin turned almost black. Gomer told me afterwards that the stench in the cottage had been almost unbearable in the last twenty-four hours of her life, and that the disease was described by others who had lost loved ones as "the putrefying disease". I can hardly bear to think of it. In protecting me from the appalling sight of Liza in such a state, I have to accept that my dear friends were very kind.

"She was not aware of anything in her final hours," said Shemi when he came to tell me the news. "That was a mercy for her, and she slipped away quietly into the tender care of her God." Tomos was being comforted by Gwenno and Gomer, he said, and Amos had gone home to sleep, having been at her bedside for thirty-six hours, praying and bringing her comfort.

Fire and Brimstone

At the Plas we were all very shocked at the suddenness of Liza's descent into sickness and thence into the grave, but Havard Medical said that was the way with these typhoid sicknesses, which lead to the deaths of almost half of those who contract them. She had been with me for most of the past 38 years, having arrived as an emergency wet nurse on the very day that Brynach was found on our front doorstep. The place seemed flat and empty without her calm efficiency and quiet and sensible talk on this, that and everything. She never was as noisy and frank as Bessie, and she was never one for scurrilous gossip. She was a truly good woman, and we will all miss her sorely. It will be especially hard for Bessie, for they were bosom friends who knew everything about each other and almost everything about me and the Plas.

I helped the family to fumigate and cleanse the cottage, to arrange the *Gwylnos* at Pantry and the funeral at Capel Caersalem, and then I helped with food and drink for the mourners. Tomos, who currently works as a labourer on the Llwyngwair estate, could not afford anything lavish, and I thought that my dear Liza deserved that from me as a parting gift, and as a sign of the love that I felt for her. She was buried in Caersalem graveyard last Friday, in the shadow of Carningli and in the presence of a very large crowd of mourners from Cilgwyn and Newport.

There have been two interesting outcomes from this latest sad event. One is that Amos has greatly enhanced his reputation in the community as a kind and faithful pastor who does not restrict his love to his own flock at Brynberian. He had no responsibilities towards Liza at all, but he chose to give her whatever healing was in him, and to bring her peace through his prayer and his presence. And my own affection for him is greatly enhanced as a consequence. The second outcome is a close bond of friendship between Amos, Shemi and young Doctor Havard. I say "young" because that is how he is spoken of in the community, having taken over from old William Havard Medical who died more than fifteen years ago. In truth I imagine that he is in his middle fifties. He is a pleasant fellow, and I have the greatest respect for him, having worked closely with him at the time of the Rebecca Riots. He lost his wife only last year, and he seems to enjoy coming to the Plas whenever he passes by or whenever there is some ailment needing attention; but I suspect that his enjoyment has more to do with the presence of Daisy than with anything else. I wish him well. And it is intriguing to think that these three fellows, known as Jones Minor

Fire and Brimstone

Prophet, Shemi Wizard and Havard Medical, give of themselves in unstinting fashion in looking after the mind, body and spirit of the local community. I would not like to have those three as enemies, for they would make a formidable team indeed, and I count it a great blessing that I have them as friends.

$$\Omega\Omega\Omega\Omega\Omega\Omega\Omega\Omega\Omega\Omega\Omega$$

1st December 1845

Today I sent off a letter to Brynach, care of Elen in America, to tell him of Liza's death. I have no address for him other than that, and I trust that he will find Elen and that the letter will eventually find its way into his hands. He will want to know about Liza, and will certainly grieve for her, since she was the one whose mother's milk kept him alive and whose motherly instincts consoled him when he suffered from the colic and from teething pains and such like. I wanted to write to him anyway, to wish him and David well and to assure the two of them that they are in my thoughts and prayers in that faraway and uncivilized land.

It is a long time since I talked to my dear friend Shemi, for he has been very busy of late dealing with ailments and mysteries, and I have had so much going on in my life that I have found relaxation almost out of the question. But this morning, on as fine a December morning as one is likely to see, I was moved to take a walk on the mountain, and to keep going westwards until I reached Werndew.

As I walked, I pondered on the many other visits which I had made to that blessed place over the years, mostly for the purpose of visiting that intriguing and wonderful man called Joseph Harries, but then later in order to help Shemi once he had discovered that it was his vocation to be a wizard. He has inherited all of Joseph's paraphernalia and books, and a good deal of his wisdom too, and is proving to be a pillar of the local community as a consequence of the help and healing he gives to other people and their animals. He does not have Joseph's erudition or sharp intellect, but he has great healing power, he is a fine herbalist, and he

Fire and Brimstone

has a natural empathy with people of all classes and ages. He has also learnt how to solve mysteries through his cunning and his great powers of observation, and his meticulous attention to detail. And in some ways he is more intuitive than Joseph, for he knows what the weather will do up to two months ahead, and he can talk to animals, which Joseph always found difficult. There is no doubt in my mind that he has special powers to a much greater extent than I -- and that, I suppose, is why he is a wizard and I am the Mistress of a failed estate. Sometimes he takes payment for his services, I know, but mostly he does not, and I wonder how he keeps body and soul together. But I suppose that his wife Sian, who used to be nursemaid to my children, brings in something from her work as housekeeper for Captain Saul Davids in Dinas, and no doubt a few pounds per year come in from their three children John, Gomer and Molly. And gifts come his way occasionally, from squires who have been particularly pleased with what he has done for them. So they survive -- not exactly in style, but comfortably enough, and they have had few costs to meet since I gave them the freehold of their cottage and an acre of land. Thank God that Brynach and I had done that, I thought, when we had the power to do it!

Suddenly, lost in thought, I was on the doorstep of Werndew. The old house looked different now, following my renovations of a few years back, but there were still roses over the front door, and I was amazed to find that some of them were still in bloom. The herb garden at the back looked as prolific as ever, and I had no doubt that now, as in Joseph's time, the plants within it, collected from all over the world, had far more magic within them than Joseph or Shemi ever had in their hands.

As luck would have it, when I walked in, Shemi was at home, crushing some strange seeds with a mortar and pestle in his little "scientific room" at the back of the house. We embraced warmly, and Shemi made a pot of tea. "Wonderful to see you, Martha!" said he. "How are you and the others coping with the loss of dear Liza? It must be difficult for you........."

"It is difficult, Shemi, but we try to honour her with our memories, and we have to get on with life."

"Good, good," said he, getting out some mugs from a battered cupboard and some griddle cakes from a tin on the mantelpiece. "Sian is in Dinas today, and will not be back till late. The Captain has guests to

Fire and Brimstone

dinner. And what brings you to Werndew on this fine day?"

"Oh, nothing in particular, Shemi. I just wanted to walk and take some fresh air."

He laughed. "Martha, my dear friend," he beamed, "you know and I know that you do nothing quite as aimlessly as that! Come now, the truth, if you please!"

"Very well then, Shemi, since you ask. What do you think of Jones Minor Prophet?"

"I thought that he might be the cause of the healthy glow upon your cheeks. Well, I find him to be entirely genuine and unaffected, and a man who carries a great love for his fellow human beings. He seems to love their failings as much as their virtues. He is certainly driven by a strong faith, and by a sense of mission to bring sinners to salvation. I do not share his scheme of beliefs, but I cannot fail to admire him. And he is funny to the point of eccentricity, as I have discovered in my conversations with him. I do not meet many jovial nonconformist pastors on my travels. Speaking as a man, I think he is as fine a friend as one can have, and I count myself lucky to know him. So that is my view. Now then Martha, what might be the view of a woman?"

I had been looking Shemi in the eye, but now I diverted my gaze, and of course he reacted instantly. "I see what I thought I might see, Martha. Not for the first time, too much heart and not enough head, if you will forgive me for saying so. I urge you to be very careful, not because you and he come from different classes, but because I sense that he is a troubled man. He is married, but obviously not happily, for he will not talk about his wife. That is trouble enough for him, for someone such as you. But then I see that there is even bigger trouble ahead, for he is too good, Martha."

"Whatever do you mean, Shemi? How can anybody be too good? Do we not all strive to be good?"

"Ah yes, but most of us learn to temper our generosity with practicality, and to modify our criticisms of evil with diplomacy. My friend Amos appears to own nothing, so he can freely give away everything that he has in seeking to alleviate suffering and in fighting injustice. Most of what he has to give away is love. And by the same token, because he owns nothing, he appears to need nothing. He does not need property or possessions; he does not even seem to need a family, or a place to lay his head, or a reputation.........."

Fire and Brimstone

"And does he not even need love, Shemi? Do we not all need love?"

"On that I cannot be sure, Martha. You might well be a better judge than I, since you see him through a woman's eyes. But I am fearful for Amos's safety, for when someone as good and kind as he sees evil, and speaks out against it, people who are in power may well see their little empires crumbling, and will seek to destroy him."

"Come now, Shemi. That is very melodramatic."

"Not at all, Martha. I hope that I am wrong. But I urge you, when you get back to the Plas this afternoon, to look at your New Testament. And while you are about it, read the Book of Amos as well."

I laughed at that, and congratulated Shemi on his knowledge of what Joseph used to call the Unholy Scriptures. And so we moved on to talk of other things. But later on, as I walked home across Mynydd Melyn with the sun on my back, my mind was even busier than it had been on my westwards walk in the morning.

ΩΩΩΩΩΩΩΩΩΩΩ

10th December 1845

I have made a resolution to be a good Christian person. I have been to church on two Sundays in succession, in spite of the fact that Rector Llewelyn's sermons are more effective than a draught of laudanum in sending one off to sleep. But I suppose that the struggle to keep awake is a virtuous thing in itself, and I gather that it says in the Bible, somewhere or other, that suffering is a very fine thing.

And in an attempt to help those in need, I have taken on Blodwen Bebb as dairymaid, and have promoted Myfanwy, in spite of her tender age, to be my lady's maid. Myfanwy is of course delighted. Blodwen is a rough sort of woman, I should say in her late forties, who started life in a hovel on Long Street as the bastard daughter of one of my enemies, one Matthew Lloyd. That evil man was one of those who killed my husband David, and he went to the gallows for that crime amongst others. Blodwen has had a tough time of it, and I am not sure how she has kept out of the

Fire and Brimstone

Narberth Workhouse, but she is a hard worker, and she has helped here on the harvest on a number of occasions. She will bring a touch of earthiness to the kitchen, and she knows how to look after herself in a cruel world; maybe she will look after me as well, should the cruel world find its way into the Plas.

Amos called in today round about noon, since the Plas lay more or less on his route between Dinas and Brynberian. He knew that he would get a bite to eat, and I flatter myself to think that he might have wanted to see me as well. He looked much better, having put on some weight and filled out those hollows in his cheeks, and he was quite tidily attired in new breeches, a well-fitting coat and shiny gaiters that would have done credit to the Bishop of St Davids. I complimented him on his appearance, and he explained that although he had no salary from the deacons of Capel Brynberian they had decided that he needed a new wardrobe so as not to bring the chapel into disrepute. Accordingly they had held five prayer meetings and had finally decided to spend £2 on clothing him. He thought that highly entertaining. He was settling in well, he said, and although his lodgings were spartan they were quite conveniently close to the chapel, and accorded a fine view of Mynydd Preseli when he sat at his desk reading his Bible and composing his sermons.

"And how does the flock enjoy your sermons?" I asked.

"Well enough, Martha. I give them plenty of fire and brimstone, and they like that. As to the theology, only a few of the elders know what I am talking about, and which doctrines I am referring to, so I can afford to be more than a little revolutionary. And the Independents are in any case far from united in what they believe. Nobody has noticed it yet, but not a single one of my texts thus far has come from the Old Testament."

"And does that matter, Amos?"

"A great deal, Martha. Almost all of the sermons preached in the revivalist meetings across Wales by other preachers are based upon Old Testament texts. Nasty, crude texts preoccupied with suffering and punishment, evil and sinners, hell and damnation. The Old Testament is a silly old testament which should be buried in a deep hole and forgotten about."

"Amos! How could you say that? We all know that the Old Testament is the word of God!"

"That may well be, my dear Martha. But it was written back in the

Fire and Brimstone

dawn of time and was intended by God as an aid to the understanding of the New Testament, which is the bit that matters. The Old Testament should be read by theologians like me, and not by uneducated people who have not been taught to think. The Bible would have been much better if it had started with the Gospel of Matthew and finished with one or two of the letters of Paul. Then we would have enough to be going on with, in the matter of knowing what to believe and how to behave. As it is, everybody is confused. Any preacher can prove almost anything by plucking a verse or two out of the Bible and taking it out of context; and look what endless and futile disputes theologians have over meaningless matters, with the ones who cite the most verses in their favour winning the arguments. Why, I could prove for you, by very careful Biblical citations, that to murder is to do the will of God, and that rape and plunder are perfectly acceptable activities. There you have it, Martha. I call it the Jones Heresy. It is much more interesting than those old Pelagian and Arminian heresies for which better men than I have gone to the stake. Let God be my judge!"

And he roared with laughter, and slapped his knees, the way men do. I had never seen him so animated before. Now I did not know what to think. Master Jones is, I thought, certainly a heretic, but is he also mad? And now that he has gone off through Tycanol Wood on his way back to Brynberian, I fear that at some stage, before too long, the Jones Heresy will find its way into the open, with fearsome consequences. Hell hath no fury like an upset deacon.

ΩΩΩΩΩΩΩΩΩΩΩ

15th December 1845

I cannot understand why, but Ireland is coming more and more into my thoughts, and whenever I get my copy of the *Welshman* the first thing I look for is the latest news of the potato blight and the fate of the Irish peasants.

Yesterday's paper carried more terrible news. The famine is now real, and widespread. With a glut of potatoes sold off cheaply during the

Fire and Brimstone

previous three months by those seeking to escape the effects of the blight, and to earn a few pounds, there now appears to be almost nothing left for people to eat. An article from "our Irish correspondent" describes how virtually all of the crop that was clamped in October has rotted away. Nobody can understand how apparently healthy tubers, carefully harvested, put away in time-honoured fashion and then protected from vermin and weather can have been so afflicted and putrefied. But it has happened, and while the peasants are already starving, government officials are wringing their hands and pleading for help from the Prime Minister and his Government in London.

According to the reports, Sir Robert Peel (whom they call "Orange Peel" on account of his Protestant leanings) has tried to do something, but instead of bringing in emergency measures for the purchase of wheat, oats and barley, he has spent £100,000 on the purchase of Indian corn from the southern part of the United States. This will now be held in various depots around the country. Some of it has been released already, but the peasants cannot mill it because it is exceedingly hard, and it has a bright yellow colour and a disgusting taste when cooked. The cottagers refer to it as an odious mess, and call it "Peel's Brimstone."

The peasants are supposed to buy the meal with money earned on various public works, but since those projects on roads, canals, public buildings and such like are not properly organized or financed, there is actually hardly any work available and hence no wages for those who have families to feed. The newspaper is thunderous in its condemnation of official incompetence; I know not where the truth lies, but I tend to believe what I read.

And as for the merchants, there is even greater condemnation. "Our Irish correspondent" reports that the merchants on either side of the water have refused either to buy or sell anything that might be used for the relief of the hungry. So barley and oats (which would be the main foodstuffs) are locked away in warehouses, and no ships are moving. The squires and traders have said that if the Government imports food into Ireland, they will not. So now the Government has to supply all of the food that Ireland needs, which is clearly impossible. It appears that the Prime Minister now has no option but to back down. He will promise that no more Indian corn will be imported, and will leave the relief of starvation to private enterprise. The prospect is truly horrible.

Fire and Brimstone

I know that there are hundreds if not thousands of tons of barley in Pembrokeshire, and I wrote to some of the merchants in Fishguard and Newport today to urge them to export at least some of the crop to Ireland as a gesture of solidarity with the Irish people. I hope for positive replies from at least some of them, but I am not optimistic, given that which old Elijah Collins has told me about the Society of Sea Serjeants and their hold over local trade.

ΩΩΩΩΩΩΩΩΩΩΩ

18th December 1845

Only one of the merchants will do as I ask -- namely my old friend Skiff Abraham, who is now wealthy enough and well protected enough to risk the ire of his colleagues in the corn trade. I had a letter from him to say that he will buy barley at a fair price from me or any others in the area, so long as he can find a buyer in Wexford, Waterford or Cork. He has written to various merchants across the water to try and organize a deal, and he will come and see me when he has a response, probably shortly after Christmas.

As for the others, I have had a whinging and self-satisfied letter from Jacob Harry, Dafydd Shinkins, Tom Transportation and various others, saying that they cannot go against the wishes of others, no matter how pressing the philanthropic arguments might be, because that would in the end be against the best interests of the starving poor in Ireland. And they urged me to work with them for the betterment of local trade and the enhancement of local wealth, which would in due course enable us to support and maybe even provide employment for "our brothers and sisters in Ireland". When I read this, steam came out of my ears and fire and brimstone from my nostrils, and I tore the letter up and threw it onto the burning logs in the fireplace.

For the moment, no matter how my heart bleeds for those who have to face a winter of starvation in Ireland, there is not much more I can do while I wait for Skiff to visit me. But I will hold myself ready to thresh the barley which is in the Plas Ingli barn at short notice, even though that is something normally left to February or March. I will also prepare plans for my ship *Mary Jane* to set off on a mercy mission to Ireland with a hold full of barley, if I can get some cooperation from across the water.

ΩΩΩΩΩΩΩΩΩΩΩΩ

21st December 1845

Amos has started to ruffle a few feathers. Yesterday, he called at the Plas, and as we sat in the kitchen drinking our cups of tea and nibbling slices of Bessie's exceedingly good apple cake, I asked him what his plans were for Christmas. Would he, I asked, be going home to his wife in Radnor for the festive season, if that could be arranged with the compassion and the cooperation of the Capel Brynberian deacons?

Immediately I saw a pained look in his eyes, and he said quickly: "Oh no, Martha. A pastor is never given time off at Christmas, nor would it be appropriate for me to ask for it, for there are sermons and prayer meetings and Christmas services to prepare, not to mention the Lord's Supper on Christmas morning. My wife is used to me being away at such times, and I dare say she will cope." He would say no more about her or her plans, and I got the clear impression that there had been no communication between them regarding the festive season.

So I said: "In that case, Amos, would you like to join us at the Plas? I dare say that your Christmas morning will be busy, but come along by all means, if you will, and join us for our Christmas dinner at five o'clock. It will be very noisy and frenetic, but I dare say you will enjoy it."

"Thank you, Martha," said he with a ready smile. "You are very kind. Yes please -- and God bless you."

So we turned to talk on other things, and I enquired as to whether he had read of the troubles in Ireland in either the *Welshman* or the *Cambrian*. "Indeed I have, Martha," said he, "and I am not at all amused. I have been talking to Havard Medical, who knows everything that goes on in town, and he has told me of the local merchants who are seeking to

Fire and Brimstone

exploit the starvation of the Irish peasants in order to line their own pockets. I am not amused, and neither, I dare say, is God in his heaven."

Then I told him of my miserable attempts to get the local merchants to break ranks with those based in Fishguard and Cardigan and to ship over barley which might be sold to men of goodwill on the other side for a fair price and then used to feed the starving. "Good for you, Martha!" he said. "It is reassuring to know that somebody around these parts understands what the Biblical exhortation to feed the hungry actually means. I must be on my way now, but you may be aware that tomorrow is a Sunday, and you may be interested to learn that at ten in the morning I will preach to the good people of Capel Brynberian a sermon that might be close to your heart."

That was an offer too good to refuse, so this morning Will drove me up to Brynberian and together we attended the service. I have to say that I enjoyed it. The hymn singing was wonderful, and the prayers were fervent, and Amos looked very imposing up there in his pulpit, raising his voice to Heaven and showing why he is already greatly loved by all in his congregation. He even welcomed me and Will publicly from the pulpit as "our friends from down there in Cilgwyn." I was not at all inclined to go to sleep, as is my wont in Newport parish church. Then came the sermon, like a blast from a battery of cannons. He preached on the text from Matthew 25, v 40: "*Inasmuch as ye have done it unto one of the least of these my brethren, ye have done it unto me*", and it was not about good deeds at all, but about greedy merchants seeking to exploit the starving peasants of Ireland and to line their own pockets. If you do evil to the poor, he said in an oblique way, you harm the Lord. And if you do it knowingly, and in pursuit of your own selfish ends, the crime is even more heinous. He did not name names, but everybody in the congregation knew of whom he was talking, and as the *hwyl* came into him, and as the pitch of his voice went higher and higher, it became clear that he was more or less accusing the merchants of dragging Christ to the cross and hammering the nails into his hands and feet. There was not much scope for cries of "Hallelujah" with such a message, but there were certainly sighs and moans, and the chapel resounded with cries of "Amen!" and "Well spoken, brother!" as the atmosphere crackled like an electrical storm.

Afterwards, having received the message, we all came down from the summit of the mountain with the lusty singing of a final hymn. We had no chance to talk to Amos before we set off for home, but we saw that there was much back-slapping and hand-shaking going on and that the preacher had clearly said something that would leave a deep impression. After all, most of the congregation was made up of labourers and small farmers, and they have no great love for squires and wealthy merchants. "*Diawl!*" said Will, most inappropriately. "That was some sermon, Mistress. Master Jones knows how to use the scriptures and move the masses, that is for sure. A pity, it is, that none of the merchants was there to hear him."

"Oh, they will get to hear about it all right, Will," said I. "You may be in no doubt about that."

ΩΩΩΩΩΩΩΩΩΩΩ

7. The Joys of Winter

28th December 1845

On the day after Amos's famous sermon was preached at Capel Brynberian, the cool weather became colder, and the wind shifted to the east. We knew that snow was on the way, and sure enough within a few hours, by early afternoon, the sky was the colour of lead and the first snowflakes had started to swirl around the Plas. The horses were already stabled, apart from a dozen mountain ponies which live on the common and which are tough enough to survive the end of the world. We left them there, knowing that if they were hungry they would find their way to our topmost field gate and that we could feed them there with hay. We got all of the other animals as close to the farm as possible. It was, in any case, time to get the cattle into the cowshed, for if they are left out in January and February they transform wet ground into a sea of mud.

By the time we had finished with the moving and feeding of the animals, the snow was coming down in a silent deluge, and visibility was down to a few yards. The ground was cold, so the snow started to accumulate straight away, and we all knew from experience that if this continued overnight we might have twelve inches or more by breakfast on the following morning. I love the snow, having never lost my childhood fascination with the quiet magic of snowflakes and the manner in which it has the capacity to transform a dull and bleak winter landscape into something of extraordinary beauty. But I hate it at the same time, for it causes chaos on the farm and leads to a good deal of digging and slipping and sliding and swearing, and also to the loss of silly sheep which are too stupid to stop themselves from getting buried alive. But the weather was calm, and that was a mercy, since snowdrifts are the worst enemies of all.

Over the next few days the snow continued to fall, off and on, and there was no thaw to remove it. The snow blanket was so thick that travel became very difficult, and we had to miss the early candle-lit *Plygain* service in the parish church which takes place every Christmas morning before dawn. But once the day had dawned, the grey clouds drifted away under instructions from Heaven, and the sun came out.

The Joys of Winter

The landscape, cleansed of the mud and filth that is everywhere during the miserable months of late autumn, sparkled and glittered so brightly that I had to narrow my eyes to look at it. Not that there was time to stand and stare, since there was much to be done, and many mouths to feed. As usual at Christmas, all of my servants stayed at the Plas over Christmas Eve -- Will and his son Gerallt sharing one room, then Bessie, Myfanwy and Blodwen in their own rooms, and Gomer and Gwenno in the room that used to belong to Shemi Wizard in his days here as a cowman. Those two struggled through the snow to get here on Christmas Eve, leaving Penrhiw in the hands of their young farmhand, because Gwenno is now so close to the due date for her first baby that I did not want her isolated and away from help should the little one decide to arrive over the festive season. She was very large indeed, bless her, and her contractions had already started; and to get her to the Plas a sledge had to be used, pulled by Gomer and two others.

This year I decided some weeks since, in deference to Master and Mistress Gwynne, that I should be careful with my household resources so as not to leave the larder entirely empty on Boxing Day. I am not quite a tenant, but neither am I entirely in charge of the estate finances from this point on, and I did not want to go to him in the New Year with my begging bowl. So I let it be known that there would be open house for Christmas lunch but that Christmas dinner at five would be for family only. The only one missing was Daisy, who had promised to spend Christmas with Amy in London and who had taken the train from Carmarthen three days earlier.

In the morning Betsi and Ioan arrived from Brithdir, accompanied by their three strong sons Benjamin, Abel and Owain, who between them pulled a sledge-load of good things. And then various tenants and labourers and their families struggled up through the snow, bearing the eggs, butter, cheeses, legs of mutton and prepared poultry that are required of them by tradition as part of their rental payment. They also carried their cutlery with them, since we did not have enough to go round. With people pouring in from all directions, and with the yard still snow-covered, the amount of snow that was carried into the house on boots and garments was truly amazing, and Rose was detailed to sweep and shovel it out over the kitchen doorstep. Had not Bessie been so organized, the kitchen might have turned into a battle zone; but most of the food was

The Joys of Winter

prepared in advance and was ready on plates and platters in the larder and the scullery. With Betsi, Blodwen and Myfanwy laying the kitchen and dining room tables and Bessie and I looking after the cooking in our big iron oven and over the open fire in the *simnai fawr*, things went smoothly enough, for we had done all of this many times before, and the only difference this year was the presence of heavy snow outside. And while the hustle and bustle was going on within, Will, Gomer and Gerallt were plodding about in the yard, checking the cattle, carrying hay and water for the sheep and horses and grain for the birds, chopping turnips, and generally ensuring that the estate did not grind to a halt. There was milking still to be done, and Ioan and Benjamin helped with that while my other two strapping grandsons took charge of mucking out the cowshed. Blodwen had to leave the warm kitchen for the cold dairy in mid-morning to put out the morning's milk, skim yesterday's milk, churn the butter, and check and turn the cheeses.

Christmas lunch was a pandemonium accompanied by a cacophony. I have not the slightest idea how many we fed, but there were able-bodied mothers and fathers from the tenant farms and labourers' cottages, ancient and retired retainers from some of the Plas Ingli tied cottages, neighbours who -- for reasons that are not entirely clear to me -- always come to the Plas for Christmas lunch, and many small children. And then, at about two o'clock, they were all gone and it was almost as peaceful as the grave. We started to clear away the debris from the feast. Bessie started to check that all the payments in kind from tenants and labourers had been delivered as expected, and she seemed well pleased that the larder after the feeding of the ten thousand was fuller than it had been at breakfast time. "Well, Mistress," she said, wiping her hands on her apron, "that went off as well as we could have expected. Thank goodness that the snow held off and that the sun shone for us, or we might have had all of them stuck here for the night!" The men went into the parlour to enjoy a quiet smoke, knowing that they would soon have to go outside again for the evening milking and animal feeding session.

That was when Gwenno went into labour. Her contractions had been getting closer and more severe during the morning, but now the poor girl was quite convinced that the time was very close. We took her up to my bedroom and gave her my bed, for the servants' rooms are too small and dark for the delivery of babies. Myfanwy quickly lit the fire and carried

173

The Joys of Winter

up a good supply of logs and small coals. I sent Bessie from the kitchen and detailed her to look after Gwenno, and Gomer stayed with her and held her hand as she became more and more distressed. Betsi, Rose and myself, and Myfanwy and Blodwen, then continued with the clearing away and the washing up, and as we did so the afternoon started to darken towards dusk. Bessie came and went, fetching towels and hot water and other necessary things, and although she was calm at first she began to get increasingly agitated. We could hear Gwenno weeping and wailing upstairs, but I stayed away, since I knew that I could not help and that Bessie knew far more about midwifery than I. Then Blodwen said she had helped at many births, so I sent her upstairs as well. She was very calm and efficient, and on one of her visits to the kitchen she said that Gwenno's waters were broken. After about an hour of increasingly frantic activity, with the poor girl's screams echoing around the house, Bessie and Blodwen banished Gomer from the bedroom, saying he was more of a hindrance than a help. "More hot water, Mistress Martha!" shouted Bessie down the stairs, and when I delivered it in a big china jug she grabbed it at the bedroom door and rushed back inside. I followed her, and stayed at Gwenno's side, holding her hand, encouraging her and mopping her brow with cold damp cloths. I gave her another cloth to bite on, and then I started to get seriously worried as she seemed to become quite exhausted. She closed her eyes, and I slapped her face and shouted at her: "Gwenno! Fight! Fight! Not long now!" But she did not respond, and I began to think that we would lose her and the baby. "Bessie," I shouted, "has she had laudanum?"

"Yes, Mistress, but I do not dare to give her more. She must remain conscious....."

Then, as we were resigning ourselves to another tragedy, a miracle happened, and Shemi, Gwenno's own father-in-law, burst into the room. He said not a word. He looked at first at the progress of the birth, and within a minute or so he had delved into his bag, laid out some things on a clean cloth on the bed, and washed his hands with carbolic soap. He pulled out a big apron from his bag, and put it on. He poured something down Gwenno's throat, which seemed to bring her back to full alertness in an instant. Then he took a scalpel and cut her, and shouted "Now, Gwenno! Push! Push! Push!" And she screamed, and pushed with an energy that I could hardly credit, and in rapid succession gave birth to twins.

The Joys of Winter

One boy and one girl. Bessie took one, and I took the other, and cleaned them and tied their cords, and wrapped them in swaddling clothes. They were both lusty and healthy, and announced to the world that they had arrived by singing a fine duet. The room was filled with euphoria, and I shouted downstairs: "Gomer! You have twins -- one boy and one girl!" He rushed upstairs like a mad thing, but Shemi would not let him in, as he had more work to do. First, there was a great mess to clear up, and Blodwen did that without batting an eyelid. Then Shemi had stitching to do, and after giving Gwenno some other medicine to ease the pain he got on with it quietly and systematically, and then bathed the closed wounds with something designed to prevent infections. Gwenno winced and shrieked, but then laughed and said that the pain was no worse than a mosquito bite, compared with what had gone before.

Then, with Gwenno washed and changed into a new nightdress with a laced-up front, we gave her the two babies, and she gave them one breast each. At last we let Gomer in to the room, and he wept tears of joy as Gwenno smiled at him. So we left them alone with their new family.

We three women had to change out of our bloodstained aprons and dresses, and then we went back into the kitchen, to be greeted with tears of joy and a great deal of hugging and kissing from the assembled company. Shemi was already washed and changed. He was the centre of attention, of course, and he was sitting in the settle at the fireside, with his wife Sian at his side, and with a grin as broad as the Teifi estuary on his face. There, I thought, sit the happiest and proudest grandparents in the world, and I embraced the pair of them and shed more tears. Then I noticed that there was somebody else in the room: Amos Jones Minor Prophet, sitting in the corner, beaming happily like everybody else. Without thinking I ran over to him and shouted: "Why, Amos! You came after all, in spite of the snow! How good it is to see you!" And I threw my arms around his neck and kissed him on both cheeks, since this was not a time for inhibitions. He looked surprised for a second, but then accepted this little offering of affection with good grace.

By now it was pitch dark, of course, and everything was greatly delayed. But I found that while Bessie and I had been upstairs Betsi and Rose and the other servants had not been idle. There was a goose in the oven, almost ready, and a suckling pig on the spit, dripping fat and crackling with goodness, and smelling like heaven. The vegetables were

175

ready, and a huge Christmas pudding was boiling in its bag. The dining-room table was laid up with all of our best china, glass and cutlery. Within an hour we were seated -- all except for Gwenno, who was already fast asleep after her ordeal, and Gomer, who would not leave his wife and little babies all by themselves in the bedroom. So we took up his Christmas dinner on a tray, and he had a little feast of his own. Amos said grace, and thanked God for the birth of his only son, and for friendship and good food and drink. Then he said a special prayer for Gwenno and Gomer, and for their two little ones, and for Shemi the Wizard. As I sat there with my eyes closed and my hands on my lap, I could not help thinking how strange it was that a nonconformist minister should say a prayer for a wizard, since wizards are normally assumed by churchmen to do nothing but the devil's work.

We had a most excellent feast, washed down with good claret and assorted other bottled beverages as well, and while we tried to remain as quiet as church mice so as not to wake Gwenno in the room above, I do not suppose that we managed to live up to our good intentions. By all accounts, Gwenno slept the sleep of the just in any case, and did not wake up until her breasts told her that the little ones needed their early morning feed. It was well after midnight that we finally shuffled off to bed. I slept with Rose, and Betsi and Ioan took over Will's room. God only knows where everybody went -- I dare say that people found space to settle down wherever they could. Will, Amos and Gerallt staggered off through the snow to the cowshed and slept in the hay in the loft above the animals, saying that it was warmer and quieter there than on the kitchen floor. And so ended our Christmas Day -- a notable one, for a number of reasons.

ΩΩΩΩΩΩΩΩΩΩΩ

20th January 1846

A long letter has arrived from Brynach, about eleven weeks after the departure of the *Emily Jane* from Cardigan Quay. I have been beside myself with worry, but can only imagine that storms and diversions have

The Joys of Winter

affected the mails and the ships that carry them across the Atlantic.

But the letter was worth waiting for, and brought me great relief. Much of it had been written on board ship during a terrible voyage which lasted 5 weeks. There were, said Brynach, many Irish peasants on board, fleeing from the famine. Conditions in steerage had been truly shocking, and typhus had been rampant. Even in the superior accommodation which he and David shared with a few others, the stench of putrefying flesh, sea sickness and dysentery had been almost unbearable. Thirty Irish peasants and three others had died on board from disease, and another twenty had been taken from the ship in New York and placed immediately into a quarantine house where medical facilities were almost non-existent. David had been ill, he wrote, but not with the typhus, and was now weak but almost fully recovered.

He described New York as a big and bustling city with building works going on everywhere, and with people flocking in from Germany, Sweden, Holland, Scotland and many other countries on sailing ships which jostled for position in the harbour. He sounded genuinely excited at the prospect of finding work and a place to live in this new land that was throbbing with life. But first he would try to find Elen. He had her address, and would call on her unannounced. He sent his love to Rose, and to me, and to all the others, and ended his letter by writing that he would immediately put it into an envelope and send it off on a ship travelling to Cardiff that very evening. It was dated on the 18th day of December 1845.

There are other matters to report. Daisy, to my great delight, is spending more than a little time in the company of George Havard Medical. He is a widower, and it is clear that he loves her dearly in spite of her unsavoury past and her three illegitimate children. Yesterday she admitted to me that for the first time in her life, at the age of 44, she is in love, and that her three offspring had each been fathered by men who wanted companionship and sex rather than love. In each case, she said, she had sought security on the arm of a fine gentleman, and had got it; and she also said that the arrival of a child in each case had brought increased allowances and enhanced security, until each of the gentlemen in turn had tired of her and cast her off. She did not complain about the harshness of life, and said that she had known full well what she was doing at the time, and had found some happiness in the process. George Havard was a very different sort of fellow, she said, with the happiest of

The Joys of Winter

smiles, and what could I do but rejoice with her?

Gomer and Gwenno are safely back at Penrhiw with their little ones, and Sian is giving them a good deal of help when she can get time away from her employer in Dinas. The babies have been christened, and have been given the pretty names Gwyn and Gwenllan.

Master and Mistress Gwynne have moved into Plas Llanychaer, and have called here to pay their respects. The old house was kept warm by the servants following Brynach's departure, and it was still fully furnished and equipped since hardly anything was taken away for the voyage to the New World. Wilmot told me the other day that all of the Llanychaer estate papers were still there, in boxes in the office, and asked whether I wanted them. But I said: "No, Wilmot, they are surely yours, since they relate to your new estate and not to Plas Ingli. They probably contain bills and receipts, and planting records, and animal pedigrees, and maps and budgets -- all very boring indeed. It is entirely appropriate that they should stay where they are." He laughed and nodded, and I did not tell him that somewhere amongst those papers were some volumes of the diary of Martha Morgan of Plas Ingli.

As for Amos, the news of his thunderous sermon about evil merchants and squires has indeed reverberated throughout the community, and he is a hero to some and a vile creature to others. He appears quite unconcerned about this, and says that it is the function of a preacher to upset the old order and challenge those who prefer vice to virtue. But there are whisperings that threats have been made against him by fellows who work with the merchants and squires whom he attacked from the pulpit, and there are other whisperings that the Society of Sea Serjeants is increasingly intolerant of criticism. A week ago, two members of Amos' congregation were beaten up after daring to criticise the merchants William Howell and Jacob Harry for refusing to send grain to Ireland.

And I have received other warnings to be careful, on the grounds that certain of the Brynberian deacons have noticed my friendship with Amos. Mean-spirited fellows that they are, they are on the lookout for anything that might be interpreted as a slip in moral standards. Already tongues have started to wag about the fact that Amos walked through the snow to have his Christmas dinner at the Plas, and that he did not return to his lodgings until the morning. Those wagging tongues were stopped eventually by assurances from my family and servants that the snow was

The Joys of Winter

far too deep for a nocturnal journey between the Plas and Amos's lodgings at Tregwynt, and that in any case Amos had slept, like Baby Jesus, in the hay above the cattle stalls.

ΩΩΩΩΩΩΩΩΩΩΩ

15th February 1846

Since the turn of the year I have had several meetings with my friend Skiff Abraham, one-time smuggler and petty criminal and now the most successful merchant in Newport. In spite of numerous letters to his contacts across the water he can find nobody to take a cargo of barley in any of the Southern Irish ports. He says that the blockade is absolutely solid, and that even if we were to send a trading vessel across with its hold stuffed with barley, and tried to give it away, we would get nobody to unload it and would probably end up with ugly confrontations in which people would get hurt. These were his last words to me on the subject: "I fear, Martha *bach*, that we will have to wait and see what happens, while more people die." I am furious, but can do no more. In the meantime my ship is anchored in the middle of the river at St Dogmael's, and my barley is still unthreshed in the barn.

Consequently my mood was black when I had a quite unexpected visit yesterday from Master Tom Foster, *Times* reporter and dear friend. I got to know him very well during the turbulent years of the Rebecca Riots, and he and I developed the sort of intimacy that exists between a mother and son. I gave him invaluable information about happenings behind the scenes, and he gave me in return immeasurable support and encouragement. But he never betrayed me in his reports, or gave any clue as to the extent of my involvement in the riots and associated events, and I learned to trust him implicitly. That was why, in the autumn of 1844, I had entrusted my diaries for the years 1832-1844 to his safe keeping, with an instruction that they were never to be released in my lifetime or the lifetimes of my children. Over the past year he and I have corresponded quite frequently, so he was aware of most of the big events in my life. He joined Daisy, Rose

179

The Joys of Winter

and me for dinner, and we gave him a bed for the night.

He told us that he had been instructed by his Editor to travel to Ireland to report on the developing famine on the supposition that it was bound to get worse and that the *Times* needed a reporter on the spot. He would be catching a ship departing from Fishguard on the morrow, and would then travel on from Wexford to the western counties, where there was a massive disaster in the offing. People were already dying in large numbers in the west. He had heard that while the Irish ports were closed against the importation of foreign food, they were fully open for exports. He wished to check reports that large quantities of grain, beef, mutton, butter and cheese produced on the big estates of eastern Ireland were being taken to the ports and shipped across to England for sale on the open market. I could hardly believe that, but he claimed that it was very likely since the big landowners needed the cash income from sales of their produce in order to resolve some of their own massive financial problems. I thought that the world was surely going mad, and said that I would travel with Tom to Ireland in order to see whether something might be done to set it to rights; but he laughed, and so did Daisy, and quite forbade it on the grounds that I was too old and too poor in any case to save even a handful of starving people.

We talked far into the night, and Tom went off this morning with an exhortation from me to report thunderingly on what he saw, with a view to bringing down the Government and putting in its place one with more compassion and more sense. "I suspect that that might happen without my help, Martha," he laughed. "I give Sir Robert two or three months, at the most. The trouble is that a new Government will not necessarily be any more sensible than the old one, so do not count on it that the state of the Irish peasants will be improved."

That left me in a black mood, but then a messenger arrived at the Plas at about midday with a bulky envelope which had just come in with the mail coach from Cardigan. It was from America, and it instantly banished the clouds and brought out the sun, for inside it was not one letter, but three! One was from Elen, the second was from Brynach, and the third was from little David. Without reading a word I knew that the three of them were together, and that a wonderful reunion between mother, son and grandson must have taken place. I shouted to Daisy and Rose, who were upstairs studying some dry history book together, and ran about the house

The Joys of Winter

laughing and giggling like a demented twelve-year-old. Bessie looked at me over her spectacles, and thought I had quite taken leave of my senses.

When they had all calmed me down, we sat down together to read the letters. All three were full of news and excitement and emotion, describing in their different ways the moment when Brynach and David had knocked upon the door of Elen's house on Fifth East Street in New York and had been taken at first for a pair of vagrants by her maid. They had apparently protested that they were there on a special mission to visit Mistress Bradshaw. At that point Elen heard the voices from upstairs, and knew instinctively who her visitors were, for she had long since received Brynach's letter and had had an intuition that they would cross the Atlantic to see her. She rushed downstairs and said "Brynach and David, from Wales?" and they had nodded, and then everything became confused in a welter of embraces and tears. Brynach said that both he and David cried, and so did I when I read about the encounter.

So all three of us read all three letters, and read them again, and then we read them out for Bessie and the other servants, and we organized a little feast in celebration.

It took me a very long time to come down from my peak of excitement after all this news, and now that I am alone at my desk with quill pen in hand, I fear that I will probably lie awake all night. I am greatly relieved by the nature of my own reaction to the news of the reunion. I have feared for weeks that on receiving news of a successful outcome to Brynach's mission, I might feel jealous or resentful, but I thank God that I am able to rejoice. And Rose is very happy too. Tomorrow I will tell the good news to Betsi and Ioan, and to Amos, and to Shemi and Sian, and to anybody else who wants to hear it. In the meantime, I will try to sleep content in the knowledge that the two lonely voyagers have found a haven in New York and can face future adventures safe in the knowledge that they have one mother there and another one here, should anything go wrong.

ΩΩΩΩΩΩΩΩΩΩΩ

The Joys of Winter

3rd May 1846

I have spent the last two months or more settling into the quiet routines of the Plas, content in the knowledge that some things, at least, are right with the world. I have had two more letters from Brynach and one from Elen, indicating that they are getting on splendidly. Elen is organizing lessons for David, for he has missed far too much schooling of late. She has given them rooms in her big and empty house, and together they are exploring assorted commercial opportunities which might pay dividends. They were very secretive about what these were, but I dare say I will be put in the picture in due course.

The big news that has to be reported is that yesterday Daisy married George Havard Medical, whose first wife died childless a couple of years ago. It was inevitable, of course, since they have been more than a little besotted with each other for months. They were married by licence, since Daisy would not have a church wedding. Her three children came to Newport for the occasion, although their various fathers stayed in London, Lancashire or wherever. The service was simple and unpretentious, and Daisy looked very pretty and more happy than I have seen her for many a long month. Rose and Amy acted as bridesmaids, and were very beautiful in silk dresses made for the occasion by Amy herself. Afterwards we had a jolly celebration at the Plas, with more than sixty guests. Notable among them were Wilmot and Delilah, for over past months Daisy and the Mistress of Llanychaer have become firm friends.

With Wilmot's cheerful blessing I gave the happy couple the feast as a wedding present, for in truth I have little else to give them in my straightened circumstances. But they were perfectly happy with that, and declared that they were in want of nothing at all, since George (as I may now call him) has a good solid townhouse which is tastefully furnished and fully equipped with the latest conveniences including water closets, baths with running water, and and a patent kitchen range with shiny iron ornamentation. Thus my old family is joined with another old family from the town, and nobody is more delighted than I.

Now just Rose and I are left at the Plas. I can watch her growing up and blooming into a delightful young woman, and she can keep an eye on me in case I should get into trouble.

8. Conduct Unbecoming

16th June 1846

On looking back over the pages of my diary it occurs to me that I have acted thus far as an observer and recorder of events, and that I have wept a lot and laughed a little as events beyond my control have affected both me and the Plas. Now, however, I have done something for which I have to take full responsibility, and I hope and pray that destruction and damnation will not follow as night follows day. I have to write this down, for if I am pilloried and condemned because of what I have done, I want the truth to be recorded. But the prospect of putting pen to paper fills me with apprehension, since my emotions are more confused than they have been for many a long year, with guilt at one extreme and elation at the other, and with resignation somewhere in the middle.

It happened like this. Yesterday, with the glass high and a haymakers' sun sailing through a cloudless sky, I decided to wait for two or three more days before starting the hay harvest. That decision was based upon the fact that we have had a cold and drizzly spell which has lasted for two weeks and left too much moisture on the ground for easy scything, raking and turning. The Irish are here, ready and willing to do my bidding, but I will not be rushed, and Will agrees with me that the harvest will be better on Thursday than today. Besides, we have only just finished shearing the sheep; that is an exhausting business, especially for the men, and they need a rest before swinging their scythes for several twelve-hour days.

So it was that Gomer, Gerallt and Will set off after breakfast with three horse-drawn gambos in a convoy, heading for Gelli Mill on the other side of Mynydd Preseli where our wool always fetches a fair price. As they went, it looked as if any of the three gambos might topple over at any moment, so high and wide were their loads of woolsacks. With the men out of the way, Bessie, Blodwen and Myfanwy immediately cleared the kitchen and embarked upon the manufacture of the breads and cakes, pies and puddings needed for the impending hay harvest, and Rose settled down at the piano for a lesson with her music teacher. I was at a loose end,

183

Conduct Unbecoming

and at first I wandered around the farmyard and lower fields in the bright sunshine. But I was in a strange restless mood, and found the cacophony of newly-shorn sheep and confused lambs in Parc Mawr irritating. I knew that within a few days peace would be restored, and that they would all be let up onto the common again, but at that moment they seemed to be stupid noisy creatures, and I wanted nothing to do with them. I knew that I would not escape from the racket on the mountain, so on the spur of the moment I decided to take a walk to Tycanol Wood, where peace and quiet could be guaranteed. It was very hot indeed, so I went up to my room and got rid of my stays, which I hate wearing at the best of times, and put on a light cotton dress. I knew that I would not meet anybody on my walk, and that appearances were not going to be important. Then I put a straw bonnet onto my head and pulled on my walking boots, and told Bessie and the others where I was going. "Very good, Mistress," said Bessie. "But there are said to be fearsome spirits in those woods, so just you take care."

I glared at her, but said nothing, and after packing a little picnic and a bottle of fruit cordial into my bag, off I went. Why did everybody insist on urging me to take care? Had I not taken care of myself ever since I arrived at the Plas? And had I not been clever enough in the art of self-protection, over the years, to have survived when others had not? But then I wiped the scowl off my face and replaced it with a smile, for I realized that Bessie was really being very sweet and genuine, and was simply expressing her affection for me in a kind and gentle way. I must learn to take things at face value, I thought, and to stop hunting for hidden meanings and unarticulated concerns in the most innocuous of expressions. So I hummed to myself as I walked down to the ford at Pantry and then up the lane past Fachongle Isaf, heading for the old oakwood.

As I walked my thoughts turned to Amos Jones, and it occurred to me that I had not seen him since my birthday party at the Plas on the 17th day of May. That had been a convivial and noisy occasion, as ever, and I remembered that Amos had been on very good form but had caused me some consternation by somehow keeping his distance from me and even avoiding eye contact. I do not suppose anybody else noticed what was happening, but I remember that later on, when everybody had gone home, my happiness was mixed in a strange way with a feeling of emptiness.

Then I was in the cool shade of the wood, with gnarled oaks all around me and with the blue sky invisible beyond and above a low canopy

184

Conduct Unbecoming

of delicate fresh leaves. So euphoria took over -- how could it be otherwise in Tycanol Wood? The air was filled with birdsong and the buzzing of little flying insects. I clambered among the craggy rocks that make this woodland so precious and so beautiful, waded through clearings overgrown with tall bracken, and followed various sheep tracks up to the cliff which was topped not just by teetering trees but also by the fortifications and hut remains left behind by our ancient ancestors the Druids. I explored among the rocks and mossy banks, squeezed through dense and prickly furze bushes, and sat in a mossy gully for a while, watching a green woodpecker. I found a little pond, and in one of the valleys there was a spring of pure clear water. I anointed myself with it, since I thought it must be no less sacred than the water of Ffynnon Brynach up on the mountain. Then I collected a posy of early summer flowers, to no particular purpose. I climbed to the highest crag in the woods and looked out for a few minutes over the treetop canopy towards Carningli and the sea in Newport Bay. Even from here I could hear those wretched Plas Ingli sheep and lambs, but they were far enough away to cause me amusement rather than irritation. It was lunchtime, so I ate my picnic and took a swig of cordial from my bottle. High above my head, almost lost in the deep azure of the cloudless sky, three red kites wheeled about lazily on slender wings, no doubt held aloft on some rising current of warm air. I wondered what it must it be like to be a red kite, and I wondered what the world looked like from up there, with its fields and cottages, and moorlands and peat bogs? Beautiful, without a doubt, and serene..........

With my good humour restored I jumped down off the rock onto the mossy bank under the tree canopy, trusting to fate since my eyes were adjusted to the brightness of the sky and not to the deep shade below me. All I knew was that the moss was soft and that the slope was not so steep as to cause me an injury. So it was that I flew through the air, stumbled down the mossy bank in the dark shadow, and collided with Jones Minor Prophet who was presumably intent upon climbing up to the same vantage point which I had just vacated. We ended up in a tangle of arms and legs, no doubt reminding both of us of the occasion of our first meeting. As on that occasion, we were both at first greatly embarrassed and apologetic, and then overtaken by hysterical laughter. Having ascertained that neither of us was injured by the encounter, I recovered my bonnet and bag, and we sat side by side in the cool shade while we regained our composure.

Conduct Unbecoming

"My dear Martha," said he, "we really must try to meet in a more polite fashion in future. All this rolling about and entwining is more than I can cope with at my age."

"Come come, sir, you are but a spring chicken, and well capable of coping with some rolling about. At any rate, it appears to be our destiny to be thrown together in the unlikeliest of circumstances. How did you know that I was here today?"

"I swear that I did not know it, Martha. Call it fate if you like. It was too hot in Brynberian today, and I decided that a walk in the cool shade of the woods would do me a power of good. I assumed that I would not meet a single soul, and that I could climb onto that little rock above the trees and look out at the world in perfect peace and quiet. It is as good a place as any for saying one's prayers. If I had known you were upon that rock, I would certainly have gone off in some other direction."

"Oh? That statement does not do much for my self-esteem, Master Jones, if I may say so."

Then Amos became very flustered. "No no, Martha." he protested. "Please do not take that remark the wrong way. Of course my instinct would have led me to give you a cheery greeting. It is just that I should also have tried to respect your privacy, given that you probably came into the wood today in order to escape from people and noise."

"Stop, Amos! You had better say no more on the matter, since you are already in danger of drowning, and if you struggle too much you will certainly sink without a trace. And that would be a great loss to me and the rest of humanity."

He laughed, and shook his head in resignation, and we both fell silent for a while. I offered him a drink of fruit cordial, and he accepted gratefully. I took a swig too, and then he said: "Shall we walk on through the wood, Martha? Every time I come here I discover new dells and rocky crags and nooks and crannies, and I am more and more taken by the magic of the place."

I smiled and said: "Why not? I have been here hundreds of times, and know it almost as well as I know the mountain. But even I keep on discovering secret places that I swear were not there on my last visit." Amos raised his eyebrows, and I continued. "Oh yes. Some say that the woodland is inhabited by ghosts and goblins, but in my view it is the place where fairies live. You are an expert on such things, Master Jones. What is

Conduct Unbecoming

your view -- if we succumb to temptation beneath these gnarled oak trees, will we be transported off to Fairyland for fifty years and retain our youthful vigour while the rest of the world decays away?"

"Temptation, Martha? It is just another thing to be conquered!" And he sprang to his feet, held out his hands, and pulled me up off the mossy bank. For a moment we stood face to face, holding hands. I looked deep into his eyes, and knew not what to expect; but I saw both fear and pain, and I found that deeply disturbing. Amos let go of my hands, and offered to carry my bag. Then he set off down the slope into the depths of the wood, dodging boulders and low branches, squeezing through little gaps between lichen-covered tree-trunks, and hopping across ditches and gullies. In such terrain we could not have held hands even if we had wanted to. I was perfectly at home in the wood, in spite of my skirts and petticoats, and I followed him without the slightest trouble. As we walked and scrambled about, we chatted about this and that, and I found it quite a pleasurable thing to watch his lean body from behind as he negotiated obstacles, held leafy branches aside for me to pass, and even pushed aside dead and rotten pieces of timber lest they should fall upon me or trip me up. He was dressed just in a light shirt and green corduroy trousers, and I remember thinking that he moved with the agility of a twenty-year-old and that he had a good healthy complexion arising, no doubt, from his life as a preacher in the open air.

For a while I was confused as to where we were, and then I recognized the sun-dappled crags of blue rock near the Druid's Cave. We examined it, and found that it was damp and dirty inside, and smelling of mildew and sheep droppings. Then I said: "Now then, Amos. I have followed you for long enough. Now it's my turn. Follow me if you can!"

I plunged into the dark shadow of the woods again, twisted and turned, clambered up some slopes and slithered down others, with Amos not far behind. After a few minutes we came to the little sunlit clearing where, long ago, before my marriage to David, he and I had first loved one another. The date was June 15th in the year 1796. Fifty years ago, to the day. That was the occasion on which I had lost my virginity and become pregnant. In our short time together David and I had made love here on many more occasions, and I had also come here for the same purpose with my beloved Owain, the man whom I had longed to marry but never did. This time, passion was the last thing on my mind, but I suddenly felt my

Conduct Unbecoming

age after all the scrambling around among the trees and rocks, and so I took off my bonnet and flung myself onto the ground in the sun, and lay on my back as I recovered my breath. I closed my eyes and said: "There now, Amos! This is my secret glade. You may count it as a great privilege to come here. Is it not beautiful?"

"Indeed it is, Martha," said Amos from not far away. "Quite perfect. A patch of blue sky and a June sun at its zenith, a surrounding fringe of old oak trees with fresh leafy branches right down to the ground, and a miniature meadow with more summer blossoms than I will ever learn to identify. No matter -- things of beauty sometimes seem even more beautiful if they do not have names."

For a while there was a comfortable silence between us. I opened my eyes and looked at him, and saw that he was lying on his back a few yards away from me, gazing at the sky.

Then I said: "Amos, can I ask you something?"

"By all means, Martha. I am in a benign mood at the moment, and will do my best to answer."

"You will be aware, Amos, that I see you as one of my dearest friends. I will go further, and say that I am very fond of you. I suspect that my feeling is reciprocated. Why, therefore, do you sometimes avoid contact with me, as you did a few weeks ago at my little birthday celebration?"

There was a long silence, and then he said: "Is it not obvious to you, Martha? You know a good deal more about love than I do. Do you not see that I am frightened?"

I rolled over onto my front, and looked at him, and our eyes met. "Yes, I have seen that in your eyes, Amos, even today. But why should you be frightened? Am I a frightening sort of person?"

"Far from it, Martha. Intimidating to some, maybe, with your beauty and your intellect and your reputation as a slayer of dragons. But not to me. No, Martha, I am as frightened as a man can be of his own emotions."

"Because you are married?"

"Precisely, Martha. I am married, and I am also a pastor, and I am watched like a hawk for almost every minute of every day in case I should deviate by one inch from the path of righteousness. Why, some of the elders of Capel Brynberian think it is a mortal sin to smile. Do you see

188

Conduct Unbecoming

that buzzard wheeling close to the sun? It has probably been trained by the deacons to spy on me, and to report on my whereabouts and activities at hourly intervals!"

At that I laughed, and so did he. We fell silent for a moment. Then I caught his eyes again and said: "Amos, you never talk about your wife. Tell me about her."

"I would rather not, Martha."

"Tell me about her. If you do not, I will have to assume that she is no more than a figment of your imagination, invented as a means of protecting yourself from emotional involvement with me or anybody else. Please. I insist."

He swallowed hard, and thought for a long time. "Very well, Martha," he said at last. "Against my better judgement, I will tell you everything, since you are the one person in the world whom I can trust. She is called Hannah, and we were married when I was very young. She is twenty years older than me, and we married because my father Edmund and her father, one Thomas Gifford, were great friends and because she came with a cottage in Radnor and a small dowry. She wanted security, and my parents wanted me out of the house because we as a family lived permanently on the bread-line. My father was away preaching for most of the time, and my mother never knew where the next meal would come from. We lived, for the most part, on charity."

"So how did you survive after your marriage?"

"Master Gifford paid for my theological training, since it was obvious to me and everybody else that I would follow in Father's footsteps. And the dowry paid for some of our living costs. We had a small garden too, and a pigsty, and I slaved away to the point where we produced at least some of our own meat and vegetables."

"Did you and Hannah learn to love one another? And were there any children? I have never heard you mention children............"

Amos gave a coarse laugh, and shook his head. "No no, Martha. There was no love, and no children. In fact, there was never even a marriage bed."

"You mean that you and Hannah have never even consummated your marriage?"

He shook his head again, and once again I saw the pain in his eyes. "Oh, Amos! I am so sorry! Have you really been denied the most beautiful

Conduct Unbecoming

gift that a man can give to a woman, or that a woman can give to a man?" He nodded. "And have you never loved anybody else, before your marriage or after?"

"No, Martha. For better or for worse, I was celibate as a young man, and since the day of my wedding I have been faithful to my marriage vows."

"So much, Amos, for all the talk in polite circles about you being "a happily married pastor". Some people seem to think that there is no such thing as an unhappy marriage. I was greatly blessed in my marriage to David, but for at least one of my best friends marriage has been little better than a life spent in Hell. Have you never thought of divorce or a nullity decree, on the grounds that your marriage never really existed?"

"Frequently, Martha. But such things are virtually impossible for a minister of religion, since they signify failure and create doubt in the minds of those who seek certainty, security and salvation. Besides, if I had sought a decree on the grounds that Hannah was and is as frigid as a Norwegian glacier that would have destroyed her as well. So we live our separate lives. She inherited a small sum from her father, and she survives, I dare say. In truth, we have nothing in common. I have heard nothing from her for several years, and since coming to Pembrokeshire I have not even made an attempt to contact her."

"But Amos, you are a charming and handsome man with a good body and a healthy complexion. Although you may have lost the bloom of youth, you are still very attractive to women. Take it from me. Do you not have -- how shall I put this -- desires?"

He laughed, and I saw at once a lightening of his mood. "Of course, Martha. I dare say that the blood in my veins is as red as that of any other man. Why do you think I am so frightened of my own feelings towards you? But I have tried to control my emotions, and to treat celibacy as a discipline and a sacrifice which I have to make in the course of my life of service to the Lord. Everybody has a cross to bear, and this is mine. If St Brynach could survive on bread, water and prayer, so can I."

"Aha, Brother Amos!" I chortled. "That is where you are wrong. My knowledge of the Life of Brynach is better than yours. Every local person knows that before he came to Nevern and became a saint, Brynach was an exceedingly wild young man who sowed his wild oats on a substantial scale, and even succumbed to the charms of a passionate

190

Conduct Unbecoming

princess somewhere on the shores of Milford Haven."

"I submit to your superior knowledge on the matter," laughed Amos. "Perhaps I will have to accept that some people have more fun than others when they are young, even if there may be a price to be paid later in life.........."

"Amos, I want to ask you another question. Have you ever dreamt of me, or imagined what it might be like to love me?"

"That is a very direct question, Martha. Why do you ask?"

"Well, you have been very honest with me, Amos, and I respect you all the more for it. I will admit to you, and to nobody else on this earth, that last Hallowe'en I performed the *rhamanta* divination at the Plas, and when I looked through the keyhole to see who was enjoying my feast, I saw you."

Amos, still lying on his back on the grass, closed his eyes and breathed deeply for a few moments. Then he said, without looking at me: "I will be honest too, my dear Martha. During the night of Hallowe'en I saw you too, as I have seen you in my dreams on many other occasions. And those dreams have been, more often than not, very interesting and worthy of remembrance."

At this, I could not resist a fit of the giggles. "Interesting, indeed!" I spluttered. "I dare say that it is the ambition of every good woman to be the subject of an interesting dream. I have succeeded in my ambition! Hallelujah! Praise the Lord!"

And I leapt to my feet and danced around the sunny glade, waving my arms in the air like somebody overtaken by ecstasy at a revivalist meeting.

"Martha! Please do not take the Lord's name in vain."

"I do nothing of the sort, Master Jones. As you have explained to me many times in the course of your discourses on the Jones Heresy, the Lord does not frown upon enjoyment or frivolity, and nor does he expect men and women to suppress their instincts."

On a sudden impulse, I stopped my silly dancing, and dropped to my knees alongside this dear, tortured, repressed preacher. Before he could react I kissed him on his lips, lingering over it for as long as I dared. His lips were soft and sweet, but he was obviously not used to kissing.

"When last did somebody kiss you on your lips, Amos?" I asked.

"Emily Evans, behind a hay barn in Radnor, when I was eighteen,"

191

he said with a grin and with a blush on his cheeks. "I fear that I am not very expert in the art."

"That much is obvious," said I, glancing down at the considerable lump in his trousers. He moved his hands to cover his indignity, and I found that both entertaining and touching. So I kissed him again, this time for even longer, and contrived to open his lips and give him my tongue. I was still on my knees and he was still flat on his back. At last I came up for air, and left him gasping and spluttering. "Martha!" he said. "This is all most irregular......"

"Balderdash, Master Jones. It is all entirely regular, and there is a rigid object in your trousers to prove it. Do you love me?"

"Martha, I cannot answer that question. I am very confused just now, quite apart from being short of breath."

"Do you love me, Amos? I want to know, because my love for you grows stronger and firmer with every month that passes. I am supposed to be too old for such things, and I know not where love will lead me, but I have to know that my affection is reciprocated."

He sat up and stretched out his hands towards me, and drew me down onto the ground beside him. We kissed again, this time properly and passionately, and the kiss led to an embrace and to exploring hands and to a rising passion of a sort that I never thought I should experience again. "Oh Martha!" he whispered. "Of course I love you! How could you ever have doubted it? It must have been obvious to you and to every other observer whenever you and I were anywhere near each other. God knows, I have fought against my passion for you from the very beginning, and fled from it on my long preaching campaign. I have prayed to be rid of this burden of guilt, and have confessed and chastised myself on more than one occasion......"

I could not suppress a giggle. "My goodness, Amos! Such guilt! Have you crawled all the way to the shrine of St Non, and taken a cold bath every night in order to subdue your passion?"

"Please, Martha. This is not a joking matter. Please remember that I am still a married man, and that according to the teachings of my church I have committed a mortal sin in thinking of you and dreaming of you, night after night and even day after day when I should have been ministering to my flock. It is called carnal desire, and I fear that I am all too familiar with it. And in the eyes of the world, both you and I are old

Conduct Unbecoming

and respectable, and that makes me feel even more guilty."

I disentangled myself, and for some reason the misery on his face made me feel more amused and even frivolous. "Come now, Amos!" said I. "You have more guilt within you than a Pope who has broken every one of the Ten Commandments. Your trouble is that you have spent your whole life giving yourself to others, to the extent that you have forgotten how to receive. Your generosity of spirit is legendary. Why, you even feel embarrassed when people give you hospitality, or congratulate you on a wondrous sermon, or provide you with a new pair of boots. You give so much love to others that you have forgotten to love yourself. And you have absolutely no idea how to receive and cherish the love of another human being. You ponder and plan too much, and suppress your instincts. Do you plead guilty to these serious charges?"

He shrugged his shoulders, but did not protest. So, acting on impulse as if I was a naughty schoolgirl, I leapt to my feet and started to let down my hair. "Well then," I said as I removed my hair clips, "the court will take silence as an admission of guilt. Rehabilitation is in order for the prisoner in the dock. I am minded to give you one or two little lessons, Amos, culminating in a little gift. Take it if you will, for the opportunity may not come again........."

Then -- I really do not know why -- I started to do a silly dance around the sunlit glade, humming a tune specially composed for the occasion. "Lesson number one," I sang out. "Be happy!" And I swirled about him, as he sat with his knees raised under his chin and a frown upon his brow. I stopped every now and then to kiss him, and his frown was at last replaced by a grin and then by easy laughter.

"Lesson number two," I whispered. "Cast off your cares." And I changed from my hopping and swirling and skipping to another sort of dance such as I imagined that the wicked ladies of an an Eastern harem might have done in days gone by. I glided about seductively, demure one second and provocative the next, and as I did so I managed, with some difficulty and many giggles, to take off my boots and stockings, and to fling them away from me with wild abandon. One of my stockings landed in a tree. Then, teasing Amos with my wicked eyes, I removed my dress, and my petticoats, and finally my undergarment. "You may be thankful, Reverend Jones, that I left my stays at home," I puffed, "for the sight of those monstrous things would surely have had a deflating effect even upon

Conduct Unbecoming

Don Juan in his prime."

Now quite naked, I continued to glide seductively around poor Amos, who must have thought me quite mad. His smile had gone, and his eyes were fixed upon my body, and especially upon my breasts and my private parts. "Have you never seen a naked lady before, Reverend Jones?" I asked. "If the shock is too great for you, you can always close your eyes." But he kept them open, and at last, exhausted by my exertions in the sunlight, I flopped down at his side.

He could not kiss me on my lips until I had recovered my breath, so I lay flat on my back, closed my eyes, and gasped: "You have my permission to touch me if you like, Amos. And I quite like to be kissed on my breasts."

Nothing happened, and I saw that the poor fellow was terrified. "Don't worry, Amos! I am just flesh and blood, like you, even though I have a different shape. Kiss my breasts if you will, and unless I am very much mistaken you will not be struck down by a thunderbolt from heaven. Even if I am mistaken in that regard, you will at least die happy."

And at last he did kiss my breasts, and then my shoulders and my stomach, and his hands started to explore a woman's body for the first time in his life. For me, that knowledge was wonderful indeed, and I felt the passion rising within me. Then his mouth was on mine again, and he was on the ground beside me as we embraced and rolled on the warm thick grass of the sunny glade. I could feel from the pressure on my stomach that he was greatly aroused, and I suddenly realised that while I was naked he was fully clothed. "Now then, Reverend Jones," I murmured in his ear, "this is very unfair, and I am being taken advantage of. Kindly allow me to help you."

So I pulled off his boots and socks, and then his clothes. That was a relatively simple business, for there were only three garments to deal with -- a cotton shirt, a pair of corduroy trousers, and a light woollen undergarment. The latter item was a little difficult to remove since there was a considerable rigid impediment in the way, but at last I managed it, by delicately disentangling the obstruction with my fingers. I flung the garment away, caring not where it landed. As I did so, I looked into his eyes, and again he looked as embarrassed as a small boy who has been caught in the middle of some mischief. I laughed at the thought that the last female to touch his private parts had probably been his mother, bathing him as a small boy. Now he lay naked at my side. I looked at

Conduct Unbecoming

him for a while, and enjoyed what I saw, for his body was lean and yet more muscular than I had expected. I ran my finger gently along the full length of his penis, which quivered like an arrow. "You are a very funny fellow, Amos," said I. "You have there a part of your anatomy of which you should be inordinately proud, and yet you look peevish. Lesson number three: be proud of your body, including wrinkles, runny nose and surplus flesh. Now you may kiss me again."

And he did, with a ravenous passion. We rolled about on the grass giggling and laughing, and exploring one another with our hands. "For a virgin, Amos, you seem to have a remarkable aptitude for this sort of thing, " I whispered. "Now try this." And I brought his hand down to my private parts, and allowed his fingers to enter me as I played with his penis. I knew that as a novice he would come soon to the peak of his passion, so I whispered again into his ear: "Lessons finished, Amos. And now for the gift........."

I rolled onto my back in the soft grass, opened my legs and pulled him on top of me. I guided his penis until it was inside me, and so, slowly at first and then at last madly, we rose together to the peak of our loving, with him gasping and sighing "Oh Martha, Martha! How I love you! Oh! Oh! Oh!" and me shouting and laughing ever higher and louder, until the sounds of our consummation echoed around the leafy margins of our glade.

Then we more or less collapsed together, quite exhausted, and I was forcefully reminded that I was quite an old woman and that he was also somewhat past his prime. My back ached, and I saw that his right knee was scratched and bleeding. "Oh dear," said I at last, "that was considerably more exhausting than turning a butter churn, but much more fun." And I could not resist bursting into laughter, and neither could Amos, as hysteria followed ecstasy.

"My dear sweet Martha," said Amos at last, lying flat on his back in the late afternoon sunlight. "That was quite the most wonderful gift I have ever received. Thank you, *cariad*, from the bottom of my heart." That was the first time he had called me *cariad*, and I found that very moving. He kissed me three times, once on my lips and once on each nipple.

"And thank you too, Reverend Jones," said I. "Do not forget that I too have received a most blessed gift today, and that I have been reminded that there is nothing on this earth more beautiful and more precious than

Conduct Unbecoming

the gift of love. You have given one sort of love to thousands of your flock, without ever counting the cost. Now you have given another sort of love to me, and me alone. You have a great talent, Amos, which might be further developed with a little appropriate tuition............."

"Discovered rather too late in life, Martha. And as for tuition, I fear that that might be difficult to arrange, given our circumstances. But even if I go to my Maker tonight I will not count this time we have spent together among the sins to be confessed at the Pearly Gates. Have we harmed one another, or indeed anybody else? Has my wife Hannah been hurt or diminished in any way by what has transpired between us? I hardly think so. If loving you has been a sin, God only knows how wonderful virtue may be."

So Jones Minor Prophet and I gathered up our clothes and stockings and boots, which were scattered all over the glade, and put them on again. Much to my amusement, Amos had to climb an oak tree to recover my missing stocking, and I found his undergarment in the topmost branches of a rowan bush. I put up my hair as best I could without a mirror, and replaced my bonnet on my head. "Do I look respectable, kind sir?" I asked, flapping my eyelashes and tilting my head to one side like a sixteen-year-old milkmaid who has just been seduced by a randy old squire.

"Respectable?" he said. "Anything but. But more beautiful nonetheless than any other woman in God's world." Then we embraced, and kissed, and declared our love for each other as the birds of Tycanol Wood started on their evensong. Then, at about five o'clock, we went our separate ways, he up the track towards Brynberian, and I down the slope towards Fachongle Uchaf and the familiar lanes of the *cwm*. I do not know what Amos was thinking as he walked, but I hope that he was happy. As for me, I walked on air with my head in the clouds. I may be sixty-eight years old, I thought, but somebody still finds me beautiful, and I still know what to do with my old and battered assets. And love still feels as wonderful as it did exactly fifty years ago, when I lost my virginity in that very same same leafy glade beneath the very same midsummer sun. Now Amos had lost his virginity too, and I thought that in gently taking it from him I had performed a charitable act; for virginity is not something that should be carried into the grave, even by a preacher.

Conduct Unbecoming

17th June 1846

Two days have passed since my adventure with Amos in Tycanol Wood, and while I suppose I should be racked by guilt, I am still elated. At any rate, thus far I have managed to steer clear of divine retribution. I trust that there have been no lightning strikes or plagues of locusts in Brynberian either. I have had one or two practical issues to deal with, but my servants know me well enough not to be too surprised by oak leaves falling out of my undergarment onto the bedroom floor and by mud and grass stains all over my dress. And I discovered that bits of moss and grass show up more clearly in white hair than in black. That is, I dare say, one of the disadvantages of old age.

When I returned to the Plas I had to cope with Bessie's raised eyebrows, as usual, when she saw how dishevelled and dirty I looked. "My goodness, Mistress!" she exclaimed. "Whatever have you done with your hair and your dress? You look as if you have been attacked by one of those Tycanol goblins, but I can see from the gleam in your eye and from your ruddy cheeks that you got the better of him. Mistress Martha emerges victorious, once again!"

"Enough of your insolence, Bessie, if you please," I replied, wagging my finger at her. "I admit to looking less prim than I did on my departure, but I have been having a fine time in the wood, exploring and clambering on the rocks, and indeed climbing trees. I am still quite young enough for such activity, I am pleased to say."

"And I suppose you went tumbling down at some stage, and purely by chance landed right on top of Jones Minor Prophet?"

"Huh!" said I. "If I was to confirm that supposition, you would not believe me anyway. So I will hold my tongue, and go and get changed."

We delayed supper until Gomer, Will and Gerallt returned with the empty gambos from Gelli Mill. They were in good spirits, having obtained an exceptional price for the Plas Ingli wool and having enjoyed a few jars of ale at assorted hostelries on the way home. I did not begrudge them that, since they are loyal friends and hard workers who have few enough opportunities for recreation.

At supper we talked of the harvest, but I found it difficult to concentrate, and kept on nodding off. At last my servants rolled their eyes and shrugged their shoulders and grinned, and Will said: "Mistress, what

Conduct Unbecoming

did you get up to in Tycanol Wood today? You appear to be uncommonly tired, for one who is usually so sprightly at the midnight hour!" I declined to answer, and so they packed me off to bed.

We resumed discussions yesterday at breakfast. Will and I agreed the order for the harvesting of each field, and we felt very relaxed about everything since the weather looked like holding, and since the ground was now dry enough for the harvesters to hold their feet and for the cut swathes to bake in the sun. The Irish came in the morning, as planned, and I gave work to four men, five women and three children. Sadly, there was no sign of the O'Connell family, and while all of those whom I interviewed had fearsome tales to tell of the famine across the water, none of them had any news of our old friends.

And today the harvest has been in full swing, with ten men swinging scythes, led by Will who is almost as proficient as my old head man Billy was in his heyday. The men cut a total of five acres, less than I would have liked, but reasonable given that the hay is heavy and leafy this year. We decided to let it lie over one night, which means that we had no need for female and child labour today; but tomorrow will be another matter, and we will need all hands on deck. There will be thirty people at the Plas, ten cutting and twenty raking and turning, not to mention various small children fooling around. That means large-scale catering for Bessie and the other female servants, and as I sit in my room at ten o'clock, with the glow of twilight still illuminating the sky, I can hear the clanking of saucepans, pots and bowls down in the kitchen, accompanied by a buzz of conversation and laughter. Will and the other harvesters are sampling the cider made from last year's apple crop, and are probably getting in the way of Bessie and the other women. There is a great deal of light-hearted banter, and the occasional gale of laughter. They are all enjoying themselves, and I am happy to leave them to it.

In any case, I am happier up here in my room all alone, gazing out towards the darkening shadows of Tycanol and Carnedd Meibion Owen, and thinking of what might next be in store for me and Master Amos Jones. What is he doing just now, in his cottage over the brow of the hill? Is he on his knees at the side of his bed talking to God, or is he beneath his sheets dreaming of me? What should I do next? What should he do next? We probably both know that we are trapped by circumstances, and that according to the law we have committed adultery. But for me what happened in the wood was wonderful, spontaneous and beautiful. It was surely a world away from the impulsive youthful liaison between Iestyn Price and my sister Elen all those years ago which resulted in her unwanted pregnancy and in the birth of Brynach. So does that make what happened acceptable in the eyes of God? Perhaps Amos will know the answer to that question, and will have the Biblical texts to support his conclusion. But whatever may happen in the future, I will always remember the first union between Amos and myself not as sacrilege but as a sort of sacrament. And that sacrament is our secret, to be guarded and cherished.

ΩΩΩΩΩΩΩΩΩΩΩ

18th June 1846

Today, at the height of the hay harvest, with scythes slicing through good grass in Parc Glas and raking and turning in full swing in Parc Bach, Amos turned up without warning. I am getting too old for the strenuous work of the harvest in hot weather, so I was in the cool kitchen at the time, up to my elbows in bread dough and with the rest of me covered in flour. Bessie, Myfanwy and Rose were also rushing about, involved in various tasks to do with the feeding of the ten thousand.

Amos greeted each of us in turn, cheerfully enough, but there was a hesitancy in his manner, and I knew that he wanted to talk to me in private. So I asked Rose to take over the kneading of the dough on the kitchen table, washed my hands, and asked Amos to walk with me to the garden. I wanted to hold his hand as we walked, but I dared not, for there were too many strangers about and too many eyes watching us. We sat on the bench in the shade, close to my favourite flower border full of purple and pink lupins. There, at least, we had privacy. He appeared quite agitated, and I asked him what was wrong.

"Nothing is wrong, dearest Martha," he replied with a weak smile. "I will not take up much of your time, and it is very inconsiderate of me to call at the height of the hay harvest when you have so much to do."

Conduct Unbecoming

"You are always welcome at the Plas, Amos, at any time of the day or night. You know that."

"You are very kind. Now, to the point, Martha........."

"Have you come to tell me that you regret what happened between us three days since?"

"No no. Do not even think it, Martha. That was the most wonderful thing ever to happen to me, and it will live with me for ever. My body is still glowing because of it, and for three nights I have thought of little else."

"But.......?"

"Yes, there is a "but", Martha," he confessed. "I have to admit to being sorely troubled. I have committed a grave sin, and all of my training teaches me that punishment -- in one form or another -- must follow. Adultery is a sin given due prominence in the Ten Commandments , and it cannot be dressed up and disguised under any other name. I am not sure that I can live a life of encouraging my flock to virtuous behaviour while knowing that I have fallen far short of the standards expected of me."

"That sounds very melodramatic, Amos. Even Christ fell short of the standards which he set for himself. Imperfection goes with humanity, I dare say, and I will not condemn it unless it hurts someone."

"My wife will be hurt, Martha, when she finds out."

"Nonsense, Amos! From what you have told me, she is perfectly impervious to the feelings or desires of others, and if anybody has been hurt within your non-existent marriage, it is you. If you were to write her a letter, and confess all, she would probably shrug her shoulders, and despise you for your naivety and honesty, rather than cry over marital betrayal. How can you betray anybody when there is no proper marriage and no bond of trust in the first place? Anyway, she need never know......."

Amos held up his hand. "Enough, enough, Martha," he grinned. "I hear what you say, and there is merit in every word. Your knowledge of the female psyche is much more sophisticated than mine, which I suppose is to be expected. But I am still troubled. I need time to think. When I leave here I will travel directly to Carmarthen, en route for Brecon, where I will visit my old mother for a couple of days. She is very ill, and I have the consent of the deacons. I will do no preaching, but as I trot along on that horrid horse of mine, I will pray a lot. God will tell me what to do."

"But Amos, I need you here. I love you, and I do not know what I will do if you are far away.........."

"You do not need me here, Martha. I will not love you any the less for being in Carmarthen or Brecon. I will be back in about ten days. With the harvest in full swing, I will only be in the way at the Plas, and I cannot mope about the place like a lovesick youth. The affection which we bear towards one another will become so obvious as to become a scandal -- would you not agree?"

I had to agree that he was right, and I was considerably cheered by his common sense. So we stood up, and found the shadiest spot under the apple trees where we could embrace and kiss without any risk of observation. Then I waved him off on that old horse of his, which is always irritated about something and which was today irritated by the flies. He dug his heels into its flanks, and tried to get it up to a trot, but it continued to walk at such a leisurely pace that I thought he would not get to Eglwyswrw and back in ten days, let alone Brecon.

I returned to the kitchen and to the preparation of the midday picnic for the harvesting hordes. Rose and Myfanwy paid no attention to me, and carried on with some discussion about the young men of the district, but Bessie gave me one of her looks, and made me blush again. She reminded me of old Blodwen Owen, her predecessor. No wonder Housekeepers are universally feared, I thought. They read all the signs, and know too much.

ΩΩΩΩΩΩΩΩΩΩΩ

19th June 1846

It is midday, and still very hot, and the hay harvest is still in full swing. But I have taken to my room, and here I will stay, for I dare not show my face either in the kitchen or in the hayfield. I am petrified with fear, since news of my indiscretion in the wood with Amos has spread like a wildfire across the parched landscape. So the time of retribution, which I dared not think about, has come.

How I wish that Amos was here with me! Or at least in Brynberian! Then at least I could send for him; and we could stand shoulder to

Conduct Unbecoming

shoulder, share responsibility for what we have done, and face a hostile world together. But he is already many miles away, and heading east, innocent of the flames which now threaten to engulf me. He will not even smell the smoke, and he will return in nine or ten days to find that everything has changed. I know not how I will cope without him, and I know not how he will cope when he returns to this parched and blighted landscape. Poor Amos -- he has far more to lose than I, and his suffering, when it comes, will be compounded by the knowledge that when I needed him most, he was not here.

I will try to control the panic in my breast by writing in my diary.

Early this morning Bessie walked down to town with her basket and her shopping-list, and returned at about ten with her shopping done and with Daisy in tow. I was in the kitchen by myself, having sent Rose, Myfanwy and Blodwen out into the hayfields to help the harvesters, on the basis that with carting starting today we needed all hands on deck. I was surprised to see Daisy, and started to give her a cheerful welcome, but then I noticed that she looked anything but cheerful, and I knew at once that something was wrong. "Mother," she said without any preamble, "will you come with Bessie and me into the parlour, where we can talk without risk of disturbance?" The two of them marched straight along the passage, and I had to follow.

I sat down in my favourite chair, and Bessie sat next to me. Then Daisy pulled up a chair right in front of mine, sat down and took my hands in hers. She looked straight into my eyes and came straight to the business in hand. "Mother," she said, "is it true that you have been sporting with Jones Minor Prophet in Tycanol Wood?"

I felt the blood draining out of my face, and I thought I might faint. "Very well then," she continued. "I see that it is true. Did he force you?"

"No, definitely not," I replied in a voice so feeble that I could hardly hear it myself. "Amos is not a man to use force."

"So it was mutual?"

"I suppose so. It just happened." And then I realized that I had to be honest, with Daisy and Bessie at least, for I could see a possibility that Amos, in the eyes of the world, might henceforth be seen as a predatory monster. I could not allow that to happen, and so I said: "I fear that if blame has to reside somewhere, it should rest with me. A strange mood came over me. I led him on, and he was too weak to resist."

Conduct Unbecoming

"A strange mood, Mother! Not strange at all, if I may say so. The most basic mood known to the human race, and one with which, by now, you should have become perfectly familiar. And is it true that prior to the act itself you danced a lascivious dance without any clothes on, and sang and laughed, and encouraged the preacher into lewd activities? "

I lowered my eyes and tried to avoid my interrogator. But at last I had to nod my head. Then tears started trickling down my cheeks. "But I love him dearly, Daisy," I whispered. "And he loves me. And what happened between us was so beautiful......."

Then Bessie put her arm around my shoulder and kissed my cheek. "Oh Mistress *bach*," she said, "what are we to do with you? Just as we thought you were old enough to become respectable, this happens. There will be complicated consequences -- you know that?"

"That much is obvious, Bessie. Will you help me? And will you, Daisy? I will need more than a little support in the days to come."

They nodded, and embraced me, and smiled, although God knows there was little enough to smile about. Then they told me where the news of the "dissolute and adulterous acts" in Tycanol Wood had come from. Daisy said she had picked it up from whispers on the street, and Bessie had heard it from Patty outside Thomas Grocer's. They both said that at first they could not believe what they were hearing, and that they had defended me furiously against mean-spirited gossip and wicked lies, but then they had picked up more whispers, and yet more, and had started to wonder whether they might be listening to something not too far removed from the truth.

Just then we three were disturbed by footsteps in the passage, and without knocking Betsi burst into the parlour, looking as if she had run up all the way from Brithdir. She was red-faced and furious. "Mother," she panted, "is this gossip about fornication true? I must know the truth, since the whole town is talking of nothing else!"

Daisy came to my rescue. "Calm down, sister," she said evenly, "and pull up a chair. It may be true, and Mother has already admitted to us that she and Amos Jones have had intimate relations in the wood. But I dare say that according to the gossip she was also involved in witchcraft and human sacrifice. One should not believe everything one hears."

"True, Daisy. And I am sorry, Mother, for my aggressive tone of voice. I see that you are upset, and I know that anger does not help."

Conduct Unbecoming

"Will you kiss me, Betsi, and tell me that you love me?"

She did as I asked, and said: "Of course I love you, Mother. I will do anything for you -- you know that."

Then Bessie said: "May I suggest, Mistress Betsi, that we establish what is being said in town, and where the rumours have come from?"

"I agree, Bessie. Shall I start by telling you what I have obtained by way of information?" We all nodded, and so she continued as I was seized by a cold apprehension. "I went to town this morning," she said, "and was bemused by the strange behaviour of various friends and acquaintances who looked furtive and stopped speaking as I approached. But I encouraged people to be honest with me, and I heard at first that there were rumours circulating about Mistress Morgan of Plas Ingli and Jones Minor Prophet. I was not greatly surprised by that, Mother, since your friendship with Amos is I suppose quite well known. But then I heard the word "fornication" and started to get concerned, and at last I picked up tales about carnal activities in Tycanol Wood. I picked up no more detail than that, but when I got home I discovered that Nellie, one of my servants, had a scurrilous note written by one of her friends from Brynberian. She showed it to me. It said that some days since, one Mary Roberts, a servant at Tycanol Farm, was going along the woodland footpath when she was attracted by "laughter, singing and certain other noises". She investigated by following the sounds, and then clearly spied on you, Mother, and your friend Amos in a wooded glade. I suspect that she spied for quite a long time. She said that you danced and sang like a naked savage, and that you shamelessly performed certain lewd acts and then took pleasure in fornication. The letter, which is still in Nellie's possession, then expresses total outrage, "she being a respectable widow and grandmother, and he being a happily married man and a reverend gentleman to boot". Another bit said: "besides, was it not an act of the most base kind, given the great age of the lady involved, and given that such carnal lusts of the flesh should have been left behind her thirty years since?" And so on, Mother. I will spare you the details."

"And the writer of the letter, Bessie?" asked Daisy.

"Does it matter? Some dairymaid or other who has learned how to write. There are probably twenty similar letters flying around the district as we speak. One of the benefits of education for the masses, Mother, as you might or might not agree. But all I am interested in is the truth or

Conduct Unbecoming

otherwise of what has been written down."

Daisy spared me any further embarrassment, and said: "From what Mother has told us, Bessie, it is mostly true."

"Tell me, Mistress," said Bessie. "Where exactly did your interesting activities in the company of Master Jones actually take place? If you were next to the footpath that was not very discreet of you."

"We would not have been so stupid, Bessie," I replied, having rediscovered the power of speech. "We were at least two hundred yards from the path. This Mary Roberts, whoever she is, must have followed us for a long way, or else heard us from a great distance and then deliberately set out upon a spying mission. And if she watched us for a long while, that shows scant regard for the privacy of others and precious little Christian charity. What happened between Amos and me was none of her business!"

"Well, we should not be too surprised, Mother. There is something of the voyeur in all of us. Young Miss Roberts probably had almost as much fun in the observance as did you and Amos in the act."

We fell silent for quite some time, and while we thought, Bessie went to the kitchen and fetched a jug of ice-cold fruit cordial with which to revive our spirits. While we sipped at our glasses the full import of the morning's events hit me with full force. I moaned, and said: "Oh, may God forgive me for this, the greatest of all my indiscretions. As far as the neighbourhood is concerned, I do not know whether to defend myself or to admit my shame. Whatever I do or say in the coming days, I must take my punishment. But my greatest regret is the manner in which this scandal will destroy the prophet's reputation and transform him from hero to outcast. Poor, poor Amos! Then I must take responsibility for what will now happen to you, Betsi and Daisy, and in particular to the younger generation -- Rose and the other grandchildren. Oh, they will be known from now on not as the proud bearers of a grand family name, but simply as the grandchildren of an adulterous and lascivious old woman!"

And with that, I fear that I burst into tears again, and required much consolation from Bessie and my daughters. We could not talk more, for there was a banging on the kitchen door, and various harvesters reported that they had come to help with carrying the picnic down to the hayfield. "Hell and damnation!" exclaimed Bessie, in most unladylike fashion. "With all of this talk I have quite forgotten about the feeding of the masses. Forgive me, Mistress, but I must go, and I fear that I will need the

Conduct Unbecoming

help of Betsi and Daisy too if we are not to have a riot on our hands."

So all three of them gave their apologies and rushed off, promising that we would talk again later. But before she went Daisy, who has become very sensitive since her return to the Plas, escorted me upstairs and insisted that I should lie down. I did as instructed, and before she left the room she kissed me and gave me a big wink. "Try to get some sleep, Mother dear. And don't you worry too much. You and Master Jones will survive to fight again another day. If you think this is a big scandal, one day I will tell you all about myself and the Bishop of Wells. Now that really was a story to cherish!"

Now I am exhausted by all this emotional turmoil, and by my reporting of it. It is still mid-afternoon, and the harvesters are still at work under a high sun. The talk in the harvest field will by now be all about the misdemeanours of Mistress Martha and Jones Minor Prophet. I will simply have to leave Bessie and Daisy to defend me, and try to sleep.

ΩΩΩΩΩΩΩΩΩΩΩ

20th June 1846

Last evening I was minded to remain in my room and miss supper, but I was surprised when my granddaughter Rose, almost fifteen years old and very wise in the ways of the world, burst into my room and said: "Come along now, Grandma. It is time for supper. You and I, and Aunts Betsi and Daisy, will eat in the dining room, leaving the kitchen to the servants and the harvesters. They will be happier without us, and we will certainly be happier without them."

"Are Betsi and Daisy staying for supper? What will their husbands think?"

"Don't you worry about them, Grandma. They have enough sense to know that we women need to chat in peace and quiet." And she smiled that angelic smile that will melt many a manly heart in years to come.

I had to laugh, and agreed to come down. Rose helped me to change and to tidy myself up. As she put up my hair for me, I said to her: "You

Conduct Unbecoming

know, Rose, about this business involving myself and Master Jones? I fear that it must be very distressing for you........"

Much to my surprise, Rose gave a very unladylike belly laugh. "Nonsense, Grandmother!" she chuckled. "I know all about it. I think it is all perfectly splendid, as do most of the others in the hayfield. Indeed, I would go so far as to say that your reputation is greatly enhanced. If I am in such good working order when I am old and grey, I shall be well pleased!" For her insolence, I grabbed her, and put her over my knee, and spanked her bottom as if she was a toddler; and she screamed blue murder, and we both had fits of the giggles.

Thus restored to something like my normal self, Rose escorted me downstairs to the dining room to find Betsi and Daisy already seated at the table, and we three generations of Morgan women enjoyed a hearty meal together. Having admitted almost everything already to my two daughters, I had to repeat some of it for Rose, hoping not to destroy her youthful innocence, but after a while it became clear that she knew a good deal more about biology and psychology than I did myself, no doubt because of time spent in Daisy's company.

Over an excellent pudding of strawberry tart and whipped cream, I thought that contrition was in order, and I apologized to my three companions for the hurt that I had inflicted on all of them and their families. But Daisy laughed, and said: "You worry too much, Mother. Now that we have had a few hours to get used to the latest news from the Garden of Eden, we are less worried than we were. Speaking for myself, there is not much nowadays that can hurt me, since I have coped with more than you can imagine during the days of my London career. This incident is thoroughly entertaining, and I suspect that most of the Newport inhabitants, of both sexes, may say "Absolutely disgraceful!" while they are out doing their shopping in Market Street, but will say "Dammo, good for them, if they have the energy for it!" in the privacy of their own homes. I must say that I am full of admiration myself.........."

"Daisy, you are being very flippant," retorted Betsi. "We are talking not about London's Regent Street but about Newport's Market Street. Mother is a free agent, and can probably cope with a little local scandal, but think of the Prophet -- he is a pastor and a married man who has now committed adultery. His career is ruined. He will never stand in a pulpit again, and he will probably be drummed out of the community. He

Conduct Unbecoming

will be blamed -- it is always the case that the man is assumed to have led the woman astray."

"I fear that that is nowhere near the truth, Betsi. As I intimated this morning, it was I who led him on, and he who was reluctant. I removed my clothes and danced naked before him. I cannot lie about that."

Daisy squealed "Good for you, Mother! The Bluestockings would be proud of you. You are a true heroine, and deserve a medal for your noble contribution to the emancipation of women."

"Daisy! Will you never take this seriously?" scolded Betsi, playing out her role as big sister. "We are talking here about the ruination of the good name of the Morgans of Plas Ingli, and the miserable end of the Prophet's career as a preacher. The shame of it may well kill him, in this day and age of fierce evangelicals who think it a mortal sin to show an ankle, or to whistle a cheery tune, or to skip across a pathway!"

"So what can we do to save Master Jones?" asked Rose. "For a start, Grandma, can we keep this from his wife?"

"I am glad you asked that, Rose. I will not tell this to anybody else, and I depend upon your discretion. But Amos's marriage is a sham, and he has no contact at all with his wife. He does not seem to know whether she is alive or dead. The marriage was never consummated, and to his eternal credit -- up to the time of our indiscretion in Tycanol Wood -- he was faithful to his marriage vows for no less than 38 years. In my estimation that makes him a saint."

"Why then," asked Daisy, "has he never sought divorce or a nullity decree?"

"Those are not options for a preacher, Daisy," I replied. "You must know that. For a start, it would involve scandal and a great deal of money. Secondly, I suspect that the Prophet is too kind to drag his wife through endless unpleasantness."

So we talked on, well into the night, and decided that we could do little other than to await developments. I agreed to stay clear of the town for the time being, and to send a message to sister Catrin in Castlebythe first thing in the morning, asking if Rose and myself might come and stay for a few days. I hope and pray that she and husband James will agree to my proposal, for I have no wish to stay here and put up with a succession of scowls, grins, nudges and winks from those who know me a little and who know even less about what actually went on in Tycanol Wood.

Conduct Unbecoming

24th June 1846

Some days have passed, and I am writing this in the guest bedroom of the grand old house of Castlebythe. Catrin and James have been perfect hosts. They have been very understanding, and I have told them almost everything. I feared that Catrin would condemn me with her eyes if not with her lips, but in a moment of complete privacy, sister to sister, she said to me: "You have my complete sympathy, dearest Martha. There, but for the grace of God, I might have gone too." I raised my eyebrows, but she would not elaborate.

Rose has enjoyed it here, for she has other young people to entertain her. In particular, she gets on famously with seventeen-year-old Maria (daughter to John and Ruth) and Bronwen (daughter to Mark and Megan) who is fifteen, and just a few months older than she. They all live within a mile or two of Castlebythe, and the three young ladies seem to spend all of their time wandering about on the moors and talking about clothes and boys. They are as pretty as pictures, all three, but I am pleased that they have inherited the family instinct for the outdoor life, and that thus far they have not whined and moaned about missing the Tenby social season.

To more serious matters. Today Ioan rode over to Castlebythe with the latest news. He reported that the Nonconformists in Newport are outraged and scandalised by the news of my frolics in the wood with Amos. He said that over the past day or two certain "respectable" people had crossed the street rather than talk to Daisy, Betsi or himself. At this I moaned and said: "Oh, no! This is what I feared.........."

"Don't you worry, Martha," he replied. "Sometimes it takes something like this to help one to sort out the real friends from the fairweather ones. We can well do without the friendship of those who pass by on the other side."

Then he said that some of those squires who have old grudges against me have accused me of becoming senile or deranged, while others have started a whispering campaign saying that I am a witch -- and that the events in Tycanol Wood were part of a pagan rite. After all, they say, is it not well established that witches dance about naked beneath the oak trees? And does not Mistress Martha have a reputation of seeing strange things and having premonitions? And while we are about it, was she not on intimate terms with that fellow Joseph Harries, who died some years

Conduct Unbecoming

back? They probably got up to all sorts of despicable things in the privacy of the Plas..... and did she not visit Werndew many times over the years? It was not seemly, come to think of it, for a respectable widow woman to go visiting single gentlemen, let alone wizards, without a chaperone. And is she not, to this day, a great supporter of Shemi the Wizard of Werndew? And was she not far too close to that Patty Ellis and other disreputable people in town when she was younger? And then that Nightwalker on the mountain over 30 years ago -- she saw him more than any other, and he must surely have been the Devil. More than likely, she and Satan dance naked upon the moonlit mountain at the time of every full moon. And does she not, to this day, disappear up onto the mountain for hours on end and become invisible? Probably Satan is still there, and she meets him for debauchery and fornication, and takes instructions, and does his bidding in spreading wickedness in the world............

I was dismayed and even terrified by all this gossip as reported by Ioan, and I must have been as pale as a ghost at the end of it; but he, Catrin and James each roared with laughter, and said that these speculations about my private life were quite the most wonderful things they had heard for many a long year. "Write them in your diary, Martha," said Catrin, "as evidence that certain sections of our community have not progressed since the Dark Ages. If anybody believes any of that nonsense, he or she deserves to be shut away in a lunatic asylum!"

I did my best to laugh, but when Ioan had gone back to Brithdir after joining us for supper, I reported to Rose what was being said about me. I felt truly miserable and so, so tired; and I held onto her as she had held onto me in the past when she had been frightened by strange shadows or noises in the night. I did not admit it to her, but I feared that I might sink downwards into black despair again, for the first time in many years. But the dear child held me tight, and kissed me, and said: "*Mam-gu*, I will allow nobody to harm you. I love you very much. You are the warmest and kindest person on this earth, and if you have given Master Jones one small moment of happiness in a life of misery and coldness, you have done a good and noble thing. I will not condemn you for it. At the very worst, you have been indiscreet, and indiscretion does not come very high on my list of sins."

At that, I smiled, and wept, and decided that in spite of everything there was still enough love in the world to keep me afloat.

9. According to the Scriptures

27th June 1846

Today at midday I returned to the Plas without Rose, determined to face the music. When I arrived, the hay harvest was over and done with, and the hay ricks were up and thatched. I was glad to see my servants again, and I embraced each of them in turn and thanked them for keeping everything in good order during my absence. "No problem, Mistress," said Will. "You have trained us well, and you have told us often enough that nobody is indispensable."

Then, early in the afternoon Amos turned up at the Plas, having arrived back at Brynberian in mid-morning and having been told by his landlord, Master George Ifans, to get out of Tregwynt by noon. He had been informed by Master Ifans that he had been sacked in his absence from his post as pastor of the Brynberian Chapel for "lewd and immoral activities". That decision had been based entirely on the testimony of young Mary Roberts, who was a chapel member. There was to be no discussion, and no appeal. Amos was confused and angry, as well as being homeless, so I embraced him and tried to comfort him as best I could, and led him into the parlour where we could exchange news. In private, we again declared our love for one another, although it has to be said that the situation was not conducive to any great displays of passion. Then Bessie fetched him some food, for he looked as if he had not eaten for a week.

I told him everything about how the scandal had broken, and about the things that were now being said about us by our enemies. To cheer him up, I told him that perversely, our reputations appear to have been enhanced in certain quarters rather than damaged; but he would not accept that, and said that those he respected most were the members of his own congregation, whom he had betrayed and before whom he would now have to appear so as to seek forgiveness. "They must give me the right of appearing before them, Martha!" he declared. "Natural justice demands it. I must appear before the whole congregation, and prostrate myself if necessary, and throw myself on their mercy. If nothing else, I will discover whether the concept of Christian charity has any meaning for the people

According to the Scriptures

of Brynberian. The elders and deacons will be as fierce and unforgiving as the fathers of the Inquisition, but thank God that there is a degree of democracy in the Independent Chapels of Wales, and in the last resort the congregation as a whole will have to decide, having heard the evidence and having assessed the extent of my contrition, whether forgiveness is appropriate. Without that, I fear that I will never again be allowed back to the Lord's Table."

"Would that be so terrible, Amos? There are those who go through life without taking holy communion, and they seem happy enough."

"For me, it would be terrible, Martha. Remember that I have given my life to the service of the Lord, and that I actually believe in the things which I preach from pulpits and hilltops. Now, will you help me to compose a letter to the deacons?"

"Of course I will, *cariad*. I admire your bravery, and your faith, for you are asking to be cast into the lion's den."

So together we composed a letter to the deacons and elders of Capel Brynberian. It was very difficult to find a form of words which expressed contrition and asked for forgiveness without actually admitting debauchery and adultery, and there is no way that I would accept any form of wording that said, in effect, "I promise on pain of death never to perform the sexual act again, until the day I die." I said to Amos that whatever our future together might be, I wanted nothing to do with a Trappist monk. So I advised him simply to ask for a Big Meeting with the whole congregation, where Mary Roberts might make a public statement as to what she had witnessed in the wood, and where he might then give his account of what transpired between us. Then, I said, he could ask for Christian forgiveness on the basis that we all fail, at certain times in our lives, to resist temptation; and that according to the scriptures salvation is nonetheless still available for those who repent.

At last we were happy with the letter, and Amos wrote it out and signed it. He placed it into an envelope and I handed it to Gerallt for immediate delivery to the senior deacon, one Stephen Lloyd. When my servant had gone galloping off on his chestnut pony, Amos collapsed into a chair and looked utterly exhausted. "Well, that is done," he said. "Now Mary Roberts will have her pound of flesh."

That statement shook me to the core, and I said: "Amos! Whatever do you mean by that?"

According to the Scriptures

"I have not told you this before, Martha, but I have been plagued by Mary Roberts ever since I arrived at Capel Brynberian. She is a spinster, aged about thirty-five, who is a good faithful member of the chapel. I dare say that she has been disappointed in love in the past, and she is not the prettiest creature on God's earth, but she thinks she is in love with me. She writes me little notes, gives me gifts, and makes sure that at all our prayer meetings and Sunday services she is positioned prominently where I can see her. I have tried not to act cruelly towards her, but on a number of occasions I have had to reprimand her and ask her to leave me alone. She arranges "chance encounters" too, and I am sure that she follows me around whenever she gets the chance."

"Do you think that she followed you into the wood on the day of our indiscretion?"

"I am almost certain of it, Martha."

"Well, this changes everything, Amos. If you have been pestered by this woman, and if she has shown you no respect and infringed on your right to privacy, the strength of her testimony at the Big Meeting will be greatly diminished. You must be honest with the congregation, and seek to discredit her as an independent witness............"

"We are not talking about a court of law here, Martha. We are talking about a congregation of simple and uneducated people. I have no wish, either within or without the walls of a sanctified building, to do anything that might harm one of my flock."

"Amos Jones!" I exclaimed, with my temperature rising. "How can you speak in that way? Has Mary Roberts not harmed you enough? You do not have to set out to harm her in return -- but you must at least defend yourself like a man!"

"But if, in defending myself, Martha, I harm another who is perhaps more vulnerable than I, what then? I think I know what Christ would have done in these circumstances."

"Amos, do you want to be a real man or a feeble saint?" I shouted. "And do you have no self-respect? And has it not occurred to you that in allowing her free rein you will be hurting me?"

He did not answer any of those questions, and it was clear that he had never seen me before in an angry mood. There was frost in the air, and we scowled at one another. I thought that Master Amos Jones was being very irritating indeed. I had to do something to reduce the tension, so I

According to the Scriptures

said that I would go to the kitchen and make some more tea. I stretched out that process for a good five minutes, making Bessie very exasperated in the process since she was trying to lay up the table for supper.

I was calmer when I returned to the parlour, and while I poured out two cups of steaming tea I managed to find the good grace to apologize to Amos for my hot temper. "No no," he smiled wearily. "I deserved a lashing from your tongue, Martha. Thank God for your strength, since I am feeling very tired today."

"That is not surprising, Amos. Since riding into Brynberian this morning you have, after all, been sacked from your position as pastor, and evicted from your lodgings without any prior warning. That is quite enough trouble for one day. Now, shall we change the subject? I want to know all about your journey, and about your old mother. How did you find her?"

Before Amos replied, I saw the pain in his eyes. "I am afraid, Martha, that she died the day after I arrived in Brecon. She was so ill when I went up to her bedroom that she hardly recognized me. But she smiled, and that is something for me to remember. I am not sure that she heard any of the things that I said to her as I sat at her bedside. I held her hand and prayed for her throughout the night, but at last her pulse weakened, and God took her away........"

His voice cracked, and I saw that there were tears in his eyes. I went and sat next to him, and put my arm around him. "Oh, my poor *cariad!*" I whispered. "I am so very sorry to hear all of this. And on top of everything else that has happened. No wonder that you are tired. Did you love her very much?"

"I did, Martha. She was a very wonderful woman, and she meant everything to me. I was a single child, and she devoted her life to me while my father was away doing the Lord's work. But she was old, and I think she had a happy life. Her housemaid said that she knew I would come to visit her at the end, and that she kept herself going until I was there to hold her hand. And then, in a perfectly peaceful way, she just let go of life."

I sat with Amos, held his hand, and rested my head on his shoulder. He wanted to talk about his mother, and her funeral in Brecon, and about childhood memories, and it would have been crass of me to have asked him to talk of anything else. As the evening progressed, he perked up a

214

little, and he enjoyed a good supper. Then we packed him off to stay with Betsi and Ioan at Brithdir, since in the circumstances it would not have been good for either him or myself if he had been given a room at the Plas. They have said that he can have a room there until matters are resolved; but after his disgrace his status is now not much better than that of a vagrant, and like me he will have to cope with the disapprobation of a sizeable part of the community.

ΩΩΩΩΩΩΩΩΩΩΩΩ

4th July 1846

Amos has received a reply from the deacons and elders of Capel Brynberian, short and to the point, agreeing to a Big Meeting on the tenth day of July. They said that they will not reconsider his dismissal as pastor, since he has chosen not to dispute the allegations made against him by Mary Roberts. Adultery having therefore been effectively admitted, they said, re-employment was out of the question. I thought that more than a little outrageous, since they were not paying poor Amos a wage anyway. But they said that after much prayer they had received divine guidance that the congregation as a whole should consider the matter of his membership and his excommunication. Divine guidance indeed! I know full well, from my conversations with Amos and from reading the chapel rules for myself, that they have to follow the course of action laid down. And if the Lord provided guidance in the writing of the rule in the first place, he surely has no further part to play in the matter.

    Amos has been back and forth to the Plas every day. He finds this waiting extremely difficult, and he is more than a little apprehensive. I have spent a great deal of time in his company, and we have sat and talked for long hours in the garden and in the orchard. I have encouraged him to help out on the farm, and it has been good to see how well he gets on with Will, Gomer and Gerallt. I tell him that if he can show me that he has green fingers, I might employ him as a gardener! We have been trying to feed him up, since he appears to have neglected himself during his

According to the Scriptures

expedition to Brecon, and now and then we have sent him off alone on long walks over the mountain in the hope that he might find peace. Our therapy seems to be working, for his shoulders are less tense than they were, and I swear that his face is less lined. He is also discovering, thank God, that his disgrace is by no means the end of the world, for people still smile at him and greet him in the street, and indeed his reputation for devotion to his flock, and his compassion for all who are in need, have stood him in good stead. He is still, when all is said and done, a good man. Many good Christian folk have considered his virtues against his vices, and having weighed him in the balance they have found him to be only a little less saintly than he was before he met me in the wood.

That having been said, I am still very worried about the outcome of the Big Meeting.

There is absolutely no doubting Amos's courage, for he is brave almost to the point of foolhardiness, and he has spent most of his life preaching in the open air, facing down thugs and sceptics, and coping with physical hardship. He has been beaten up and sent packing on more occasions than he cares to remember, and still comes up smiling and praising the Lord. I am lost in love and admiration, and I suppose that his extraordinary resilience is one of his most endearing characteristics. But there is one thing that I do not admire, and that is his instinct for self-abasement and even self-sacrifice. For a start he wants to take full responsibility for what happened in the wood. I will not let him do that, and I have repeated to him that if blame lies anywhere it lies with me. If necessary, I will say that publicly before a hostile congregation. Then he is almost obsessed with the fact that he has committed adultery, and will not contemplate any mention in a public forum of his wife's frigidity or failure to provide him with either loving support or a warm home. He says that she is harmed enough by his betrayal, and that he will not harm her further; and when I argue about that (as I try to do frequently) he will not budge. He is a very stubborn fellow, this Master Jones. And finally he will do nothing to diminish the reputation (if she has one) of that mean-spirited and vengeful woman called Mary Roberts, who followed him and spied on us and then started a hateful campaign of whispers and innuendoes throughout the district. He says that when she speaks before the congregation he will not challenge her, or mention her unwelcome attentions, or seek to belittle her in any way.

According to the Scriptures

So if the man whom I love will not defend himself before his accusers, it is down to me. Amos does not want me to attend. He says that he will face his Inquisition without assistance from anybody, and that this is just a private matter to be settled between people of goodwill who happen all to be members of Capel Brynberian. A private matter? Private no more, I fear, since the whole district knows about the meeting, and hundreds will be there for the entertainment. And people of goodwill? There is more good will in the Black Lion on a Saturday night than there is among those frosty deacons and elders, and those who follow their lead. And I will be there, come hell or high water, to say what I have to say, even if I leave with my reputation in tatters. There is not much left of it anyway.

And if the Brynberian deacons can make their plans, so can I.

ΩΩΩΩΩΩΩΩΩΩΩΩ

11th July 1846

The Big Meeting in Brynberian took place yesterday, and it turned out to be considerably more exciting than the normal Thursday evening prayer meeting.

It was scheduled to start at eight o'clock -- late enough for small farmers and labourers to finish their evening milkings and other tasks and to grab a bite of supper before heading for the chapel. I saw nothing of Amos during the day, and he travelled up to Brynberian with Betsi and Ioan in the Brithdir chaise. It was just as well that we did not meet beforehand, for we would surely have infected one another with irritability and doubt. So rather as a bride and groom keep apart on the day of a marriage, we each pottered about beneath our separate roofs, each supported and encouraged by those around us, and each perspiring and mulling endlessly over options and possibilities. For myself, I was glad Amos was out of the way, for I was very glum and ill-tempered, and had to apologise several times to Rose and Myfanwy, who were both doing their best to keep me calm. I knew that I would speak in the chapel, and I went

According to the Scriptures

over my words again and again. I tried to eat some breakfast and lunch, but could not. At last, at the end of a day in which every minute felt like an hour, Will shouted up the stairs: "Mistress Martha! Time to go!" And off we went in a convoy, using almost every wheeled vehicle we had, and leaving only Blodwen behind to keep an eye on the Plas and the animals.

As we splashed across Trefelin ford and clattered along the lane past Cilgwyn Church, it soon became apparent that the Big Meeting was going to be very big indeed, for there was a constant stream of traffic. There were people in carriages and coaches, people in carts and on gambos, people riding horses and even donkeys, and many more on foot. They were all dressed up in their Sunday best, stiffly starched and with shining faces. I recognized most of them, but tried to avoid eye contact for fear that I might be turned to stone. In any case my heart sank, and I thought: "Oh my God! Every adult from within a radius of ten miles is going to be there! And almost all of them will be straining to hear the salacious details of what went on in Tycanol Wood! And what is more, they will all be there to relish the ritual humiliation of Jones Minor Prophet and Mistress Martha Morgan, who always were too happy and too big for their boots.............

We reached Brynberian at about seven-thirty, to be greeted at the chapel gate by Ioan. Amos was already settled into the chapel, he said, and Betsi was in the back row of the pews keeping places for us. There were people milling about everywhere, jostling to get into the chapel, wandering all over the graveyard, and climbing up outside the windows so as to get a better view of the proceedings. Some even had ladders with them. The deacons were trying to admit members only, but that was a hopeless task, and those who were most determined simply refused to be turned away. Outside there were some groups of people singing hymns, and there were two groups of demonstrators waving placards and chanting. One group was shouting "An end to fornication and adultery!" and the other countered with "Let him who is free of sin cast the first stone!" and "Martha and the Prophet! Martha and the Prophet!" Oh dear, I thought, this is going to be more like a gladiatorial contest than a prayer meeting, for reverence had clearly been abandoned long since.

I went inside with Rose and Daisy and her husband George Havard Medical, and Ioan led us to the seats that had been reserved. One or two of the deacons smiled at me as I entered, and one or two others scowled. Once

According to the Scriptures

seated, I bowed my head and tried to pray, but that was near impossible with all the noise and jostling going on around me. So I simply asked God to save Amos and not to abandon me, and resigned myself to my fate. Rose sat on one side of me, and Daisy on the other, and I thanked the Lord that they were with me. I saw Amos at the front of the chapel, and he turned his head and gave me a little smile. Was he, I wondered, as calm as he looked?

So the Big Meeting started, thirty minutes late. It was chaotic from the beginning. The four senior deacons -- Stephen Lloyd, Thomas Jones, John Thomas, and Jacob Jobbins -- tried to open the proceedings with prayers, but that was a shambles since there was so much chanting from outside. Then Master Lloyd, acting as spokesman, climbed into the pulpit and announced that it was the duty of the deacons and elders to uphold virtue, to denounce sin generally and to condemn "sins of the flesh" in particular. He announced the decision to eject Amos from his living, and then asked if Sister Mary Roberts would come forward to give witness as to the reasons. There was no reply, and after a minute or two of turned heads and whispers it had to be concluded that she was not present. No matter, said Master Lloyd; and he then proceeded to recommend to the members of the congregation that they should "cast out" Pastor Amos Jones from the church into the darkness of night since he had decided of his own free will to "inhabit the domain of the devil."

Immediately there was uproar, with the crowd shouting that Amos should be allowed to speak. At first Master Lloyd refused, but at last he had to accede. So Amos stood up, turned round and faced the massive crowd in front of him. "Into the pulpit! Into the pulpit!" shouted the crowd, and they would not be quiet until Master Lloyd gave way and allowed Amos -- no doubt for the last time -- to stand in the hallowed place to which he had grown so accustomed. He looked very striking indeed, strong and upright and good-looking, and fashionably turned out in Ioan's Sunday best. He stood still and said nothing at all until the chapel was as quiet as the grave. The old devil, I thought; even at the greatest moment of crisis in his life, he still knows how to work a crowd. I could hardly suppress a grin, in spite of the gravity of the situation.

So Jones Minor Prophet spoke for about twenty minutes, without notes and without a single slip. He talked movingly and with great dignity, accepting that he had made one error of judgement in his life, for which he

According to the Scriptures

now repented and for which he had already spent many nights in prayer. But he did not know exactly what he was accused of, he said, since Mary Roberts had not met him face to face and since she had apparently refused to come to this meeting. Nobody doubted, he said, that she had been the person who had started the rumours and spread the gossip about Mistress Martha Morgan and himself. "What slander has she spread?" he pleaded. "I do not know, because she will not tell me. And what other wickedness has she committed? It may not be a crime, but is it not sinful and cruel to spy upon a man and a woman who have a right to their privacy and a right to be unmolested and untroubled by scandalous gossip? Is it not a sin to take pleasure in reporting the misdemeanours of others? What sort of a world would we inhabit, my dear brothers and sisters, if we all spied upon each other, and claimed to be virtuous in so doing, and reported each other's little misdeeds and moments of weakness to the deacons and the constables and the magistrates? But I bear Sister Roberts no ill-will, and in my heart I have forgiven her, for she lives in sin and struggles for salvation, just like the rest of us."

Then he turned to face the deacons and elders in the front row of the pews. In a voice which I thought remarkably calm and controlled, he said: "You have judged me already, gentlemen, without giving me the privilege of a hearing, and you have taken away my living. I can still preach, to those who may wish to listen to me and who may seek salvation, but I am no longer a pastor, and I feel the loss of that privilege as deeply as I might feel the loss of my right arm." Then he turned again to the congregation. "I turn once more to you, my beloved brothers and sisters," he said. "I have sought to serve you all to the best of my ability, with God's help. I repent before you, having already been vilified and humiliated. I ask for your forgiveness and your love. And my last point is this. I leave you to judge where sin lies, brothers and sisters, and it is now for you to determine where, on the scale of things, I have offended against God and the good name of this chapel congregation by giving love to a good woman and receiving love in return."

By now he was as white as a sheet, and shaking with emotion. He descended from the pulpit, holding on desperately to the handrail. I thought he was going to pass out, and come crashing down. I could not look, and covered my eyes. But at last Daisy squeezed my hand, and I opened my eyes again and saw that he had regained his seat in the front pew. There

According to the Scriptures

was dead silence, apart from sniffles and much blowing of noses. I saw that many tears were being spilt in the congregation.

Nobody broke the silence, but at last the tension became unbearable, and I could not resist leaping to my feet. "For you gentlemen who are deacons and elders in this House of God, I have to say that I cannot be still and silent for another moment. What is happening here today is a gratuitous humiliation of a good and holy man, and an outrage committed against simple human decency and dignity! This man........."

"Mistress Martha, you may not speak!" shouted Deacon Lloyd. "You are not a member of this congregation and you do not have my permission!" Then, the silence having been well and truly broken, there was uproar, with the congregation chanting "Let her speak! Let her speak!" After several minutes of pandemonium, the deacons consulted and had no option but to agree. So I continued.

"I want to say just this to all those whom Reverend Jones calls his brothers and sisters. This gentleman is the purest and most saintly man I have ever met. I dare say that he has spread more love and kindness in this world than the rest of us beneath this roof put together. But to describe him as "a happily married pastor", as I have heard him described, is to assume that happiness and marriage are one and the same thing. Many of us beneath this roof know that not to be the case. I will say no more than that about his personal life. But I will say, for anybody who wishes to listen, that I love this man with all my heart........"

Then I had to stop, for emotion was getting the better of me. Daisy took my hand again, and squeezed it, and gave me the strength to continue. "What happened beneath the oak trees in Tycanol Wood was sinful according to the Bible and the canons of the church, and you gentlemen who are elders may in your smug security call me seductress, fornicator and adulteress. Yet I will not apologize for what I did. I take full responsibility for it, and I will make my own peace with God. I led Master Jones on, and the blame is all mine. All mine! Punish me as you will, gentlemen, if you feel that you have not already had your pound of flesh............" Then I fear that I really did break down in tears, and had to resume my seat while Rose and Daisy tried to console me.

So far as I recall, there was another tense silence, followed by animated whispered conversations all over the church The deacons and elders consulted for a few minutes. Then Deacon Jobbins stood up and called

According to the Scriptures

for silence. "Brothers and sisters," he announced in stentorian tones, "this is a truly terrible matter, the like of which this church has never before encountered since the day of its foundation in the Year of our Lord 1690. In the past, we have had to deal with members of our congregation who have fallen from grace, but never has this happened to one of our own pastors. The sin of Pastor Amos Jones is therefore compounded, since he has betrayed not only the holy name of God, but this church and this people. He, of all men, should have known where the boundary lies between human frailty and the gross blackness of sin. Master Jones has said that he recognizes his fall from grace, and that he repents his sin, but we do not see in his person, his words or his demeanour true repentance and mortification. Indeed, he sits there silent and impassive even as I speak, with no sign of guilt on his face, and no awareness of the wrath of the Almighty. And as for Mistress Martha, she has admitted her part in this act of gross indecency, and has sought to take the blame for it, but she has signally failed to ask us for forgiveness, or to show us true repentance. Our instinct for tolerance is limited, much as we might wish it otherwise, for no church can exist without discipline, and our rules are laid out in the church governing document of 1690. Let Master John Thomas read from it, brothers and sisters!"

So Master John Thomas read the following from a big book, in tones fit to signal the end of the world: *"Rule Nine: Of Scandalous Persons guilty of gross Acts of Immorality. If any member fall into any gross acts of sin, as swearing, lying, drunkenness, fornication, covetousness, extortion, or the like, and it is known and publicly spread abroad to the great scandal and reproach of religion, and of the holy name of God, his Church, and people; the said offender so charged, the church must send one or two brethren to him to instruct him to come before the congregation. When he doth appear, his charge is to be laid before him, and the witnesses called; and after he has made his defence, and said all he hath to say, and the congregation finds him guilty, then there is only one censure to pass upon him, to the end that he may be brought to unfeigned repentance. Thus the name of God shall be cleared, the honour of Christ and his church vindicated, and the congregation shall manifest to the world its just indignation against notorious offence and wickedness. Though the offending person be penitent, yet because his sin is open and scandalous, he ought to be cast out for the honour of Christ and the church, and his just*

According to the Scriptures

punishment shall be the ordinance of excommunion..............."
He paused for effect, with such tension in the air as I have never
experienced, before delivering the coup de grâce. He thundered out the
last sentence of Rule Nine: *"If the offending person shall be a pastor, so is
his offence compounded, and he shall never again be readmitted to
communion no matter what remorse he may show during the rest of his
life."*

Then he sat down, and in a terrible silence his colleague Master
Stephen Lloyd got to his feet and climbed into the pulpit. As he did so, his
boots squeaked and his heavy footsteps on bare boards echoed around the
chapel. He turned and for a full minute he looked into the white faces and
terrified eyes of the congregation, to right and left and straight ahead,
and then up in the balcony. This was his moment of ultimate authority,
and his opportunity to make his mark on history. He relished it in a
manner that made me sick in my stomach. He fixed Amos with his gaze,
and pointed to him with his right hand. He spoke in a sepulchral voice,
with all those present hardly daring to breathe, and with fear dripping
from the rafters: "Therefore, in the name of our Lord Jesus Christ and
before this Congregation, we find you guilty of adultery. We pronounce and
declare you, Amos Jones, excommunicate and shut out of the Communion of
all faithful Christians. And may Almighty God, who by His Holy Spirit
has appointed this sentence for removing of scandal and offence out of the
Church, and for reducing of sinners to a sense of their sins and danger, make
this censure to all the good ends for which it was ordained. And that your
Heart may be filled with fear and dread, that you may be recovered out of
the same and out of the power of the Devil, and that your Soul may be
saved, and that others may be warned by your sad example not to sin nor
continue in sin so presumptuously............"

"Nonsense, sir!" came a shout from somewhere up in the balcony. I
recognized the voice straight away. It was Shemi Wizard. There was a
considerable commotion as he went to the staircase, descended and strode
past the door towards the pulpit. With his wild and bushy beard, and
with a stout staff in his hand, he looked like Moses just down off the
mountain. "Stuff and nonsense!" he declaimed. "Mistress Jones is dead.
She died upon the fourteenth day of June, horribly scalded by hot water in
her own kitchen. Whatever sin Pastor Jones might have been guilty of on
the fifteenth day, it was certainly not adultery. Further, I venture to

suggest, sir, that your excommunication is null and void, since you have not heard the one independent witness to this supposed indecent act, namely Sister Mary Roberts. Why is she not here today to make her accusations to the face of Pastor Jones and before this congregation? Neither have you sent one or two brethren to talk to him. Neither, sir, have you sought the opinion of your congregation, and nor have you established the difference between fact and fantasy. You have therefore not followed the very rules upon which you place such store!"

There was uproar in the church, with people cheering and stamping their feet. Shemi started to enjoy himself, and waved his staff in the air before confronting the row of deacons. He waited until it was quiet again, and then continued: "And where, gentlemen, is your Christian charity? I see precious little of it, either in those old words written down a century and a half ago when old Oliver Cromwell was still warm in his grave, or in your mean-spirited and vicious humiliation of these two good people. You should cringe before your vengeful God and whine for his forgiveness! I know your Bible as I know the Koran and the Kabbalah and many other ancient books beside, and in its pages does it not say *"let him who is without sin cast the first stone"*? You have pointed at Pastor Jones. Let me therefore also point the finger!" Again he paused for effect, with none of those present in the pews daring to blink. He slowly raised his arm and pointed at the senior deacon and then at the others. "Master Stephen Lloyd!" he thundered. "Did you not in the summer of 1805 fornicate with a certain married lady of our mutual acquaintance in the hayfield of Hafod Tydfil? Thomas Jones, did you not steal a bag of turnips as a young man from the Squire of Henllys, and place the blame on a vagrant named Billy Wilson, and cause him to be transported to the colonies, and to die an innocent man upon a convict ship? John Thomas, did you not sow your wild oats not once, not twice, but thrice following your marriage to your late-lamented wife? And Jacob Jobbins, you who take it upon yourself to act as God's messenger and to represent the conscience of all those here today beneath this roof, did you not, at the age of twenty-nine, travel to Pembroke and try to kill a fellow called Tom Fancy with a knife, leaving him terribly injured for the rest of his miserable life? Hypocrites! Hypocrites, all four of you! Mean-spirited, miserable fellows who revel in your own petty power and who have forgotten that there are such things in this world as beauty, and love, and forgiveness! Do you deny the charges

According to the Scriptures

which I have placed before you? If so, place your hands upon your precious Bible, each of you in turn, and swear your innocence before God and this mighty congregation! Do it now! Do it now!" he bellowed, with a voice that almost brought the ceiling crashing down. The four deacons sat still, each one as white as a sheet.

Then the whole place was transformed by disorder, with cheering and clapping, and laughter on all sides, and from the balcony, and even from outside on the forecourt and in the graveyard. "Three cheers for Mistress Martha and the Prophet!" shouted somebody, and there were three roaring cheers. "And three cheers for Master Jenkins the Wizard!" shouted somebody else. Again the cheers reverberated to the rafters. I realized afterwards that that was no doubt the first time for a practitioner of the black arts to be applauded and cheered in Brynberian Chapel. The crowd streamed out into the cool night air, and the occasion ended with a carnival atmosphere, with torches sending sparks towards the stars and with revellers dancing round the headstones in the graveyard. Amos and I were dragged by laughing crowds out into the fresh air and carried shoulder-high three times round the chapel.

At the end of all of that, Amos and I were utterly exhausted. I was ecstatic, but he was having to come to terms with the sudden news of his wife's death, and he did not know what to think or how to behave. We settled onto our assorted vehicles illuminated with candle lanterns and blazing torches, and joined a mighty throng of people on the lane back towards Cilgwyn and Newport. People were singing and laughing, and the hubbub of animated conversation could no doubt be heard from the summit of Carningli. As we clattered along I wondered whether the angels of the mountain were laughing or crying, since the events of the evening must certainly have set back the cause of Christianity by a century or two. But then I thought that on balance the angels were probably laughing; and the more I thought about it, the more I came to realize that the cause of Christianity might actually have been advanced. In what was supposed to be a straightforward casting out, bigotry and hypocrisy had been exposed by Shemi, who was of course the hero of the hour; and that stupid rule book from 1690 will, I dare say, now be thrown onto the bonfire by the Capel Brynberian faithful who have shown themselves to be remarkably fair-minded. And as for the four deacons, whose reputations are now sunk without trace, they will have to make their peace with God.

According to the Scriptures

I suppose that once we were back down into the *cwm*, we should all have retired to the Plas for a wild party; and indeed that is what the younger ones and the servants did, together with Shemi and Sian and many of our neighbours. But I could not keep my eyes open, and went straight to bed. Before doing that, I kissed my beloved Amos goodnight, and Ioan took him to his room at Brithdir and to his widower's bed.

ΩΩΩΩΩΩΩΩΩΩΩ

13th July 1846

Two days have passed since the dramatic events at Capel Brynberian, and I have to admit that for most of that time I have been wandering about like an idiot. I must have used up more of my resources of energy than I realized at the time, and I suppose that is one of the penalties of old age. Yesterday I rose very late, and spent most of the day snoozing in the shade of the garden, while Rose and Bessie dealt with a string of well-wishers who wanted to congratulate me on a successful outcome and to gloat over the discomfiture of the deacons. Well, I was in no mood for gloating, and Bessie told me at supper that some of the gloaters were those who had refused to acknowledge her in the street just a few days earlier. People are fickle indeed, but in this case I will not complain.

I have also gathered from my servants that as a result of all this gossip about my antics in the wood with Jones Minor Prophet, and the infamous events at Capel Brynberian, I am not considered any longer to be the respectable Mistress of a fine estate, but simply as an eccentric old woman with an unusual and amazing appetite for sex. So I dare say I have lost something in respect and respectability. Again, I am in no position to complain, since it is better to be considered eccentric than wicked, and since the community at large appears to place some value upon the entertainment that I have provided. But I hereby declare, in the pages of my diary, that I have had enough of entertaining people, and that I will henceforth be old and graceful.

My dear Amos came to see me today, having spent the whole of

According to the Scriptures

yesterday in prayerful retreat at Brithdir. We met on the driveway on a bright and blustery afternoon with big white clouds tumbling over Carningli, and we talked as we walked about in the newly-cut hayfields. He told me that when he got home from the Capel Brynberian "casting out" service, he had been too tired even to take his clothes off, and that he had fallen into bed and slept for fifteen hours. So he too is feeling his age, I thought. I asked him about Shemi's revelations, and what he made of them, for they have been exercising me considerably, and make me more amazed the more I think of them. When, and how, did Shemi learn about the date of Hannah's death and the manner ot it? And how on earth did he know about the sins committed, but never acknowledged, by the four deacons? When I asked about this, Amos laughed, and said: "Why, Martha, you have seen enough of wizards to know that you should never ask about such things. I know Shemi very well, and I have the greatest respect for his integrity. He is a true *dyn hysbys*. If he says these things, they are true -- take it from me."

"But Amos, have you never wondered whether he might have been giving a theatrical performance at Capel Brynberian, or simply throwing out wild speculations in the hope that they might be more or less true?"

"Not for a moment, Martha. Remember that I am a prophet myself, but my powers are piffling as compared with those enjoyed -- or endured -- by Shemi. He does not say things unless he is certain about them. And you have special powers yourself, which you could have developed to a greater extent had you been minded to study more and give freer rein to your intuition. Did you not tell me that you studied quite seriously many years ago under Joseph Harries, the most famous of wizards in these parts?"

"You are quite right, *cariad*," I replied. "I must trust more and think less. So if this is all true, where does this leave you? A month has now passed since Hannah's death, and she must by now be in her grave. I trust that she had a decent burial. But why had you received no notification of it? Did she and her family not know where you were?"

"They must have had a rough idea, Martha, and they did indeed write several letters addressed to *"Reverend Amos Jones, Brynberian in Pembrokeshire"* but never, sadly, delivered to me. Ioan kindly offered to investigate this matter on my behalf yesterday. He rode up to Brynberian and spoke to Mistress Ifans at my former lodgings. She admitted, upon

According to the Scriptures

being pressed, that letters for me had found their way to Tregwynt after the breaking of the scandalous story about our liaison in the woods, but she said she was so angry and upset about the whole business that she simply said to the fellows delivering them that I had gone off to Brecon and would probably never return. So I dare say that they all got sent back again to those who had sent them. I still do not know who they might have been -- perhaps some of Hannah's distant relatives or her neighbours."

Amos was really quite upset about all of this, for he saw his ignorance as a dereliction of duty, and I had to embrace him and encourage him to accept that he was simply the victim of circumstances and that he had absolutely nothing to feel guilty about.

"But I do feel guilt, Martha," he sighed. "Guilt about what happened in the wood between us -- even if it was not technically adultery -- and then more guilt about the fact that I fled from the scandal to Brecon. If I had not been in Brecon, I would have received those letters, and I could have immediately set off for Radnor so as to oversee the funeral arrangements and give succour to those who grieved. I might have even grieved myself.........."

"Really, Amos, this is preposterous! This is mortification and repentance taken to absurd lengths! I dare say that self-flagellation comes next! I do not think you have ever fled from anything in your life, and that is one of the many reasons why I love you. Let me remind you that you set off for Brecon before the scandal broke, and at a time when we both assumed that the events in the woods were strictly a matter for you and me. You went because your mother was ill, and you had to deal with her death while you were away. You had quite enough grieving to do as it was. You could not possibly have behaved in any other way, *cariad*, and I would be grateful if you would refrain from any further talk on the matter."

At last Amos did manage to laugh, and he held his hands up in a gesture of surrender. "I give up, Mistress Martha," he grinned. "You are right, as ever! Now then, do you think that Bessie might rustle up a nice cup of tea and a slice or two of *bara brith*? All this guilt makes one hungry and thirsty!"

So with Bessie promising to organize refreshments for us in the garden, Amos and I sat down together on my favourite bench and cuddled

According to the Scriptures

and kissed for a little while. That was very pleasant, for I had all but given up hope that such activities would ever be possible again; and in truth it was even more pleasant because I did not care whether we were observed by anybody else. We managed to talk of things other than adultery and scandal, and although the conversation did come back more than once to the events in Capel Brynberian I am pleased to say that at last we could laugh rather than wince with horror as we recalled the occasion.

Then my dear sweet granddaughter Rose appeared, carrying a tray of refreshments, and upon our invitation she sat with us in the shade, as we all three nibbled and sipped, and chatted and laughed. Suddenly we heard the clatter of hooves and the rattle of wheels on the driveway, and we knew that a four-horse coach was approaching. I could not resist looking over the garden wall to see whose coach it might be, and saw at once that the snorting beasts were black and magnificent, and could only have come from the stable of Plas Llanychaer. My heart sank. For Master Wilmot Gwynne and Mistress Delilah to arrive unannounced at the Plas did not bode well, and their visit could only be related to the scandal involving Amos and myself, and the events at Capel Brynberian. "Oh dear," I moaned to Rose and Amos. "We are blessed with a visit from the Master and Mistress of our estate. That means trouble."

I need not have worried, for when I greeted them, and they stepped down from the coach they were both grinning like Cheshire cats. "Why, Martha," boomed the Squire, "how good it is to see you! And Master Jones and Miss Rose too! And all looking so well! I trust that you are, all three, feeling as well as you look?"

"Yes indeed, Wilmot," said I. "Speaking for myself, tired but otherwise well, after the excitement of recent days. A very warm welcome to you. We have been sitting in the garden, drinking tea and eating *bara brith*. Will you join us?"

"How can we resist, Martha?" laughed Delilah, with her large bosom wobbling like a jelly. "If the cake is one of Bessie's, it will have been worth the visit for that alone. I always think that good food is one of life's little pleasures. Would you not agree?"

I had to agree, while thinking that Delilah might have benefited from a little less *bara brith* in her diet, and Rose ran off to the kitchen to organize extra supplies whilst Amos and I accompanied our guests back to

According to the Scriptures

the garden. Delilah, scented like a field of lavender, took Amos's arm, and I walked with Wilmot. We explored the greenery for a little while, talking of flowers and shrubs and vegetables, and then Rose and Bessie delivered extra supplies of refreshments and went on their way.

In spite of my own animated conversation with the Master of the estate I could not help noticing how natural and easy was the flow of chatter and laughter between Amos and Delilah. I had forgotten that already, after less than a year in residence at Plas Llanychaer, the Gwynne family has not only settled in well but has also established many happy links with my own circle of friends and family members. Delilah, for a start, is very friendly with Daisy and has clearly visited her a number of times in Newport. Rose has been to Llanychaer several times, and greatly enjoys the company of those who now occupy her old home. Then Daisy's new husband George Havard Medical is on excellent terms with both Amos and Shemi Wizard; and I know that both Delilah and Wilmot have heard Amos preach, both in Swansea some years back and then more recently in Fishguard, and have provided him with hospitality at Plas Llanychaer; and finally I am aware that Shemi has visited Llanychaer several times at Wilmot's behest in order to treat one of his black mares and in order to provide medication for his own severe breathing problems. Wheels within wheels, I thought. I have been so preoccupied with my own difficulties, and with those of my sister Elen and my son Brynach, that I have failed to notice that those around me have been living their own lives and have probably exchanged much interesting information as the months have passed. So, I thought, there is not much that Wilmot and Delilah do not know about Amos and me.

So it transpired, and when Wilmot and I had finished talking of finances, the size of the harvest and other estate matters, the conversation at last turned to the events at Capel Brynberian. I thought that there might be at least some hint of disapproval from Wilmot and Delilah, if not relating to the pantomime in the chapel then at least to the events in Ty Canol Wood, but no -- they were both thoroughly entertained by those happenings, and Wilmot gurgled, with intermittent loud guffaws, that he had not been so royally entertained for many a long year.

I was a little worried by that, and said: "Well, Wilmot, I am grateful that you are not one of those who will cast stones at Amos and me for what has happened. We, too, are learning to laugh about the whole

According to the Scriptures

saga, but in all honesty it was not all that funny at the time........."

"Come come, Martha. I quite understand that the casting out service was a truly terrible matter, but surely your liaison in the woods must have been a very funny business indeed, and well worth the subsequent trouble?"

At that I think I must have blushed while Amos turned as white as spindrift snow, and Delilah jumped to our rescue. "Now then, husband," she scolded, "you are a very coarse fellow, and must learn to choose your words more carefully in polite company. What transpired between Martha and Amos in the wood may have been very beautiful and even enjoyable, but "funny" is certainly not the right word. Kindly apologize at once."

"Yes yes, my love," he said, rolling his eyes. "I must remember that this is Cilgwyn and not Gorseinon. I am sorry, my friends -- no offence meant, and I hope none taken. As for the business in the chapel, I should like to have been there. Of course I knew about it in advance, since the talk in our district was of nothing else, but not being a religious sort of fellow, and not being local, I thought that my attendance would not be appropriate."

"That was very considerate of you, Wilmot," said Amos. "On the other hand your presence would not have led to a black mark against your name, since I dare say that three-quarters of those present were not from the regular congregation at all."

Then Delilah looked me in the eye, and said: "There is one great mystery that has puzzled Wilmot and me over the last couple of days. Our friend Shemi Wizard was the hero of the hour. He is not a man for churches, and yet, by all accounts, there he was, fully prepared to do battle with the forces of darkness. Why was he there? Who asked him to come? Would that, Martha, have been anything to do with you?"

That caught me somewhat by surprise. One has to keep certain things out of the public domain, so I feigned innocence and said: "Now why on earth should you think that, Delilah? I will say nothing on the matter, except to pronounce that it is incumbent upon all of us to do what we can for our friends. Would you not agree?"

ΩΩΩΩΩΩΩΩΩΩΩΩ

According to the Scriptures

16th July 1846

Just as I was becoming used to having Amos here as company, and was beginning to enjoy the experience, he has gone rushing off again. I suppose it was inevitable that he would have to go off to Radnor at some stage, in order to pay his last respects at the grave of his late wife, but yesterday he received a letter from an attorney in that little place informing him of his wife's death and reminding him that he had a house and other matters to take care of. In truth, Amos is such an unworldly fellow that I am sure he had forgotten that he was a man of property. Indeed, I was happy to remind him that he is a more substantial property owner than I, and that he would make a fine catch for an old widow like me who might be looking for a husband. He found that very entertaining, and said that one day he might well preach a sermon on the chimera of wealth and status.

So today off he went on that horrid horse of his, intent upon the disposal of the house and its contents, if Hannah's relatives have not already stripped the place bare. Before he went, I asked him whether he had thought that he might keep the house and even contemplate moving back to Radnor himself.

"If I did that, Martha, and asked you to marry me and move back to Radnor with me, what would your reply be?"

"You know, Amos, that I would have to decline." I replied. "I love you dearly, but you know that I can never leave the Plas. I would die of *hiraeth* within a week of leaving. Besides, I still have Rose to think of, and an estate to run even if I am no longer the owner of it."

"Answered exactly as I knew you would, Martha. That decides it. I will sell the place and then hire a wagon to transport my goods and chattels, such as they may be, from Radnor to here. Then, with money in my pocket, I will find a place to rent. Perhaps you will help me in that regard?"

"I will see what I can do, my dear Reverend Jones," said I, with a twinkle in my eye. "I am sure we will find you a space somewhere." And we left it at that. We embraced as I whispered in his ear that he must return soon -- very soon -- before anything else happens in this topsy-turvy life of mine.

With Amos gone and with the prospect of more lonely days

According to the Scriptures

stretching out before me, I realized that I had not visited my cave of late, and neither had I thanked the angels of the mountain for the good fortune which had recently saved me from spending the rest of my life as a disreputable, despised and bitter old crone. I told Bessie that I was minded to take a walk, and she said: "Very good, Mistress. Take the opportunity while you can. You have had a hard time of it lately, and the summit wind will surely cool your brow and refresh your spirit. The Irish will be here soon, looking for work on the corn harvest, and once that starts you will have no time to think of anything else for a month or more. Off you go then, but don't be late back. I have a rather special salmon pie for supper."

With my walking boots on my feet and a shawl around my shoulders to protect against the keen breeze, I set off up the track from the farmyard, but I had not gone two hundred yards when I glanced back and saw a female figure hurrying up the driveway from the Dolrannog Road. She saw me and waved, and I waved back. Then she shouted: "Martha! Martha! Come quick!" There was nothing for it but to turn and retrace my steps, and as I drew closer I could see that the visitor was none other than my old friend Patty, from the Parrog. We met and embraced in the lane behind the cowshed. "My goodness! How good to see you, Patty!" I exclaimed. "What brings you here at such haste?"

My dear friend, who is a sprightly seventy years old, was red-faced and exhausted after trotting all the way up the hill from Newport, but at last she had enough breath in her body to say: "You must come straight away, Martha! Something terrible has happened! Shemi Wizard is in prison!"

"In prison? You mean in the Newport lockup? Whatever has he done? Shemi never breaks the law, and makes a point of maintaining good relations with everybody."

"That's true, Martha. I can hardly believe it myself, but he is accused of witchcraft and murder!"

"Murder? But that is preposterous, Patty! Shemi would never harm a gnat, let alone a human being."

"True, Martha. You know that, and so do I. But I was walking up Long Street and saw Shemi being dragged along in manacles by a couple of constables before being slung into the lockup. When he was locked away, I demanded the right to see him, but they told me to clear off since they

According to the Scriptures

were under orders to allow no visitors. So I asked the fellows what was going on, and they said that Master Jenkins was a witch and a murderer, and would be brought before a Petty Sessions tomorrow in order to face the full weight of the law."

"And who are his accusers? And who has he supposedly killed?"

"The constables would not say, Martha."

So confused was I by this shocking news that at first I knew not what to do. But I knew that I had to get an interview with Shemi if there was to be any chance of saving him from terrible injustice and from incarceration in Haverfordwest Gaol. I knew only too well, from personal experience, that a Petty Sessions conducted by two or three local magistrates could be as corrupt as an unsalted herring and could lead to Shemi being remanded in custody for weeks if not months while awaiting trial at the Assizes. We could not let that happen, so I called Gerallt from the barn and asked him to harness up one of the ponies to the light chaise immediately.   Ten minutes later, with both Patty and myself calmed by a few sips of brandy, we went off at a lively pace on our errand of mercy.

When we arrived at the lockup, there was a mute crowd outside, all just as confused as Patty since the constables had remained tight-lipped ever since she had set off up the road to the Plas. I have an intense and instinctive dislike of tight-lipped constables, and so I hammered on the door and demanded to see whoever was in charge. The senior constable, one Gwynfor Griffith, unlocked the door and poked out his head, "Oh, it's you, Mistress Martha," said he, not looking at all happy to see me.

I took that as a compliment, and said; "Now look here, Constable Griffith, I insist that you tell me what is going on here. Why is Master Shemi Jenkins being held here against his wishes?"

"I cannot say, Mistress. My lips are sealed."

"Well, I had better unseal them then. May I remind you, Constable, that it is an offence to deprive a man of his freedom unless all proper procedures are followed. If they are not, it could be you who ends up in a foul dungeon in Haverfordwest Castle, and not Master Jenkins."

"Oh, I assure you, Mistress, that this fellow is properly arrested," said the constable with a smirk, "and that all procedures have been duly followed. I have been around for long enough to know what to do and what not to do."

Now if there is one thing I have learned since my arrival on this

According to the Scriptures

good Earth, it is that while I may not know much about the law, most other people know even less about it than I do. So I said: "Constable Griffith, can you read and write?"

"Moderately well, Mistress, since as a child I was privileged to attend Madam Bevan's school, thanks to your good self."

"No thanks are necessary, Gwynfor. I do what I can, and seek no reward. But since you read well you will know that according to the *Lord Lieutenant's Code of Conduct for Justices and Constables,* 1845 edition, the legal representatives of prisoners are entitled to full sight of all documents, and to private interviews with prisoners, in advance of any court proceedings. You are aware of that?"

With a little frown on his brow, and with his eyes darting about hither and thither, I sensed a degree of uncertainty in the constable's manner. "Well, yes, Mistress," he mumbled. "I am not sure of the wording in the book of rules, but that is in general my understanding."

"Well then, we are agreed. Excellent! So kindly let us in, and prepare the documents for our examination."

At this, Master Griffith roared with laughter. "Now then, Mistress," he chuckled. "You are joking with me, that's for sure. You do not look in the least like an attorney. For a start, you are the wrong sex."

"Now that is where you are wrong, Gwynfor. Rule forty-five, paragraph six, clause two states with all the clarity in the world that a prisoner may choose whomsoever he wishes to be his legal representative." Then I raised my voice, so that Shemi could hear me from inside the building. "I always act on behalf of Master Jenkins in matters relating to the law," I bellowed. "Is that not correct, Shemi?"

"Of course, Martha," came another bellow from within. "Come inside. What took you so long?"

But Gwynfor stood his ground, and said: "Not so fast, Mistress *bach.* I truly believe you are trying to pull a fast one on me. You just hold on while my friend Billy Webb goes along to the Clerk to the Justices in order to check this in the rule book......."

Then I produced my most withering look and my most icy voice. "Now then, Gwynfor," said I. "I have no wish to get you into trouble. But you may take it from me that the new Clerk to the Justices knows next to nothing about the law. He will not even have the new book of rules in his possession. I have it at home, left behind by Master Brynach when he

235

According to the Scriptures

went off to America. Remember that he was an experienced magistrate, and well informed as to the law. If I have to go all the way home to fetch the regulations, and then come all the way back down to Newport, that would count as a most unreasonable delay in the application of the rules and in respect for the prisoner's rights. Now that is indeed a serious offence, likely to result in a mandatory sentence of three weeks in gaol. If you please, let us come by you, and let us into the prisoner's cell without further ado."

So with the constable's mouth opening and closing like that of a half-dead fish, Patty and I pushed past him into the dark passageway. "But Mistress Nicholas?" he protested feebly. "What is she doing here too? You said nothing about **two** ladies............"

"Gwynfor, please be assured that when on legal business I go nowhere without my clerk."

We were let in to Shemi's cell, and the door locked behind us. Billy stood outside the door, listening and watching lest anything untoward should happen, while Gwynfor reluctantly went into his little office to fetch the arrest warrant for me to inspect. Shemi embraced both Patty and myself, but having been prepared to give him moral support and to drag him out of the depths of despair, I was amazed to discover that he looked not at all discomfited. On the contrary, he seemed to be enjoying himself hugely. "Isn't this exciting?" he enthused. "I always did want to experience a spell in prison, and now here we are, with my wish fulfilled."

"Kindly be serious, Shemi," I said. "This is not a frivolous matter at all. I gather that you are accused of murder, and if that is not serious, I do not know what is. Remember, if you please, that if you are found guilty by a process more likely to be corrupt than fair, you will be strung up on the gallows."

He laughed again. "Nonsense, Martha! There is not the slightest chance that I will be convicted, since I am as innocent as a newborn babe."

"Do not count on that being of assistance to your case," I replied, "since the justices will in all probability be firm believers in the doctrine of original sin."

"Point taken, Martha. But this is all a misunderstanding, down to the fact that certain justices and other members of the community do not understand special powers."

My heart sank, and I thought that Shemi, in deep enough trouble as

According to the Scriptures

it was, might seek to argue in his defence that he had special powers not enjoyed by ordinary mortals. I did not see how that was going to help him, especially since he was apparently accused of witchcraft as well as murder. Then Constable Griffith arrived with the arrest warrant in his hand, and reluctantly handed it to me through the bars of the lockup door. "Please be careful with it, Mistress," he said. "It is a very valuable document."

"On the contrary, Gwynfor," I replied. "I suspect it is not worth the paper it is written on." So I read through it, and was staggered to see that charges were being brought against Shemi by Master Jacob Jobbins and Master John Thomas, both resident in Brynberian, "for the felonious use of spells and witchcraft in the execution of a most heinous crime, viz the murder in cold blood of Mistress Hannah Jones of Radnor, at the behest of Master Amos Jones, late of that town."

I was utterly amazed, and showed the document to Patty. "Can this really be true, Shemi?" she spluttered. "This sort of thing might have been appropriate in the Age of the Druids, but I can hardly credit it in our Age of Enlightenment."

"It is true enough, Patty," laughed Shemi, "and the wording there accords exactly with what was read out to me by these two honest constables when they came to arrest me. Do you two not find the whole thing thoroughly diverting?"

I looked again at the document, and saw that it was signed by Squire Mefin Owen of Gelli Fawr and Squire Dafydd Laugharne of Pengelli Fawr -- each one young and inexperienced in legal matters, and each one an enemy of the Plas Ingli estate. My heart sank. "Will they be in charge at the Petty Sessions?" I asked the constable standing by the barred door of the lockup.

"Why yes, Mistress. That stands to reason, seeing as they were the ones who signed the warrant. They are good friends of Master Jobbins and Master Thomas, and will therefore be keen to see justice done."

"Justice?" retorted Patty. "Revenge, more like, since those fellows have had their reputation sorely dented by Master Jenkins here, in that episode in Capel Brynberian. When will the Sessions be held?"

"Tomorrow morning at nine, Mistress, in the upstairs room of the Llwyngwair Arms."

"Oh, no!" I moaned. "That gives us hardly any time, Shemi, to organize our defence. And Amos cannot appear as a witness, since he is miles away en route for Radnor, and is quite oblivious to all of this. I fear that the outcome could be a disaster for all of us........."

"Come come, Martha," grinned Shemi. "I expect support from my attorney, instead of which I have a long face and a prediction of doom. I do not need Amos to be at the Sessions, and neither do I need you or any other legal person. I hereby release you from my service, and declare that I will conduct my own defence. The whole matter will be over in ten minutes tomorrow. May I then invite myself to lunch at the Plas, in celebration of a famous victory?"

"You seem remarkably confident, Shemi," I said, managing a feeble smile. "I hope your confidence is not misplaced. If you are a free man at the end of the morning, of course I will be only too happy to provide lunch for you and Sian and the family. I might even open a bottle or two of wine, if the occasion demands it."

"Is there anything you need for the hearing?" asked Patty. "Witnesses? Evidence? Letters or other communications?"

Shemi shook his head, and said with a toothy grin that he was protected by the sword of righteousness. So we embraced, and Constable Griffith let Patty and me out into the bright afternoon, leaving Shemi to demand his rights, including a mug of water and a bowl of soup as laid out in the statutes. As we left he shouted out: "Don't forget to turn up in the morning!"

"Never fear, Shemi," I shouted back. "We would not miss it for all the treasures of the Orient!"

ΩΩΩΩΩΩΩΩΩΩΩ

17th July 1846

The Petty Sessions are over and done with, and as I pick up my pen late at night I am still chuckling at the sheer effrontery of Shemi Wizard. His esteemed predecessor Joseph Harries could not have done better.

When I turned up in the morning in the upstairs room of the

According to the Scriptures

Llwyngwair Arms, the place was packed with people. There must have been fifty or more crammed in, including many from the congregation of Capel Brynberian. Daisy and her husband George were there, and Betsi and Ioan from Brithdir, and Patty and Jake from the Parrog, and even Wilmot and Delilah from Llanychaer. Then Shemi's dear wife Sian was there, and their three grown-up children John, Gomer and Molly. Gomer should have been at the Plas for the day, but I rearranged things for him since his father was, after all, being tried for very serious crimes. We were all quite apprehensive, since we had no idea how Shemi might defend himself, but there was a hubbub of animated conversation prior to the arrival of the justices. I noticed that Shemi's accusers, Master Jobbins and Master John Thomas, were sitting very quietly on the front bench, looking nervous.

"Silence in court!" shouted the Clerk, one Bobby Toms. "Be upstanding for the entry of the Justices!" So we all stood, and in they came, Squire Mefin Owen of Gelli Fawr and Squire Dafydd Laugharne of Pengelli. I knew both of them to be corrupt and hostile, but I was intrigued to see apprehension on their faces. Maybe, I thought, they have some concern as to whether they have acted wisely in bringing this matter to court. They sat down. "Bring in the prisoner!" shouted Squire Laugharne, who was obviously going to be in charge of proceedings. The two constables led Shemi in, with his hands shackled in front of him. He was grinning broadly, and obviously felt quite at home. Although he was not dressed in his wizardly outfit, he looked very imposing nonetheless, for he is a big man with massive shoulders, flowing locks and a bushy beard. He greeted many of those present with expressions such as: "A very good day to you, Willy *bach*! How are you, Ifan? That old knee better, I trust? Good morning, Mistress Sally! And how is that old porker of yours after the change of diet?" Willy and Ifan, and Mistress Sally and the rest of them, replied with cheery greetings of their own, and Squire Laugharne grew very red in the face. "Order in court!" he roared. "I will not have it! This is contempt of court, and if I do not have silence and respect I will have the court cleared!"

At last there was something approximating to silence, and upon the invitation of the magistrate the Clerk identified the prisoner and asked him to confirm his name. "Come now, Bobby. Jenkins Werndew, as you know full well," said Shemi.

According to the Scriptures

"Who appears for the defendant?" asked Squire Owen.

"I appear for myself, sir," said Shemi. "I dare say I can cope."

Then Master Toms read out the charge brought by the two deacons, to the accompaniment of a good deal of hilarity from the assembled company. Master John Thomas was called, and after swearing the oath he was asked to explain the basis of the charges against the defendant. He looked around him like a cornered rat, and then swallowed hard before launching into a catalogue of Shemi's wizardry. Shemi objected at once, and much to everyone's surprise the objection was upheld. "We must follow procedures, Master Thomas," said the justice. "Now then, what is the evidence upon which you base your accusations?"

"Your honour, it is known that wizards such as Master Jenkins can cast evil spells and strike people down even though they may be a great distance away. It is well known ...."

"Your evidence, sir?"

"Well, it is simply known to be a fact. If wizards can do it, then Master Jenkins had every reason to place a curse upon Mistress Hannah Jones, because he is friendly with the Prophet and with Mistress Martha Morgan. It is our contention that those two were intent upon fornication and possibly marriage, and that they hired Master Shemi Jenkins to place a curse upon the Prophet's wife and thus to kill her unlawfully."

Shemi knew that he was going to enjoy his morning's work. "Your lordships," said he, knowing full well that these two relatively junior squires on the bench were not lordships at all, "I insist upon defending myself. If friendship is now a crime, sirs, we live in a very sad world. Pray tell me how this long-distance cursing may work; if you know of a special method of killing people who are a hundred miles away, I would be greatly intrigued to hear of it."

"Well, I admit that I know nothing of such matters."

"Anything else, Master Thomas, which we might actually consider to be evidence?"

"Aha, now we have him, your Honours. How was it that Master Jenkins knew that Mistress Jones was dead, when even her own husband, namely the Prophet, did not know it? And not only that, but he knew intimately about the very means by which she died a most horrid and lonely death!" Then he turned towards Shemi, with triumph in his eyes. "Tell the Court, sir," he shouted. "I challenge you!"

According to the Scriptures

Shemi did not bat an eyelid. Then, slowly and theatrically, he dug deep into his jacket pocket and pulled out a battered newspaper. He handed it to the justices. It was, said Squire Owen, a copy of the *Cambrian* dated 17th June 1846. "Sirs," said Shemi, "this is a little newspaper to which I subscribe together with five other gentlemen in Dinas. It is my good fortune always to read it first. I received this edition on 20th June. I could not draw the sad news to the attention of the Prophet at the time, for he had set off, as I believe, to visit his old mother in Brecon. If you look at the marked piece of page three, you will see the following words: *Tragic Death in Radnor. It is with great regret that we report the unfortunate death on 14th June of Mistress Hannah Jones, beloved wife of Pastor Amos Jones who has recently answered a call to the Independent Chapel at Brynberian in Pembrokeshire. It is understood that she was found dead on the floor of her cottage terribly scalded by a cauldron of boiling water, having slipped whilst carrying it from her fireplace to her washroom. The distressing discovery was made by her kitchen-maid some three hours after the event. An inquest has been held, and since foul play is not suspected, the body has been released for burial on Friday next. We extend our heartfelt condolences to Pastor Jones and to other family members in their sad loss."*

"Word perfect, Master Jenkins. You have a good memory. So that disposes of any mystery surrounding the date of Mistress Jones's death. Any more witnesses for the prosecution? No? Then you may speak in your defence, Master Jenkins. First of all, take the oath."

"Thank you Squire. I decline to take the oath on the Bible, since I am a student of all religions and a follower of none. I do, however, give you my word that the evidence I shall give is the truth, the whole truth and nothing but the truth."

Squires Owen and Laugharne scowled, and put their heads together. Then Squire Laugharne said: "This is most irregular, Master Jenkins. One must swear on the Bible. It is laid down in the statutes. However, we will allow you to speak not as the defendant in this case but as the defendant's legal representative. Now then, what do you have to say on behalf of Master Jenkins?"

This solution having been found to a mighty legal dilemma, Shemi grinned and continued. "Now then, your lordships," he said, "my unfortunate client has been arrested, detained and charged in a most

According to the Scriptures

malicious fashion by two gentlemen towards whom he bears no personal ill-will. But it is plain to see that they do bear great malice towards him, because of certain disclosures about their private lives made at a recent Big Meeting at Capel Brynberian. Sirs, my client does not kill people, and neither does he harm them, for I have it from him personally that his code of honour does not permit it. But I will say this on his behalf: he knew of Mistress Jones' death within one hour of it happening. The newspaper report was simply by way of confirmation. Do not ask me how my client knew, for I cannot explain it, and neither can he. I rest my case."

"Sir, I must warn you that you and your client are on very dangerous ground. You have admitted on his behalf that he knows things which others do not know, through some wicked communion with the spirit world. If Master Jenkins can obtain messages from this contact with demons, can he not also instruct them to do his bidding? What do you say to that?"

"I repeat, sir, that my client does not understand this strange power," said Shemi, relishing this unworldly exchange. "All I can say on his behalf, having consulted with him at length, is that he has this power, and that it sometimes troubles him. Let me give you an example............."

Shemi paused for effect, while all those in the room held their breath. Then he raised his manacled hands in front of him and pointed his index fingers directly towards the two justices. He closed his eyes, and mumbled something strange under his breath while the colour drained out of their faces. "Now then," he intoned, contriving to make his voice echo round the room as if it was some magic cavern. "My client instructs me as follows. If you two gentlemen will kindly give him the dates on which you were born, he says that he will instantly tell both of you the dates on which you will die."

Two justices exchange glances, and I noticed to my great pleasure that each of them was as white as a sheet. Without further ado Squire Owen banged the desk with his little hammer. "Case dismissed!" he bellowed. "Not guilty! Furthermore, those who have brought this case are found to have done so frivolously and maliciously. Master Thomas and Master Jobbins, you are charged to pay one pound each to this court for wasting its time, and one pound each to the defendant for unlawful imprisonment. The prisoner is released forthwith!"

"The court will rise!" shouted the Clerk, but he might as well not

According to the Scriptures

have bothered, for all those present were already on their feet, shouting and laughing and clapping. Once again, Shemi was the hero of the hour. Now with black scowls on their faces, the justices folded up their papers and went downstairs to the bar for a stiff drink. John Thomas and Jacob Jobbins stayed in their seats as if petrified, having been comprehensively humiliated and having to face the prospect of finding two pounds each as decreed by the two justices whom they had previously counted as friends.

As for myself and my family and friends, I had to be as good as my word, and we all came back to the Plas for a celebratory lunch. When we arrived after a bracing and noisy walk up from town, we found that Wilmot and Delilah had arrived ahead of us, having travelled in their pony and trap; and they were both hard at work laying up the table with Bessie and Myfanwy. I was duly impressed by that sight, not simply because I like to see a Master and Mistress who are capable of hard work, with servants telling them what to do, but also because they did not stop for a moment to think about what this extravagance might have been costing the estate. At times such as this, I thought, one's faith in human nature is restored. Now it is late at night, and our lunch party has only just come to an end. I have eaten too much, and drunk too much, and I have lost my voice and have suffered from stitches in my side as a consequence of too much laughter. How I wish that Amos could have been here! He would certainly have enjoyed himself. However, I declare that when he returns I will tell him all about Shemi's murder trial, and he and I will have a little celebration all on our own.

ΩΩΩΩΩΩΩΩΩΩ

10. Hard Times

30th July 1846

It is late at night, and pitch black outside. Not for the first time, and probably not for the last, elation has been followed by horror. I face the task of describing the events of the day with considerable apprehension, but I have to do it, and in doing it I will seek to slay some of my demons.

This morning, soon after breakfast, I found myself alone in the kitchen. It was around seven-thirty, and it was already uncomfortably hot. Outside, I could see steam rising from the nearest fields as the sun melted off the dew. Bessie and Rose had gone off to the town market with a lengthy shopping-list, planning to obtain some of the essentials required for the feeding of the barley harvesters who will soon be busy in our fields. Blodwen was busy with the morning's milk in the dairy, and Myfanwy was upstairs dusting and tidying up the bedrooms. Will was doing things with the horses, and Gerallt was mucking out the cowshed. I should have been thoroughly contented, but I was seized by a feeling of unease, and I knew that I would soon be guided to take some action which would most likely prove to be uncomfortable. I closed my eyes and allowed intuition to take over, and immediately I knew that I must take a walk to Tycanol Wood.

I had not been to the wood since that beautiful and terrible day in the middle of last month, when I had enticed my dear Amos to my private dappled and secluded glade and had danced naked before him before introducing him to the full joy of union between a man and a woman. As I recalled that moment, a flood of warm pleasure spread through my body, and I dare say that a flush appeared on my cheeks. I looked round furtively in case anybody should notice, but then I realized that I was quite alone, and laughed to myself. In any case, I thought, why should I feel ashamed of our pure and gentle passion? If I was excited and stimulated by the memory of his body joined with mine, and by the knowledge of love given and reciprocated, that was my business. As the deacons of Brynberian had reminded me and the rest of the world in the Big Meeting, I had admitted to no sin, had shown no remorse following the events in the wood, and had asked for no forgiveness. Nor will I in the

Hard Times

future, either before man, or before God when I stand before Him at the Pearly Gates.

So why was it now required of me to go back to the rocky crags and gnarled oaks of Tycanol Wood? Was it so that I could sit quietly in that sacred place and seek to understand the concerns of others about my behaviour? Was that to be my penance? If so, I thought that I could cope with it, for I know only too well that certainty and self-belief have sometimes in the past led me into arrogance, and that in seeking to be good I must confront that impostor and seek to put it behind me.

I shouted upstairs to Myfanwy that I was minded to take a walk to Tycanol Wood and that I would do it now before being overtaken by the rigours of the barley harvest. "Very well, Mistress," she shouted back. "Just you take care, and try to be back for twelve noon, since Bessie and Rose will be wanting to talk to you about baking and such things."

Five minutes later I was on my way, striding down towards Pantry ford as the golden orb of the sun climbed ever higher into a cloudless sky. I greeted various neighbours who were out and about, and their friendliness did more than a little to reduce my sense of foreboding. I looked back at Carningli, its jagged profile proud against the western sky and its old blue rocks already shimmering in a heat haze. The world looked very beautiful, and I was surrounded by high summer birdsong. Indeed, by the time that I climbed over the last stile at Fachongle Uchaf and entered the wood I felt quite cheerful.

Then I saw and heard the birds. They were crows for the most part, and I could see through a gap in the canopy of oak leaves that they were wheeling about and squabbling in a very agitated state. There must have been at least thirty of them. There were buzzards and kites too, circling high above the wood, as silent as death. I was surprised that I had not noticed them before, as I had approached the wood from the *cwm*, but I knew enough about birds to be certain that there was carrion on the ground below them, and substantial carrion at that. A dead sheep maybe, or even a cow which had got into the wood and perished after sinking into one of the bogs in the valley beneath the rocks? I was intrigued, and not particularly concerned; but then as I continued towards my secret glade in the deep shade of the oakwood, I noticed that the sound of the angry birds was growing louder, and I realized at last that the object of their attentions was in the glade itself.

245

Hard Times

I wanted to turn back, for I was now fearful of what I might encounter when I emerged from the cool shade onto the grassy bank where I had loved David, and Owain, and Amos. But something a great deal stronger than curiosity drove me onwards, and I found myself shivering with fear in spite of the exertions of my climb into the upper part of the wood. At last I came out into the full glare of the sun, and even before my eyes had adjusted to the light I saw that I had walked into a nightmare. There were so many crows on the ground, and wheeling about between the trees and swooping down from the sky above, that I did not at first see what had made them so excited. They did not pay any attention to me, and indeed appeared not even to have noticed me, but I clapped my hands and shouted at them, and with a great cacophony of protests and a wild flurry of wingbeats they wheeled away into the sky. Black feathers swirled about them, and then floated gently to the ground as the air stilled. Then the stench of death hit me, and I saw what was left of a human body, swinging gently on a rope which had been tied to one of the low branches of the biggest oak tree on the edge of the glade.

I saw from what was left of the clothes that it was the body of a woman, and I knew at once that I was looking at the mortal remains of Miss Mary Roberts, servant at Tycanol Farm and faithful member of the Brynberian congregation. The crows had long since taken her eyes and her cheeks, and most of the flesh from her neck, and most recently they had ripped away her dress and had started on her breasts and stomach. Her torso and limbs were puffed up and coloured red and blue, and as I watched I saw that her bodily fluids were dripping onto the ground below. Her feet were gone, probably taken by foxes, and I surmised that they must have been no more than twelve inches off the ground when the tightened noose crushed the life from her body. Grotesquely, her hands dangled nonchalantly and undamaged at her sides, and her long hair was still tied up in a neat bun at the nape of her neck. With the crows gone, the only sound I could now hear was the mad buzzing of a million flies, and I knew that the flesh of the corpse must be crawling with maggots.

I am amazed that now, many hours after the event, I can recall any of these details, for within just a few seconds I was overtaken by a combination of nausea and sheer terror. I had never seen or smelt anything so appalling in my long life. I collapsed onto the ground and was violently sick. At last I plucked up the courage to look again into the glade, and I

Hard Times

saw that most of the crows had returned. They were sitting silently on the leafy branches of the surrounding oak trees, waiting for me to go. Horrified as I was by the thought that they would resume their feast as soon as my back was turned, I could do nothing for poor Mary Roberts, and neither did I have the courage to stay for a moment longer. So I scrambled to my feet and fled.

I was old enough and sensible enough not to run, and as I hurried along I concluded that the most obvious source of assistance was Tycanol Farm, right on the edge of the woodland. I was there within ten minutes, hunting for somebody with whom I might share the news of my macabre discovery. The kitchen door was wide open, and I fear that as soon as I went inside I must have fainted, for my next recollection is of concerned faces above me and smelling salts under my nose. "Why, Mistress Martha," said somebody, "you look as if you have seen a ghost."

"Much worse than that," said I, shivering uncontrollably. "There is a body swinging from a rope in the wood. I have never met her, and know not what she looks like, but I fear that it might be the body of Miss Mary Roberts."

Then the farmer, Master Charles Ifans, came in from the yard and took control of the situation. He gave me a tot of brandy to calm my nerves, and insisted that I should describe what I had seen as accurately as I could. He nodded. "I fear that you might be right in your supposition as to the identity of the deceased," he said. "Mary Roberts was very agitated towards the end of last month, but refused to explain her state of mind to anybody. We were seriously worried about her, and I had to warn her that if she did not pull herself together I might have to terminate her employment. Then one day she went out and did not come back."

"Would that have been at about the time she spread the news of my activities in the wood with Reverend Jones?"

"Somewhat later, Mistress. We all knew that she was spreading gossip about you and the pastor, and that she had reported the matter to the Brynberian deacons and elders. I rebuked her for it, and she appeared to be contrite."

"Oh may God forgive the poor creature!" I moaned. "So she disappeared when the Big Meeting was announced, and when she knew that she would have to appear before the congregation and bear witness against the pastor?"

Hard Times

"Correct, Mistress. That would have been a few days after the start of the month. We were concerned, but not unduly so. We thought that she had simply run away, back to her family in Narberth. I was not minded to go after her, since she did too much mooning about and too little work anyway."

We reasoned that if the body was indeed that of Mary Roberts it might well have been hanging in the woodland glade, in the full heat of the summer sun, for the best part of a month. The fact that it had been undiscovered for so long was not really surprising, since high summer is a time of hard work in the farms, cottages and gardens of the *cwm*, and since few people have the time or the inclination to wander in the woods.

Master Ifans decided that the body would have to be collected immediately. He called in two of his men from the fields and asked if I could face another visit to the wood, in order to lead them to the site of the tragedy. I hesitated at first, but had to agree, and a few minutes later I led the three men back into the wood. They carried a short ladder, a shroud and a large oilskin bag -- and soaking wet kerchiefs to wrap around their faces, since I had warned them that the task of cutting down what was left of the body, and wrapping it up, would be gruesome indeed. While we went into the wood, another of the Tycanol servants mounted a good horse and went galloping off to Newport to summon the constables and to notify both the Clerk to the Justices and George Havard Medical that a body had been found in the wood.

There is not much more to tell about this unutterably sad event. I led the men to the glade and remained in the shadows while they chased away the crows, cut the body down and wrapped it up with as much respect as they could manage, given its advanced state of decomposition. They confirmed from the shreds of clothing and from the hair colour and ring on her right index finger that the body was indeed that of Mary Roberts, and they confirmed that she must have taken her own life by climbing out onto a low branch, tying the rope around her neck, and then dropping to her death. That must have involved careful planning and much determination, but the men agreed that a healthy young woman could have done it without too much difficulty. Not far from the body, resting in the long grass, Master Ifans stumbled upon a corked glass bottle which contained a rolled piece of paper. I had not spotted it from the far side of the glade on my earlier visit, which was not at all surprising given that I

Hard Times

had been about twenty yards away. The farmer showed me the note, which read as follows, with many spelling mistakes which I have, out of respect, corrected:

To whom it may concern.

I am Mary Roberts of Tycanol, late of Narberth. I cannot live more, for there is no good thing left to live for. I have truly loved Master Amos Jones, a married man and a pastor and a pure and kind gentlemen, but in loving him and in lusting after him I have truly sinned against the Lord and against his wife and against my brothers and sisters of Capel Brynberian. He has rejected me, not with harsh words but with true humility, and I place no blame upon him. Then I declare that to my eternal shame, and in a manner surely leading me into the fires of Hell, I have followed him, and bothered him, and tried to tempt him, and then spied upon him and the Mistress of Plas Ingli as they did such things as I can only dream of in this very glade.

In Christian charity I should have let things be, but I was so filled with rage and hate that I spread word of what I had seen, and complained to the deacons of the house of God so that retribution might be brought down upon the heads of those who had according to the teachings of the prophets committed mortal sin. And what good did it do me, the most miserable wretch that ever walked this earth? No good at all. Torture and torment indeed, that is the truth of it. I will not stay on this cruel earth to see a good man now destroyed, and a good woman with him. Because of me. Because I loved him.

This is a good place to end it all, since it is where he sinned in fornicating and I sinned in spying and hating. Now, one more sin as I go to my fate.

May God forgive me, and those whom I love.

Mary Roberts
Tycanol, 4th day of July 1846

When I read these words, I felt tears rolling down my cheeks, and I am weeping again now as I think of this poor, lonely woman and the

249

torture she must have endured as a consequence of her unrequited love for Amos and then following her ill-judged and spiteful revelations to her "brothers and sisters" in the faith. She must have suffered indescribable anguish; I know something of it, for as a young woman I was once as close as may be to taking my own life. I was saved by Joseph Harries the Wizard, who then became a truly wonderful friend. Mary Roberts had nobody to save her, for the one man who might have done it, namely my beloved Amos, was the object of both her long-term affections and her short-lived hatred.

It is true that she has sinned in taking her own life -- but was her sin so heinous that a supposedly benign God allowed her lifeless body to swing for almost a full month in the summer sun, providing a feast for crows and foxes and maggots? I know that such things happen to murderers and robbers in the colonies, where an example has to be made of them, but is West Wales not supposed to be a place of civilisation and enlightenment?

I am too exhausted and confused to write more tonight. I must wipe away my tears and put down my pen, and try to sleep. How I wish that Amos was here, and that I could fall asleep in his arms! But he is more than a hundred miles away, and ignorant of all of this. Instead of sleeping, I dare say I will spend what is left of the night gazing at the ceiling and wondering how he will react when he returns and discovers this latest consequence of our chance encounter in Tycanol Wood.

ΩΩΩΩΩΩΩΩΩΩΩ

31st July 1846

Another day has passed. I am restored to something approaching equilibrium, and can continue my narrative.

As soon as we returned to the farm with the body borne on the ladder, I told Master Ifans that I must return home, since it was now two o'clock and I knew that Myfanwy and the others would be very worried about me. He appreciated that I could do no more at Tycanol, but he would not contemplate for a moment the idea that I should walk home, and

Hard Times

insisted that I should be transported in his trap. I was grateful for this kind offer, for in truth I was exhausted. While one of his men fetched a pony and harnessed it up, Mistress Ifans tried to get me to eat something, but I was quite incapable of swallowing even the smallest morsel of bread after my horrific experience, and I had to decline.

With one of the Tycanol men driving the trap I was soon on my way home, but the journey was by no means a smooth or speedy one, for we kept on meeting people who were rushing in the opposite direction, towards the farm where the body now rested. First we met the two constables, Gwynfor Griffith and Billy Webb, travelling on a pair of ancient ponies. We had to stop and talk to them, of course, and they told me that I would have to make a statement about my discovery of the body, but they were sensible enough to appreciate that that could wait, and offered to call in at the Plas on their way home in order to complete the formalities. Then, a quarter of a mile further on we encountered Master Bobby Toms, the Clerk to the Justices, galloping along on a fine hunter, and had to talk to him too. Then my dear son-in-law George Havard Medical appeared on his chestnut mare, and when he saw my face he insisted on dismounting and helping me down from the trap so that he could give me a long embrace. I needed that, and having held myself together since reading Mary Roberts' suicide note in the glade I now wept long and passionately onto the lapels of his jacket. He was patient and tender, and in the midst of my tears I thanked God that such a good man was now a member of my own family through his marriage to Daisy.

At last I finished with weeping and sent George on his way, grim-faced and apprehensive in the knowledge that he had a partly decomposed body to identify and to examine in the hope of establishing a cause of death.

When I reached the Plas I discovered that the news of the body in the wood had travelled ahead of me. Both Daisy and Betsi were in the kitchen, and all of the residents of the Plas stopped whatever they were doing to greet me as I dismounted from the trap. I thanked Master Ifans' man for his trouble, and gave him a quart of cider by way of refreshment, for the day was now at its hottest. Off he went, and I had the miserable task of telling my family and servants the whole harrowing story of my day in the wood. They packed me off to bed, and I managed to sleep for a few hours before Master Bobby Toms called by and asked to see me. To his credit, and having seen the corpse himself, he expressed his sympathy concerning the ordeal that I had been put through during the morning, and asked if I was now strong enough to give him a statement. I said that I was, and while he sat by my side I wrote down everything that I had seen, concentrating on the facts and leaving speculation to one side. I have dealt with quite enough deaths to know what is required. When I had finished, I signed and dated the sheet of paper, and he witnessed it.

Bobby told me that the body was now in the mortuary down on the Parrog, having been examined both by Havard Medical and by Shemi Jenkins. Neither of them had been able to establish a cause of death, but they had agreed, on the evidence before them, that Mary Roberts had most likely died from asphyxiation, since her fall from the branch had not been a long one and her neck was not broken. Her death had therefore not been instantaneous, but had most likely been slow and agonizing. I was not sure that I wanted to hear that, and said as much to Bobby. He apologized for his insensitivity, and went on to say that the Inquest would be held at nine o'clock on the next morning since the Coroner wanted the body buried as rapidly as possible.

"Is it your wish, Mistress, to attend the Inquest as a witness?" asked the Clerk.

"I would prefer not to, Bobby, if I can be excused. I do not think I could keep my composure in the face of all the dreadful details which will be relayed to the court."

"I quite appreciate that, Mistress Martha. The Coroner has already indicated to me that he has three adequate witnesses in Master Ifans and his two men, and they saw more than you did since they cut down the body and transported it back to the farm. Constables Griffith and Webb have also visited the scene of the tragedy and have made a record of the circumstances. I dare say that this is a straightforward matter, and that there will be no criminal proceedings. At the Inquest I will take it upon myself to say that you are excused on the grounds that you are greatly shocked by what you have seen, and I will read out your statement to the court. The Coroner and his jury will be understanding, of that I am sure." And with that he jumped to his feet, gave me a polite bow, and took his leave.

The inquest was held this morning at the Llwyngwair Arms as planned, with Coroner Will Daniels officiating and with a jury of eight gentlemen of the town in attendance. Betsi and Daisy attended, and said that the proceedings had lasted no more than an hour. According to their narrative, the room was packed with people, including some of the Capel Brynberian congregation. The three men who had recovered the body gave their testimonies, and then the Clerk explained my non-attendance and read out my witnessed statement. The Coroner and the jury all nodded sagely and asked that their good wishes might be transmitted to me following the great trauma which I had experienced. Then George and Shemi gave the evidence from their post-mortem examinations, which was so graphic and upsetting that several ladies and gentlemen had to leave the room. They both declared the cause of death to have been asphyxiation, "on or around the fourth day of July in the Year of our Lord 1846." The deceased person's suicide note was then read out, and two servants from Tycanol confirmed that the writing was hers. There were various questions from jury members and from the Coroner, but no attempt was made by anybody to explore the circumstances surrounding poor Mary's death, although it was common knowledge that she had been infatuated with Amos Jones and that the trigger which caused her death was her observation of the act of love between Amos and myself. When Daisy told me this, later in the morning, I became quite emotional, for it demonstrated two things -- first, that the goodwill which I once enjoyed in the town has not entirely disappeared, and second, that the community has now had quite enough of this business and wants nothing more to do with recrimination and retribution.

The verdict was not long in coming, said Betsi. The jurors declared that Mary Roberts had, with a high degree of probability, died from asphyxiation occasioned by a rope tied around her neck, and that she had taken her own life while the balance of her mind had been disturbed. The Coroner formally accepted and recorded this verdict, thanked all those involved in this unfortunate matter, and discharged the jury. Then he released the body for burial, and asked whether any relative or any member of Capel Brynberian might wish to take responsibility. There was no relative present, and Master Ifans Tycanol said that he had sent word to Mary's old father in Narberth but had had no reply. Those members of Capel Brynberian who were present mumbled about the need to "take instructions" from the chapel elders in view of the fact that the deceased had taken her own life. At this, the Coroner became very agitated, and announced that the body would be left for a further forty-eight hours in the Parrog mortuary, and that in the event of it being unclaimed it would be buried and covered with lime in an unmarked grave, in the interests of public health.

In the street afterwards, Betsi and Daisy organized contributions from assorted townspeople and managed to raise enough money to pay for a coffin, which will be ready by tomorrow morning. In the meantime, what is left of Mary's body lies on a cold slate slab in the mortuary, soaked in carbolic acid. If nobody claims it tomorrow, it will be dumped into an unmarked grave on Thursday. If nobody else will do it, I have told Daisy and Betsi that I will try to give the poor thing some sort of a Christian burial, but where should it be done? And where should the grave be dug? With Amos still away, and with no other minister of church or chapel prepared to become involved in the disposal of a rotting corpse, is it all down to me? Oh God, have I not had punishment enough? Is this Mary's revenge, or my purgatory? When will it all end?

ΩΩΩΩΩΩΩΩΩΩΩ

1st August 1846

Amos has returned, and my penance is over. He came back to the Plas today around noon, in the middle of the thunderstorm which has been threatening for some days. Not for the first time, he was soaked to the skin, and not for the first time he came into the kitchen cursing that old horse of his which has still not learned to cope with thunder and lightning. When he appeared I flung my arms around his neck and hugged him for several minutes, and neither he nor I could understand the floods of tears which I released onto his already sodden collar. They were probably tears of joy and relief, and I recall wailing "Oh Amos! Amos! Thank God you are back! How I have missed you, *cariad*! I know not how I have survived without you! So much has happened -- I know not where to start. Oh Amos, how I love you! Do you still love me? Tell me that you do, *cariad*! Tell me now, or I will surely die!"

Hard Times

Since this outburst occurred in the presence of Rose, Bessie and Myfanwy the dear man was perfectly bemused and had no idea how to respond. He mumbled something or other, and when I looked into his eyes and at his weatherbeaten face I could not decide whether his ruddy complexion was down to embarrassment or sunburn. Then I laughed, and he lost his inhibition, and said: "Of course I love you, Martha. Did I not tell you that before I left? And why should anything have changed? Now then, first things first. Are there any dry clothes in this house? And might I trouble you for a bowl of soup or some such thing? I have not eaten for twenty-four hours."

So we clothed him and fed him, and Gerallt stabled his horse and gave it a bucket of crushed oats. For an hour we talked -- or rather, I talked and he listened -- for he knew nothing of either Shemi's murder trial or of the death of Mary Roberts. His face registered surprise, amusement, shock, incredulity and a good many other emotions during my narrative. I knew that he too had much news for me, but I correctly surmised that his news could wait, for there were pressing matters to attend to. Then without any prompting from me, he leapt to his feet and said: "Martha, I will claim Mary Roberts' body and give her a Christian burial. It is the least I can do. Will you accompany me to the mortuary? We have not a moment to lose. No churchyard will have her, so will you give her a corner of your garden? From the wall near the barn there is a wonderful view across to Tycanol Wood and Carnedd Meibion Owen, which I know she loved. Her spirit will be sorely troubled, but there at least she might find peace, and she will be helped on her way if you and I, the causes of her distress, can find it in our hearts to do this last kindness for her. Will you agree? Please, Martha, do this for me."

"Of course, Amos. Your wishes in this matter are identical to mine. The soil near the top wall is deep and sandy, and it will take a grave. I will ask Will and Gerallt to start digging immediately. If they work hard, the grave will be ready by the time we return with the coffin."

So we went to town with Amos driving the light gambo, and by signing a piece of paper at the mortuary we obtained the release of the body. Mercifully, the stench of death had been deadened by copious quantities of carbolic acid, and we were able to return home with the coffin on its makeshift hearse at a sedate and respectful pace. We passed some of our neighbours, who knew instantly whose body was being transported, and to their credit they stood still as we passed, and doffed their hats.

Now Mary is at rest, six feet down with a simple cross and a vase of flowers to mark the site, not far from the white lilac tree which reminds me of dear departed Owain Laugharne. Amos, fully aware that he was risking the disapprobation of clerics and churchmen across a wide area, conducted a simple and beautiful service, in the presence of my family and servants. As the coffin was lowered into the ground I saw that tears were rolling down his cheeks. Was this dear man truly a sinner worthy of excommunication? I thought that in the eyes of God he was already a saint, and I loved him more, and shed tears of my own.

ΩΩΩΩΩΩΩΩΩΩ

8th August 1846

During the last week Amos and I have spent much time in each other's company, for our mutual consolation. With time to reflect, the death of Mary Roberts has made a deep impact upon him, increasing the sense of guilt which he carried around like a great wooden cross even before he set off for Radnor. He is sorely troubled that his actions -- and mine -- should not only have caused upset through the community and particularly among the members of the Capel Brynberian congregation, but that others have now been gravely harmed. The deacons and elders of the chapel have lost status and self-esteem, and through their ill-judged actions Masters John Thomas and Jacob Jobbins hardly dare to show their faces in Newport. And Mary Roberts is dead. She was a foolish woman, and was responsible to a great degree for her own misfortunes, but Amos still feels that he has her blood on his hands, and I dare say that it will be many months before that blood is washed off.

As for me, the shock of recent events struck me with great force on the day after Amos returned. I suppose that up to that point I had kept going on my reserves of energy, such as they are, and that in a strange way everything was released when my dear friend was back at my side and when the little cross was placed on Mary's grave. At any rate, for two or

Hard Times

three days I behaved like an imbecile, weeping a lot, refusing my food, sleeping until all hours, and being very irritable with family and servants. I even became angry and rude with poor Amos, and gave him sharp lashings with my tongue on two occasions when he was trying to be helpful and supportive. But he, and my servants and family, have forgiven me, as they always do, and today I feel much better. After a few days of grey and windy weather, with spells of rain, the sun has returned and the Plas Ingli barley harvest has started. The weather damage to the standing crop is not too great to bear, and with twenty-three harvesters to be organized and fed there is no time to be morose.

And so to practical matters. During our recent walks upon the mountain Amos has told me his story.

When he arrived back at Radnor, after preaching a few sermons and saving a few souls on the way, he had found a somewhat complicated state of affairs. The first thing he did was to find his wife's grave in the local churchyard and to pray awhile and pay his last respects. Then he had visited his cottage and found it locked and barred, with the garden looking like a tropical jungle. So he had talked to the neighbours, and had discovered that towards the end of her life Mistress Jones had behaved very erratically, and had upset many of her erstwhile friends and those few members of her own family who were still alive. She had also apparently run up considerable debts. They had confirmed the newspaper report of the date and manner of Hannah's death, and had said that her funeral had been organized by her solicitor and two distant cousins from Presteign.

Amos had called to see the solicitor, who had been trying for more than a month to communicate with him via a string of letters; and now Master Absalom Carter (for that was his name) had welcomed him like a long-lost brother, and with a happy smile on his face had told him of the extent of his problems. He was the executor of Mistress Jones's will, he had said, and indeed proved it by showing the document to Amos. He had used Hannah's meagre cash resources to pay for the funeral but had then been bombarded with demands for money from all manner of people, including tradesmen and distant relatives, who had showed him invoices and statements and other bits of paper. So far as he could see, said Master Carter, most if not all of the demands were genuine, and matched up with items found in the cottage and with documents found in a pile in a bedroom

257

cupboard. In order to keep the bailiffs at bay, and to prevent a distraint sale of the contents of the cottage, he had allowed some of Hannah's creditors to take away furniture, clothes and other items which they had sold her in the past. He had kept the cottage locked, but some distant relatives had appeared there one day without his knowledge and had taken away almost everything of value, including jewellery, china and cutlery, pictures and books.

"But that is preposterous!" Amos had exclaimed. "How could you or the neighbours have allowed that to happen?"

"My dear sir, I was powerless to prevent it," the attorney had replied. "My office is more than a mile from the cottage, and I could not have stood guard over it all day and every day. Neither could the constables. As you have seen, the will was a quite useless document, which your wife wrote out herself many years ago with two witnesses. Almost everything in the house was legally yours, and not hers, and had you turned up shortly after her death matters of inheritance might have been resolved. But after the funeral certain cousins, male and female, from far and wide, decided that you were unlikely ever to return, and started to compete over the spoils. Sad to say, that is human nature for you, my dear Reverend. They broke in and cleaned out the house."

"Including my library of philosophical and theological books?"

"Afraid so, Reverend. They left the family Bible, out of respect for the Almighty."

When he related all of this, Amos became quite upset and agitated, and I was moved to put my arm around his shoulder by way of consolation; but there was little I could do to reduce his misery at the loss of hundreds of valuable books collected and studied both by his father Edmund and by himself as a young man.

After that meeting with Master Carter, Amos said he had been given accommodation by a kind neighbour and had gained access to the cottage, which was, as he had feared, stripped almost bare and in a filthy condition. There was not even a bed for him to sleep on. He had spent several days cleaning it up and trying to sort out the garden, and then he had advertised it for sale. There had been plenty of potential buyers, and he obtained £28 for it. Having disposed of the property, he had insisted on settling Hannah's outstanding debts and on paying the solicitor's fees, which added up to a grand total of £24/10/0d.

Hard Times

"So, my dear Martha, I am today not a wealthy fellow at all," he said, with resignation on his face and sadness in his eyes. "After paying something for my food and accommodation, I have a grand total of £3 in my pocket, a few clothes, and a disobedient horse. If you were thinking of marriage, then forget it, for I am currently not a very good prospect for even the lowliest woman in the Narberth Workhouse."

"But Amos," I said, "you do have possessions, and the things taken by Hannah's cousins are rightfully yours. Your books, in particular, mean a lot to you emotionally as well as being valuable in cash terms. You must pursue these people and recover everything!"

"Quite impossible, Martha. I do not know who most of these distant cousins are, or where they live. I could find out from Master Carter, I dare say, but is it a sensible use of my time, or anybody else's, to go rushing about all over East Wales, issuing summonses for the recovery of stolen property, and chasing people through the courts? My £3 would be gone in no time at all. No, Martha, I do not have a stomach for it."

So it appears that Jones Minor Prophet is destined to remain destitute, and I am coming to accept that maybe poverty goes with his calling. I am not in a position to do much about it, but I love him, and while I live he will not starve. Neither will he go homeless. He cannot live here at the Plas -- at least, not yet -- for emotions are still raw following our misdemeanours in Tycanol Wood. But Betsi and Ioan have invited him to stay at Brithdir in their spare servant's room, and he has been happy to accept their offer. He needs a cottage of his own, and I am minded to ask Wilmot Gwynne if he can find one for my wandering homeless preacher, in an attempt to settle him down.

ΩΩΩΩΩΩΩΩΩΩ

15th August 1846

With so much going on in my life, I have omitted to mention the news from the American branch of the family. It appears that Brynach and David have settled in better than they dared to hope, and with almost nine

Hard Times

months having passed since their arrival in New York they are enjoying excellent relations with sister Elen. I have received happy and effusive letters from all three of them, and of course Rose gets many letters from her little brother. We read out loud our letters from across the ocean to each other, and have become very close in the process. Although she is still only fifteen years old my sweet granddaughter has accepted her separation from her father and brother with surprising equanimity, and when I ask her often if she is truly happy here at the Plas, she insists that she is, and that she has no wish at all to follow them westwards across "those horrid heaving trackless wastes of salty water." She truly hates the sea, and maybe that is because she knows that long ago it claimed the lives of my brother-in-law Griffith and my son Dewi. I dare say that things are safer now, and that the emigrant ships are secure and sound, but we still read in our papers about shipwrecks and the gruesome conditions that have to be endured by those seeking a new life in the New World, and Rose is intelligent enough to draw her own conclusions as to risks and benefits. David misses his sister, and has pleaded with her to come to New York, but she appears quite impervious to his cajoling.

So Rose and I enjoy each other's company and indeed provide much mutual support here at the Plas. Over there, Brynach has set up his own business as a merchant, with the aid of some money (he insists that it is borrowed but not given) from his natural mother. Elen is very excited about it, and says, with a mother's pride, that her son has an instinct for managing people and money, for buying low and selling high, and for spotting trends in the market ahead of others. That surprises me not a jot, for he has after all managed a sizeable estate at Llanychaer, and I have trained him well. The skills that are so lauded by Elen are taken for granted here in West Wales, but of course I share her mother's pride. I can only hope that Brynach has learned some lessons from the collapse of his estate and becomes so successful that before long he will come back and pay us a visit on one of his fine trading vessels!

Elen is, by her own admission and by the accounts of Brynach and David, now fully recovered from the death of her beloved husband Tom more than a year ago. Indeed, she appears to be rejuvenated, and although she is now more than seventy years old she has taken up her old career as a music teacher once again and is giving piano lessons to various elegant young ladies and gentlemen. Her star pupil is David, and she claims that

Hard Times

he has an instinct for reading music and finger dexterity the like of which she has never seen before. I knew that he was musically talented before he and his father set out for America, but if the extent of his talent is as great as claimed by his American grandmother that is exciting indeed, and perhaps opens up the possibility of a career in music. Then again, I suppose that caution is in order, for I know only too well that one's grandchildren (unlike other people's grandchildren) tend to be the most talented and beautiful of all the creatures ever to have walked on God's earth.

So I am happy, not to say relieved, that all is well across the water. Truly, with so much happening here, I would find it hard to cope if news were to come of sickness, unhappiness or some other disaster afflicting those whom I love in foreign parts.

Amos has finally got a cottage of his own. A week ago I sent a message to Wilmot, explaining the straightened circumstances in which Amos now finds himself, and asking if he could find a home for the preacher somewhere either on the Llanychaer estate or close to the Plas. I suggested in the most gentle and diplomatic fashion that a ruinous cottage near Garfeth might fit the bill, since it has been uninhabited for a year and has been used off and on by vagrants and travelling Irish harvesters. It lies up the hill on the other side of the road from Cilgwyn Church, on a parcel of land that belonged to Gelli Fawr until I bought it following the conviction and hanging of Squire John Owen last year. I told Wilmot that the property was deteriorating, and that if it remained unoccupied he would very shortly have a problem with squatters. To his great credit, my good friend wrote back immediately, expressing his sympathy and admiration for Amos and saying that he could occupy the cottage at a peppercorn rent, to have and hold until the end of his days, on condition that he undertakes the renovation work himself and charges no future maintenance costs to the estate.

This was a perfect solution. When he heard the news Amos was very moved, and travelled over to Llanychaer to thank Wilmot personally. On his way home across the common he fell off his horse and injured his shoulder. He blamed the horse, of course, but I know Amos well enough to know that he and Wilmot probably enjoyed a tipple or two or three at Llanychaer in the shady orchard, and that the incident on the mountain was down to his own imperfect balance rather than the wild behaviour of his steed. Wilmot is a rough diamond, but there is no doubting his inestimable worth, and he sees, from a man's perspective, what his friend Amos actually needs if he is to recover from the traumas of recent weeks. For a start, he needs more male company, away from this household dominated by strong females. Second, he needs to pray and preach less and enjoy himself more if he is to get used to a life above and beyond that of the church. Without having the duties of a pastor, and with no flock to be shepherded, I am sure that Wilmot appreciated a grave danger that Amos might become at best irritable and at worst introverted and depressed. He still carries far more guilt on his shoulders than is good for him. Third, Wilmot has given Amos the security he needs, in knowing that he has a roof over his head for life, whatever might happen to me or the Plas, or indeed to the Llanychaer estate. And finally the wise fellow has decided that Amos needs a building project which will keep him out of mischief. My beloved preacher is still only sixty years old, and is quite young and fit enough to move stones, mix mortar, and cut timbers. He is not the most practical fellow in the world, but the exercise will do him good, and he will enjoy the company of many willing helpers. Indeed, I might help him myself now and then over the coming months by turning up at Garfeth and giving instructions. That will make him very angry, and I will remind him -- before he sees the sparkle in my eye -- that anger keeps a man on his mettle.

ΩΩΩΩΩΩΩΩΩΩΩ

20th August 1846

The harvest is still dragging on, and it has been one of the most bothersome I can remember, with spells of hot sunshine interspersed with heavy rain and high winds. There has been a lot of stopping and starting, with harvesters sheltering in the barn more often than I, or they, would have liked, and with some areas of ripe standing corn flattened and destroyed. The harvest will not be a disaster, but by the time the gleaners come it will have cost me a lot, and the barn and the rickyard will have too much empty space in them for comfort.

Hard Times

Tom Foster has been to see me. He was on his way to Ireland for another of his reporting visits, and by now he will be halfway across St George's Channel between Fishguard and Cork. He has told me more about the situation in that benighted land, and since I have of late failed to keep up with the reports in my newspapers I was amazed and horrified by what he told me.

He said that throughout most of Ireland the early part of the year had seen great hardship among the peasants, with virtually no potatoes surviving in their clamps and with deaths on a large scale prevented only by the distribution of Indian corn meal from Government depots. There have been riots at the food depots and more trouble because of the unpalatable and disgusting nature of the meal itself. The squires and merchants, quite impervious to the suffering around them, have maintained their blockade and have continued to export their agricultural products to England and the continent, while refusing to import anything that might go to feed the peasants. Their protest is against "government interference in the market", and they want an end to government feeding programmes based on bulk purchases of Indian corn at the American ports. They want an end to "secret" government storage depots. They want to arrange the imports themselves, and they want to retain the right to sell into the feeding programmes.

I frowned when Tom tried to explain all of this, but he said the matter was really quite simple. "Thus far," he said, "the government has bought the corn in bulk, so as to reduce the cost to the Exchequer, and has cut out the middlemen at the Irish ports. Now, with the fall of Peel's government in June and the arrival of a new austere Chancellor, Sir Charles Wood, a promise has been made that last year's official purchase of corn worth £100,000 will not be repeated. "Laissez faire" is the new philosophy, and private enterprise has already taken over. In future the merchants will do the purchasing themselves, and the new free market arrangements will be politically acceptable, but I dare say much more expensive when the real costs are added up."

"And very convenient for the merchants, who will monopolise the market and make a tidy killing?" I asked.

"Correct, Martha. And thinking of the market, whatever happened to your plan to send barley across to Wexford at a fair price?"

"I am afraid, Tom, that although my intentions were good, and

263

Hard Times

although I had Skiff Abraham on my side, we never did find a buyer for our barley in Ireland. When March came along I had to thresh my barley as usual, and after keeping my seed I had to release it for the best price I could get. And the captain of my ship tired of waiting in the river at St Dogmael's and went off to Bristol with a cargo of slate from the Cilgerran quarries."

"A pity, Martha, but one or two idealists can do little against the might of the government and the Irish squires."

"Come now, Tom. We did not do too badly, did we, when we took on the government and the Welsh squires in the matter of the turnpike trusts? I dare say that the Irish squires are no more formidable than their cousins in Wales?"

At this, Tom roared with laughter at the recollection of our adventures with the daughters of Rebecca. "Agreed, Martha!" he grinned. "They may even be less formidable and less organized. But in case you are tempted to sort out the problems of Ireland, may I remind you that there is a considerable quantity of salt water between here and there, that the Irish peasants speak a language that you do not understand, and that neither you nor I can come close to appreciating the political and religious subtleties that complicate what might otherwise be a simple matter of economics and agriculture." Then he became serious again. "I advise you to stay out of Ireland, Martha. If you try to get involved, you will surely get hurt. No -- do what you can, but I urge you to do it on this side of the water."

"Very well, Tom. I will take your advice, at least for the time being. But why is your Editor sending you across to Cork just now?"

"Because, Martha, word has reached us that the government is steeling itself for an even greater tragedy than that of last winter. Corn prices have started to rise, and this has caused trouble up and down the land. There are protests because the peasants cannot afford to buy food in the markets and because there is not enough Indian corn in the government stores to go round. There is supposed to be a government work programme on roads and bridges and so forth for all those who are fit for work, but the organization of it is a shambles. So there are long queues and much irritation, but little work actually going on. And most ominous of all, Martha, after a warm and wet summer reports are now coming in that the new potato crop is turning black. That was probably inevitable, given that most of the seed potatoes planted in the spring were already infected with the blight."

"Starvation again, Tom, and on a greater scale than last year?"

"Absolutely inevitable, Martha. I fear that many thousands will die, and that many thousands more will flee."

And on that miserable note Tom took his leave, fearing that if he stayed longer he might miss his ship for Cork and upset his Editor.

Since he left, I have pondered on his words at length. I know that the situation in Ireland is none of my business, but concern for the Irish peasants is always there in the back of my mind, and I cannot understand why. My intuition tells me that the stench of rotting Irish potatoes will somehow reach my nostrils here in West Wales, and that I will have to take some action to minimise my own discomfort, let alone that of others.

ΩΩΩΩΩΩΩΩΩΩΩ

20th December 1846

Winter has come early this year. In the middle of last month the wind shifted to the north and then to the east, and I knew from experience that this heralded snow. Sure enough, when I woke up on the morning of 20th November there was a blanket of snow upon the ground, and since then we have had bitter winds, more snow, hard frosts in the coldest spells and icy rain when the weather has been relatively warmer. Here at the Plas we will cope, since we have good supplies of oats, barley straw, turnips and hay laid up for the animals, and cabbages, potatoes, apples, parsnips, salted meat and pickled herrings put away for the human residents. Rarely do I need to buy in supplies, and I have learnt over the years that this little estate cannot produce an abundance of any one crop but that its peculiar combination of soils and weather enables me to grow modest quantities of almost anything I choose to plant. As Grandpa Isaac taught me many years ago, the secret ingredients of good husbandry are rotations and manure.

Much as I would like to write a learned treatise on agriculture, I

Hard Times

have more serious matters to report to my diary. For a start, Amos is not well, having caught a chill by working on his cottage at Garfeth in the most inclement of weather conditions. He has been putting up a new roof, and since the place is open to the elements he has been living in a scruffy hovel next door. He has been very stubborn, and although I offered him a room at the Plas when the weather turned bitterly cold he declined to move in, declaring that the Lord would protect him and that the snow would not last. In any case, he said, he needed to spend every daylight hour sawing and measuring and heaving great beams about so as to make the place habitable and cosy at the earliest opportunity. I suppose that is very laudable, and have to remind myself that he is tired of charity and wants to become a fully independent gentleman again. I also have to remind myself that his current regime of hard labour is a sort of penance for past misdemeanours and an attempt to recover the esteem of the community. People are indeed full of admiration for him. That having been said, I just wish that he would recognize his own limitations and listen to those of us who know the weather in these parts. When I went to visit Garfeth a few days since, following a horrid blizzard, I found the dear man sheltering under some soggy blankets in his hovel, with a little fire smoking in the corner and providing virtually no warmth. He was shivering uncontrollably, with a flush upon his brow and a nose dripping like a defective tap. So I disregarded his protests and Gerallt and I dragged him out of the place and through the snowdrifts down to the church, where we had left our sledge.

Now the preacher is in bed in one of the downstairs rooms, well wrapped up and complaining about the taste of some foul potion that Shemi has prescribed for him. He is at least warm and well fed, and since his years on the road have made him as tough as my oldest walking boots it is clear that he will survive. He will still be here over Christmas, and while that may cause raised eyebrows and shaking heads in the community, I am past caring. After all, he is here on strictly humanitarian grounds, and I would be a heartless creature indeed were I to send him packing to the other side of the *cwm* in this horrid winter weather. God will surely agree that preachers and prophets have to be preserved and protected, for the greater good.

There are two deaths to report. Dai Darjeeling is dead, having been caught out in a blizzard on Preseli at the end of November. They say that he was frozen to death, like his horse, and that travellers found him and the poor creature huddled together in a snowdrift, five days after they died. There was a funeral at Caersalem. Bessie was and is distraught, for she and Dai were very close for as long as I can remember. There is no doubt in my mind that they loved one another dearly, and that their relationship was by no means of the platonic kind. I was always surprised that they did not marry, but I dare say that Bessie was too attached to the Plas for that to happen, and that Dai was too attached to the life of a wandering tea merchant. He was a lovely man, and he will be sorely missed. I will also miss my old friend Elijah Collins, who died a week ago at the age of ninety-six. The cause of death was, says Havard Medical, difficult to discern, but no inquest was held since it is always assumed that fellows who survive beyond their allotted span can quite easily die of nothing in particular. At any rate, the squires and merchants whom he scourged and bothered endlessly will all, no doubt, sleep easier in their beds as a result of his passing.

And one more serious matter, beside which those reported above appear to be piffling and pedantic. Tom has written me a long letter from a place called Limerick, describing the conditions which he has encountered during the last month. He says that there has been so much snow in the western districts that travelling around has been impossible at times. But his problems have been as nothing when set against those of the poor cottagers. They are used to rain and wind in the winter, but not snow, and they have been quite unable to cope with it. They are ill-clothed and ill-housed, quite apart from being exhausted and starving. As predicted, the potato crop has been entirely wiped out by the blight, and in desperation the peasants have used up their meagre resources of oats, cabbages and turnips (which very few of them grow in the first place) and have actually been selling "spare" clothes and blankets in order to buy market produce at ever-increasing prices. For many families, every penny is gone, so they have long since slaughtered and eaten their family pigs, and near Tipperary Tom saw horse meat and dog meat being cooked and eaten in some hovels. The people are ranging across the desolate countryside gathering everything edible -- dandelion roots and leaves, nuts, berries, charlock and nettles. Some have died from eating rhubarb leaves. Foxes, rats, hedgehogs and even snails are being hunted and eaten. Bird-catching is a frantic and largely unsuccessful occupation for children, since they

Hard Times

have hardly enough energy to walk, let alone run. They wait for the spring, when there will be fresh plant growth and small eggs in the hedgerow nests; but Tom says that thousands of small children will not last that long. He has already lost count of the dead bodies he has seen at the roadside which cannot be buried until the ground thaws.

For those who can get it, the disgusting yellow gruel made from Indian corn meal will be their Christmas fare this year. For others, their feast will be made from blood taken from cattle, mixed with cabbages and a little oatmeal and baked to make a sort of revolting black pudding. And for others, death will arrive before Christmas, relieving many devout people from the need to celebrate the birth of their Saviour.

There was more from Tom, but I cannot bear to repeat it in the pages of my diary. Not for the first time, I feel unutterably miserable and also impotent. We will, I dare say, do our best to enjoy Christmas here at the Plas, and indeed I owe it to my family, tenants and servants to make it as grand and hospitable as may be; but I fear that my roast goose may stick in my throat when I recall that less that sixty miles away to the west a tragedy of gigantic proportions is unfolding out of sight and (for most of our political masters) out of mind.

In a grotesque coincidence of events, on the day after the arrival of Tom's letter a cheerful Christmas epistle arrived from New York, written by Brynach and bearing news of assorted exciting events. My dear son included in his letter the following words:

"My new business is growing by the day, and I am very pleased with progress. I trust, dearest Mother, that you will be proud of me when in due course I have an opportunity to explain all of my transactions to you. For the moment, the thing that gives me most pride is my purchase of 2,000 tons of maize, or Indian corn as we call it, from Mississippi, at £2 per ton and sold on to certain Irish merchants at £5 per ton. After costs, that means a profit of £5,000 from just a few days of wheeling and dealing! This truly is a land of milk and honey. You may not be aware of it, but there is a great need for food in Ireland to offset the failure of the potato harvest. Is it not a fine thing, Mother, to be able to help the starving through the provision of this excellent food and at the same time to make an honest living?"

Hard Times

So it is that the fortunes of the next generation of the Morgan family appear to depend upon the trading of a foul and unpalatable corn meal produced by starving slaves in the deep south of America and fed to starving peasants in Ireland. It is clear that I must write to Brynach on this matter, but not yet, for in my present state of mind I am quite incapable of unravelling the moral complexities of this new situation.

ΩΩΩΩΩΩΩΩΩΩΩ

11. Long Memories

22nd December 1846

I have broken into my Christmas preparations by having a long talk with Amos. He was not very talkative, poor fellow, since he was still coughing and sniffling and suffering from a mild fever; but he assured me that listening to me was more interesting than reading the collected sermons of John Wesley. It was cosy enough in his room, with a good fire glowing in the grate, and as I sat at his bedside I felt that my attentions and ministrations would perhaps do him some good.

In any case, I wanted to share with him my concerns about Ireland and the tragedy that they now refer to in the newspapers as "The Great Hunger". I wanted to know whether he, as a committed Christian, felt any obligation to do anything to help the starving Irish peasants. He replied that he did indeed, and that so should any civilized and compassionate individual on this side of the water, regardless of religious belief. "Those who are suffering are of course Papists, Martha," he croaked, "and they suffer from the effects of bigotry as well as from lack of food and work. As you know, I have preached sermons in which I have urged people to help the Irish, and I think some have been moved to send subscriptions, but sadly the effectiveness of my sermons has diminished of late, as a result of our activities in the wood. When I thunder these days about morality, I fear that the echo comes back and deafens me, in the form of cheap jibes from my listeners. I wish I could do more, but with no money I can neither travel to Ireland nor finance the sending of food parcels."

"But I could do more, Amos."

"True, Martha. But you are no spring chicken, and you are on the wrong side of the water. Neither you nor I can take on all the troubles of the world, much as we might like to. We can only act within our own spheres of influence. For example, you have already given succour to the Irish, through providing regular employment during the hay and corn harvests, year after year. You have fed them and given them your barn to sleep in. You have taken risks in doing that, and have been heavily criticised in some quarters for your "Papish sympathies". Your willingness

Long Memories

to take risks, and your wonderful generosity of spirit, are two of the reasons why I love you."

"Thank you, *cariad*. I can, and will, say exactly the same about you. But have I been so heavily criticised? I was not aware of it."

"Thank God that you are not aware of everything, Martha. You know too much for comfort as it is, what with your avid reading, and your inquiring mind, and your extraordinary powers of recall. But take it from me that Rector Thomas has campaigned for years to get the Irish banned from the parish, and blames you for inviting them back again, every time they reappear."

"But I am not the only one to use the Irish, Amos. There must be a dozen other squires in the neighbourhood who use them when they move on from the Plas."

"Quite so. The Rector blames them less, saying that they give work to the Irish because they are cheap, whereas you give them work on principle!" He made a strange noise, which in retrospect was probably a chuckle from a man with a sore throat. "Llewelyn Thomas is an idiot, if the Lord will forgive me for saying so. But don't you forget the power of the Nonconformists in this area, Martha. They hate the Pope and his faithful flock even more vehemently than the members of the Established Church do, and go so far as to say that the Pope is in the thrall of Satan, and has been seduced so as to do the devil's work."

"I know, I know. There is much about the Baptists, the Methodists and the others that I admire, but I cannot abide their smug self-satisfaction or their bigotry. Seeking salvation is one thing, but passing judgement on other human beings is quite another."

"Now then, Martha, you are being smug yourself. Do you not also pass judgement on others? Do I not do it? God forgive us, but in the last resort we all think of ourselves as better than others."

I thought it best to change the subject, and asked Amos if he could guide me on the matter of Brynach and his profiteering out of Indian corn. "Profiteering, Martha?" he croaked. "That implies a degree of cynicism and dishonesty. From what I know of your dear son, he is as honest as a June day is long, and is trying to make a living for himself and your grandson David. If he buys and sells commodities on the open market, that is what traders do -- and you should wish him well."

"But Indian corn is produced by the big landowners in the Deep

South, Amos, using black slave labour. Brynach must know that. He should refuse to have anything to do with foodstuffs produced under such conditions, and I am ashamed that he should be so naive."

"Perhaps it is you who are naive, Martha. If the products of the Deep South are not traded by the New York merchants, I could argue that prices and incomes would drop, and that the miserable lot of the slaves would become unbearable. There would probably be uprisings. Do you want revolution and bloodshed, or a quiet transformation of the American way of doing things?"

"But the Americans in the north hate slavery, Amos! I have read as much in *The Times* newspaper."

"Let the Americans sort matters out for themselves, Martha! I should not be at all surprised that Brynach has strong views about slavery, given the values that you have fed into him since he was a small baby. And while you are about it, you might be wise to let the Irish sort things out for themselves too. You have your opinions about the palatability of Indian corn, but Brynach knows that it is cheap and edible, and thinks he is providing a valuable service by shipping it to Ireland. As for me, if I had to choose between eating a bowl of Peel's brimstone and starving, I would probably choose the former."

So Amos comprehensively demolished my prejudices and reduced my concerns about Brynach. But I have to admit that after our conversation I was very irritated, and spent the next hour, while Amos was fast asleep in his warm bed, in a black mood. I knocked over a jug of milk and issued a string of expletives that made Myfanwy blush. Men are very useful at times, but they appear to look at the world with a degree of pragmatism and tolerance that is quite beyond my female comprehension.

ΩΩΩΩΩΩΩΩΩΩΩ

1st February 1847

Christmas and New Year have come and gone, and we celebrated those happy occasions well enough. Amos recovered from his chill just in time to

Long Memories

enjoy his Christmas dinner, and since the weather continued cold and snowy I refused to allow him to return to his flimsy hovel at Garfeth until it was safe for him to do so. In that, I dare say that I was being very self-indulgent, for I would prefer him (in an ideal world) to be in my house and in my bed than shivering and sneezing on some draughty and damp building location. As for the prophet himself, he had a thoroughly good time here, and showed all of us that in spite of his ascetic leanings he is perfectly capable of eating and drinking too much, with suitable encouragement. Some of my labourers and tenants who were with us on Christmas Day were surprised to observe this lighter side of him, having previously seen him either as a thundering and ferocious preacher or as a fallen holy man with a permanent frown upon his brow.

He was at the Plas for about three weeks, and I must admit in the private pages of my diary that I loved having him here. I dare say that that was obvious to all who had eyes to see, and while I was careful not to allow him anywhere near my bedroom, the many hours spent in each other's company reminded me of some of the pleasures of having a good man about the place. We talked endlessly on all manner of things, sometimes in private and sometimes in the company of family and servants. We walked several times on the mountain, on several afternoons plodding through thick snow and once having to brave a real blizzard which sprang up without warning. He was not at all discomfited by these natural hazards, and indeed seemed to be energized by them, reminding me that in his long life he has spent more nights under a canopy of stars than under a slated roof.

After three weeks at the Plas Amos started to become restless and irritable, and he and I started to get on one another's nerves. He is instinctively a wanderer in the mould of that hairy old fellow called John the Baptist, while I am rooted like an ancient oak in the stony soil of Carningli. I love him, and he loves me, and we have declared our love openly, in public, on more than one occasion. We have talked of marriage, but we both know that it would never work, and while we are very comfortable in each other's company and share many beliefs, I doubt that I could ever share his deep faith or tolerate his tendency to wander off every now and then in order to save more souls for the Lord. Probably I have my idiosyncrasies too, and if Amos were to take me on as a wife he would suddenly be burdened with responsibilities -- for the running of an estate which balances precariously on the edge of extinction, for the welfare of servants, tenants and labourers and their families, and for the education and nurture of a young granddaughter. His life, which is currently very simple indeed, would become more than a little complicated, and he would be faced with the need to make decisions, and more decisions.

So while our bond of love may well deepen and strengthen, I doubt that Amos will ever occupy my bed. I am sure that a part of him wants it, and I know that I want it too, but we have both been so seriously burned by the consequences of our infamous encounter in Tycanol Wood that the spontaneity and joy of that occasion would be impossible to recapture. So we will kiss and cuddle, and grow old together and yet apart, comfortable in each other's company, and sharing our memories..........

ΩΩΩΩΩΩΩΩΩΩΩ

7th February 1847

I suspect that before we go to our graves Amos and I will have to share experiences as well as memories, for something has happened that gives me a deep sense of foreboding.

Rose, my beautiful and sensitive granddaughter, has seen a battle in the sky. Yesterday I went up to Garfeth in the afternoon to check that Amos was well and to take him a parcel of food. I found that he was making admirable progress on his cottage, with the roof timbers now all in place and with the positioning of slating battens almost complete. He had two young fellows from Brynberian helping him, in reciprocation for some kindnesses given three months back. That is how Amos works; he gives and receives, without the inconvenience of coins and bank notes. We chatted amiably for a while, and then I set off for home, humming a happy tune. I arrived just as darkness was falling. Rose was not there, but that was no cause for concern, for according to Bessie she had walked down to town to visit two of her girl friends and had said that she would be back by five o'clock. So she was, but when she walked in through the kitchen

Long Memories

door Myfanwy, Bessie and I had to abandon our task of setting out the dinner things for fear that she might faint and hurt herself on the slate slabs. The poor girl, normally so ruddy-cheeked and vivacious, was ashen-faced, and there was a wild look in her eyes. We grabbed her before she could fall, and removed her cloak and bonnet before sitting her down on the settle by the *simnai fawr*.

"Good gracious, Mistress Rose," said Myfanwy. "You look like a ghost, or somebody who has just seen one. Are you all right?"

She nodded, and a fear common to all women of all ages came in to my mind. "My dear child," I said, taking her hands in mine and looking into her eyes, "has somebody intercepted you on the Cilgwyn Road? Have you been........?"

"No no, Grandma, nobody has interfered with me or attacked me. I saw nobody at all between Greystones Farm and the Plas. But I fear that I am greatly upset."

"That much is obvious, *cariad*. So what has happened?"

She did not answer, but looked around her with a mixture of puzzlement and horror still writ large across her pretty face. We gave her a glass of water, and for a few minutes she sat looking at the flames in the fireplace and breathing deeply. Then, having recovered her composure, she said: "Grandma, I should like to talk to you privately, if I may. May we go through to the parlour for a few minutes?"

"Of course. There is a good fire in there. Bessie and Myfanwy, please see that we are not disturbed." My servants nodded, and Rose and I went along the passage to the parlour, arm in arm. We closed the door behind us, but before we sat ourselves down I knew that Rose had seen a battle in the sky or some such thing, for I have been aware since she was a small child that she has special powers. The memories of my own supernatural encounters came flooding back to me. "You have seen the battle, Rose?" I asked.

She looked startled, and then swallowed hard and nodded. "It was truly terrible, Grandma! Such a cacophony of shouting and screaming and dying, and of clashing weapons, and of screeching clouds of arrows, and of horses falling! Oh, I hope to God that I never see such a thing again. If I do, I will surely die from the horror of it............"

"No no, child, nothing of the sort will happen. What you saw was in another world and from another time. I have seen it, and so has Shemi,

275

Long Memories

and so have others in these parts. Where were you at the time?"

"On the side of Carningli. What I saw was in the west, high above the glimmer of the setting sun."

"Mynydd Morfil again. And the light in the sky after the fading of the battle? What colour was it?"

"Red, Grandma. An unusual sort of red, somewhere between the colour of fresh blood and the crimson of an angry sunset."

At this, I fear that my task of consoling Rose was over and done with, and she had to console me, for I felt the blood draining from my face as panic gripped my breast. "Grandma!" exclaimed the sweet child. "Are you all right? Have I said something that you would prefer not to have heard?"

I confirmed that she had indeed done just that, and so I had to tell her all that I know about the battles in the sky and what they might mean. I then swore her to secrecy, for those who have special powers and who suffer the agonies of premonitions have a duty to care for those whose fate hangs in the balance. I was able to reassure Rose that it was most unlikely that she herself would be harmed in the coming weeks or months because of what she had seen, but I knew full well that somebody would suffer, and my experience told me that the finger of fate pointed at me.

ΩΩΩΩΩΩΩΩΩΩΩ

8th February 1847

Hard on the heels of my unsettling conversation with Rose, my discomfort has been compounded by revelations and remembrances. I had a visit in mid-morning from young John Wilkins Legal. It was good to see him, since he is a pleasant and efficient fellow who has helped me in the past to escape relatively unscathed from various crises. But solicitors, in my experience, do not turn up out of the blue bearing gifts on rainy winter mornings, and I knew before he opened his mouth that he was the bringer of bad tidings. We gave him a cup of tea to warm him up, and then he and I sat in the parlour together.

276

Long Memories

"My deep apologies, Mistress Martha," said he. "I like to make appointments for the conduct of official business, but today I have discovered something which I thought required immediate action, so I thought it best to come along directly to the Plas."

"I am all ears, Master Wilkins," said I, with a flutter in my breast.

"As you know, Mistress, old Elijah Collins died almost two months back. The circumstances surrounding his death were somewhat mysterious, and his servant Mary said at the time that he had not been ill before she found him dead in his favourite chair. Havard Medical examined the body and was puzzled, and decided in the end that he had died from heart failure. He was after all extremely ancient, and nobody was surprised at his passing. Doctor Havard wanted a post-mortem and an inquest, but the Coroner would not agree to it."

"I imagine that with very old people, unnatural deaths are very rare, Master Wilkins?"

"Correct, Mistress. When the Coroner made his decision neither Doctor Havard nor I had any basis on which to challenge it, and Christmas was approaching, so the dear old fellow went to his grave. I thought that that was that. Since Christmas I have been helping with the administration of his estate, and Llysmeddyg is about to go on the market. With the assistance of two old spinster cousins of his, and his servant Mary, I have been clearing the house, selling furniture and going through his possessions."

"I was aware of that, Master Wilkins, having recently received the latest small news from town. But what has this got to do with me?"

"Just this, Mistress Martha," said the young fellow, fishing into a deep pocket and producing a folded piece of paper. He handed it to me. "It is for you -- read it please."

The paper contained a short scribbled message, as follows:

For Martha Morgan Plas Ingli.

Dear Mistress Morgan
I cannot put my finger on it, but I sense a certain danger. You know that I have enemies, and you know who they are. If anything should happen to me, I beg you to recall our conversations in the spring of last year, and to keep away from Irish matters.

Long Memories

Some families have very long memories.
Sincerely yours

Elijah Collins Llysmeddyg
5th December 1846

When I read this, my blood ran cold, for I realized that the note had been written not long before his death. And I recalled only too well our conversations related at the beginning of this diary which had, in truth, until that moment gone out of my mind. I looked at the piece of paper again, and noticed that in the corner of it there was a little symbol, drawn in a shaky hand, which could only be interpreted as a ship's anchor.

I looked at Master Wilkins with questions in my eyes. He nodded. "Let me explain further. The note was found yesterday, in the middle of a great pile of papers on Master Collins' desk. I am not sure why he never sent it to you, or whether indeed it was meant simply to sit on his desk in case anything should happen to him. At any rate, when I found it Mary was with me, rummaging through various drawers. I showed it to her, and she frowned and said: "That little sign, sir. There's a funny thing for you, but when the Master died, and I found him in his chair, there was a crumpled scrap of paper on the floor by the side of the chair, with a little anchor drawn on it." She thought it was some little doodle he had been drawing, and thought nothing more of it, and threw it in the fire."

"And what does the sign mean, Master Wilkins? Have you seen it before?"

"Yes, Mistress, I have. You do not need me to interpret it for you, of that I am sure."

"The Society of Sea Serjeants? Oh no! Are you thinking what I am thinking?"

"I am, Mistress. And just for the record, I am not a member, even though I have been urged many times to join. Sadly, while this evidence might point to murder, we have absolutely nothing to go on. Elijah might simply have been deranged -- he might have drawn little anchors every day of his life, for all we know. And the members of the Society may all be as innocent as newborn babes."

"Have you drawn this to the attention of the Coroner, or the magistrates, or even to Doctor Havard?"

Long Memories

"No, Mistress. The letter was for you, and my priority was to see that you got it with all haste. Elijah has been in his grave for six weeks or more, and I doubt that an exhumation would tell us anything. In any case, permission for it would have to be granted by the Coroner and by the magistrates, who are all, purely by chance, members of the Society."

Shortly afterwards Master Wilkins went on his way, with a deep bow and the words: "Farewell, Mistress. Let me know if I can be of further assistance. And just you take care."

When he had gone, I sat alone in the parlour for a while, seeking to come to terms with the situation that has now arisen. I could not understand it twelve hours ago, and nor can I understand it now, as I sit in my room with my diary open before me and a quill pen in my hand. I have read Elijah's note over and again, and I have re-read my diary entries from 17th May and 25th May in the year 1845. I have also tried to recall my discussions with Skiff Abraham and the local squires and merchants over the last year or so, during which time I have urged them into philanthropic activity and tried to break the embargo on grain exports to Ireland. Apart from Skiff, they were all uncooperative, and some of them were rude to me and told me to mind my own business, but none of them actually threatened me, and at no stage during my conversations did I feel in danger.

And yet it is as clear as a crystal spring that Elijah Collins felt threatened before his death, and for a good many months beforehand, and that in his view I am threatened as well. If he was murdered by some fellows belonging to the Society of Sea Serjeants, could it be that they have it in mind to murder me too? But what would their motive be? Even the most evil and scheming of squires do not go around killing people, or paying others to do their dirty work, just because they are urged by some meddling woman to do something that they are disinclined to do. Now I am even more confused, and more than a little apprehensive, given Rose's recent sighting of the battle in the sky.

I will sleep on it, if I can, and in the coming days I will seek advice and undertake some research into the shadowy organization which employs the sign of the anchor. Twenty years ago I would have tackled this business alone, but I am older and wiser now, and do not have the strength to take on a battalion of squires and merchants single-handed.

Long Memories

9th February 1847

I did not sleep well, which is hardly surprising. But the day dawned bright and clear, and I took that as an omen that the world was not about to end and that I needed fresh air and sunshine in order to clear my head and refresh my spirit. So straight after breakfast I set out for a walk upon the mountain.

It was one of those February mornings which defy all the midwinter odds and remind me and the other inhabitants of the *cwm* that God is in his heaven and that spring is just around the corner. True, the sun was neither high nor hot, but there was warmth in it, and the crags of Carnedd Meibion Owen and the distant hills of Preseli were sharply etched against a sky of milky blue. There was no wind, and as I looked above my head I saw that thousands of seagulls were winging their way, high and silent, from their inland roosts towards the coast. That was a good sign, I thought, on a day when I needed encouragement.

I climbed up the trackway between our top fields, followed the edge of the common across the mountain face to Ffynnon Brynach, and anointed myself with a handful of its icy water. That old spring, I knew, had been blessed by Saint Brynach many centuries ago, and had healed many pilgrims in the bad old days, and had more recently provided the clean and healthy water for generations of the Morgan family and their servants and animals. Without the pipe that joined the spring to the farmyard and house, the Plas would never have survived in such a hostile environment, and would have been abandoned and rebuilt lower down on the bank of some river or stream, like all the other grand houses of the area. But here was the old place, still shining white on its rocky hillside, still sheltered from the Cardigan Bay gales, and still taking advantage of every ray of sunshine available to it from dawn to dusk.

How I loved this house and this mountain! I cursed my own negligence in failing to climb to the summit or to my secret cave for many months, and thought that had I done so I might better have coped with the momentous events which have brought me, more than once, to the edge of despair. And yet now, as on hundreds of previous occasions, with every step of my climb I felt energy rushing back into my body as the fog cleared from my mind. Soon I passed from the grassy mountain track to the tumbled blue boulders of the slope leading to the summit. Up and up I went, closer

Long Memories

to Heaven with every step, until I was scrambling over rocky slabs and boulders and banks of rubble, caused, I dare say, by the frost breaking up the living rock of the mountain since the beginning of time. I had to be very careful, since in February the rock surfaces are wet and slimy, even when the sun shines on them. There were five ravens on the mountain, settled on their favourite crag near the summit, and looking quite unperturbed as I approached. The oldest and biggest one looked at me with his beady eyes and moved his head from side to side; he was, I thought, scolding me for failing to pay him a visit in recent weeks.

I climbed to the summit and looked down on the coast and on the little town of Newport, and the port of Parrog at the mouth of the estuary. It was low tide, and there were three vessels beached on the sand, each one of them alive with the unloading of cargo onto horses and carts. In the streets near the castle, as ever on breathless winter days, smoke rose straight up from more than a hundred chimneys, showing me which houses and hovels burned wood, and coal, and peat. Here and there in the sunny and shadowy streets I could see people moving about. If I had had Grandpa's telescope, I should have been able to recognize most of them. Down there, I thought, are my friends and my enemies, getting on with their lives, unaware that I am up here on the summit with the angels, observing them and thinking about them, and pondering on the things that drive men and women to do good or evil.

Then I had an urge to visit my cave, and I scrambled down from the summit on the south side of the mountain and followed my familiar route along narrow ledges and crevices, past great pillars of rock and finally to the little rowan tree and the cluster of ferns that masked the entrance. I squeezed through the slit in the rock face and found my sanctuary quite unchanged -- cool and dark, with a few glimmers of sunlight filtering through cracks in the roof, and with my sheepskin and blankets neatly folded in the far corner, just as I had left them on my last visit. I sat down against the rough backwall of the cave, pulled a blanket over my knees, and pulled my knees up to my chin. I closed my eyes and watched my troubles rolling away over some invisible horizon. I did not sleep, but stayed in that position for maybe thirty minutes, mulling over the news which had recently come in to my possession and working out in a serene and orderly fashion what I might do next.

Twenty minutes later I was back at the Plas. It was soon time for

281

Long Memories

lunch, and for talking over the afternoon tasks with my servants. But when we had all eaten well and everybody had left the kitchen except for Bessie and me, I asked my beloved housekeeper and friend if she would sit with me for a while in the parlour. She did not look at all surprised, and said: "Certainly, Mistress. It has been quite clear to me that you have had something substantial on your mind since Wilkins Legal came here yesterday. You have been more than a little distracted."

When we were seated before the fire in the parlour, and had given instructions to Myfanwy that we were not to be disturbed, I said to Bessie: "Now then, my dear friend, you know me better than anybody else under this roof, and you have been more than a little involved in my escapades over the years. I need your help, since I am convinced that I face some danger, without knowing what it might be or whence it might come."

"Well, Mistress? Kindly explain. I will help you of course, if it is in my power to do so."

"Bessie, you go to town often, and seem to know everything that happens in the streets in the light of day and behind closed doors at dead of night. I want you to tell me who my enemies are."

"Mistress, what a strange demand!"

"Not strange at all, Bessie. Please put your mind to this, for my life, and yours, and the future of the Plas, might depend upon the accuracy of your reply."

So Bessie frowned, and thought hard for several minutes, while gazing into the crackling heat of the log fire. I looked at her, and thought her still uncommonly petite and pretty for her age, notwithstanding her grey hair and spectacles. What would I have done without her, I thought, during the time when I was trying to bring up a young family following the death of David, or during the years when I suffered from deep melancholia, or more recently during the intrigues of Rebecca and her daughters? She has certainly been too insolent and too honest with me at times, and sometimes she bosses me around as if **she** is Mistress of the Plas, and not I -- but she is truly an angel, and a guardian angel at that...........

I was dragged out of my reverie when Bessie lifted her eyes from the flames and looked at me over the top of her spectacles. "Very well, Mistress," she said. "In my estimation you have about a dozen enemies, and they are all men. That is interesting in itself, given your liking for male company."

Long Memories

"Enough of that, if you please, Bessie. Can we get to the matter in hand?"

She grinned, and then became serious again. "For a start, there are several squires who would be only too pleased if you were to be struck down by the plague or run over by a herd of bullocks. Squire Mefin Owen of Gelli Fawr, for a start, who is young and impressionable, and who runs a diminished estate following the death at the gallows of his father John. He probably blames you for his father's death, and for his other misfortunes............"

"But that is preposterous, Bessie! The old squire killed two men in cold blood, and I had nothing whatsoever to do with it!"

Bessie looked at me as a fierce schoolmistress might look at a little girl who has failed to do her lessons. "Mistress," she said, "I am not accusing you of anything. Do you want me to give you my opinion, or do you not? If you do not want to hear the truth as I see it, I can give you some fantasy instead."

"I am sorry, Bessie. Pray continue, and I will try not to interrupt."

She looked at me over the top of her glasses again as if she did not quite believe me, and continued. "Then there is Thomas Watkins, Squire of Ffynnonddofn, the nephew of the monster Alban Watkins who caused you such trouble when you were young. He is mean-spirited and ambitious, and the members of his family have long memories. Another one is Jacob Harry the merchant, who lost buildings and corn during the Rebecca Riots and who was greatly upset by your attempts to reform the local turnpike trust. He knows you were involved in the riots, and I have heard it said that it is one of his ambitions to teach the Mistress of Plas Ingli a lesson or two."

She paused as if expecting me to intervene again, as indeed I was about to, but I managed to bite my tongue and she continued. "Jacob Harry is a burgess of the town and has ambitions which are greater than his talents. He also has cronies including James Jobbins, the Squire of Holmws, with whom you have also crossed swords. As for him, he belongs to a close family which has fallen on hard times, and he is the brother of Master Jacob Jobbins, deacon of Capel Brynberian. This latter fellow, far from being an upstanding Christian gentleman, is narrow-minded and vindictive, and he has recently seen his reputation reduced to tatters as a result of the Big Meeting at Capel Brynberian and the ill-conceived court case involving Master Shemi. The other day, in town, I saw the two brothers talking intently on the street corner, and when they saw me coming they stopped and looked very furtive indeed. Another who was in their little group was William Howell, and another was Madoc Huws. The former is the illegitimate son of John Howell, who went to the gallows for the murder of your husband David. He calls himself a merchant, but he is nothing more than a thug who is involved in most of the skulduggery in the dark streets of the town. His father's family was once rich and powerful, but now virtually nothing is left of the estate; and for that, Mistress, I dare say you are to blame. The Huws estate at Bayvil was also once large and powerful until its decline was precipitated by Master Madoc's father Solomon. You crossed swords with the old father as you have with the son, Mistress, and they have always come out of these encounters with their reputations reduced. Have you heard enough?"

I moaned. "Oh my goodness, Bessie, I never realised that I had so many enemies. Have you still not finished?"

"I am almost done, Mistress. Others whom I would stay well clear of include Squire Dafydd Laugharne from Pengelli Fawr, who is not much better than his nasty old father who died a couple of years back and who on one memorable occasion tried to get me into his bed........."

"Really, Bessie? You never told me about that."

"It was a long time back, before I married my dear Benji. As I recall, Benji rescued me and gave the squire a black eye and knocked out three of his teeth for his trouble. He never did recover his good looks. Unlike the Laugharnes of Pontfaen, those who belong to the Pengelli branch of the family are not very nice people, Mistress, and they too have long memories. Returning to religious gentlemen, you can probably count among your enemies John Thomas, Thomas Jones and Stephen Lloyd from Capel Brynberian, all of whom have been humiliated as a result of the events at Capel Brynberian. I hear that they have all recently resigned as deacons, and you may take it as a Biblical certainty that they blame you and the Prophet for their misfortunes. Passing from the Nonconformists to the religious establishment, Rector Llewelyn Thomas is by no means an admirer of yours, and it is common knowledge that he is greatly irritated by your reluctance to pay your tithes and by your other attempts to break down the old order. He lost some corn ricks too, during the Rebecca Riots, and I know it as a fact that he still blames you for that. He is a traditionalist, and has many cronies among the burgesses and successful merchants in these parts. And last but not least, Mistress, you may know that Richard John Rice is back in town. You do not need reminding that he is a cousin of Joseph Rice, who was killed by his fellow conspirators in Haverfordwest Gaol many years ago. He was headed for the gallows anyway, as one of those who killed David and tortured your beloved Owain. Old Benjamin Rice, another whom you defeated and sent to his grave when the world was young, was of the same family. I hear that Master Richard was set upon a sparkling career in the army, but that he has been dishonourably discharged in recent weeks. There is some doubt as to the cause, but his superiors will have been mindful of the fact that he was more or less accused, in an inquest which you will remember well, Mistress, of causing the death of your servant Bryn Williams through neglect and brutality when the Rebecca Riots were at their height. He was also reduced to a laughing stock by Rebecca's daughters on a number of occasions. He knows that you were somehow involved in heaping these misfortunes on his head, Mistress, and he is furious that he cannot obtain hard information which he can use against you. He is an arrogant young man who is reduced to impotence and poverty, and I imagine that he would not be too sad to see you in your grave."

I suspect that Bessie might have continued with her catalogue of enemies, but at that point she decided that her list was long enough to be going on with. I sat in my seat for a very long time, trying to come to terms with what Bessie had told me, and incapable of words. She came and put her arm around my shoulders and kissed me on my cheek. "There now, Mistress," she said, "don't you take this too hard. You asked me to be honest with you, and I have given you my truth. I may be quite wrong in my assessment of certain gentlemen............."

"No no, Bessie, I am sure you are right in almost everything you say. But I had absolutely no idea that I was so universally hated!"

"Nonsense, Mistress! You are held in the highest esteem by the great majority of people in the neighbourhood. Your reputation is perhaps a little dented as a consequence of your dalliance with the Prophet in the woods, but for every dozen who have condemned you there is another dozen who have supported you and admired the manner in which you have stood by Amos and have attempted to shift the burden of blame and recrimination from his shoulders onto yours. You have hundreds of friends who will move heaven and earth to help you, should it be needed. Me, for

Long Memories

a start, and your other male and female servants, and friends like Ellie and Mary Jane. Then your daughters Betsi and Daisy. And your beloved Amos, and Shemi Wizard, and Ioan at Brithdir, and George Havard Medical, Skiff Abraham, Patty and Jake down on the Parrog, Master Wilmot Gwynne and his wife Delilah, not to mention Master Hugh Williams and John Wilkins Legal, and Squire Nicholas Lloyd, Squire Mostyn Gittins, Squire Alexander Williams, Squire John Collyer, and all your tenants. I could go on, Mistress, but I will refrain. Take it from me that in your circle of friends you have an invincible army."

"I do not want a war, Bessie, and would prefer not to require invincibility."

"That may well be, Mistress, but in my long life I have observed that those who are successful, and happy, and beautiful will always be hated in certain quarters. Jealousy is a particularly nasty vice, but there is a lot of it about. The same can be said of pride. And if a woman such as you is strong enough and determined enough to stand up for her beliefs and seeks to protect those whom she loves, then certain gentlemen will be humiliated in the process. We live in a man's world, Mistress, and almost all of those whom I have identified as your enemies have been humiliated by you at some time or another. Some of them, I suspect, have even been in love with you."

Then my dear housekeeper kissed me again and jumped to her feet. "Will that be all, Mistress? I have potatoes to peel and three cakes to bake." I managed to smile, and thanked her for her honesty, and she gave a curtsy and went on her way. I sat where I was, gazing at the flames in the fireplace and with my thoughts racing hither and thither, until I noticed that the room was getting dark and that dusk was spreading its fingers across the cwm outside. I cursed the day that Cruel Fate had snatched my young husband away from me more than forty years ago and had decreed that I should never marry again. If only I could have spent my life as the sweet and supportive wife of a good man, I thought, I would at this moment be thinking of cross-stitch or the colour of my new dress, instead of pondering on a strategy for the defeat of my enemies.

ΩΩΩΩΩΩΩΩΩΩΩ

Long Memories

12th February 1847

Today I implemented the second part of my plan by entertaining my most precious male friends to afternoon tea. Following my conversation with Bessie I sent notes to them begging them to come, and to their great credit they all dropped whatever they were doing and joined me, despite the fact that it was a miserable damp and drizzly day. Amos came of course, since I had to have him at my side. Then Shemi arrived from Werndew, riding in the Llanychaer trap with Wilmot, the Master of the estate. And finally my two sons-in-law , George Havard Medical on his pony and Ioan as ever plodding up the hill on foot. I asked Will to join us too, since after forty years at the Plas I count him as a dear friend and as a source of valuable information as to what is going on in criminal circles.

I love all of these good men, and know them well enough to dispense with formalities, so as we settled into the parlour over our cups of tea and slices of currant cake, I told them straight away why I had asked them to come. My days of secrecy are over, and I had decided on total honesty. So I told them everything -- about Rose's vision of the battle in the sky (which Amos and Shemi understood perfectly, having experienced such things themselves), about my discoveries relating to the death of Elijah Collins, and about my own sense of unease. I showed them the note written to me by Elijah shortly before his death. I told them about my recent conversation with Tom Foster, and my conviction that there was some connection between the "Great Hunger" in Ireland and events much closer to home in Newport. And finally I told them of my conversation with Bessie, and named all of those whom she had listed as my enemies.

"So there we have it, my dear friends," said I. "Something is going on, and I do not know what it is. That makes me very frustrated and a little scared since, like any woman, I like to be aware of things. Am I correct in my assumption that this all has something to do with the Society of Sea Serjeants?"

I noticed that glances were exchanged by several of those present, but luckily they were all disposed to total honesty, and it seemed to me that nobody held anything back.

"You are probably right, Martha," said George, a medical man who has been around for long enough to know most of Newport's secrets. "The Society is getting too strong for either your comfort or mine. It is a sign of

Long Memories

the times, with many squires and merchants in financial trouble. What used to be a social club and mutual admiration society is now , I fear, something much more sinister."

Then Wilmot said: "Correct, George. In my short time at Llanychaer I have been approached several times by those who want me on board, but when I make inquiries as to the Society's objectives they become very evasive, and it is clear to me as an outsider that those in charge have more in mind than annual picnics and talks about antiquities."

"And who are the men who make these approaches, Wilmot?"

"Some of those mentioned by your housekeeper, Martha. So far as I can see, the leading lights are Thomas Watkins, James Jobbins, and Dafydd Laugharne, all three of them experienced squires, magistrates and -- in their own eyes at least -- pillars of the local community. They are also burgesses, and are well in with the Lord Marcher. Thomas Watkins has been mayor once, and I dare say that the other two have ambitions to fill that office before long. I have met their wives too, and I am sorry to say, Martha, that Delilah judges all three of them to be ambitious and mean-spirited."

"Do you think that they might be jealous of me, Wilmot?"

"No doubt about it, Martha. Following the episode in the woods involving you and Amos, Delilah happened to meet them at some sociable gathering, and it is best that I do not repeat some of their comments about your morals."

Then Ioan chipped in. "You may not have been aware of it, Martha," he said, "but those three ladies were responsible for spreading malicious gossip in the days prior to the Big Meeting. We did not tell you at the time, since you had enough on your plate."

"I knew that too, Master Ioan," said Will. "My contacts in town were so angry that they offered to teach the three ladies a lesson. Told them to back off, I did, since there was enough trouble already."

I was amazed by this, and admitted as much, saying that I prided myself on keeping abreast of developments in female circles. At this, all the men laughed, and dear Amos explained that I had been so preoccupied over the past six or seven months that I might not even have noticed the disappearance of Mynydd Preseli from my bedroom window, had it happened. "Besides, Martha," he said, holding my hand, "you forget that in your own interests, certain information has been withheld from you by

288

Long Memories

your servants and friends."

Nobody wanted to go down that particular route, and Shemi said: "Back to this nasty little Society, Martha. I have been watching them for some time. To the best of my knowledge, every single person mentioned by Bessie when she spoke to you the other day is a member. Membership is not widely advertised, but I have my sources."

"The Brynberian deacons as well?" I asked, with incredulity in my voice. "The Nonconformists normally have nothing whatsoever to do with the gentry, and indeed seek to diminish their power and status at every opportunity."

"They were invited to join, Martha, after the Big Meeting and the ill-fated court case in which they sought my conviction for murder."

"Shemi, that is incredible!" I whispered, suddenly very afraid. "Do you mean that the leading lights in the Society have gone out to recruit those who might have reason to hate us? That would imply the darkest sort of conspiracy............."

"That may or may not be so, Martha," said Ioan. "I do not think that the Society exists for the purpose of taking revenge upon the Mistress of Plas Ingli. But Watkins, Jobbins and Laugharne have long memories. Watkins in particular is a very nasty fellow who holds you responsible for the gruesome death of his Uncle Alban and for the collapse of the Watkins estate at Llannerch."

"But that all happened forty years ago, Ioan!"

Wilmot laughed, and said: "The gentry have long memories, Martha! I have dealt with them for long enough to have realized that pride and honour are more important to their way of thinking than integrity and honesty. Family feuds can go on for generations. Why, have you not told me yourself of the great feud between the Morgans of Plas Ingli and the Lloyds of Cwmgloyn?"

"Safely resolved, thank God," said Ioan. "But the Society does recruit religious gentlemen now and then, for the sake or respectability. Reverend Llewelyn Thomas is a member, and is indeed the Society's Chaplain."

At this, Will hooted with laughter. "The man is a clown!" he chuckled. "He may be Rector, but I don't know anybody who respects him, Mistress. You don't have to worry about him. But if I were you, I would worry about that smooth-talking snake called Richard Rice, and Joseph

Long Memories

Harry and William Howell. If I can hazard a little guess as to how the Society works, I would say, Mistress, that the squires provide the brains, and the deacons the respectability. Then the three I have just named are the ones who do the dirty work."

Everybody in the room nodded. I asked the obvious question: "Including murder?"

All eyes turned to George, and Shemi said: "I was very sorry not to have examined Elijah Collins's body. You did George, and although you were suspicious you found nothing that would obviously point to murder. Now Master Wilkins has provided information that seems to confirm that the death was not a natural one."

"I agree, Shemi," said George. "Now, in retrospect, I wish that I had insisted on an inquest and a fuller post mortem examination. Sadly, I received no cooperation from the Coroner or the justices............."

"I think we all know why," said Wilmot.

"Can we obtain an exhumation?" I asked.

"I would advise against it," said Amos, who had been remarkably quiet up to this point. "I am no medical man, but I would have thought that after the passage of two months the body will be somewhat decomposed, and if George did not spot anything the signs of harm done by the hands of evil men will have been very subtle to begin with and will have disappeared entirely by now."

"I am not sure of that, Amos," said Shemi. "George and I have our methods, and we might pick up some clue. But I agree that on balance we should leave the body at rest, and not alert suspicions by making a great palaver. If evil has been done, and if we are ever to catch those responsible, it is best that they are unaware of our interest."

"And the sign of the anchor?" asked Wilmot.

"Well known as the sign of the Society," said Ioan. "I have seen certain communications between Society members in the past, and in addition to their silly games with passwords and codes, they use the anchor as a sign of brotherhood."

"How very charming!" said I, with as much sarcasm in my voice as I could manage.

"There is much more to it than that," said Shemi. "I know it for a fact that the sign is sometimes used as a "visiting card" when a member is disciplined, and I have also seen it used on non-members as a threat, or as a curse, in order to create fear in the heart of the recipient. Very primitive, but we wizards know all about the effectiveness of such things."

"So the anchor sketched onto that piece of paper near Elijah's chair might have been an assassin's visiting card, or else a warning?"

"Correct, Martha. At present we have no way of knowing which."

"And the Irish connection? Why did Elijah mention Ireland in his note to me? He seemed very keen that I should keep away from Irish matters."

This caused great discussion amongst my friends as we drank more China tea and ate some more slices of Bessie's excellent cake, and in truth we got nowhere. Wilmot thought that the squires and merchants involved in the Society might be upset about my attempts -- and those of Elijah Collins -- to influence their buying and selling strategies; but I could not for the life of me work out why they should be so upset as to threaten either of us. And why should an argument about grain exports and the starving peasants of Ireland be viewed in such a serious light as to require threats, or revenge, or even murder? Nothing quite added up, and at last we concluded our meeting with an agreement that we would each keep our eyes open, and our ears to the ground, in the hope of obtaining enlightenment.

When my other dear friends had gone home, I was left alone with Amos. As a relative newcomer to the district, there was much that he did not understand about local politics and the families mentioned in our discussions, and he wanted background information from me. He was also keen to talk further about the revelations of the afternoon, and indeed I wanted to explore further with him what might be going on. It gave us the opportunity to sit in the parlour alone, in front of the blazing fire, well into the evening. We cuddled and we talked, and indeed my burden was considerably lightened as he listened sympathetically to my meanderings and speculations, and gave me gentle and wise advice. Whatever may happen in the future, I know that Amos will stand at my side. He may even stand in front of me and take whatever missiles might be aimed at my heart by my enemies.

ΩΩΩΩΩΩΩΩΩΩΩ

Long Memories

15th February 1847

Today, on a sudden inspiration, I took a walk to town, intending to do a little shopping and to visit assorted friends and acquaintances. I called in first to see my old friend Patty on the Parrog. She was very happy to see me, and for a while we talked of family and friends, and of small news from the community. Then I asked her about Richard John Rice, lately a Lieutenant in the Light Dragoons and even more lately dishonourably discharged and seen hanging around the inns of Newport. I knew that she would know whatever there was to know about him, because she has a special interest in the members of the Rice family dating from the time, more than forty years ago, when an evil monster called Joseph Rice forced her into prostitution and lived off her earnings. I apologised for reminding her in this fashion of an unsavoury past which would have destroyed a lesser woman, but she laughed and said that it was all a very long time ago, and that that part of her life had taught her a great deal and had turned her from a feeble servant girl into a woman with the guile and the guts to survive in a cruel world.

"Richard John Rice?" she laughed. "Of course I know all about him, Martha. A distant cousin of Joseph Rice. He has lodgings on West Street, and drinks in the Royal Oak. Jake drinks there too, and sees him quite often. Slim and good-looking he is, and quite a dandy, but he is so affected and arrogant that most of the locals cannot abide him. He is teased mercilessly by all the regulars at the bar, and great amusement is caused because he is totally unaware of what is happening behind his back. His Welsh is not very good, and that does not help the poor fellow."

"Is he evil, Patty, or as capable of wickedness as your persecutor Joseph Rice?"

"I would think so, Martha. He is certainly not a gentleman, although he clearly thinks that he is. I have seen no wickedness from him since his arrival some weeks back, but he does keep unsavoury company."

"And who might his special friends be?"

"A very interesting assortment of friends, Martha, as Jake remarked to me the other day. That brute William Howell for a start, whom I would not like to meet in a back street on a dark night. And then Jacob Harry, whom we know only too well down here on the Parrog as a man who would sell his grandmother for a few crowns. And then those

Long Memories

sanctimonious deacons from Brynberian who lurk about in the Royal Oak but refuse to touch a drop of the Evil Drink. Is that not highly entertaining? I forget their names......"

"Masters Jobbins, Thomas, Lloyd and Jones?"

"Yes yes, the very same, Martha. The ones who spoke and made fools of themselves at that Big Meeting. Jacob Jobbins and John Thomas were the two mentioned by Jake as being in the inn just the other day."

That was enough to keep my brain occupied, and I thanked Patty for her information and asked her if she would kindly keep me informed of the activities of the fellows mentioned.

Then I went to see Skiff Abraham, and explained my concerns about the Society of Sea Serjeants. I also told him most of what I had divulged to my friends at the Plas a couple of days ago. He was intrigued, to put it mildly, and clearly shared my suspicion that certain members were up to no good and were seeking to exert influence over the Barony and over other groups such as the Court Leet and the Association of Commoners. After a long and detailed conversation he agreed to set some of his spies the task of finding out what was being planned in the Royal Oak and in other drinking places frequented by the Society faithful.

And after making a few purchases in town, I made a point of visiting the little cottage on College Square where Mary Ifans lives with her old mother. Mary was the housemaid who looked after my old friend Elijah Collins in the last few years of his life at Llysmeddyg. As luck would have it, Mary was at home, and invited me inside. I declined her kind invitation and said: "Forgive me, Mary, but I must be back at the Plas very shortly. I just have one thing to ask you, and hope that you will not think me impertinent. It is just that Master Wilkins Legal has recently shown me that note written by your old master shortly before he died, and I wonder whether you can recall any visitors who might have called in to see Elijah on the day of his death?"

"Well, Mistress, there was Havard Medical, whom I called to the house when I found the poor master in his chair. And then later on there was Davy Death who came to do some measurements for the coffin, and later still the master's old cousin Mistress Sally Collins who came over from Dinas."

"And before he died, Mary?"

"Oh yes, Mistress Martha , now that you come to mention it. In the

293

morning it was. Three gentlemen who came to see him now and then to talk business. I don't think he liked them very much. One of them was Master Harry, the merchant from the Parrog, and another was Squire Thomas Watkins Ffynnonddofn, and the third was some fellow new to the town, with a fancy way of talking. I remember the others referring to him as "Lieutenant", so I suppose he must be a sort of soldier."

I thanked Mary for her help, and went on my way. I was thinking so deeply on my climb up Greystones Hill and along the Cilgwyn Road that I hardly noticed the weather, or the time of day, or the beauties of my beloved *cwm*. When I arrived back in the kitchen I found that Rose was there, chatting to Myfanwy in a very animated fashion. By all accounts she had just been for a walk down to Pantry Fields with one of her girl friends from town. "Oh Grandma," she chirped, as excited as a little sparrow, "I have just been for a lovely walk, and have come back with a ravenous appetite. I can hardly wait for supper! And do you know what? When I approached the house along the lane, guess what I found nailed to the gatepost at the entrance to the yard? This little picture! Is it not pretty?"

And she handed me a rough piece of paper which had been folded into four, and which had on it a rough sketch of a ship's anchor.

ΩΩΩΩΩΩΩΩΩΩΩ

12. Flotsam and Jetsam

8th November 1847

Not for the first time in my life, I have looked into the black jaws of death, and have lived to tell the tale. For more than two months I have been in my sick-bed, hovering between life and death, and on several occasions I quite lost the will to live, only to be pulled back by the love of Amos and the rest of my family and servants, and the medical skills of George and Shemi. I am still very weak, but now I want to live, for there are things to live for and things that I have to do.

My misfortune -- in the form of the typhoid sickness -- was entirely of my own making, and my enemies had nothing to do with it. I must briefly set down what happened, omitting many details, since the best part of nine months has passed since I last took up my quill pen.

In the spring of this year I was in a strange mood, and although I did not plunge into the deepest sort of melancholia (such as I have experienced too often in the past) I was listless and uncertain of myself. I could not understand what was happening in my life, or in the lives of others such as Amos and Brynach, and in truth I felt afraid. That feeling of fear and foreboding might have been deep in my breast before the Society of Sea Serjeants left that sign on my gatepost, but to my shame I treated it as a curse and convinced myself that the powers of darkness were out hunting for me and that it was only a matter of time before they caught up with me and devoured me. Amos, Bessie and Shemi all saw ominous signs, and told me not to behave like an idiot. "Martha!" said Shemi on one occasion at my bedside. "You have laughed at such primitive tricks many times in the past, and now you allow a silly piece of paper to turn you into a snivelling wretch! Pull yourself together if you please!" Even Rose, young and innocent as she was, reprimanded me and tried to help me.

But I could not pull myself out of my lethargy and misery, and in a perverse sort of way I enjoyed it, since it gave me an excuse for forgetting the world and all its troubles and turning inward upon myself. Why, I thought, should I worry about the downfall of Amos, and black slaves, and Brynach's future, and Rose's prospects of a good marriage, and the hunger

Flotsam and Jetsam

in Ireland? Why, I thought, should I not let others worry about **me** for a change? I felt that I had given of myself, and given again until there was nothing left to give -- and now it was high time to receive and to recover my capital. So ran my thoughts -- silly, conceited and self-indulgent though they were, and articulated to nobody but Bessie in one of many tearful episodes.

So I wrote nothing in my diary as week followed week, and as the harrow followed the plough and as the harvest followed seed-time. I observed events from a distance, but did nothing to influence them; and indeed I felt as Tom Foster must feel in his life as a reporter for a great newspaper, recording and commenting on the news but taking care never to become the story or even to be involved in its fashioning.

But things did happen in my world, and I do recall some of them. Around Easter I became aware, through my friends and my little network of spies, that the Society of Sea Serjeants was tightening its grip on Newport and the surrounding countryside. Membership increased substantially, and the leading lights in the Society took control of key institutions including the Barony, the town council and the Court Leet. It came to my notice that Thomas Lloyd of Bronwydd, the Lord Marcher and owner of the castle and thousands of local acres, had become a member. Others who were not members, including Coroner Will Daniels and the Mayor and constables, were pressurised in a number of ways and were "encouraged" never to step out of line or to take actions against Society stalwarts. Petty crimes which should have gone to court were overlooked or not deemed worthy of pursuit, which was very convenient for the perpetrators but miserable indeed for the victims. Extortion and blackmail followed, and a number of people who stood against the Society were beaten up. Some of the local thugs who had laid low for a number of years suddenly found themselves in great demand, and one of their jobs was the collection of protection money. My friends were disgusted and depressed by what was happening, and to their credit they resisted the bullies and blackmailers and managed to maintain a sizeable opposition of honest townsfolk. But Bessie and Ioan told me that law and order in town had almost broken down, and that they could hardly believe that such a thing could happen in the space of just a few months.

Looking back on it now, the seizure of local power had probably been going on insidiously for years, through elections and appointments, with

Flotsam and Jetsam

nobody realizing that those moving into power all belonged to the Society, while those moving out were non-members.

My friend Wilmot, supported by Jake Nicholas, Skiff Abraham, and a number of squires including Gwilym Mathias, Aaron Voyle, Mostyn Gittins and Joshua Lloyd, sent several submissions to the Lord Lieutenant and to our Member of Parliament complaining that there was virtual anarchy in Newport, with thugs ruling the streets and with honest people hiding behind their shutters; but they would not intervene, saying that the administration of local affairs, and the effective working of the judicial system, were matters that had to be resolved locally. Wilmot was furious, and became convinced (though he could not prove it) that both of those august gentlemen were themselves members of the Society. I was urged over and again to help in the attempts to restore peace and civility to the town, but I felt too tired and too personally threatened to do anything.

At first it was hard for anybody to identify the "invisible masters" of the town, but gradually they came out into the open, and by May they were flaunting their new-found power and enjoying the adulation of their cronies and the servility of almost everybody else. As Will predicted back in the early part of the year, the brains behind the operation belonged to Thomas Watkins, Dafydd Laugharne and James Jobbins, with William Howell, Richard Rice and Jacob Harry acting as their lieutenants.

In retrospect, and on pondering why this group of corrupt and power-hungry men should have targeted Elijah Collins and myself, it was probably because we were both considered to be strong and incorruptible. Maybe they thought that if they could subdue us, preferably through threats and subtle pressure, then their hold on the town might be consolidated. My thinking on this was confirmed one day by Skiff, who has his sources. According to him, Squires Dafydd Laugharne and Thomas Watkins had been overheard in the Black Lion agreeing that if an alliance of independent-minded residents including myself, Wilmot and Ioan should be created and maintained, then the ambitions of the Society might be thwarted. They were greatly afraid of that, and agreed that at some point it might be necessary for things to "get rather dirty." I also received a report from Patty, who keeps a close watch on Richard Rice, that he and Watkins have sworn an oath on the blood of their ancient families that they will settle old scores with the Mistress of Plas Ingli.

Flotsam and Jetsam

In the light of all of this, and looking back on it, was it surprising that I should feel as threatened as a fragile snail with a booted foot poised above it, and retreat into my shell?

And as if this was not all bad enough, word started to circulate in Newport at about the time of the hay harvest that certain stalwarts of the town, portraying themselves as the guardians of virtue, were minded to "make an example" of Mistress Morgan and Jones Minor Prophet. Skiff told me that Rice and Watkins were at the source of this message, and that they shortly afterwards started to put out another message, along the following lines: "Old Elijah Collins was a very uncooperative fellow who talked too much and interfered in matters that were none of his business, and look what happened to him!" That was as close to an admission of murder as may be imagined, but of course the leaders of the Society knew, after the passage of more than six months, that they would get away with it -- as indeed they did.

Malicious gossip started to circulate again about my encounter in the woods with Amos, and word was put about that he and I shared a bed and fornicated quite brazenly at the Plas in the full knowledge that my tender and innocent granddaughter Rose was living beneath the same roof. It was also put about that I had manipulated Wilmot and obtained the remote cottage at Garfeth for Amos, so that he and I could use it for "dalliance and debauchery." I was shocked by the evil that lay behind these rumours, and jolted by the realization that not just I, but Amos too, might be threatened by these fellows. I could not work out why they should be so interested in him, but then I remembered that he had on more than one occasion thundered against them from his pulpit.

Suddenly, towards the end of June, I decided that enough was enough, and I dragged myself out of my apathy and went onto the warpath. I do not know to this day why that happened, but maybe it was because Amos was getting himself into deeper and deeper water by giving wayside sermons on corruption and the abuse of power. Three times he was hit and injured by flying stones, and once he was so badly beaten up by some of the Society's paid thugs that he had to be given medical assistance and carried back to the Plas on George Havard's chaise. I remember Amos saying to me: "Well, Martha, if you will do nothing to defend yourself, I will do the defending for you. If I get killed in the process, so be it." So with more fury in my breast than was good for me, I decided that I had

Flotsam and Jetsam

nothing to lose by demonstrating my contempt for the Society. At the beginning of June I ostentatiously advertised for Irish labourers for the hay harvest, by nailing a notice on the door of St Mary's Church according to local custom. That caused Rector Llewelyn Thomas and others to become incandescent with rage, since never before had anybody used the church door to encourage Papists into the neighbourhood. He ripped the notice down, but by the time he did that it had been read by quite enough local people to have become the main talking point in town. Predictably, I then received more pieces of paper with ship's anchors on them, but I refused to be cowed or diverted from my course, and later in the month (having got the Irish labourers I needed) I placed another notice on the church door telling the Society of Sea Serjeants to stop pestering me and to "desist from playing silly games." That caused even more of a stir, since that was the first time that the Society of Sea Sergeants had been named publicly in writing; and the *Cambrian* and *Western Telegraph* newspapers both carried stories about "secret activities and the decline of law and order in Newport." That caused Watkins, Rice and their cronies to go underground for a while, and to some degree law and order were reasserted.

In July news came that the Irish Potato Famine had become worse, although God only knows that it was bad enough already. The people themselves started to refer to it as "Black Forty-seven". I was kept abreast of developments not only by the reports in the newspapers but by detailed letters from my friend Tom Foster, who was travelling about mostly in the western districts. He told me that after a cruel winter the new potato fields were all black and stinking. All public works, said he, had been suddenly stopped by the Government. Many of those works had been useless in practical terms, for example through the building of roads where they were not needed, but they had at least provided a modest income for those who needed money and food. Now, on a political whim, 700,000 people had no money at all. Soup kitchens were being set up everywhere, said Tom, and whatever self-respect the poor labourers might have had before, through being able to work and buy the food they needed, had inevitably disappeared. Typhus, scurvy and other diseases spread through the population at a frightening rate.

I still cannot account for my fascination and involvement in the affairs of the Irish, but I was greatly moved by the news of suffering and death on an unimaginable scale. News came from other sources of great

Flotsam and Jetsam

numbers of people fleeing across to Liverpool and into Fishguard and the other ports of West Wales. This caused problems, for when times are hard (as they are in this neighbourhood) there are limits to the tolerance and benevolence of people when confronted by hordes of sick and penniless refugees. And when the refugees are Papists, even the charitable instincts of church and chapel members tend to be greatly diluted.

In the month of August, prior to the start of the corn harvest, I decided on a short visit to Ireland. Tom Foster was passing through, having been back to London for a few days for meetings with his Editor, and so disturbed was I by his reports of the brutal behaviour and political posturing of those who presume to call themselves our elected representatives, and of the situation across the water, that I became obsessed with the idea of seeing for myself. Tom and my family and servants tried to discourage me, saying that there was little I could do to help, and that I might be placing myself in danger, but I refused to be diverted. I promised that I would be away for no more than a week. Bessie agreed to come with me.

With Tom acting as our guide and companion we took the packet vessel from Fishguard to Wexford. There were very few travellers on board, and the crossing was smooth and easy. That gave me the chance to talk to the captain of the ship, who said that of late the journeys in the opposite direction had been chaotic, with scores of poor Irish peasants trying to buy places on board or even trying to sneak past his crew and to get to Fishguard as stowaways. I could believe that, since I knew that many of these frantic souls were now on the streets of all the towns of Pembrokeshire, begging and pleading for work.

We spent our first night in a good little inn in Wexford, and then travelled westwards on a road recently repaired in the Public Works programme. Soon we were passing crowds of poor ragged shoeless people trudging eastwards, and both Bessie and I were horrified by their emaciated bodies and sunken cheeks and by the fact that they were carrying virtually nothing. "They are fleeing from certain death," said Tom. "They are carrying nothing, Martha, because they own nothing." I could not work out how such distress could afflict a land so lush and green, but then as we approached Kilkenny Tom pointed out the little patches of land which were owned or rented by the peasants and which were used for the growing of potatoes. Many of those little plots were already

Flotsam and Jetsam

abandoned, and those which were still cultivated (if that is the right word) were covered in a black stinking mess of rotting foliage. Underground, said Tom, the tubers which should have been plumping up for the October potato harvest were already destroyed by the deadly blight.

We passed Kilkenny and saw a place where a thick broth of Indian corn and other ingredients was being fed to long queues of people, and Tom then directed our carriage away from the main road and into the hills. "You wanted to see the full extent of the tragedy," said Tom. "My Editor wants me to send a report from the far west, but I hear rumours of great hardship near Tipperary. Let us see what we find here."

I can hardly bear to describe what we did find at the end of the dirt track, for I had never before encountered such human degradation. Along the street of what might pass as a village there were rows of little hovels or cabins, made of bits of wood, sods and stones. There were no chimneys, but here and there peat smoke was filtering through roughly thatched roofs. The sun was shining brightly, and in some respects it was a perfect breezy August day when all should have been well with the world. The street was quite deserted, and the place had an eerie feel about it since there were no dogs, no chickens and no pigs rooting about.

Tom knocked at a flimsy door of one of the hovels and we heard some little noises from within. I hesitated to enter, but at last I did, and once my eyes adjusted to the darkness I was terrified by what I saw. In a space no bigger than ten feet by fifteen there must have been a dozen people. Near the embers of a turf fire an emaciated woman was crouched, listlessly seeking to stir up the flames. It was impossible to tell how old she might be. Next to her there was a cooking pot containing a broth of green leaves. In a dark corner, almost invisible, at least three children were huddled together, apparently too weak to rise. One of them raised its white face towards us and pleaded with its eyes. It opened its mouth, but no sound came out, and I suppose it must have been in the last stages of starvation or disease. The other children might well have been dead. Although it was warm outside, the inside of the hovel was damp and smelling of urine and faeces, and the stench of typhus. The floor was sodden and muddy. On a patch of straw lay an old woman, so shrivelled up that she might have been a small child, moaning piteously and rocking gently back and fore. In her arms lay a small baby, showing not the slightest sign of life. The only man in the place was a very old fellow lying on a raised platform that presumably served as a bed, partly covered with rags. In between his coughs he cursed us with as much energy as he could summon, and when we fled outside again into the sunshine I was shaking like an aspen leaf, and understood well enough why he should hate us and all the other well-dressed and well-fed well-wishers who passed momentarily into his life and then passed out again...............

We tried to do something to assist that particular family by obtaining supplies at Tipperary market and returning later with them, but when we got back to the hovel we found that members of the local Relief Committee had called and had taken four bodies away for burial and the rest of the family to the workhouse. We hoped that they would be fed and saved, but we knew that the workhouses and their associated fever wards were fearsome places where only the strongest survived. I asked Tom if he would take Bessie and myself to visit the Tipperary Workhouse. He was very reluctant, and said that those who inhabited the place were suffering from a number of diseases including scurvy and typhus. But I insisted, and could not resist going into the foul vapours of the fever ward and trying to give some small comfort to those who were dying and some small encouragement to those angels who were trying -- often without any hope of success -- to save them.

That was when I became ill. I do not know how or when I contracted the disease, but Bessie thinks it might have been even before our visit to the Workhouse. I went down with a very high fever, and although I have only the haziest of memories of the following days and weeks, Bessie tells me that I became delirious and started to vomit, and that I later developed a rash and horrid sores all over my body. Tom insisted that I should return to Wales immediately, for there were few facilities for nursing me in Ireland, and so he took me and Bessie back to Wexford and sent us off across the water on the first ship he could find that was destined for Fishguard. Ironically it was a tidy Irish cargo ship carrying exports of butter, cheeses, barley, and wheat flour in sacks, all destined for sale in the markets of Fishguard, Haverfordwest and Newport. If I had been capable of it, I would have wept.

Flotsam and Jetsam

10th November 1847

In October, having recovered some of my strength and having become capable again of rational thought, I tried to do something to alleviate the suffering of those poor people starving in their hovels across the water. I greatly admired the work of the Society of Friends who raised great sums through their Irish subscription and who bought food, clothing and seed to be distributed among the poor. From my sick bed I wrote to all of my female friends and started a Newport Subscription for the Relief of Irish Distress, and with their enthusiastic support we managed to touch the hearts of local people. Daisy put on a play in town which was wonderfully popular, and Rose and her girl friends organized a bazaar with musical entertainments. We raised a grand total of £846, and were very proud.

Then Tom wrote to me and said that in many respects the famine was stayed, and that the soup kitchens all over the country had fed many thousands who otherwise would have died. Indeed, he wrote that many of these feeding stations had now closed, with charitable gifts of food flooding into the country to take their place. That did something to restore my faith in human nature. So what should we do with the money we had raised? After consulting with Tom, I decided along with Patty, Betsi and Daisy that we must send turnip, cabbage, flax and barley seed which could be used to encourage the Irish peasants away from potatoes and towards the growing of a wider variety of crops which would make them less vulnerable to the effects of disease or the vagaries of the weather. I tried to buy seed as cheaply as possible, and had a major row with the squires who belonged to the Society of Sea Serjeants, who were intent upon playing the market. Some of them had seed for sale, but they, like me, had read of the large sums of money raised in London and elsewhere through the Irish Subscription, and they wanted to wait until the agents of the charitable organizations came to Fishguard with more money than sense, looking to fill ships with food and to send them to Wexford and Cork. So we by-passed those squires completely, and with the help of Ioan and Wilmot and some of the squires with whom I was on good terms we set fair prices for the seed that we wanted and bought it from those who were willing to forego their normal profit margins. In this way we increased the size of the shipment by maybe fifty percent. Since I was still very weak, and

Flotsam and Jetsam

since Bessie would still not allow me out of the house, Skiff Abraham organized the shipment, and Ioan and Wilmot travelled with it to Ireland and coordinated with the Quakers to see that it reached those who needed it in the west. To my intense satisfaction, Tom saw to it that fifteen bushels of seed went to the very village in which we had observed such destitution and degradation as I had never dreamt of.

ΩΩΩΩΩΩΩΩΩΩΩΩ

14th June 1848

It has taken me a very long time to recover fully from the effects of the typhoid fever which I contracted in Ireland. I suppose that had I been afflicted in my days as a young and sprightly woman I would have fought the sickness off with a toss of my head and the wave of an arm, since I had no time to be ill; but I fear that age is taking its toll, and that I have less energy than I would like. Having felt somewhat stronger in November (at the time of the last entry in my diary) I fear that I felt very weak during the winter, and that I was so susceptible to chills and other ailments that Christmas and New Year were occasions that all but passed me by. I was also too ill to attend the wedding of my grandson Abel in the early part of December, which should have been a great occasion in my life. That was very frustrating, for my melancholia had quite disappeared and I was angered by my own frailty.

In the spring, with the sun reasserting itself and bringing warmth and comfort to both me and my beloved landscape, I felt much more like my young self again, and assisted in obtaining signatures for the great Chartist Petition presented to Parliament on the 10th day of April. I would dearly have loved to be in London for the mighty rally on Kennington Common, but my family would not allow it on the grounds that I was still too weak for such excitement. They were probably right. Nonetheless, in May I celebrated my 70th birthday in some style. All of my family and friends came, and we had a splendid feast in the garden, for we were blessed with a perfectly warm and still May day. Amos, Shemi and Betsi made little

Flotsam and Jetsam

speeches about me, which made me very emotional, and I have to admit to shedding tears as I was reminded of the love which enfolds me and nurtures me at the Plas. And in the evening, we kept alive an ancient tradition by taking a long nature walk on the common and down towards the coast, with Shemi leading us and talking about birds and flowers and rocks in a manner no less erudite than his predecessor Joseph Harries all those years ago when I was young.

So I felt better, much to the disgust of the faithful members of the Society of Sea Serjeants, who had probably wished me dead. They probably wish Amos dead too, since he has taken up much of the past twelve months -- when not sitting at my bedside and ministering to my needs -- in preaching from his wayside pulpit and attacking corruption and greed at every opportunity. Since he cannot now preach at Capel Brynberian or in any other chapel, he does his preaching in the open air, and appears to enjoy it. He is no strutting bantam, and I have urged him to settle into a quieter life, but there is a sort of mad energy about him, and he relishes controversy and risks. So where he sees injustice in the magistrate's court he writes letters and preaches about it and then seeks to help the victims in any way that he can; and where he sees deprivation he pesters those who are wealthy for "contributions" so as to achieve a modest redistribution of wealth. He has no money himself, so there is a limit to his own munificence, but he is truly a pastor in the best sense of that word, and he does seem to be able to bring succour to the needy in a spiritual sense if not in a practical one. He is greatly loved by the poor, of that I am in no doubt. He is, after all, one of their number.

The cottage at Garfeth is finished, and Amos is very proud of it. He put a great amount of work into it, and so did many of his helpers, and it is now as cosy as may be, with four small rooms (each lit by a good-sized window) and a central passage connecting front and back doors. I gave him some furniture and crockery, and Wilmot gave him a bed and a table with four chairs. He might have bought some items very cheaply from distraint sales, where the bailiffs have removed items from the homes of poor people who have defaulted on their tithe payments or their rents, but he refused to have anything to do with such sales, saying that he would not benefit from the misfortunes of the poor. He even has flowers in his little garden at the front of the cottage, and a vegetable patch with cabbages and potatoes at the back. He has painted the cottage red, and from the

Flotsam and Jetsam

window of his dining room he can see the Plas very clearly across the *cwm*. So comfortable is he that he now has time on his hands, and I dare say that those who see him as an enemy are quaking in their boots at the thought of what he might choose to do with his empty hours.

There has been another wedding in the family, just one week ago. This time the happy young man was Benjamin, the oldest son of Ioan and Betsi, who married the oldest daughter of Squire Mortimer of Stone Hall. His new wife Sally-Anne brought with her a good dowry, and although the couple will live for the time being in a cottage on the Brithdir estate they will no doubt have other ambitions and may choose to find a larger place of their own which they can populate with children.

The hay harvest is late this year, and as I write the rain is hammering against the west side of the house and sluicing down off the slate roof. That does not augur well, for much of the grass in my three hayfields is already flattened. The Irish have been knocking on my door, but as yet I have no work for them. Thinking of Ireland, the news from Tom is that the famine is easing off, but with hundreds of thousands dead and with hundreds of thousands more fleeing to America, Canada and the other colonies in search of a new life, it is clear that things will never be the same again on that benighted isle. That is no bad thing, for there was a great need for land reform and for changes in agricultural practices, but under the new "laissez faire" philosophy land is changing hands fast, and the new breed of squires and land-holding merchants are evicting tenants legally (or illegally with the connivance of the courts and the government). So starvation and disease are replaced by homelessness, and those who are not so weak as to be apathetic are stirring and demanding rebellion. Troops are pouring in and there is much antagonistic comment in the press, even from Tom, who feels that if they are not careful the Irish rabble-rousers will quite lose the goodwill of those who currently keep them alive through charitable subscriptions and gifts of food.

So there is going to be trouble in Ireland, and there is apprehension in my breast as I read in the *Times* of unrest and even revolutions all over Europe as ordinary people seek justice and increased rights in the choosing of their rulers. I am tempted to go and sort out the Hungarian Republic; but I gather that the climate is hostile in those parts, and on balance I think I will go shopping in Cardigan instead. I doubt that there will be revolution here, but our silly government appears very nervous indeed.

Flotsam and Jetsam

20th July 1848

I have just read Tom's report of the Irish Rebellion in the *Times* newspaper. It was expected, I dare say. However, it appears to have been a farce rather than a real threat to authority, involving but a handful of quite incompetent people, but Tom (who becomes more opinionated, and less of a reporter, as he gets older) has thundered against it, and he is now convinced that sympathy for the plight of the Irish will ebb away. Support for Ireland was always very fragile anyway, with large groups of influential people in England feeling that the Irish have been the architects of their own misfortunes and that they should solve their own problems, even if the price of reform is a million people dead. Others, especially within the church, adhere to the primitive belief that the Great Hunger was, and is, an act of divine retribution for the misdemeanours of a whole nation. One of the misdemeanours is apparently the production of large numbers of babies. And others, adhering to even more primitive beliefs, believe that the Irish people are being warned by God to give up their blind loyalty to the Pope and are being encouraged to walk in the bright and shiny light of Protestantism instead. I have seen letters in the newspapers expressing exactly these sentiments, and I sometimes feel that old-fashioned tolerance has been entirely replaced by bigotry in our modern and progressive world.

There are other reports from Ireland that the warm wet weather has been perfect for the blight, and it is being predicted by the experts that virtually the whole of the potato crop is already ruined. With no help from the government or the British public, the country will be left to cope as best it can. According to new legislation, all the poor relief which came in the past from the government now has to be charged to the rates -- and I fear that the only way the squires can find the money they need is by enlarging the size of their tenancies and reducing the number of tenants they have to deal with. That means evicting thousands of peasant families who have occupied their pathetic plots of land for generations. So the tragedy rolls on like a giant boulder shaken loose from a hillside, crushing a whole nation.

So concerned have I been about Ireland that I have sought to reactivate the Newport Subscription for the Relief of Irish Distress. However, I am sad to report in the pages of my dairy that it has been very

Flotsam and Jetsam

difficult to obtain donations, and I have raised only £23 thus far. This compares very badly with my earlier efforts. Even my good friends say that they "cannot afford to help just now", which means that they are not prepared to treat Irish starvation as a priority. I have given this matter much thought, and I have been to Amos's cottage to ask him whether my concern for starving people is rational or irrational. He and I talked for several hours, and I had to admit to being somewhat obsessed with the Irish question. He laughed and said: "I love you for it, Martha! It is no bad thing that you should attach yourself to some great cause, and since Irish typhoid fever almost killed you a short time ago it is perhaps not surprising that Ireland should still be in your thoughts. Better that than worrying about silly squires and their secret society, and -- dare I say it -- better than worrying about the breeding potential of your new bull or the yield of a new variety of turnip!"

"But I do feel some guilt about my obsession, Amos, and also anger that others do not share it with me."

"That is natural enough, Martha," he said, putting his arm around my shoulder and giving me a little kiss. "I feel exactly the same when I preach the Gospel and others throw stones at me instead of appreciating the profound wisdom of my words."

"But you are a saintly fellow, Amos, and are used to coping with setbacks and adversity. You seem to be able to sail along serenely through life, no matter what happens to you. I do not, I fear, have that sort of resilience."

"Oh, but you do, Martha. I understand, from what you and your family have told me, that you have bounced back on many occasions in your long life from situations that would have destroyed lesser mortals. Just be patient -- if you want to make a grand gesture for those in need, your chance will surely come. In fact I am sure of it."

I was surprised by that, and raised my eyes to meet his. "Now then, Master Jones, is that your minor prophecy for today?"

"It is, Martha. Accept it if you will." Then he changed the subject, and refused to talk further of prophecies or of Ireland. I was most irritated, but by way of a peace offering he gave me a cup of tea and some very hard black barley-flour scones made palatable through the addition of large quantities of honey. I had to grin, and complained about his cooking, and the rest of our conversation was frivolous to the point of being absurd. But my dear friend knows me well, and is perfectly familiar with my tendency to worry too much and to get too involved in matters outside my control, and he knows how to make me laugh. At any rate, when I left an hour or so later I had a much lighter step and a longer stride, and that was not just because I was walking downhill.

ΩΩΩΩΩΩΩΩΩΩΩΩ

18th August 1848

High summer has been truly awful, with one storm after another roaring in from the west and with driving rain causing the virtual destruction of the grain harvest. It is almost too late for me to harvest my three fields of barley. Much of it is flattened, and seeds are already starting to germinate on the ground. I fear that unless we get a miraculous change to warm and dry conditions within the next few days, the wheat harvest will go the same way. I have only half as much hay as usual in the rickyard, and whatever barley and wheat I do get into the barn will have to go for animal feed. I will have to slaughter more beasts than usual, sell more than usual, and buy in both grain and hay before next winter is out. Those are all miserable prospects indeed, but I have faced similar catastrophes before, and I dare say the Plas will survive.

That was Mistress Martha the farmer reporting on practical matters and collecting her thoughts. Now to the real news, which relates to the fulfilment of Amos's prophecy of last month. I had been wondering what might happen to me and what opportunities might open up before me, but now there has been a most amazing and terrible occurrence.

We have had a giant of a storm, with such winds as I have not experienced for fifty years or more. It started yesterday and continued this morning. Trees came down not only up here on the edge of the common but also in Gelli Wood and the other woodlands in the *cwm*. Slates flew off our roofs, and although we did our best to keep the shutters closed in the house, many panes of glass were smashed in our windows. According to the news reaching the Plas, more than twenty animals belonging to my tenants

Flotsam and Jetsam

have been killed by falling trees and by the floods which followed eighteen hours of continuous and torrential rain, although so far as we can gather there has mercifully been no human loss of life in the neighbourhood. There was no thunder and lightning, but the wind screamed in, first from the west and then swinging round from north-west to north. That gave the Plas some degree of shelter from the great bulk of Carningli, but I knew that the coast of Cardigan Bay must have been battered by mighty waves, and we all knew that any vessels caught offshore by the shifting of the wind would have had little chance of survival, even with all sail furled and with sea anchors out.

By four o'clock in the afternoon the rain had stopped and the wind had eased off a little, and I decided that Will and I should make a tour of inspection on the estate so as to assess the damage done. We were walking across the bottom fields, looking for three missing sheep, when we saw a young man running towards us. I recognized him at once as my grandson Benjamin, who works with his parents Betsi and Ioan at Brithdir. He was dressed in heavy oilskins, and he had a soft felt hat on his head, tied under his chin with twine. "Grandmother!" he shouted above the wind, as soon as he was within earshot. "Thank God you are here and not away on the common! A most dreadful thing has happened!"

"Tell me about it, Benjamin."

We met up, and I gave my dear grandson a kiss, noticing at the same time that he looked exhausted, and that he was soaked to the skin in spite of his oilskins. "Three or four hours since," he said, "a ship was smashed onto the rocks at Aberrhigian. I was out on the coast with some of the other coastguards, since we knew that there would be shipwrecks. At least four vessels, so we hear, between here and Fishguard, and God knows how many along the whole coast between St Davids and Aberystwyth. At any rate, as chance would have it we were on the cliffs near Aberrhigian when this one came in, driven by waves the like of which I have never seen before. More of a boat than a ship it was, Grandma, made of canvas, and maybe twenty-five feet long with just a little section covered with decking. There might have been a small mast and a crude sort of sail, but the wind and the waves had taken them."

"A sort of curragh, Benjamin, like they have in Ireland?"

"Correct, Grandma. Such a vessel has never been seen on this coast before. Jake Nicholas was with us, and he knows these things. It came

Flotsam and Jetsam

onto the rocks just to the east of the cove. We could see that there were people on board, screaming with terror although we could not hear them for the noise of the wind and the waves. We scrambled towards the place where the boat was on the rocks, but the cliffs are high just there, and we thought that we would never be able to get to them with our ropes and rescue equipment. Well, we had just about given up hope of rescuing those poor souls when I stumbled through a gap in the furze bushes and fell down to a little grassy platform halfway down the cliff. I never knew it was there, Grandma, although I know that coast well!"

Then the dear young fellow paused in his narrative, which had been tumbling out of him in a veritable torrent. "Grandma! Are you all right?" he asked. "You look suddenly very distressed. Is my narrative upsetting for you?"

"No, no, Benjamin," said I, hanging on to Will's arm. "I have suddenly realized that I know that particular ledge on the cliffs rather well. Pray continue."

And continue he did, although in truth my recollection of his words is hazy from this point on, since memories of a picnic with my beloved Owain Laugharne on a perfect May day, a long time since, kept on flooding into my mind. That was in 1807, if I am not mistaken. More than forty years ago .... and what an occasion that had been, filled with love and beauty, and spoiled by my wild imaginings of a creature called the Nightwalker just as we were coming to the peak of our loving! Dear Owain, poet and romantic, the kindest and gentlest of men, and long since in his grave! How I had loved him, and how he had loved me!

I pulled myself out of my reverie and tried to concentrate on what Benjamin was telling me. But the dear young fellow was shivering uncontrollably now, and I insisted that we had to get back to the Plas where he could warm himself by the fire and get out of those soaking wet clothes. We talked urgently as we walked, with the wind still howling about us, and by the time we got back to the kitchen I had discovered that Benjamin and his heroic colleagues, with the aid of their rockets and ropes and harnesses, had managed to rescue eight people from the doomed canvas boat as it was smashed to pieces at the foot of the cliffs. At least eight others were lost, including a small baby and three other children, and several elderly people who did not have the strength to hang onto the ropes that reached them from the cliff. Two of the children who died

Flotsam and Jetsam

were actually pulled up onto the grassy ledge, but they were so weak that they could not be resuscitated.

"Oh no! What terrible loss of life, Benjamin!" I said, as he changed out of his wet things. "Where are the survivors now?"

"In a hovel near the turnpike road, Grandma. The old couple there, Tom and Ginny Jenkins, are trying to warm them up and get some hot soup into them, for they are in a truly terrible state. Just skin and bones, all of them. And battered, bruised and bleeding from being thrown about on the rocks. I think two of them have broken limbs. It's a miracle that any of them are alive."

"And the dead?"

"Taken by Jake and the others back to the mortuary on the Parrog. Only two bodies so far, but no doubt others will be washed up."

"Who are these people, Master Benjamin, and where have they come from?" asked Will.

"That is why I am here, Will. They are from Ireland, and from what I can gather they set out a week ago, seeking to escape from the Great Hunger, from a place called Arklow just up the coast from Wexford. They had no money, and virtually no food on board, and it seems that they just set off with a westerly wind behind them, hoping to land somewhere on the coast of Wales."

"Desperate times and desperate measures, Benjamin," said I. "And so providence swept them onto the cliffs at Aberrhigian........."

"They see it as providence, Grandma, for they say they know this coast well, and claim to know you."

I was greatly surprised by this, and said: "Do they indeed? Have they told you their names?"

"Yes, Grandma. They all belong to one family. The father is one Brendan O'Connell, and his wife is called Mary. I'm afraid I cannot recall the names of the six children. They are all very shocked and terrified, as you can imagine, and say that those who perished in the wreck were all related. Brendan is quite inconsolable, and says that the eight of them are now all that is left of the O'Connells."

"Oh, that is truly terrible, Master Benjamin!" said Will. "That family has been coming to the Plas to help with the harvest for as long as I can remember, and maybe back to the time of Grandpa Isaac or even earlier. Good friends they have become, over the years, and they are hard

Flotsam and Jetsam

workers too. A sad thing it is if they have almost died out, because of the Hunger and other misfortunes."

At this point Rose got some dry clothes for Benjamin and Bessie made him swallow some hot soup, while bombarding the poor boy with questions about the rescue. I sat silently in my favourite settle by the fire for some minutes, gazing at the flames. Was this the same Brendan O'Connell whose life was saved by Joseph Harries Wizard after a hayfield accident all those years ago? Then, as I recalled, he was a lively little boy aged five or six; now he must be in his late forties. He was a very special friend to Daisy, I knew, and it was while they were playing together that Brendan slipped and almost cut his leg off on a sharpened scythe. Was it his fate, or mine, that had now brought his family into Aberrhigian, one of the special places in my life, and had brought news of the catastrophe straight to the Plas?

Again I was disturbed from my thoughts of the past, and of the meaning of things, by Benjamin, who suddenly asked: "Grandmother, what is to be done?"

"Is that down to me, Benjamin?"

"Why yes it is, Grandma. This poor Irish fellow seemed to come alive again, having looked like a drowned rat, when I told him where they were on the Welsh coast and told him that I was related to the Morgans of Plas Ingli. He pleaded with me, with tears in his eyes, to come straight to you and to tell you of the plight of his family. "Tell Mistress Martha," he said to me. "She will know what to do." So here I am. It is down to you, Grandma, since the parents and the six children cannot possibly stay in that hovel down by the turnpike road. The old folks who live there can hardly feed themselves, let alone a family of starving Irish. We will have to get them out of there by nightfall. If we do not, they will be picked up by the constables and either sent packing, to make their way in the world, or transported to the Cardigan Workhouse on humanitarian grounds. If I may be so bold, Grandma, neither course of action will do them much good."

So it was that ten minutes later we set off from the Plas at the gallop, with a view to transporting the shipwrecked Irish mariners back to the Plas. Will and Benjamin were in attendance, each one driving a trap. On the road we had to dodge many obstacles thrown down by the storm, but after thirty minutes or so we arrived at the old people's cottage

Flotsam and Jetsam

not far from Dinas. When I went inside I thanked God that it was still August and that the air was quite warm, for there was no decent fire in the grate, and Brendan and his wife Mary, and the six children, were sitting in a huddle together, trying to keep warm. Two of the littlest ones were wailing inconsolably, and another one, a girl aged maybe eleven or twelve, was sobbing and appeared to be deeply shocked. Her arm was horribly twisted, and I was sure it was broken. Their sodden and ragged clothes were hanging on a line draped across the width of the cottage. Tom and Ginny Jenkins were clucking about them like old chickens, mopping up the blood from their injuries, indubitably kind but very ineffectual.

"Why, Mistress Martha!" said Brendan when he saw me, with his green eyes shining. "May God bless you! I knew that you would come, and that you would help us if you could."

I hardly recognized him, so small and thin was he. He struggled to his feet, grabbed my hand and fell to his knees, in the manner of actors in grand theatricals, while his wife handed over the small baby she was nursing to one of the other children and gave a deep curtsy.

"I am truly sorry for troubling you, Mistress," he whispered, "being already greatly in your debt.........."

And as if the poor fellow was not wet enough already, tears started rolling down his cheeks. I pulled him to his feet and put my arm around him. "Why, Brendan, what is the meaning of this? Whatever Doctor Harries and I might have done for you when you were a small boy was spontaneous and exactly what you, or any other civilized person, would do for somebody in need. There was no debt, and even if there was you and your family have repaid it a hundred-fold through your honest toil at my harvests over the years."

It was apparent that this was no time to talk of harvests, or of anything else, for these people needed warmth, food, and medical attention as quickly as possible. So we wrapped all of them up in the pile of blankets which we had brought with us, got them packed onto the two traps, and after giving our thanks to the old people in the cottage set off for home. We made a diversion past the house belonging to Daisy and George Havard Medical, since three of the smallest children were shivering uncontrollably and clearly needed skilled help. George was out looking after other victims of the storm, but Daisy said she would send him on to the Plas as soon as he returned, and all I could do was hope that

Flotsam and Jetsam

that would be sooner rather than later.

I need not have worried, for when we got back to the Plas twenty minutes later Shemi Wizard was there, having received some sort of guidance that he was needed. His medical knowledge is almost as great as that of a trained doctor, and he can also heal with his hands and with herbal remedies which George dismisses as "scientifically dubious." We got the eight refugees into the warmth of the kitchen, wrapped them in yet more blankets and went hunting through the house for old clothes that would fit two small and thin adults and six small children all under the age of twelve. We threw their old clothes out, since they were no better than rags. Shemi examined each member of the family in turn, tenderly and efficiently, cleaning and bandaging the wounds received in the battering on the rocks, and checking them for fever or other injuries. Communicating with them was not easy, since the children speak no English or Welsh, and cannot easily describe their symptoms. But Shemi diagnosed as best he could. He made temporary splints for the two children with broken limbs, and they both screamed in agony as he tried to manipulate them pending later treatment. He was very worried about the oldest child and one other, aged about five, and thought that they might both be suffering from scurvy or some other ailment related to malnutrition. He gave them some herbal tonic and said that he looked forward to getting a second medical opinion from George when he came.

Then, once the O'Connells were all warm and as settled as circumstances would allow, we gave them some food. Bessie had already prepared a steaming hot broth and some slices of barley bread, on the assumption that she would need to feed the starving; but ravenous as they were she would not allow them to gobble down too much, saying that they were so thin and undernourished that they would be violently sick if they were not tended carefully. "Small quantities, quite frequently, is what starving people need, Mistress," she said to me. "Just you trust me."

We sent Benjamin back home to his wife at Brithdir to get some tender loving care and, above all, some sleep. The poor boy was so tired that he could hardly stand, and I dare say that he was exhausted from his efforts on the cliffs even before he came to the Plas with his message from Brendan. He and Jake and their coastguard colleagues are truly heroes, and had it not been for them it is obvious that the whole of the O'Connell clan would have been wiped out.

315

Flotsam and Jetsam

During the course of the evening I was able to snatch a further conversation with Brendan. I remembered that Benjamin had talked of the loss of other members of his extended and prolific family. So I asked him who else had been on board their flimsy craft, and who had been lost.

"My father and mother, Mistress, two of my uncles, two of our own children, and three of my brother's children, who came under our roof when they were left alone in the world............." His voice cracked, and I saw that there was a look of unspeakable desolation on his face.

"Oh, you poor things!" was my inadequate and banal response. "Your parents Molly and Michael? They were with you? I had assumed that they were dead long since, for we have not seen them here at the Plas for some years."

"Well, now they are flying with the angels, Mistress. They had the chance to get ashore when Master Benjamin and his friends kept on sending that harness of theirs down from the cliffs, but they declined time and again, and insisted that Mary and me and the children went first. Eight of us got ashore, thanks be to God, but then a monster wave swept in and what was left of the boat was smashed to smithereens. God only knows what happened to those still aboard. I suppose their bodies will be washed up on Berry Sands when the storm has abated."

There was a long silence. Then I asked about the ages of the children lost, and discovered that the youngest was just one and the oldest sixteen. The older ones were swept away because they insisted that the little ones got ashore first. "And your two uncles, Brendan -- was one of them named Daniel?"

"He was, Mistress. He was not my real uncle, but he took our family name and became a member of the family. Always on the run from the English, he was, and he swore that a bullet or a bayonet would take him; but now the sea has done for him instead."

I wanted to talk more, but this was neither the time nor the place. Now it is late at night. I have given Brendan and his exhausted and traumatised family Gerallt's room, which is the the biggest downstairs room in the servants' quarters. They are so confused at present that I do not want to separate them, so they are crammed together in the manner to which they are accustomed. George turned up at dusk, dog tired after visiting a dozen other people injured in the storm, and he and Shemi gave some sort of sedation to the two children with broken limbs and tried to reset them as best they could. In the case of the oldest child with the broken arm, they had to operate on the kitchen table, and they say that the bone is so shattered and the damage to soft tissues is so great that an amputation may be necessary.

Now the house is as quiet as may be expected in the circumstances, and we must all try to sleep. George has gone home, and will return in the morning. Shemi is asleep or awake on a temporary bed in the parlour. Gerallt has gone to sleep in the hayloft above the cowshed. Every now and then the wailing of one of the children disturbs the black silence of the August night, and as I write I can hear Mary humming softly as she tries to get him or her back to sleep. It is a serene August night with a full moon sailing high overhead, but it has a mocking grin on its face, as if it knows that I am faced with an unspeakable tragedy and know not how to cope with it. So when I go to bed I will probably lie awake, watching the pool of moonlight passing slowly across my bedroom floor, with a single question going round and round in my mind: "What must I do? Oh, what must I do?"

Ω Ω Ω Ω Ω Ω Ω Ω Ω Ω Ω Ω

23rd August 1848

In the night following the rescue of the O'Connells from the cliffs at Aberrhigian, the tragedy was compounded, for two of the poor little children died. At three in the morning, when it was still dark, I was wakened by a commotion downstairs, and I knew that Shemi was up and about. I went down and found him ashen-faced in the dimly-lit kitchen, with two little bodies laid out on the table. Brendan was sitting by the fire, moaning and rocking gently back and fore, and I could hear sobbing coming from the room in which the Irish family had been sleeping. That was Mary, grieving and at the same time trying to console her four children who were still hanging onto life. "There was nothing I could do," said Shemi bitterly. "Brendan came and knocked on the parlour door ten minutes since, asking me in a whisper to come quickly. He was afraid, poor

Flotsam and Jetsam

fellow, that he might wake the rest of the house. It was too late. I think both of the children died in their sleep at least an hour ago, Johnny from shock and disease, and little Martha from the injuries to her arm........."

"Did you say Martha, Shemi?"

"Yes, Martha. Brendan told me she was named after you. I fear that the poor girl had very little chance of fighting through the crisis brought on by her injuries; if she had been a normal well-nourished child, that would have been a different matter."

Then Bessie appeared, followed by Rose, Blodwen and Myfanwy, all woken by the shuffling feet and whispers and moans. I will forbear to describe in detail what happened during the rest of that day, except to say that it was largely taken up with the business of death. We had to inform the Coroner, Will Daniels, about the two new deaths at the Plas, and we had to take the two little bodies on the gambo to the mortuary on the Parrog to join those of the two other children who had died on the cliffs during the rescue. When we got there we found that there were five other corpses too; three new bodies had been brought ashore by the high tide on the little beaches near the sea quarries, and two more on the wide expanse of Berry Sands near Parrog. There was one child, but the other four were adults. I looked at them, and thought that I recognized all four. There was a woman who looked familiar, but whose name I could not recall. Next to her lay Molly and Michael, greatly aged and now serene in death. And then I saw the grizzled and battered face of Daniel O'Connell, who had entered my life briefly more than forty years ago when he worked on the Plas Ingli corn harvest. He had also brutally murdered Squire Alban Watkins, the worst of my enemies, in a revenge killing, in retribution for atrocities committed by the squire while he was in the Australian penal colonies. Later on he had written to me, admitting the murder and saying that he would never see me again. In that he was right, as he was right to say that he would not die in his bed. But in his letter he also said that I would not see him again, and in that he was wrong. I still have the letter, buried deep among my papers.

I sent a message to Amos, and he came and ministered to the needs of the bereaved and shocked family. He knelt and prayed with them on many occasions, which I found strange and wonderful, given the animosity which most Nonconformists feel towards Papists. He talked at great length to Brendan and Mary, and although there was no common language

318

Flotsam and Jetsam

he managed to communicate with the children, and to make them smile.

With so many bodies there had to be post-mortems and inquests, and Will Daniels, George and Shemi had two days of gruesome activity. Brendan and Mary were the only ones who could identify the bodies with any certainty, and I stayed with them and tried to support them when they passed, looking as pale as death themselves, from one corpse to another laid out on the cold slate slabs of the mortuary. The Coroner, who is a decent if feeble fellow, was very sympathetic, and arranged a single inquest at which all the deaths were examined. It was decided that some of the deceased had been drowned when swept away from their battered craft and that others (including Johnny and Martha) had died from "injuries sustained during the shipwreck, and from disease, hunger and trauma." It was a mercy to the parents, and a relief to the rest of us present at the inquest, that the amount of detail required in evidence was minimal, and that the Coroner showed great kindness and sympathy towards those who were left alive after the tragedy.

So with the Inquest over and done with, nine coffins were transported to Fishguard on three of the Plas Ingli gambos, for a funeral mass and burial at the Catholic Church of St Mary. Rose and the servants looked after the surviving four children at the Plas, and Brendan and Mary travelled with me and Amos in the chaise. Throughout the proceedings they behaved with a dignity and stoicism which I could hardly believe. That is, I dare say, a characteristic that all the poor people of Ireland have acquired. Although I shed tears at the funeral, they did not weep, but remained stony-faced throughout, and I was glad that they were supported by many of my friends and family including George and Daisy, Ioan and Betsi, Wilmot and Delilah, and Shemi and Sian from Werndew. Patty and Jake were also there, along with Benjamin and the members of the coastguard watch who had tried so desperately to save the shipwrecked family. Most of those present in the congregation had never been inside a Catholic Church before, and understood little of what was going on, but the grief was shared and genuine.

The burials of the dead took place yesterday. I am still undecided as to what to do, and the six survivors have been given a space in the hayloft above the cowshed. That is not as primitive as it might sound. It is warm and dry there, and the room, boarded in with rough planks, is used quite often as a retreat or a refuge. We have made up four beds there and two cots for the smallest children, and the family has privacy, which I deem to be a necessity just now. There are also twelve small kittens for the children to play with.

This morning two more bodies were washed ashore at the far end of Berry Sands. More grief, more funerals............

ΩΩΩΩΩΩΩΩΩΩΩΩ

24th August 1848

At last I have decided what to do, and as I write this there is a mixture of fear and excitement in my breast.

For days, whenever I have been able to snatch a few moments to myself, I have been mulling over the tangled web of connections between the O'Connell family and myself, without being able fully to understand the significance of any of them. At last, with the harvest still delayed because of yet more rain, I decided to climb up to my cave and to ask the angels where the shipwreck tragedy was leading me. On the way up, with the rain lashing down from a leaden sky and sluicing off the blue rocks around me, I doubted the sanity of my decision to go out on such a day, but then a sort of elation came over me. Once I was inside the cave, in the cool darkness, I took off my sodden oilskin cape and hat and left them near the entrance. I settled down on the sheepskins and blankets near the back wall.

I drew my knees up to my chin, closed my eyes and breathed deeply. I tried to focus on the matter in hand, and gradually the clouds cleared from my mind. I realized that I had had links with Ireland, and with the O'Connell family in particular, since my earliest days at the Plas. We had got to know Michael and Mary O'Connell as shy and gentle people during one harvest after another, discovering that they had been evicted from some pathetic patch of land and were effectively homeless wanderers, travelling around Britain and Ireland and working on one regional harvest after another. They had gathered up hay, corn, potatoes, turnips, apples and other produce for countless squires, travelling between Wexford and Fishguard at least once a year for fifty years or more. They

Flotsam and Jetsam

probably knew more about agriculture than I did! Their children worked with them, and their wages, measured at each location in pennies rather than shillings or pounds, somehow kept them alive during the winter and spring. The episode involving Brendan and the scythe had brought their poverty and their subservience into sharp relief. But there was an independent and rebellious side to the family too, and while I was not sure whether Brendan or his father Michael had ever been involved in riots or disturbances across the water, his Uncle Daniel certainly was. He travelled with the family in the year that Brendan was injured, specifically with the object of finding and executing Squire Alban Watkins in revenge for the deaths of his four brothers. He had done that, with considerable planning and much brutality; but when he wrote to me later it became clear that he was a cultured fellow who was much more than a political assassin. He was certainly in contact with subversive organizations, and received and transmitted information within a considerable network of spies. No doubt he was motivated by the desire to obtain political freedom from the English, and I will not blame him for that. He was a handsome and even charming man, and I think he was in love with me..........

Then I remembered that Daniel had been friendly with Jake Nicholas, and that Jake had not only picked up news of Alban Watkins's sadism and perversion in Australia during his days in the Royal Navy, but had also sheltered Daniel and helped him on his mission of execution. Now Jake had been involved in the rescue mission on the cliffs at Aberrhigian, and, I suppose without knowing it, had tried to save his old friend. Had he looked into Daniel's eyes and recognized him through the maelstrom of flying spray before that last wild and monstrous wave had snatched him away? Jake has thus far not mentioned anything to me about the connection, but he was at the inquest, and is well aware that one of the names of the deceased was that of Daniel O'Connell.

Then there is the connection with Daisy. When she was a little girl Brendan was one of her special friends, and since the tragic arrival of the family at the Plas she has been back and forth many times, ministering to their needs and talking to Brendan at great length. There is a barrier of class and age between me and Brendan, but not between him and Daisy -- although it is ironic in the extreme that my dear daughter, who once shared a bed with the Prince Regent and who moved within the most

Flotsam and Jetsam

fashionable circles in London, should now be so friendly with a penniless Irish peasant who has every reason to hate every single member of the English establishment.

And there is a connection with Brynach too. I had forgotten it, but now recalled that when he was left on my doorstep on an April day in 1807, I was convinced for a time that the child's natural mother was eighteen-year-old Kate O'Connell, wife of Jamie O'Connell and one of seven members of the Irish family who were in Pembrokeshire at the time, looking for work. As it happened, my suspicions were unfounded, but at the time Kate lost her own baby and was saved from death herself by the medical skills of my friend Joseph Harries. I must remember to ask Brendan what his relationship might be with Kate and Jamie...........

As for the fact of the recent clifftop rescue being effected from the very ledge on which Owain Laugharne and myself, following his return from the dead, made passionate love in 1822, I could only speculate on its significance. Perhaps that was pure chance, connecting me to happy memories, but with no other significance? Perhaps **all** of this was pure chance, with me reading great things into simple situations and reacting emotionally to a tragedy that was really none of my concern? Perhaps, if I waited a few days, common sense would return and I would be able to relax and get on with my life?

But then the ghost of Alban Watkins started to haunt me again, and for some reason my mind turned to the Society of Sea Serjeants. That monster of a man had been responsible for many of the misfortunes of the Morgan family in my early days at the Plas. He had wanted the Plas so badly that he had been involved in a corrupt court case in order to get it. He had been shipped off to the penal colonies after being found guilty of a whole range of crimes, but had later returned, murdered my husband David and tortured my beloved Owain at the time when we were betrothed. In the end, Watkins had died at the hands of Daniel O'Connell, but had he not had something to do with the Society of Sea Serjeants? I racked my brains, and recalled at last that on several occasions when I was young, Grandpa Isaac had expressed fury at the self-serving activities of the Society and had been involved in quite serious disputes with them over trading matters. I am sure that the name of Alban Watkins had come up on more than one occasion. Now the Society was threatening me again, with the last of the Watkins clan, the thuggish Thomas Watkins, playing a leading role in their operations.

And why had Alban Watkins returned to the scene of his downfall, at great risk to himself, after serving time in the penal colonies? To find the Plas Ingli Treasure. Ah yes, the treasure. A plan started to form in my mind, but before doing anything about it, I needed to say farewell to my angels for the moment, and leave the sanctity of my cave so that I could make further inquiries.

ΩΩΩΩΩΩΩΩΩΩΩ

25th August 1848

Today I have done what I promised myself to do, and that involved much rushing about and a lot of talking. A week has now passed since the tragedy at Aberrhigian, and I see with increasing clarity what my course of action must be; indeed, as I sit at my little desk late at night, my heart is beating wildly as I look forward to the events of the coming days.

First, as soon I had finished my breakfast, I set off along the Cilgwyn Road towards Garfeth, walking under a canopy of dripping trees. The sun was trying to come out, and as I walked I pondered on the chances of saving some of the harvest, but in truth my mind was really elsewhere. When I arrived at the cottage I looked through the window and saw that Amos was on his knees, saying his morning prayers. I left him in peace, and sat quietly on the bench in his new little garden, enjoying the colours and scents of his flowers and herbs. There was one particularly beautiful rose, transplanted from my own garden at the Plas, which clearly enjoyed the soil at Garfeth, and I thought that its scent appeared more delicate and pervasive than it ever had up there on the edge of the common. At last Amos came out through his front door, yawned and stretched his arms, and was greatly shocked to see me sitting quietly on his garden bench. "Why, Martha!" he exclaimed. "What a pleasant surprise! How long have you been sitting here?"

"Minutes or hours, Amos -- I know not which. No matter. I have been enjoying the peace and quiet of your garden while you have been

Flotsam and Jetsam

talking to God. I want to ask you something."

"You are very welcome. But first, I need an embrace and a kiss, and something to eat. I dare say that you ate your farmers' breakfast ages ago. Will you join me in taking a slice of bread and cheese and a cup of tea?"

So I gave Amos his embrace and his kiss, which was no hardship at all, and shared in his simple breakfast. Then I said to him: "Now then, Amos, may I turn to the matter in hand? Not long ago you received a premonition and gave me a prophecy that my chance would soon come to make a grand gesture for those in need. You know all about the shipwreck and the plight of the Irish family who are still in my hayloft. May I talk to you about the situation which now confronts me?"

"Indeed you may, Martha, if it will help you."

So I talked to my dear friend at considerable length, outlining the connections between the O'Connell family and myself and the Plas over the years, and even revealing to him the gruesome story of the murder of Alban Watkins by the man who called himself Daniel O'Connell. I thought there was no harm in that, now that both of the players in that particular drama were dead. I revealed the connections between Daisy and Brendan and between my son Brynach and another branch of the O'Connell family. I even talked about the Society of Sea Serjeants and speculated on the long-standing animosity felt towards the Morgans of Plas Ingli by the Watkins family -- now extinct but for the bastard Thomas Watkins. Was there some long-standing animosity towards the Irish in that family, I wondered, going back to the days when Alban Watkins had sent a group of them (including four O'Connell brothers) to the gallows? And might all of that have had a bearing on my instinct towards compassion and tolerance with respect to the shipwrecked family? Did providence have a hand in all of this? What did he think, as a prophet and man of God?

Amos laughed. "Stop, stop!" he pleaded. "My dear Martha! Questions, questions and yet more questions? Do you really think that I know the answers to any of them?"

"Well, Amos, you know a lot about me already, and I have now told you a lot more. I value your advice, and I want you to tell me what to do."

"I cannot do that, Martha. And you know perfectly well why, so please do not press me........"

"But I know you have had a premonition, Amos. You already know

Flotsam and Jetsam

what I will do, and you probably know the consequences."

"Precisely. But you know the rules as well as I do. I will never share the contents of my premonitions, and nor will you, or Shemi, or Rose, or any other with special powers. The result would be chaos. What I know will go with me to my grave. For better or worse, Martha, the decision is yours and yours alone."

"But this might be a matter of life and death, Amos."

"Quite so, *cariad*. You have made life and death decisions before. If there is now another one to be made, weigh up the costs and the benefits, my dear, and get on with it. Whatever you decide, I will support you."

I was very irritated by that, but I knew that Amos was right, and in my heart of hearts I never really expected him to tell me what to do. So I suppressed my irritation, gave Amos a kiss, and went on my way with a promise that I would keep him informed as to developments.

Next I went back to the Plas and talked to Brendan, who is getting stronger by the day and who is already able to help around the farmyard in spite of the limp inherited from that scythe accident many years ago. He was mucking out the cowshed when I called him over and asked if I might have a word in the orchard. We sat beneath our best apple tree, which had somehow managed to hang on to most of its crop during the terrible gale that blew the Irish ashore.

"Brendan," said I. "I have some questions for you. Will you help?"

"By all means, Mistress, if I can."

"What was your relationship with Kate O'Connell, who lost a baby and almost died herself many years ago when she was in this area looking for work?"

"My aunt, Mistress. Her husband Jamie and my father Michael were brothers. Jamie died of the typhus a year ago, and Aunt Kate saw all her children and grandchildren die of the Hunger. She was the last of her line of the family. She was with us on the boat when we went on the rocks. Her body was one of the two washed up after the other funerals were over and done with."

"And there was one other woman, Brendan. I recognized her face when I saw her on the slab, but could not put a name to her."

"Daniel's wife Sara. She was a Collins to start with, who came to Wales and worked at the Plas often, with her children, when Daniel was off doing secret things."

Flotsam and Jetsam

"Did you say Collins?" I spluttered.

"Correct, Mistress. A big family, and great patriots. Sara had an uncle in Newport, which is why she insisted on coming with us in the boat. She knew the chances of drifting into Newport Bay were a million to one, but she took the chance anyway. I think the old fellow had some Biblical name -- I never met him myself."

"Elijah, maybe?"

"Yes, that would be it. Master Elijah Collins. He was very old, I think, and is probably dead long since."

I nodded, with my mind racing. I would follow up that particular matter on another occasion, but for now I had another priority. "And talking of secret things, Brendan, what do you know of the Society of Sea Serjeants?"

"Too much, Mistress Martha. Their members are monsters, all of them. Many of the squires in County Wexford and in Connaught belong to it, and when they join they have to swear that they will revenge themselves upon the Papists for some ancient wrongs that have, they say, been done to the Protestants. And if any new "crime" is claimed to have been done by a Papist to a Protestant who is a member, then there is a blood oath that all of the brothers have to take, promising to extract revenge upon the perpetrator."

"This all sounds positively prehistoric, Brendan! I cannot believe that men think this way in this day and age!"

"But I assure you they do, Mistress. Many of the poor people believe that the Society -- whose members are in London as well as in Ireland -- want the Hunger to continue for as long as possible, so as to wipe out the Irish."

"That is preposterous, Brendan! No group of men, no matter how powerful, could possibly orchestrate a famine and wish death upon millions of poor people. The causes of hunger and disease are much more complicated than that, as you well know. There is the small matter of the potato, for a start....."

"Quite right you are, Mistress. We have brought some of our problems down on our own heads, I dare say. But take it from me that the members of the Society will work wherever they can to prevent help from reaching those who are still left in the blackened countryside we have left behind, and when you hear talk of "divine retribution" for Irish stupidity

326

Flotsam and Jetsam

and incompetence, you may be sure that the Society is behind it."

"You make it sound as if the Society is very big, Brendan."

"It is big, Mistress. There are even members here in Newport."

"I am aware of that. But how did you know it?"

"My Uncle Daniel told me, more than once. In this area, we always knew that we would have problems getting any work on the harvest from squires who were members. Some of them were very aggressive, and even set their thugs on us." Then he grinned and added: "But we O'Connells know how to look after ourselves, Mistress, as you might have noticed."

"And your Uncle Daniel. You knew, of course, that he was an assassin and that he came to Newport once in order to kill a squire named Alban Watkins?"

"I knew it, Mistress, although many others in our family did not. That evil bastard probably joined the Society when he was in Australia, and did unspeakable things to my countrymen. That is why he had to die."

"You seem to know a great deal about this Society and about its members, Brendan. Will you promise me that you have not been involved in secret or revolutionary activities yourself?"

"I cannot lie to you, Mistress, since you are the kindest person I have ever met, along with Master Jones Minor Prophet. I have kept clear of trouble and troublesome things, being too busy trying to keep my family alive. That is the truth. But I did, to my shame, take part in that stupid Rebellion a month or two back."

"Oh, Brendan! That was the last thing I wanted to hear. Are you on the run from the authorities?"

"Yes and no, Mistress. I turned up at Ballingarry to find out what was going on. It was a shambles. I threw some stones at the soldiers and then ran away. I didn't know anybody else who was there, and nobody knows I was involved except my wife Mary. But I have to admit that the shambles at Ballingarry was one of the reasons for us choosing to flee from the country. Uncle Daniel **was** involved in the planning, and he had much more reason than me to flee."

"Do you think that any of the Society members in Newport will know of your Uncle Daniel and his activities?"

"I doubt that, Mistress. They may be evil, but they are not so organized as to know the names of all the revolutionary leaders. In any case, in Ireland Uncle Daniel always used the name Mick O'Grady, and

327

Flotsam and Jetsam

that was the name known to the authorities."

"Thank God for that. And one last thing, Brendan. If I have it in my power to find some way for you and your family to stay in this area, I will do what I can. But will you promise me that you are not here with some subversive or vengeful purpose in mind, and that you will, if you settle, stay entirely clear of politics and all other controversial matters?"

"May God be my judge, Mistress Martha, but I will give you my word on both matters. I swear that I wish no harm to any man or woman, and I swear that all I want out of life is the means to live quietly and honestly on the land and to keep my family alive. I know nothing of politics and commerce on this side of the water, and nor do I want to."

"That is good enough for me, Brendan. Leave things with me, and I will see what is to be done about you and your dear little family."

Our interview was at an end, and Brendan returned to the cowshed while I walked by myself for a while in the garden. I had learned more than I wanted to learn about the Society of Sea Serjeants and about the Great Hunger, and about things that go on in the dark, unobserved and unreported.

I needed to talk to Jake Nicholas, in order to confirm some of the things that Brendan had told me. So after taking an early lunch, I walked down to the Parrog, thinking so earnestly as I walked that I cannot remember, now that it is late at night, whether I walked in sunshine or pouring rain. Jake was at home, sitting in his little office doing sums about cargoes and crew's wages and the price of commodities. He was glad to see me, as I was glad to see him, for he is a rough and lovely man of whom I am very fond. We talked of this and that, and of the shipwreck, and then I asked him about Daniel O'Connell. He looked genuinely shocked, but then I explained that I knew all about the manner in which he had helped Daniel to capture Alban Watkins all those years ago. I also looked for confirmation that the evil squire had joined the Society of Sea Serjeants in the penal colonies and that his hatred of the Irish is what lay behind his persecution of tens if not hundreds of Irish convicts.

"No no, Martha," said Jake. "This is not something that I have spoken of before, but I know it as a fact that Watkins was a member of the Society before travelling to the penal colonies. When I was out there as a sailor, I picked up on the fact that he started an Australian branch of the Society, and fomented hatred against the Irish. I would go so far as to say

Flotsam and Jetsam

that much of the brutality against the Irish convicts in the years after Watkins was there was down to his legacy."

"But that is hard to believe, Jake. He was a convict himself. How could he have had that much influence?"

"Remember that he was a squire, Martha. He was well educated and intelligent, and he knew how to ingratiate himself with the prison governors and guards. He was also a pervert and a sadist, and did whatever was necessary to curry favour. It worked, for he got his ticket-of-leave and got out of the place, leaving chaos and misery behind him."

"Not to mention the rotting corpses of the four O'Connell brothers."

"Precisely. When Daniel approached me and asked me to help him capture Alban Watkins, all those years ago, I was only too pleased, for I had seen the results of his evil activities for myself."

"You knew, Jake, that one of the victims of the shipwreck tragedy was Daniel O'Connell himself?"

"Yes, I knew it, Martha. I tried to save him, along with Benjamin and the other fellows from the coastguard, but we do that for all shipwrecked mariners. I did not know it was Daniel until I saw him on the slab in the mortuary. That gave me a shock, but I kept my emotions to myself and said nothing to anybody -- not even to Patty. I thought it best to let the past stay in the past."

"And what do you know, Jake, about the manner in which the Society of Sea Serjeants organizes itself in Newport, and about the things they believe in?"

"Very little, I am afraid, Martha. The members help each other, and have oaths and secret ceremonies, but God knows what they believe in. The only thing I have noticed is that they seem to hate the Papists even more than they hate the Nonconformists."

And so my interview with Jake was at an end. I talked for a while with Patty, and we enjoyed a cup of tea together. Then I walked home, once again deep in thought. I have learnt much during the course of the day. But nothing I have heard has done anything to change the plans which are forming in my mind. I am more and more determined to proceed, and tomorrow I will talk to my family and bring things to fruition.

13. Old Scores, New Tunes

27th August 1848

I have dug up the Plas Ingli treasure. It has been lying in the ground, not ten feet from the wall of this dear house, since 1796, known only to me. Many years ago I swore that I would never touch it until its recovery was vital for the survival of the Plas and until all other means of rescue had been tried without success. But things have changed. The Plas is no longer mine, and it does not need rescuing. Neither does my family need rescuing, for apart from Rose they are all settled and as happy as can be. Even Brynach, far away across the wide Atlantic Ocean, is thriving and happy, if his latest letter is to be believed.

The time was right, and the circumstances were right. So with the ghost of old Alban Watkins gazing at me from a safe distance, and with others still alive in the community who remember the great treasure hunt of 1806 and the Battle of Parc Haidd which led to the incarceration of eight of my enemies, I decided to proceed. The news is already out, and no doubt certain members of the Society of Sea Serjeants (especially those named Rice and Watkins) will be apoplectic with rage; but what is done is done, and I feel that I am walking on water.

To start with, I had to talk to my nearest and dearest. So yesterday, straight after breakfast I sent urgent messages to Daisy and George and to Betsi and Ioan, asking them to attend at the Plas at eleven in the morning to discuss a matter of the utmost importance. They turned up obediently, having dropped various other urgent tasks, and I was very grateful for that. We all sat in the parlour together, and I invited Rose in as well, since although she is very young she is in effect the representative of the recently established American branch of the family. Bessie brought us some tea, and I asked that we should not be disturbed.

"Now then, my dear people," I said, "you have stood by me through more than one crisis in my life, and I love you all dearly. I trust your advice more than any other advice I might receive from another quarter, and I have called you together to ask you what I should do in a very difficult situation."

Old Scores, New Tunes

"To do with the shipwrecked Irish family, Mother?" asked Daisy.

"Yes, Daisy. God knows they have suffered enough, and we cannot throw them out. But neither can we allow them to stay in the barn indefinitely. If I had enough money to help them, and the opportunity came along, would you object if I was to try and provide for them in some way?"

"Not at all, Mother," said Daisy. "George and I have all that we need, and my children have too much support from their natural fathers as it is. I will speak for them and say that if money was to come raining down from Heaven, you should give it to the poor. Brendan and I were childhood friends, and having renewed my acquaintance with him I judge him to be a kind man, a good father, and as straight as a hazel rod."

"Are you expecting sudden wealth, Martha?" asked Ioan. "Perhaps if not a gift from God, a legacy from some rich aunt of whom you had no prior knowledge?"

"Oh, that would be exciting!" said Rose. "But we are all comfortable enough, and if I had a thousand pounds I think that I should seek to help poor Brendan and his family before doing anything else."

I laughed. "No rich aunts or manna from heaven, I promise! But Betsi, I want your view too."

My oldest daughter frowned for a moment, and then said with a smile: "Ioan and I are not wealthy, Mother, as you know. But you have saved us from bankruptcy in the past, and saved our sanity and self-respect, and Ioan and I agreed long since that whatever else happens in our life we will not take another penny from you, but will make our own way in the world. Both Benjamin and Abel have made good marriages, and they are secure and happy. Therefore you have our blessing in whatever enterprise you might have for the saving of the O'Connells."

That was all I wanted to hear. Ioan and George, my sons-in-law, nodded in agreement. "Thank you one and all," I said. "Your reactions are all that I had hoped for. Now to the matter in hand. Betsi and Daisy, you were very small at the time, but do you remember the Battle of Parc Haidd, in which we managed to capture all of the enemies who had been responsible for the death of your father and for the misfortunes of the estate?"

"I remember it very faintly, Mother," said Betsi. "But it is a part of family lore, and I have heard the story many times from our servants and

331

Old Scores, New Tunes

from Great-grandpa Isaac, even though you yourself were very reluctant to talk about it. It was all to do with an orchestrated treasure-hunt and a non-existent treasure, was it not?"

"There was no treasure in Parc Haidd, Betsi. But there is a treasure, and I know where it is."

Rose squealed with excitement. "Oh Grandma, this is very thrilling!" she gushed. "Shall we have a real treasure hunt? Shall we start now?"

I did not answer, and there was a long silence during which all those present in the parlour came to terms with the information which I had just dumped upon them with very little warning. I thought I had better explain. "I have reason to believe that there might be a sum approaching £2,000 in gold and silver coins hidden in the ground not far from the north wall of this house. The money represents the saved fortune of the Morgan family as it was in the year 1795. In that year there was a terrible fire which destroyed the old Plas and killed five members of the family. The money was stolen by a certain manservant and buried in great haste in the hope that it might later be recovered. I will tell you no more about what happened, and I will not tell you how and when I obtained this information. Those details are things which I shall take to my grave. Will you all promise never to press me for details?"

They all nodded. "And are you all still with me if we now go and seek to find the treasure, and dig it up, and treat it as a first priority to save the O'Connells by giving them a house and a new chance in life?" They all nodded again, with a palpable sense of excitement in the air.

We finished our tea, and without further ado we trotted out into the kitchen just in time to meet all our servants, who were coming in for their lunch. So I told Bessie, Will, Gerallt, Myfanwy and Blodwen all they needed to know about my plans, while they sat open-mouthed around the kitchen table, letting their bowls of cawl get cold. I asked for their blessings too, although in truth I did not need them. They gave them willingly, and so it was that at one o'clock in the afternoon on a showery day when we should have been harvesting wheat, we dug up the treasure.

It did not take long to find, for I knew where it was, to within five yards or so. All the men set to with their shovels and picks, flinging soil and stones in all directions, and I promised a golden guinea to the man who first heard the sound of metal upon metal. As luck would have it, that honour fell to Gerallt, the youngest and poorest of the diggers, and he shouted: "Mistress! It is here! My pick has just hit something that isn't a stone!" So all the diggers concentrated on Gerallt's patch, getting in one another's way as the rest of us cheered them on. Then the coins began to appear in the shovelled soil, dirty and encrusted but recognizable as old crowns, half crowns and guineas. They shone like the sun when they were cleaned, which I thought amazing after so many years underground.

After about thirty minutes we had obtained all the coins that had been buried by Moses Lloyd, thief, murderer and devil incarnate, at the height of the Plas Ingli fire. We threw them into two big buckets, washed them in the yard, and carried the treasure into the kitchen. There, on the scrubbed kitchen table that has seen too much of my life for comfort, we counted it out. Two thousand one hundred and twenty-five pounds and five shillings. Then, since there was nothing else to be done, I gave Gerallt his guinea and asked Will to fetch a few bottles of the best sparkling wine that he could find in the cellar. We all drank a great deal, and I fear that nothing much was achieved in the way of work on the Plas Ingli estate during the rest of the day.

I dare say that in the late afternoon cows were milked and horses and chickens and geese were fed, and that later on somebody locked the animals in for the night, and that somebody else dealt with the milk in the dairy, and that somebody else made some supper. My memories are very hazy, and I put that down to old age.

ΩΩΩΩΩΩΩΩΩΩΩΩ

31st August 1848

Having dug up the treasure, and having duly celebrated its recovery, I spent the greater part of the following day with a sore head. But there was some urgency if I was to get the matter of the O'Connells sorted out, and so I put the treasure in a box under my bed and travelled with Will in the chaise to Llanychaer. I needed to talk to Wilmot, sooner rather than later. He was out taking his morning constitutional when we arrived, so I spent an hour in the pleasant company of Delilah, who becomes more eccentric by the day. Perhaps she thinks the same about me.

When Wilmot arrived back he greeted me warmly, as ever, and since he refuses to discuss anything without Delilah being in attendance, the three of us sat down in his study to talk over my cunning plan. I did not need to tell them anything about the plight of the O'Connells, since they knew the details already, but I did talk to them about the Society of Sea Serjeants, and said that I was disgusted by the bigotry displayed by them and other pillars of the local community when it came to the treatment of the Irish. They nodded in agreement, as I knew they would, for Wilmot has done a great deal to establish warm relations with Ireland and to help the poor starving people of that island through generously participating in my subscription scheme. Then I moved to the matter of the treasure, and told them how it had been recovered. They were truly amazed and delighted. "Martha my dear!" gushed Delilah without thinking. "Spend it please on something exotic and luxurious! A fur coat made of silver fox, if you will, or a grand tour to see the romantic ruins of Greece! You spend little enough on yourself, and live a frugal life. You work too hard and play too little. Now is your opportunity to have fun! Insist upon it -- I am sure your family will not begrudge you a little frivolity, after all you have done for them."

"No no, Delilah. It is kind of you to suggest a little self-indulgence, but I have other plans, and they are made with the full agreement of my family. If you will, I want to buy ten acres of land from you at Garfeth, up the hill from Amos's cottage. I want no generous gesture, since you have been kind enough already in helping the prophet. I insist on paying the market price per acre. Then I will build a good cottage on the land, and I will give land and cottage, and a few cows, sheep and poultry, to Brendan O'Connell and his family. I might even give them a horse and some implements if the money will stretch to it. They will become freeholders, beholden to none, and able to make their own way in the world on the basis of their hard work and their skill as farmers. Will you agree?"

Wilmot looked at me over the rims of his spectacles, and I saw that there were tears in his eyes. "My dear Martha," he said, with a catch in his voice, "you never cease to amaze me. You suddenly get your hands on a small sum of money, and the first thing you want to do is give it away! You may be mad, but you may also be a saint -- I cannot tell which. How can I

Old Scores, New Tunes

refuse you? The loss of the upper Garfeth land would mean little to the workings of my estate, but it is well drained and sheltered. I will get my attorney to complete a valuation, and I will respect your wishes that it should be a fair one involving no favours. And now, my dear lady, will you allow me to fetch you a drink? I could do with one myself, and so could Delilah. Is that not right, my sweet? Yes indeed. We must toast the generosity of the Mistress of Plas Ingli, and the good fortune of Brendan O'Connell and his family. And we must trust that others in the community will celebrate in similar fashion without jealousy or resentment."

So we drank assorted toasts, and for the second day running I over-indulged. That left me, next day, with another sore head. But now the deal is done. Papers are signed, and money is paid over. The land cost me £200, but that is just the start of it, since I now have building materials to buy and labour to pay for if the new cottage is to be habitable by the time that winter sets in. Then there will be animals, furniture, implements and so forth to be paid for, and food to keep the family going over their first winter. I suppose that at the end of it I might, with luck, have £1000 left.

As soon as the contract was sealed, I went to see Brendan and Mary in their little room above the hayloft. They and the four children are doing very well, and they now have colour in their cheeks and flesh upon their bones as a result of Bessie's campaign to fatten them up. When I descended upon them by climbing up the ladder the parents looked apprehensive at first, for they probably thought I was about to fling them out of the Plas to survive as best they could in a wicked world; but when I told them my news they were literally rendered speechless. At last they recovered the power of speech and were simultaneously overcome with emotion, doing their best to thank me through a torrent of tears. Probably for the first time in their miserable lives, they were tears of joy. I had to embrace them, for I was moved to tears too, and they clung to me as shipwrecked mariners might cling to a piece of flotsam or jetsam.

During the past day or two, in between the times devoted to the spending and committing of money, I have been pondering on the instincts and the emotions that have driven me -- for better or worse -- to this particular course of action. Idealism and compassion for my fellow human beings? Bloody-mindedness, designed to show the Society of Sea Serjeants that they will not dictate to me how to behave, and that I will not adopt their hatred of those who have beliefs different from their own? Defiance in the face of threats emanating from the last of the Rice and Watkins families? When I look deep into my own heart, I have to admit that there is more to it than all of this. I have refused to admit publicly to any guilt over what happened between me and Amos in Tycanol Wood; but I know that deep down in my soul, there is guilt, and that it has to be assuaged. Maybe my mad determination to help the O'Connells is my penance and my fate.

ΩΩΩΩΩΩΩΩΩΩΩ

10th November 1848

The cottage at Garfeth is built, and Brendan, Mary and the children are installed in it, as cosy as may be. Most of my money is gone, in spite of the temptation to save much of it in the light of the miserable harvest and the prospect of a tough winter ahead. I have a little more than £800 left. But to their credit, neither my family nor my servants have criticised me or questioned my judgement, nor have they sought to move me from my course. And I have received solid support from my best friends, who have all proved to be angels.

However, I have to admit with sorrow in my heart that the response of certain people in the *cwm* has taken me by surprise. Some of my tenants have been jealous because they are still tenants whereas the O'Connells, who were pathetic and starving Irish peasants not so long ago, are now freeholders or yeoman farmers who have a higher status than they do. Within a few days of the news getting out of the recovery of the treasure and the purchase of land for Brendan and Mary, a deputation of labourers came to see me. They complained that they too were close to starvation, and that they had to clear their own miserable patches of land and work for a pittance in order to survive from one winter to the next. But I became furious with them, and reminded them that the O'Connells had had to cope with misery that was far beyond their comprehension. Brendan and Mary would now have to sink or swim, I said, just like everybody else. And I asked them how often I had waived their rents when times were hard,

Old Scores, New Tunes

and how often I had subsidised them through gifts of seed and other supplies, and how often I had helped them far beyond the terms of our contracts. How often, I asked, had I turned a blind eye when they had brought brothers or cousins to the Christmas feasts at the Plas, and how often had I tolerated their absences when they should have provided me with labour? I sent them packing with their tails between their legs, but I suspect that there is still a simmering resentment, for people do find it hard to be delighted at the good fortune of others.

Then there has been the predictable response from some of the Nonconformists to the fact that a family of Irish Papists has settled in their midst. Although the good folk of Brynberian are for the most part kindly and fair-minded, some of the older chapel members have been particularly mean-spirited, spreading rumours about Brendan and Mary, sending them notes inviting them to "go home to Ireland", and seeking to encourage local traders to have no dealings with them. Thank God that Amos is their nearest neighbour. He has proved to be wonderfully supportive in advising them and defending them as they find their way around the locality and learn who is who and what is what; and my family and servants have also shown themselves to be good friends. A couple of weeks ago some feeble attempt was made to sabotage the cottage by setting it on fire while the whole family was out, but luckily there was a heavy downpour of rain which put the fire out. We do not know who was behind this despicable act, but we have our suspicions, and some of my spies in town are on the trail. Amos was very angry when he found out about it, and immediately set up his wayside pulpit in the middle of town and thundered against jealous and bigoted people who should not moan and whisper but should rejoice in the good fortune of others. And as for attempts at arson as a means of heaping further misery upon the heads of those who had already been through Hell, he roared that no words could describe the depravity and evil that lay behind such acts. "Whoever you are, go on your knees and pray for forgiveness!" he shouted, with his voice echoing round the streets. "If you call yourselves Christians, I say that you are insulting the Lord and his church! If you say you are acting for God, may God forgive you, for you are surely the agents of the Devil in seeking to compound misery and to extend suspicion and hatred when you should seek to do good! Where there is fear, may God give us trust! Where there is conflict, may God give us peace! Amen!"

5th December 1848

I am not sure whether I need to thank God or the forces of the market, but we have settled in to a somewhat more peaceful routine -- ironically, because of the miserable failure of the West Wales harvest. There is real hardship around. I have had to spend some of my savings in buying in fodder and other supplies, and most of the merchants and squires have turned inwards as they try to balance their own books and to make their own resources stretch through the winter and into the hungry months of the spring. I know that the members of the Society of Sea Serjeants are angry with me and with Amos, and will be looking for any opportunity that might arise for doing us harm, but idle hands are the ones that do mischief, and there are few idle hands in Newport at present. The news is that Howell, Harry and Rice have gone over to Ireland in pursuit of "business opportunities", and until they come back I feel reasonably safe. The other leading lights in the Society, including Laugharne Pengelli, Jobbins Holmws and Watkins Ffynnonddofn are all in financial difficulties, and chasing after me is not an activity likely to improve their fortunes. In any case, they are getting a lot of resistance from Wilmot, Ioan, and some of the other honest squires, who feel that they are managing, with the help of the newspapers, to force the Society of Sea Serjeants into retreat.

So there is a breathing space, and many months have passed since I received any pieces of paper with the sign of the anchor scribbled onto them. And there is good news to report. My beloved granddaughter Rose is in love with one Henry Evans, the son of a local sea captain. She is only seventeen, but she is already a beautiful, accomplished and graceful young woman. The sons of half of the squires in the neighbourhood are desperately in love with her, and indeed I have to protect her from unsolicited and unwanted messages and visits. If I did not put on my fierce grandmother act, she would surely be entertaining these ambitious and pompous young fellows to tea every afternoon of the week. She is invited frequently to winter socials and balls, but she is quite uninterested in all of this superficial social activity, and all she wants to do is spend time with Henry. I have talked to her, of course, and have warned her of the dangers of infatuation, and I have told her to be careful about entering into situations where unbridled passion may lead from one thing to another.

Old Scores, New Tunes

But she laughs at me and tells me not to be old-fashioned, and indeed she is a very stable and sensible young woman who knows far more about the world than I did at her age. She even winks at me cheekily when I urge caution, reminding me without saying a word that she knows perfectly well that I married very young, and that I was pregnant at the time of my marriage. And after my own indiscretions in the past with Owain, and Hugh Williams Solicitor, and more recently Amos Prophet, who am I to advise or pass judgement on others? In any case, Henry is a splendid upright young fellow, fresh-faced and fair-haired like my own husband David, and I shall watch the progress of their love affair with interest.

ΩΩΩΩΩΩΩΩΩΩΩΩ

28th October 1849

I am surprised to see, on looking into the pages of my diary, that the best part of a year has passed since my last entry. I have to admit that of late I have been on the edge of despair, with many of my old friends in their graves and others lost as a consequence of my own mistakes and misfortunes. We have had another disastrous harvest, and my cash reserves are almost exhausted. But there is good news to report, and my spirits have been lifted by the reminder that I still do have friends, some of them in quite high places.

At the beginning of the month young Henry Evans came to me in the company of his father, Captain Billy Evans, to ask for Rose's hand in marriage. They were both very nervous, and were not sure of my consent, for it is not often that the daughter of a gentleman marries a tradesman, even if he is young and successful and has good prospects. As we sat in the parlour drinking tea I asked Henry whether he had written to Brynach in America to seek his blessing. He replied that he had, and indeed showed me the letter recently arrived from across the ocean. In it, Brynach said that if he and Rose were genuinely in love he would willingly give his consent and his blessing; that if they wished to marry soon he would not stand in their way; and that he would seek to send them some monetary

Old Scores, New Tunes

help as soon as his own circumstances allowed. He ended his letter with these words: *I know that you are a good man, Henry, and it is clear to me that Rose has a great affection for you. My own greatest regret is that I shall be unable to be with you on your big day. But go ahead, and make a good life together. I hope that I will be able to return to Wales and visit you within the next year or two. I leave all decisions and arrangements in the hands of my mother, and trust her judgement in all things. Sincerely yours, Brynach Morgan.*

I knew that behind those words there were probably tears, for Brynach loves Rose dearly, and to miss her wedding day would be a mighty burden for him to bear. But to his credit, he is wise enough to know that Rose's happiness is more important than his disappointment. So I swallowed hard, and smiled. "Well, Henry, that seems like a blessing to me. And of course you have mine as well." Then I turned to the young man's father. "Captain Evans, you are aware that there will be no dowry? As you know, this estate has fallen on hard times, and ownership has passed out of the hands of the Morgan family. I fear that I cannot even offer a modest financial settlement, since I own no property and after another miserable summer I hold virtually no cash reserves. Brynach is far away in America, and it is clear from his letter that he currently has no reserves either. Is that a situation which you can accept?"

"It is, Mistress Morgan," said Captain Evans. "I am aware of your personal situation and of the misfortunes that have afflicted the Plas. But if these young people are determined to wed, as they obviously are, I will help them as best I can; and I know that you will as well, should circumstances change. If you agree to it, we will arrange a bidding, and that will give them a good start to their married life."

Then we discussed where the couple might live, and I promised to talk, not for the first time, to Wilmot Gwynne in case there might be a cottage somewhere on the estate which might be available for rent. There was room in the Plas for them as a last resort, but I felt sure that they would want a place of their own. So we left it there, and Rose (who had of course been waiting in the passage and listening at the parlour door) rushed in and screamed with delight, and embraced me, and her future husband and father-in-law. We have had little enough to celebrate lately, so we organized a jolly betrothal celebration on the following evening, and Bessie and the other servants did the young couple proud.

Old Scores, New Tunes

So plans were set in motion for the wedding at Caersalem Chapel (which is Rose's place of worship) at the end of the month, and for the bidding. I put my mind to the sort of gift that I might give the young couple, apart from the best wedding feast that could be conjured up, and I regretted immediately the fact that my treasure had been dug up and mostly given away to the O'Connells. But what was done was done, and I knew that nothing was to be gained from misery or recrimination. So I went to see Wilmot. He was pleased to see me, as ever, and was delighted when I announced the news of Rose's betrothal. He was even more delighted to hear that she would be married to a local tradesman, and that she would not be moving to some fine house far away from Newport.

"So the young couple are, as of this moment, homeless, Martha?" he asked.

I confirmed that they were, and asked whether they might move into the Plas with me if that should be necessary. He giggled with delight and rubbed his scarred hands together. "Not necessary, Martha!" he beamed. "Not a good idea and not needed either! It is all arranged, as a result of my delicate sensitivies and my capacity for planning far ahead!"

"Whatever do you mean, Wilmot? I am mystified."

"So much the better! I like to see a woman mystified! Let me explain. As you know, I am extremely fond of that young lady, for she is very gifted and very beautiful. Young Master Henry Evans is a lucky fellow. I knew that Rose was in love some little time ago, for she told me so herself. That was about the time that old Annie Gittins of Trefelin died. She had been in the cottage all by herself, and I had it in mind to put in another labourer and his family. But then I had a brilliant idea! I like having brilliant ideas! Trefelin is on the edge of the estate, down by the ford and near the mill. I never dispose of properties within the estate, but on the edge, I can make an exception. Rose and Henry shall have the cottage, freehold, as a wedding present from me and Delilah! They shall also have four acres of tidy land along the river, south-facing and suitable for a good garden and some animals. Is that not a fine idea, Martha?"

"Oh, Wilmot!" I squealed as he beamed like the midday sun. "I love you! Thank God that there are gentlemen such as you left in the world!" And I flung my arms around his neck and kissed him, with Delilah looking on approvingly.

Old Scores, New Tunes

"Please, please, Martha," said he with mock disapproval in his voice. "Such displays of emotion are not considered polite in the best of circles. And by the way, I am not a gentleman, as I have frequently been reminded."

"Oh, you are, sir. Take it from me. You are a true gentleman and a true friend, and I know not what I would have done without you, over these past few years."

So there was a second celebration on the following day when I travelled with Rose and Henry in the chaise over to Llanychaer, so that Wilmot could give the news of his wonderful gift to them personally.

Then there was another quite extraordinary stroke of luck. Two days after our visit to Llanychaer, which left Rose and Henry cooing like a pair of turtle doves, I received a letter. It was from Master Lloyd Davies of Glynsaithmaen on the other side of Mynydd Preseli. He is a cousin of Will's, and he and I worked together in the early days of the Rebecca Riots some years since. I have the greatest respect for him, as an honest man who has taken great personal risks in the pursuit of justice. This is what his letter said:

Glynsaithmaen, on the 4th day of October 1849

My Dear Mistress Martha,

I have been saddened by the misfortunes that have overtaken you during recent years, and wish that I could have done more to help you. But I have not been in the best of health, and my farm has had problems of its own.

I send you some interesting news. Master Ianto Llewelyn, who used to be a drover in these parts, has just returned from England a wealthy man. He has bought a farm called Garnmeini, not far from Mynachlogddu and hard against the mountain, and he has taken a long lease on five hundred acres of grazing from the Barony. He is also betrothed to be married, somewhat late in life, and his happy day will be in the parish church in five weeks' time.

I thought you might like to know.

I send you my warmest greetings
Lloyd Davies

Old Scores, New Tunes

The letter was extremely interesting to me, for it was clear that Will must have told cousin Lloyd at some stage, maybe many years ago, that in 1830 Ianto Llewelyn took my prize cattle and sheep on a drove to London, leaving me with a promissory note for £800. That was not exactly common practice, but it was not unheard of in the droving trade. He presumably sold my animals for a good price at Smithfield and then disappeared without trace, with my money in his pocket. Now I may be old and forgiving, but I have a long memory, and I am also organized enough to keep all of my old records -- including promissory notes -- in my office next to the parlour. I went to search among my papers for 1830, and there I found the vital document, with Master Ianto's florid signature written in black ink.

I could not work out why Ianto had returned to the district, since he presumably owed money to others as well as me, but maybe he thought his creditors from the north would not notice him if he settled in quietly on the south side of the mountains; and maybe he thought we were all dead or decrepit after the passage of so many years. But I am neither dead nor decrepit, and I knew exactly what to do. First, I made some inquiries in town and discovered that Ianto's intended bride was the oldest daughter of Squire Hugh Jenkins of Llandissilio. It transpired that she would bring to the marriage a substantial settlement. So after the wedding Ianto's wealth and standing in the community would be greatly increased.

With fire coming out of my nostrils, I sat down and penned the following letter:

Plas Ingli, Cilgwyn, Newport
6th of October 1849

My Dear Master Llewelyn,
I write to welcome you back to the district after so many years, and to offer my felicitations in the matter of your forthcoming marriage. It is always pleasant to see an honest drover making his way in the world.
I remind you that I have in my possession a promissory note written in your hand, dated 20th September 1830, in the sum of £800. That sum should have been paid to me by the spring of 1831 at the latest, and through the application of a very modest rate of interest I calculate that the sum owing is now £1500. I look forward to receiving this sum from you,

343

in cash, within three days of the date of this letter.

If I do not receive the money owed, I will do two things. First, I will place the matter in the hands of my attorney, with instructions to take out summonses against you for theft and deception in the Newport Magistrates Court, and then another summons in the Court Leet of the Barony of Cemais for the recovery of the full sum due. That will also have the effect, as you will be aware, of nullifying any agreement you may have with the Barony regarding the rental of grazing lands on the mountain. As you will appreciate, a criminal conviction in the County Court and a debt collection order from the Court Leet will not greatly enhance your reputation.

Finally, I understand that the first banns in advance of your wedding will shortly be read out in Mynachlogddu Parish Church. If I have not received my money by Sunday I shall be forced to join the church congregation on what should be a joyous occasion, and formally object to your marriage on the grounds that you have debts that are undeclared and undischarged.

I look forward to receiving the sum due at your earliest convenience.

Yours most sincerely,
Martha Morgan (Mistress)

Having finished that letter, I wrote another -- this time in a somewhat calmer frame of mind -- to Lloyd Davies, offering him my heartfelt thanks for the information recently provided. When I sent Gerallt off on the grey hunter to deliver my messages to Garnmeini and Glynsaithmaen, I told him to take his stout leather saddlebag, since I had every reason to expect that he would return with notes and coins stuffed within it. If there is one thing I know about drovers, it is that they deal in cash, and that they always have large quantities of it hidden away.

Gerallt returned with a look of utter amazement on his face. "Now there's a wonderful thing for you, Mistress *bach*," he said, with his eyes as big as mushrooms. "As soon as I got to Garnmeini and gave the letter to that gentleman, and told him that I would wait for a reply, he opened it up and read it, and went as white as a goose's breast. *Diawl!* I thought he was going to faint! He asked me in for a jug of ale, and disappeared upstairs as if the devil was after him with a red hot poker. Then he asked me to come upstairs without the servant girl, and took me into his bedroom, and there on the bed was all this money! Notes and golden sovereigns, in a pile! *Diawl!* Not long ago the treasure, and now this, Mistress! He counted it out again, and I counted it too, and we agreed that there was £1500 in the pile. I stuffed it into the bag, and he more or less pushed me out of the house, as fast as he could get rid of me. White as a sheet, he was. He said to please give his kindest regards to Mistress Martha, and slammed the door, and I came back home over the mountain. Here is the money, Mistress. Now was not that a very funny thing?"

I could not contain myself, and having giggled during the recounting of this tale I now roared with laughter, and danced a gig with Gerallt round the kitchen table, much to his surprise and to the consternation of his sister Myfanwy who was at that moment trying to wash the floor. I immediately called in all of my servants and swore them to secrecy concerning this manna from Heaven. Then I gave each of them a golden sovereign, and I put the rest under the bed where it will be quite safe.

It has been there now for three weeks. Rose and Henry will be married tomorrow, and I will have something to give them after all. I will keep some of my new-found wealth for eventualities, but the young couple will have £500 which will be enough to pay for some good animals for their little holding and for timber, stone, slates and mortar for the rebuilding and improvement of their new home.

And by the way, I do not feel in the least bit sorry for Ianto Llewelyn. He has enjoyed my money for far too long, and it is good to get it back. Thieves and tricksters meddle at their peril with Mistress Martha Morgan.

ΩΩΩΩΩΩΩΩΩΩΩ

12th June 1850

My sweet granddaughter Rose is happily settled at Trefelin, and she and Henry are as happy as can be, with the cottage now substantially extended and their little patch of land by the ford nicely cultivated. I dare say they will get from it most of what they need in the way of fruit and vegetables, for Rose is not afraid of getting her hands dirty and Henry is as strong and sprightly as a bullock. With a little help from his father Billy and myself, Henry has started a new business of a most surprising kind, manufacturing and selling strange machines for doing agricultural things. He has two partners in the enterprise -- my grandson Abel from Brithdir, and my grandson William (Daisy's youngest son) who is moving to Newport from Birmingham. They will do well, for Abel is a practical fellow who has acquired great skill in the working of metal, while Henry knows about trade, and William has such an inventive mind that I become exhausted after talking to him for ten minutes. This all started at the wedding of Rose and Henry, when the three young men started chatting together about "the industrial future", whatever that might mean. So animated were their discussions that poor Rose might have felt quite neglected at the wedding feast, had it not been for the fact that she was the queen bee of the occasion, with worker bees buzzing about her and attending to her every whim. At any rate, the new industrialists have an eager investor in my dear friend Wilmot, who knows about working with metal and who sees great opportunities in making machines to do the work of men and horses.

There is more news from America. Following an interesting and protracted correspondence with Brynach on the ethics of trading the products of slave labour, my beloved son has started to involve himself in local politics and in the anti-slavery campaigns now sweeping the northern states. He says that he is involved with something called the "underground railway", and assures me that it has nothing to do with trains in tunnels. There is talk of great antipathy between north and south on the slavery issue, and if the parties become entrenched, and conflict ensues, I trust that he will stay well clear of it. On the business front, he has taken up some of the activities of Elen's husband Tom, who died some years back. But he is also looking for opportunities connected with agriculture, and like the younger generation in Newport he is obsessed with machines. He says that America is a great place for invention, and tells me in his letters that he is minded to export to England machines for dealing with the harvest. That is a strange coincidence indeed, and it may be that his friendship with Wilmot has something to do with it; but there is a great flow of correspondence between Brynach and his nephews Abel

Old Scores, New Tunes

and William and his new son-in-law Henry. There is talk of patents, agencies, licences and other things that I do not fully understand, and excitement is in the air.

So all is well on the family front, and as a proud grandmother I am quite sure that the bright young members of my family will change the world. They will have adventures too, and disasters and triumphs, and maybe I will be informed about some of them. But other momentous events in their lives will quite pass me by, unless they choose to tell me about them. So all of a sudden I have few responsibilities in life. There are no children or grandchildren at the Plas, and I can see as much or as little of them as I like by visiting them or inviting them to visit me. Although I manage the estate, I do not own it and nor does my family, and when I die I have no idea whether Wilmot will retain it or sell it. That is his business. I have looked after the Plas for so long now that I could truly do it with my eyes closed, and so long as Bessie and Will and the other servants are here with me we will cope with fat years and lean years as we have always done, and find food for the table and clothes for our backs. Having dug up the treasure and recovered my missing money from Ianto Drover, and having spent most of it on the O'Connells and on Rose and Henry, I now have modest savings under the bed. So I am reasonably secure, and in truth I want for nothing. My health is not as good as it used to be, and I suppose that is not surprising since I passed my seventy-second birthday last month. But Amos is at my side when he is not off preaching or helping the poor, and I am happy enough.

The other day, as the prophet and I sat on my favourite garden seat and pondered on life and on the simple pleasures of old age, I told him that I was done with adventures and excitement and was minded to fade away gracefully if that was my fate. He laughed and said: "Martha, was that really you talking? I fear that you are bored. Fading away is not your style. You still have enemies, as I do, and your awareness of injustice is so acute that if your family and your precious Plas are threatened in any way, you will probably die on a white charger, with sword and shield in your hand!" I smiled and did not respond, but not for the first time I got the feeling that Amos knew something that I did not.

14. Seeing through the Mist

3rd September 1854

After four years of contentment and comfort at the Plas, something has happened which has jolted me out of my complacency and forced me to confront my demons, real or imagined. I have a deep intuition that what is happening to me now may well lead me to my grave, but I have had a good life, and I am ready to confront the Grim Reaper, even if I have to hand him victory. I will fight him anyway, for it is not in my nature to submit meekly.

I am not sure whether the events of recent days have happened because of the activities of my beloved Amos, or in spite of them. Let me explain. Some years since, with the departure of Rose from the Plas and with serene old age beckoning me with a smile on his face, I was more or less resigned to a life free of stress and devoid of activity. The Society of Sea Serjeants did not threaten me at all, and indeed its members lost even more influence in the town. William Howell, Jacob Harry and Richard John Rice seemed to spend most of their time in Ireland, and indeed over the course of a few years they were each reputed to have accumulated modest fortunes. That got them off my back, and petty crime in the town noticeably declined. Amos reduced his travelling and preaching commitments, and appeared to be perfectly happy tending his garden at Garfeth and chatting to me about the meaning of life. Then something happened which caused him to become very aggressive towards the Society of Sea Serjeants, and he started to attack them at every opportunity from his wayside pulpit. He seemed to me to be asking for trouble where he might have been wiser to let sleeping dogs lie, and I remember remonstrating with him on a number of occasions. Each time he simply shrugged his shoulders and said that injustice must be confronted. More than once he said this: "Martha, all that is needed for evil to triumph is for good men to do nothing."

So he upset Laugharne Pengelli, Jobbins Holmws and some of the other squires, and even contrived to upset squires and magistrates who were not members of the Society. I became very irritated with him, and after

Seeing through the Mist

one ill-tempered confrontation between us he took to the road again, and I did not see him for several months. He did not even come back to Garfeth, and his garden became a jungle in spite of the best efforts of the O'Connell children to look after it for him. He preached all over South and West Wales, no doubt thundering against inequality and social injustice and helping the underprivileged where he could. There was a great Revival going on in Swansea and Neath, and he went there and helped to fan the flames of the Holy Spirit. He sought shelter wherever he could find it, and often slept in barns and under hedges. That made both of us miserable, for we still loved one another dearly. I wanted him at the Plas, and I know that he wanted to be here too. Then he turned up in the middle of the wet spring of 1851, sick with rheumatism and pneumonia, and disillusioned to boot. He complained that the common people had no time for his sermons, and no place in their hearts for his message of love and tolerance. That was not the first time I had heard that particular story, so I shrugged my shoulders and took him in. He agreed at last to give up his life as an itinerant preacher, and to stay closer to home. Bessie and I nursed him for many months, and although he recovered from the pneumonia he was, and is to this day, greatly afflicted and debilitated by rheumatism.

Inevitably Amos and I started to get on one another's nerves, trapped as we were between the four walls of the Plas, and he moved back to Garfeth. That improved matters considerably, and we saw as much or as little of each other as we fancied. While all of this was going on, the production of great-grandchildren was in full swing. In 1850 Abel and his wife Susan had a little daughter; then Benjamin and Sally-Anne had a son in 1851; and John and his wife Molly had a daughter in 1852; and in the same year Rose and Henry had a son, whom they christened Levi. That all brought me great joy, and I saw a good deal of the three little babies who were growing up in the neighbourhood of the Plas. My only regret is that just one of the new generation bears the Morgan family name -- Elizabeth, the daughter of Daisy's son John, a young man born out of wedlock but using his mother's surname. With Elizabeth's marriage, in due course, the name will be lost, but there is still time for John, or William, or David in America, to produce a Morgan grandson for me...........

Within the last year Amos and I have spent much time together, both here and at Garfeth. We no longer have any fears about scandal, and

349

Seeing through the Mist

when the fierce deacons of Capel Brynberian or Capel Caersalem see us hobbling along the lanes of Cilgwyn together, hand in hand, they probably think that we are incapable of nefarious activity between the sheets. And on that matter they are mostly right. Our relationship has become serene, mature and even comfortable. We talk often about our dreams and our memories, about the spirit world, about miracles and divine intervention. We talk even more often about social justice and tolerance, and I have developed a somewhat eccentric attachment for the little Book of Amos which we have studied together at great length. I have not been a great one for Bible study in the past, but now that I have time on my hands it is a pleasant enough diversion, and keeps my mind active and alert.

And so to the present. There is another farming crisis, brought on by poor weather and erratic farm prices. I have coped with such things before, and I am not so worried about them as to lose any sleep. But I am losing sleep because after a period of non-intervention in the affairs of others, Amos has suddenly started to interfere in the Barony and the Court Leet, and in the Petty Sessions. He attends public hearings when he can, and sends letters to selected squires, accusing them of sustaining the old order. He has even started to act as an advocate for assorted poor people accused of petty crimes or of defaulting on piffling debts. He is untrained as an attorney, but he is intelligent and quick-witted enough to make a considerable nuisance of himself. I have told him off more than a few times in past weeks, and yesterday I asked him whether he was intent upon self-destruction. In answer to that question he simply gave me a little smile, and my heart was suddenly stopped by ice.

That reminded me that I am feeling my age, and I am not sure how I will cope with any new crisis in my life. Hardly any of my old friends are left alive, and my contact with Brynach and Elen is very erratic. I still have my large family in the neighbourhood, of course, but children and grandchildren are all busy with their own lives and sometimes days and even weeks go by without my seeing any of them. Will is back at the Plas, following the death of his wife Tegwen. Poor Bessie is seriously ill at the moment, and as she has nursed me in the past I am now nursing her, arranging visits from Shemi Wizard and George Havard Medical and seeing that she gets the recommended medications at the right times. She is even older than I, and at her next birthday she will be 79, so she does not

Seeing through the Mist

resist ailments as well as she used to. She has a high fever which comes and goes, and neither of my medical friends appears confident of any diagnosis. So Myfanwy is acting as housekeeper just now, reluctantly receiving orders from Bessie's sick-bed.

So it was that I was seized with panic when I received in an envelope this very morning a single piece of paper with the sign of the anchor scribbled upon it. I was preoccupied with looking after Bessie at the time, and my thoughts were elsewhere. I was not expecting a letter, let alone a secret sign, and whereas I have received many such threats in the past and have thrown them onto the fire, this time I was truly seized by a cold fear. I knew that I had no reason to be more afraid now than in the past, but somehow I was **much** more afraid. I decided that secrecy should be a thing of the past, and that honesty should now be my watchword, and so I told Myfanwy and my other servants about the sign and expressed my irritation about it. "Somebody in town is still playing silly games with me," I grumbled. "One would have thought that he or she would have better things to do, with hard times afflicting all of us."

"Yes indeed, Mistress," said Will, with a strangely furtive look on his face. "If I was you, I would pay no attention to it. You have more important things to worry about, what with poor Bessie being sick."

The others nodded, and talked of other things, and would not let their eyes meet mine. Immediately I suspected that they knew more than I did, and that made me feel uneasy. So later on, when I was giving Bessie her medicine, I asked her what might be going on. She was flushed already as a result of her fever, but I could have sworn that she blushed, and mumbled something about previous notes meaning nothing in particular, and about letting things be. Then she closed her eyes and coughed, giving me a perfectly clear impression that the cough and the weariness were both affectations unrelated to her actual state of health.

I did not press the matter with Bessie as that would have been unkind, but I determined that I would ask Amos if he knew anything that I did not know. So this very afternoon, on a warm and quiet September day, I walked up to Garfeth and found him picking blackberries in the lane leading from the church. He gave me an embrace that was a little less spontaneous than normal, and then I said to him: "Amos, may I ask you something?"

"Go ahead, Martha."

351

Seeing through the Mist

"I have received another of those silly signs from the Society of Sea Serjeants. They -- or perhaps just one or two of their number -- are threatening me again, quite out of the blue and unrelated to anything in particular. My servants tell me to disregard it, but I am sure they are hiding something from me. Do you know anything, Amos, that I do not know? If you do, I beg you to be honest with me."

As I spoke, I saw Amos stiffen, and his face became white. He thought for a little while, and I knew that he did not want to tell me an untruth. At last he said: "Martha, I urge you not to let this upset you, or to over-react. You have enough to worry about, with dear Bessie's illness, and it will be best for all of us that you concentrate on nursing her back to health."

"You have not answered my question, Amos."

"Forgive me, Martha. I cannot say anything more, except that we all love you, and that you should not worry."

At that, I had to grit my teeth in order to prevent my fury from infecting my words, and no matter how much I tried I could get nothing further from the prophet. So now here I am in my room, pen in hand, trying to record the events of the day and at the same time trying to work out why those around me are being so secretive and protective. I have a deep sense of foreboding that enemies are closing in on Amos and myself, and I do not know enough to act in self-defence, let alone go onto the offensive. Ignorance and impotence are terrible enemies indeed, and I hate and fear both of them.

ΩΩΩΩΩΩΩΩΩΩ

14th September 1854

I have been in this situation once before, when my family and friends all conspired to keep from me certain information about that dark and ominous figure called the Nightwalker. That was a very long time ago, when Brynach was a small baby. Then, I thought that my nearest and dearest were conspiring against me, or at least conspiring to protect me from some

Seeing through the Mist

outside danger that I did not fully understand; in fact, it transpired that they were doing their best to save me from myself and from my own personal demons. I do not know whence the danger comes on this occasion, but no matter how I have pressed my servants they have remained tight-lipped, and during two further conversations with Amos all he has done is tell me, over and again, that he loves me. That is all very pleasant to hear, but it does nothing to calm my nerves.

So I have been undertaking some investigations. On a number of occasions I have been to town, and from talking to many of my spies -- and indeed to shopkeepers and the like -- certain information has come into my possession. I know that if there is any threat to me, or to Amos, or to the Plas, it is going to come from the members of the Society of Sea Serjeants, so I have concentrated on those gentlemen. I have discovered that they are very offended and angry with Amos, and have threatened several times that they will "deal with him" if he does not keep out of their affairs and desist from mentioning them by name in his wayside sermons. He has made specific accusations of corruption against them, and has challenged them to take him to court if they wish to test the truth of his allegations. They will not do that, for they know that what he says is true, and that there are more than enough aggrieved people in town who will stand up and give evidence in his defence. This was all news to me, but I have to say that I was not too surprised by it. More seriously, I fear that Amos's foolhardiness and bravery will lead to violence, not against me but against him. That leads me to conclude that I might have to try to rescue him from a situation largely of his own making. Why, therefore, do I have the feeling that **he** is trying to rescue **me**?

The answer to that question might have been provided when I discovered that William Howell and Richard John Rice have returned to Newport for good, having been forced to leave Ireland under mysterious circumstances. They came back without their friend Jacob Harry, and the news is that he was murdered in Kilkenny by an angry mob following an incident involving a girl. Ireland is a lawless place just now, in which big fortunes can be made and lost, but those who seek to profit from the hardship of others run big risks, as they know full well. I have made enquiries as to the nature of the business activities of Howell, Rice and Harry across the water, and have it on good authority from Patty and Jake that the three of them were operating as hired bailiffs, helping to evict

353

Seeing through the Mist

poor Irish peasants from their pathetic hovels and patches of land during the government's "land redistribution programme." That probably made them unpopular enough, but then I also discovered from Brendan O'Connell (whose friends in Ireland still come over to Pembrokeshire for the harvest) that the three of them were known throughout the South-East of the country for fraudulently selling tickets for vessels travelling from Liverpool to New York. By all accounts they extracted the last pathetic shillings and pence from families desperate to emigrate, in exchange for worthless bits of paper, for places on sailing ships that did not exist. Brendan said that many families were taken in by this cruel deceit, travelling under the greatest of difficulty to Liverpool from Dublin or Belfast only to find on their arrival that they had been duped. Most of them had neither the resources nor the energy to return to Ireland to extract revenge, and ended up on the streets of Liverpool or in the workhouses, destitute and miserable. None of the victims realized the dream of making a new life in the New World, and many of them were overcome by disease or apathy, destined to end up in unmarked graves in the city.

Brendan said that it was inevitable that in due course word would get back to Ireland about the despicable activities of this trio of evil men, and he suspects that Jacob Harry was a marked man even before he raped the young daughter of an Irish miller. He said that Harry was lynched by a mob and that Rice and Howell were lucky to escape with their lives. He also told me that the death sentence has been passed on the pair of them, and that they will in due course be called to account. When I heard this I moaned, and said to Brendan: "But Brendan, you promised me years ago that you would never again be involved in politics......."

"And I have kept my promise, Mistress Martha," said he. "I will not lift a finger against another man, nor will I pass on information to others that might lead to death and destruction. Let God be my judge, and let me rot in Hell if I lie. But I hear things, Mistress, and nod my head, and keep my counsel. Then I get on with saving my little harvest and feeding my family."

On the day after my conversation with Brendan, I walked over the mountain to see Shemi. The September sun was warm and high on my left side, and the common was ablaze with golden yellow furze and red and purple heather. I did my best to let my spirits soar with the skylarks, but that was difficult, and my mind kept on returning to evil men and their

Seeing through the Mist

designs, and to my dear Amos and his instinct for attracting trouble. Questions kept on running around inside my head. Is the prophet just too good to survive in this cruel world? Why should he now be provoking the members of the Society of Sea Serjeants when their power is in any case in decline? What does he know about some threat directed towards me, and why will he not tell me about it? And why are my own servants showing greater loyalty towards Amos than they are towards me?

Then I was on the doorstep at Werndew, rejoicing in the usual warm welcome from Shemi Wizard. Sian was out at work, so Shemi organized some tea and *bara brith*, and the two of us sat together in the shady garden as we had done many times before. Shemi knew that I had questions for him, and immediately signalled his disinclination to cooperate with me. "My dear Martha," he said. "I think I know why you are here, for I have recently talked to Amos on matters of mutual interest.........."

"About the Society of Sea Serjeants?"

"Yes indeed, among other things."

"Very well then, Shemi. Something is afoot, and I know not what it is. Amos is involved, and of that I am certain. I may be old, but my memory is long, and as you know we have both been threatened in the past through the issue of anchor signs on bits of paper. I thought that was all over and done with; and then suddenly, a couple of years ago, Amos started to behave very provocatively towards Laugharne Pengelli, Owen Gelli Fawr, Jobbins Holmws and others. To this day, I do not know why he did it, and neither do I know how he got away with it. Then things went very quiet, only to gather momentum again recently. It is almost as if Amos, racked with rheumatism as he is, is intent upon self-destruction. He is sorely trying the patience of the squires and merchants who keep in the background; but now that William Howell and Richard John Rice are back in town, I fear that he will take them on too, and get his throat slit in the process. Shemi, I need your help if I am to save him from himself."

Shemi sipped his tea and munched on his slice of *bara brith* for what seemed like a very long time. At last he said: "Martha, you are very perceptive and very persistent, and since you love Amos dearly I well understand that you want to curb his excesses. But believe me, he is doing what he believes to be right, and in doing that he is serving his God. I do not share his beliefs, but I respect them. I will have words with him and will urge him to be careful. Will that be acceptable to you?"

355

"No, it will not, Shemi!" I shouted, losing my self-control. "You are one of my dearest friends, and I expect honesty from you. But all I get from you, as from everybody else, is procrastination and obfuscation! All I want from you is the truth! Shemi, please -- just what is going on?"

"I am not at liberty to say, Martha, for I have sworn to others that I will hold my tongue. When the time is right, everything will be revealed, and I will pray to your God, on your behalf, that both you and Amos will come out of it unscathed."

"Come out of what, Shemi? The collapse of the empire? The end of the world? You are talking in riddles!"

Then Shemi, blessed fellow that he is, put his arm around me and gave me a little hug, and kissed me on the cheek. "Enough, enough, Martha," he said. "You will get nothing more out of me. I beg you to let matters rest, and to get on quietly with your life. You have my assurance that those who love you -- and they are numbered in scores -- are intent upon your protection, and will do whatever is necessary to ensure that you enjoy your remaining years in peace and security."

I had to forgive him for his obstinacy, and to recognize his loyalty and his love for me, so at last I calmed down and managed to talk of other things. When it was time to go, I carried the cups and plates back into the cottage for Shemi, and gave him a fond farewell. As I embraced him, I glanced out of the corner of my eye a large bundle of stamped envelopes on a shelf near the fireplace. I recognized the envelopes, for I have received many such myself. And I recognized the florid handwriting on the topmost envelope, illuminated in the rays of the setting sun, as that of my son Brynach.

ΩΩΩΩΩΩΩΩΩΩΩ

15th September 1854

Today I have done further research, and I have had a chance meeting with Dafydd Deliverance. He is the excellent fellow who collects the incoming mail from the Cardigan and Fishguard mail coaches and who delivers

Seeing through the Mist

letters and packets (for a small fee) to those who might or might not be expecting them. He also takes outgoing items to the mail-coaches and sees them safely on board, and is personally responsible for a great deal of mail traffic within our local area. He knows all about everything, and although he is supposed to be a model of discretion I have found that even discretion has its price. And while he is partial to a few silver shillings now and then to supplement his meagre income, he also owes me a favour or two for services rendered.

So it was that on this very morning, in the wind and the rain, I chanced upon him on the Cilgwyn Road, knowing that he would pass along it at ten o'clock. I held up my hand as he approached. "Why, Mistress Martha!" said he, pulling up his horse. "Good morning to you! You are doing a passable impression of Master Dick Turpin, if I may say so."

"No no, Dafydd," I laughed. "My cloak and wide-brimmed hat are simply intended to keep the rain at bay. I trust that you are well. I will not keep you out in this inclement weather, but I wonder if I might ask you a question or two? I know that I can always count on your discretion......."

"Anything for you, Mistress. What do you wish to know?"

"You may know that I have had certain problems in the past with the gentlemen who belong secretly to the Society of Sea Serjeants, and whose names we all know. You have had trouble with them yourself, as I recall, having been beaten up by some of their thugs three or four years since.........."

"Correct you are, Mistress. Bastards, the lot of them. I will get even with them some day."

"Perhaps sooner than you think, Dafydd. I am quite interested to know of any interesting correspondences there might have been in recent years between them and, for example, Ireland."

"Well now, Mistress, as you know I am sworn to secrecy as to the mails, and I am not known as "Dafydd Discretion" for nothing. However, I am also a very observant sort of fellow, and when I am off duty I cannot resist pondering to myself on the great frequency of mails passing between Masters Howell, Rice and Harry -- may he rot in Hell -- and certain squires of our mutual acquaintance."

"To hazard a few guesses, Dafydd, might they have been Laugharne Pengelli and his cronies?

"You took the words right out of my mouth, Mistress. Oh yes, and I

Seeing through the Mist

might add to your little list Gwynne Llanychaer and Jones Minor Prophet."
I could hardly credit this. "What?" I spluttered. "Do you mean
Master Wilmot Gwynne and Amos Jones? But they are good friends of
mine! What purpose might they have had in communicating with those
three petty criminals while they were in Ireland?"

"Don't ask me, Mistress. I dare say that your guess is better than
mine. And as for those other fellows being petty criminals, "petty" might
not be the right word. I delivered many bulky packages that came in from
the three of them on the Rosslare to Fishguard packet ship, addressed
mostly to Watkins Ffynnonddofn. I think that they contained paper
money, in considerable quantities."

"How do you know that, Dafydd?"

"Oh, one day one of them burst open. Purely by chance, you
understand. I was very apologetic to the Squire, and he gave me a guinea
for keeping quiet about it. After that, they avoided me and sent the
packages by special courier, which means my friend Waldo Perkins. Me
and Waldo have no secrets between us, Mistress, but I dare say Watkins
does not know that............"

"And then one other matter, Dafydd, if I may. I understand that
there has been some correspondence between Shemi Wizard and my son
Brynach in America?"

"Oh yes indeed, Mistress Martha. Very frequent letters, and more in
these last few months. Good friends they must be, to be sure. I gather that
Master Brynach must be doing well, for the envelopes that he uses are of
the finest quality, being very difficult to see through even under very
strong light."

"I will take your word for it, Dafydd," said I with a grin, handing
him a crown. "Thank you so much for your help. My lips are sealed, as
ever. Any other interesting correspondences that I should be aware of?"

"Just a lot of very uninteresting correspondences, Mistress, containing
small news from here and there." Then he frowned, and smiled, and said:
"There is one thing that might be of interest, though. Now that I come to
think of it, there have been a number of letters back and forth between
Laugharne Pengelli and somebody in Wexford by the name of Seamus
Collins. Now there's a funny thing -- this time the bulky envelopes have
been going from here to Ireland, and the thin ones have been travelling the
other way. And the writing on the envelopes sent by this Master Collins is

identical, if I am not very much mistaken, to that on the envelopes that used to come for dear old Elijah Collins, when he was alive. Elijah and Seamus were not brothers, but I would hazard a guess that they might have been cousins. That is probably not of the slightest interest, Mistress, but there it is, for what it is worth. Now then, please forgive me, but I must go at the gallop to Eglwyswrw, or I will miss the Cardigan mail coach!"

And off he clattered along the Cilgwyn Road in a cloud of muddy spray, having left his discretion in my tender care.

ΩΩΩΩΩΩΩΩΩΩΩ

18th September 1854

I probably still know less than everybody else about what is going on, but as a result of my researches I am now in possession of some very interesting information. I have put two and two together, and I dare say that I have come to a total of five, but I am more than ever convinced that Amos is in danger, and I am now set upon a course of action which I hope will save him. He is truly his own worst enemy, and his reckless disregard for personal safety is his greatest vice and his greatest virtue. He is truly a good man, and I love him, and if it is necessary for me to sacrifice myself to save him, then so be it. He still has work to do, and a Gospel to preach; but I am increasingly coming to the view that I have done all I want to do with my life.

This morning, having sent out urgent invitations yesterday, I entertained four men to afternoon tea. I did it without informing my nearest and dearest, in the knowledge that had I consulted with them they would have tried to discourage me or even intervened to prevent the meeting. Those invited were Squires Laugharne Pengelli and Watkins Ffynnonddofn, and their henchmen William Howell and Richard John Rice. Gerallt was bewildered yesterday when I asked him to deliver secret invitations to them, and all my servants were horrified when they turned up together at the Plas today, all smiles and courtesies but no doubt

Seeing through the Mist

with death and destruction at the forefront of their minds. However, I had asked my servants to be courteous, and to provide an excellent tea for our guests, and while Bessie grumbled from her sick-bed Myfanwy and Blodwen did us proud, with three teas to choose from and an assortment of delicious cakes and sweetmeats on the parlour table. Having made small talk for a few minutes, I asked Myfanwy to put some specially selected logs onto the fire and to ensure that we were not disturbed. Then we got down to business.

I had not met these fellows for a very long time, for I keep away from the normal social circuit and so do they. But they were very much as I remembered them: Laugharne elegant and urbane, with sleek silver-grey hair and eyes as cold as those of a dead fish; Watkins rough and crumpled, and obviously a bachelor, with stubble on his chin and stains upon his coat; Howell sporting exotic whiskers and seeking through his speech and his mannerisms to disguise the fact that he is really nothing more than a brute and a bully; and Rice slightly built and sharp-faced, still speaking with the affectation that I remember in him as a young officer in the Dragoons.

"Now then, to what do we owe this pleasure, Mistress Morgan?" asked Master Laugharne. "Your invitation was a pleasant surprise, and it is a constant cause for regret that we seem to move in different social circles."

"Indeed, Master Laugharne. Life goes rushing by, and then, too late, we all realize that we have missed out on opportunities for delightful social intercourse. Would you not agree?" I gave them as dazzling a smile as I could manage, and all four of them nodded and mumbled in polite gestures of agreement. I continued in response to the expectation writ large across their faces. "To the point, gentlemen. You are all leading members of the Society of Sea Serjeants -- that much is common knowledge, and I take it that you do not deny it?" There was a long silence. "Good, good. It has come to my notice that the Society has recently been making serious threats against my good friend Amos Jones, who has been openly attacking some of your activities. Your threats follow a silly campaign of sending little notes with the sign of the anchor upon them to me and others in the community of whom you disapprove. As you recall, I have in the past asked you to desist from such childish activities, but they have continued to this day, and I have to say that I am disappointed. Why, Master

Seeing through the Mist

Laugharne, have you allowed such eccentric behaviour to go on? It does no credit to your Society."

Master Dafydd Laugharne's eyes narrowed, and he said: "Why do you assume any involvement on my part in this activity, Mistress Morgan? I really do not have the faintest idea what you are talking about."

"Come come, Master Laugharne. You are the Grand Master of the Society, and have never denied it. Do you deny it now?" I paused, and as I expected, there was no denial. "Nothing happens without your knowledge. I know a good deal about the workings of the Society from talking to certain members, and am in possession of much information that is supposed to be contained within the four walls of your cosy little lodge. My information could lead each one of you to the gallows."

In truth that was a wild exaggeration, for I know very little about the workings of the Society, and I hold none of its secrets. But my comment had the desired effect. The four men exchanged nervous glances, and Thomas Watkins spoke for them. "I hope that you are not going to make any wild allegations about myself and my friends, Mistress Morgan. If so, I urge you to bear in mind that we take slanderous comments very seriously indeed, and will take appropriate actions to defend ourselves."

"Is that a threat, Master Watkins?"

"Take it as you will, Mistress Morgan. I will simply remind you, between these four walls, that others have spoken out of turn in the past, and have been called to account."

"And might those "others" include Master Elijah Collins Llysmeddyg?"

I noticed that Richard John Rice had beads of sweat upon his brow. "Are you suggesting that he was murdered?" he asked, with a break in his voice. "Everybody knows that he died of natural causes."

"Come now, Master Rice. On the contrary. Everybody knows that he was murdered. In fact, you and your brave colleagues in the Society practically boasted of it some years back, when the Society was at the height of its powers in the town. And everybody knows that the three men who visited Master Collins shortly before his death were you, Master Watkins, and you, Master Rice, and your late lamented colleague Master Jacob Harry. I have further evidence that I will not divulge."

That truly put the cat amongst the sparrows, and all four of my guests looked at each other and at the walls of the parlour, on the basis

Seeing through the Mist

that walls might have ears. Rice and Watkins were as white as death, and Laugharne and Howell turned an interesting shade of green. "How did you know that?" hissed Watkins. "That cannot be common knowledge. We were very careful to go by the back door.........."

"Be quiet, you fool!" spluttered Squire Laugharne. "Have you taken leave of your senses? She knows nothing. This is all pretence." Then he turned to me and sought to seize the initiative. "Mistress Morgan, I take the gravest exception to what you are doing here this afternoon. You invite us to tea, and then spend your time hurling insupportable accusations against us. I warn you that I am very displeased, and that I am not a very forgiving man. I am minded to take my leave rather than listening to more of this nonsense." He stood up, and nodded to his colleagues. They stood up too, and placed their tea cups on the table near the fireplace. I sat still for as long as I dared, and then delivered my coup de grace. "Very well, gentlemen. Do as you will. But I thought that you might be interested to hear what else I know, about such matters as fraudulent tickets between Liverpool and New York, and about fat parcels of money arriving at Ffynnonddofn, and rape in Kilkenny, and about your interesting correspondence with Seamus Collins. If you will be patient, I will even tell you about the death sentences recently passed upon you, Master Howell, and you, Master Rice, by certain interested parties in Ireland."

The four of them stopped in their tracks, and now all four were as white as newly laundered sheets. "How did you know all of that?" growled Master Rice. "Damn you, Martha Morgan. That cannot possibly all have found its way back to Newport."

"Oh, but it has, Master Rice. At the very least, it has found its way out here to the Plas, so I dare say it is all common knowledge in Newport as well."

There was another tense silence, broken only by the spitting of wet logs in the fire, as each one of the four loathsome creatures sought to gather his thoughts. They now realized that there was not much to gain from the pretence of innocence, and Laugharne said to Watkins: "Hell and damnation, Watkins! Why did you ever allow the Irish money to come back here to Wales? You should have known that those three idiots would create chaos out of the best-laid of plans. Harry is dead, and now the Irish are probably hunting for all of us!"

" I heard that, sir!" shouted Rice. "You call us idiots. But at least

Seeing through the Mist

we were brave enough to risk disease and hardship in order to earn some precious paper money while you two miserable bastards stayed at home, comfortable and cosy, waiting for the parcels of cash to arrive. And by the way, so far we have only seen fifty pounds each out of the eight hundred sent. We should have had a hundred and sixty each, Howell and me, and in our view we should share the part that was due to that fool Harry.........."

"Enough! Enough, the pair of you!" shouted Howell, who looks like a brute but who must have a grain of common sense between his ears. "Have you forgotten where you are and who is listening? Have you taken leave of your senses?"

They had indeed, thought I, but I was not complaining, for I found these exchanges more than a little diverting. There was another long silence, during which each of the four villains drew breath sharply. Then Dafydd Laugharne reasserted his authority over his squabbling fellow conspirators. "Very well, Mistress Martha," he said at last, with his voice shaking. "It is clear that you now know far too much either for your comfort or ours. What do you want?"

"Do you think that my purpose is blackmail, sir?"

"That is a reasonable assumption, Mistress. Information is a commodity, and is always worth money. Every little piece of information has its price."

"Very well. You gentlemen have stolen eight hundred pounds from the starving peasants of Ireland, and the least you can do is give it back. So by one o'clock tomorrow I want all of it deposited in the Black Lion Bank in town, credited to the account of the Newport Subscription for the Relief of Irish Distress. The account has been somewhat run down of late, but the trustees will appreciate a substantial new donation, and you may be sure that it will be put to good use........."

"But some of the funds have already been, shall we say, dissipated........" said Watkins feebly, glancing towards Rice and Howell.

"That is your problem, sir, and not mine. The offer is there. Take it or leave it."

"And in return for this generosity, Mistress Martha?"

Then I truly lost my self-control, and fury raged through my body. "Generosity, sir?" I raged. "How dare you use that word -- you common criminals who have stolen the hard-earned pennies of starving people

363

Seeing through the Mist

through some cruel deceit? They are all human beings, deserving of respect and dignity, and you have treated them in a manner that is beneath contempt! I despise you, all four, as I despise the other members of your sordid little secret society. Get out of here now, all of you, and I hope to God that I will never have the misfortune to meet any of you again! I make no promises, and I make no deals. When I see the money in the bank, I want a statement on the church door, signed by all four of you, stating that you are pleased to return £800 recently taken from the starving people of Ireland, and that you wish it to be used for the relief of distress wherever it may be found, regardless of race or creed. When that is done, I will decide what to do next. You will have to hope, gentlemen, that by two o'clock tomorrow I will be feeling more benign than I do at this moment!"

And I chased them out of the Plas as an angry mother might chase out a rabble of small children who are getting under her feet. When they were gone, I was shaking like a leaf. I took a little while to calm down, and then returned to the parlour and shouted: "Master Billings! They have gone. You can come out now. Did you get all of that?"

"Yes, Mistress," said Billings Scrivener, emerging from behind my heaviest tapestry screen. "It was difficult at times, but their voices were quite distinctive, and I think I will have all the right attributions. Most interesting, it all was. I will write it out again tidily in the morning, and you will have both the original and the copy, signed and dated, by tomorrow afternoon. I was worried about the scratching of my pen, and was most impressed by your use of wet logs, hissing and spitting, in the fireplace. Not much heat, but plenty of noise. There was enough heat anyway, from the brows of those four worried bastards. Now then, Mistress, after all that hard work, is there any chance of a slice of that nice cake and a cup of tea?"

ΩΩΩΩΩΩΩΩΩΩ

15. Endgame

23rd October 1854

Following my interesting meeting with the forces of evil, £800 in paper money was paid into the bank in Newport exactly as I had politely requested. On the same morning, a notice appeared on the church door with the approximate wording I had required, and with four rough signatures on the bottom which could just about be deciphered as those of Laugharne, Watkins, Howell and Rice. I was not really satisfied with that, and I was still shaking with fury even though almost a full day had passed since our encounter. So I added a note of my own, which said:

> *To whom it may concern*
>
> *I am grateful that Squire Laugharne Pengelli, Squire Watkins Ffynnonddofn, and Masters Thomas Watkins and Richard John Rice -- all leading members of the Society of Sea Serjeants -- have seen fit to return £800 stolen by them without mercy from the poor people of Ireland. The money will now be used in that country for the relief of distress among the starving and the dispossessed. I trust that all those who know the meaning of common decency will rejoice in this development.*
> *I herewith request that the evil organization SSS will desist from any further activities in this town or further afield, and will allow people of goodwill to get on with their lives.*
>
> *Martha Morgan*
> *Mistress*
> *Plas Ingli*
> *dated this day 19th September 1850*

That might have been considered libellous, and it was certainly risky, but I knew that there would be no immediate repercussions. The note stayed on the door until a sizeable number of townspeople had read it, and then it was torn down. Afterwards, Amos and my family were furious with

Endgame

me, and asked if I had taken leave of my senses in entertaining four such dangerous men all alone at the Plas, and then provoking their anger in this blatant fashion. But in truth I never felt threatened during the whole of the encounter, and I knew -- and still know -- that I am stronger than the four of them put together. Besides, only my servants and I know that Billy Billings Scrivener was here on that afternoon, and that I have his sworn transcript of the proceedings in my desk. That gives me no power over the leaders of the secret society, but it is a tidy little insurance policy, and if it should become necessary I might even let them know that I have it.

In the days following my meeting I still had a considerable number of questions that required answers, including the nature of the correspondence between Brynach and Shemi, the reason for the payments made by Dafydd Laugharne to Seamus Collins in Ireland, and the truth behind Elijah Collins's death. Also, I was mystified as to the real reason for the animosity shown by the Society of Sea Serjeants towards Amos, and as to the cause of his denunciations of the Society's members. I would not go so far as to say that he hated the Society, but certainly his attacks had more than a little venom in them, and I could not see how he could sustain them while at the same time claiming to believe in love, tolerance and forgiveness. I confronted him on this matter on several occasions, but he always evaded the question and gave me some pat and unconvincing response. Then I wrote to Brynach in America to ask him about the nature of his correspondence with Shemi. I received a reply this very morning, referring to other items in my letter but pointedly failing to mention the matter in which I was really interested. So I am still frustrated, still mystified, and still confronted by a wall of silence on which are perched my friends and my family.

In the past month I have had no further contacts with Squire Dafydd Laugharne or his henchmen, and the news from town is that the local branch of the secret society is in considerable disarray. It was clear from my meeting with the four leading members at the Plas that there were frictions and disagreements bubbling to the surface, but that is always the case with greedy and evil men. They mistrust even their own brothers, and would sell their grandmothers for a farthing apiece. They know that I know too much for their comfort, but they may also think that I have had my pound of flesh, and that I have no stomach for further conflict. So -- and this is my fervent wish -- they may leave me alone.

366

Endgame

This afternoon my ship *Mary Jane* returned from Wexford carrying a cargo of Irish wool destined for the woollen mills at Drefach Felindre. Ioan and Benjamin were also on board, having safely disposed of a cargo of seed (barley, turnips, flax and clover) destined for the poor labourers and their families in Ireland. That was where the £800 went after its receipt from Laugharne and his cronies. The seed is a gift, and must not be sold. The use of my vessel was also a gift from me. All of the seed has to be planted, and Ioan and Benjamin -- in their capacity as representatives of the Newport Subscription -- met the Quaker Irish Relief Committee and laid down the conditions for its distribution and use. The Quakers are good people, and will do exactly as we have requested. I dare say that will be the last of my involvement in Irish matters, since things are now becoming more stable across the water.

That having been said, the influence of the Irish upon the lives of certain residents of this district may still not be at an end. I will sleep soundly in my bed, but others may not, for it has just been reported by Patty and Jake that two strange Irishmen with money in their pockets have taken lodgings on the Parrog, and have been asking questions about the whereabouts of certain gentlemen whom they are keen to meet.

ΩΩΩΩΩΩΩΩΩΩΩΩ

29th October 1854

Two corpses have been found, hanging from a tree on the shore of the estuary downstream from the stepping-stones. The bodies were those of Richard John Rice and William Howell. At first it was thought that the dead men had committed suicide together in some grotesque pact, but when my son-in-law George Havard was called upon to conduct post-mortems he discovered that they had both been dead prior to having nooses placed around their necks and being hauled up so that their feet were well clear of the ground. At the inquest held yesterday, both deaths were recorded as due to "unlawful killing by a person, or persons, unknown", but George told the Coroner and his jury that he was mystified as to the precise cause of death. He said that the last death which had confused him in this fashion was that of Master Elijah Collins, a few years ago, who had had no marks on his body and no obvious signs of distress or violence against the person. That was very interesting, since each of the victims had a piece of paper stuffed into his mouth, with an anchor sign and the following words written upon it: "Inasmuch as ye do it to one of the least of these, my brethren, ye do it unto me."

The constables are on the case, but those poor fellows have no knowledge of how to solve a child's puzzle, and would rather spend their time polishing their boots than tracking down killers. Given the wording and the anchor signs on those scraps of paper, there is a strong possibility that the killings were conducted by those responsible for discipline and retribution within the local branch of the Society of Sea Serjeants. On the other hand, the strange Irishmen who were on the Parrog are no longer there, and it is widely assumed that they are already back in Ireland and lost in the crowd. Of course they used false names. They might have been the killers, and they might have belonged to some Irish revolutionary group. Then there is the third and even more intriguing possibility that the killers were from the Irish branch of the Society, whose members had become displeased with the Rice and Howell manner of doing things. I am very confused and intrigued, as is Shemi, to whom I have talked at length.

So the last two members of the Rice and Howell families have gone, destined for Hell rather than Heaven. All deaths are terrible, but they were evil men, and I will not grieve for them. That leaves Squires Laugharne, Watkins, Huws, Jobbins and Owen to maintain the local operations of the Society. I will forget about the Brynberian deacons and the Rector, for in my estimation they are foolish and vengeful fellows, but not capable of doing serious harm. But the squires must be quaking in their boots just now; and the one who will be quaking most will be Thomas Watkins, who is the last man left alive who was present at the death of my old friend Elijah Collins. I must watch each of them very carefully, for I have learnt over the years that evil men who are cornered can become very unpredictable and hence very dangerous.

ΩΩΩΩΩΩΩΩΩΩΩ

Endgame

17th December 1854

I know that the end is near, and that I will not die in my bed, for I have seen the *aderyn y gorff*. It happened this morning, very early, before the first light of a frosty dawn. I was awoken by a gentle tapping on my window pane, and when I raised my head, at first I saw nothing. Then I got up and lit my bedside candle lantern, and saw outside a small brown bird, about the size of a sparrow, tapping away at the glass, stopping occasionally to look through into my bedroom. Three times it fluttered away, and I heard the sound of its wings very clearly. Each time it came back again, and continued with its busy tapping on the glass. Then finally it looked inside again, cocked its head, and fluttered off into the darkness, leaving behind the sound of silence.

I know the signs, and I knew that this one was for me. Strangely, I was not upset, but I lay back on my pillow with my eyes wide open and with my mind meandering across a landscape populated by beloved people, some dead and some still alive, and across the decades of my life, some bad and others wonderfully good. I breathed deeply, and felt quite calm. I was pleased about that, for I have always known that this moment would come, and now I coped with it well.

The morning sounds came up the staircase from the kitchen. Bessie, mercifully recovered from her long illness, hummed a little tune as she poured water into the cauldron over the fire. Gerallt cleared his throat and spat into the embers. Then he pulled on his boots and stamped his feet, put on his thickest winter coat and went out into the pitch blackness to start tending the animals. Blodwen emerged from her room, slamming the door behind her as she always does, and fetched some logs from outside before stoking up the fire. She pulled up a chair in front of the flames for a few minutes, warmed her hands and loosened up her fingers, and then went outside to join Gerallt in the milking of twenty cows. Myfanwy appeared, trotted across the flagstones in her clogged feet, and then started to fetch cutlery and crockery from the scullery for the laying of the breakfast table. Will emerged last of all, as is his privilege, and shuffled across the flagstones in his stockinged feet. Then he stretched his arms, gave a mighty and noisy yawn, and poured himself a mug of ice cold water from the big jug beside the door. I did not need to see any of this. I knew it all from the sounds. Thus far there had been no conversation at all, but as they

Endgame

all woke up my beloved servants became more like human beings, and the low hum of early morning banter began. Snippets of conversation and snatches of laughter echoed along the passage and up the stairs. Dawn came, and the early morning noises intensified, and at last Myfanwy burst into my room, gave me a cheerful greeting, and lit my bedroom fire.

Later on, at breakfast, Bessie said to me: "You are very quiet and distant this morning, Mistress, if I may say so. And that smile on your face is very intriguing. A beautiful dream, was it?"

"No no, Bessie. I might well have dreamed, but the details are quite gone from my head. I am just relishing the moment." She looked at me, and shook her head, and continued her conversation with Blodwen about the scandalous activities of a certain Mistress Ifans down in town.

I was moved to visit Amos at Garfeth, and as a hazy sun lifted itself above the craggy rocks of Carnedd Meibion Owen I left the Plas to its morning activity. Wrapped up well against the frost, I strode off along the Cilgwyn Road. Strangely, the colours of the *cwm* were brighter and more intense than I could remember, and the sounds of birds and farm animals sharper and more distinctive. On hundreds of previous occasions I had passed this way without observing anything; but now this beloved place seemed to be imposing itself upon my consciousness in a way that I found mysterious and almost sacred. Then a sort of panic seized me, as I realized that it was now my destiny to leave the *cwm*, and the Plas, and the old blue mountain of Carningli behind as I went on some new journey which would lead me to an unknown land. But I loved this place too much! How could I leave it, at the whim of the Grim Reaper, without tearing my heart out and going out of my mind? Had I not sworn, over and again, to others and to myself, that I would never, never leave this place? But now perhaps it was my destiny to leave, and perhaps I could take it all with me, in my mind and in my soul............

"You have seen an omen, Martha?" said Amos, as I met him on his doorstep.

"How can you possibly know that, *cariad*?"

"I simply know it. And I see it in your eyes."

He gave me an embrace of such intensity that I was at first frightened, and then we both relaxed, and continued to hug each other on the doorstep for several minutes, rocking gently as if we were standing on the deck of some rolling and pitching ship. Then I raised my face from his

Endgame

collar and realized that I had been weeping. I looked into his eyes.

"Tears, *cariad*?" he said. "For the past or the future? Surely not for the present?"

"Not for the present, Amos, for we are together, and that cannot be a cause for sadness."

"Then smile, and think of a good life, and make the future good, for as long as you have left."

"A day? A week? Who knows, Amos? Do you know?"

"I have no idea, Martha, concerning either your fate or mine."

Then I knew that he too had seen a sign, for there was a sort of resignation and contentment in his eyes which told me that he was done with fighting. "You have had a sign yourself, Amos?" I asked.

He took my hands in his and looked deep into my eyes. Then he nodded. "The *tolaeth*, early this morning, before dawn."

"Will you tell me about it?"

"No, Martha, I will not. At first I was frightened, and then I was overcome by a sort of warm pleasure as I realized that I will soon stand at the Pearly Gates and meet my maker. Could there be anything more wonderful for a man such as I, having striven for justice and having given my life to God?"

"Did you not give a little part of it to me, Amos?" I whispered.

"I did indeed, Martha, with my whole being," he replied, giving me a long kiss on the lips. "And I still do, even now. My love for you, *cariad*, is undiminished, and even grows by the minute as you stand before me in your full beauty. You are truly a gift from God..........."

"But Amos, I am old and tired, and I feel at this moment that even my face is as grey as a winter shadow."

He laughed. "Nonsense and balderdash! Take it from me, Mistress Martha, that your eyes still sparkle, and that your complexion is as bright as that of your lovely Rose on her wedding day. You are still the sweetest blossom in a meadow of flowers. No self-pity, if you please. Now then, come inside, and sit down. I will make you a cup of tea. We need to talk."

So I went inside. Amos and I sat together for most of the day, and in a strange welding together of the banal and the spiritual we came to terms with our fate. As I left, he said this to me: "Martha, if I go before you, all I want is a shroud. Promise me, please, that you will not trap me in a coffin." I swallowed hard, and had to agree.

Endgame

18th January 1855

My last Christmas at the Plas (I know that to be the case) was a truly memorable one, with no expense spared. Bessie raised her eyebrows over the top of her spectacles on more than one occasion as I gave my instructions for catering and invitations, and said "Can you really afford this?" so many times that in the end I had to scold her. "I do not have much left under the bed, Bessie," I said, "but if I choose to use it for having fun, then so be it."

All of my family came for Christmas Day, including my children Betsi and Daisy and my grandchildren Benjamin, Abel and Owain from the Brithdir family and Amy, John and William from the Newport branch, and Rose from Trefelin. And the great-grandchildren too -- Jane who is now four, Joshua who is now three, and Anna and Levi who are both two years old and who are my special favourites. Then there were all the husbands and wives and assorted other relatives, bringing the Morgan family in total up to around thirty-five souls, not counting Brynach and David in America. We longed for those absentees, and gave them many a toast during the Christmas season, but there was little time for nostalgia since, with so many children around and with such a massive catering task in hand, quietness was something frequently longed for but never attained. My dearest friends were all invited for Christmas Dinner, and they all came -- Shemi and Sian, Amos of course, and Wilmot and Delilah, and Patty and Jake, and Skiff and his wife Maria, Brendan and Mary and the children from Garfeth. Gomer and Gwenno came, as did their twins (now ten years old) and their other children Robert and Jenny. Then -- and it exhausts me even to record all of this -- all my servants and their relatives, and my tenants and their families, and my labourers and their families, and assorted individuals whom I had never seen before but who were, I dare say, related to somebody or other. Bessie counted a hundred and sixty-three people inside the Plas at lunchtime on Christmas Day, and that made even the great Christmases of 1799 and 1802 pale in to insignificance.

We went to the Christmas morning *Plygain* service, of course, and that was as serene and magical as ever, and was spoiled only to a minor degree by the scowls thrown by Rector Llewelyn Thomas towards Amos and myself as we left the church hand in hand. I have long since stopped

Endgame

worrying what that silly fellow thinks or says, and indeed I find that upsetting him (for example by refusing to pay my tithes) is quite a pleasurable pastime.

There was such noise and music as I can never remember at a Plas Christmas, and there was dancing too, for Amy and John insisted on teaching all of us the latest London dances. And then the *Mari Lwyd* came, for the first time in many years, no doubt at the instigation of Will and his cronies, and that was another episode attended by much horseplay and frivolity. God only knows how many people slept beneath our roof for the Christmas and New Year week, but there seemed to be a great many every morning at breakfast. I cannot even guess at the quantities of food and drink consumed, but at the end of it Bessie sighed, and wiped her hands on her apron, and said: "Well, Mistress, that was a Christmas the like of which I have never seen in fifty years! I thought that such Christmases were but distant memories; and although I say it myself the food and the drink were better than anything ever conjured up by old Mrs Owen!" I had to agree with her, and we embraced like the old and comfortable friends that we are, and promised each other that we would never reveal the full cost to Master Wilmot for fear of giving him a heart attack.

Looking back on it, now that Christmas, New Year and *Hen Galan* are all behind us, the whole festive season had something of the wake or the *gwylnos* about it. Good humour was everywhere, and sometimes it approached hysteria; and while Amos and I knew that this was the last time that either of us would celebrate the birth of Christ, I have a feeling that others knew it too. Nothing was said even by my nearest and dearest, but I could swear that some of the farewells at the end of it all were more tearful than usual, and that some of the embraces were longer and more intense than the occasion warranted. No matter. If this was my swan song, I am resigned to my fate.

ΩΩΩΩΩΩΩΩΩΩΩ

16. Flying with Angels

12th February 1855

First David, then Iestyn, and then Owain and Joseph. And now Amos, fifty years to the day since the death of David. Five brave and wonderful men who gave me their love, and all except Amos cold in their graves, waiting for me. God knows whether Amos will get a funeral or a grave, but that is a problem for tomorrow. In the midst of my tears I am gritting my teeth, for I am angry with him, having convinced myself that I would go first.

I thought that I could calm myself by writing of the dreadful events of the day; but I have discovered that grief does not get any easier with the passing of the years, and I cannot write more.

ΩΩΩΩΩΩΩΩΩΩ

13th February 1855

I am calmer this evening, and though I am unutterably weary I will try again. It happened like this. Yesterday it was Ash Wednesday, and the day after the annual *cnapan* contest on Berry Sands. I had planned to walk down to visit Rose and Henry and their little boy Levi at Trefelin, and to join them for supper, as I always do on a Wednesday. That little routine of mine was, I dare say, well known to most of the people in the *cwm*, and to others as well. I was about to set off, shortly before dusk, when the small son of Brendan and Mary turned up at the Plas bearing a message from Amos. It urged me to delay my departure for a little while, for reasons that would soon become clear. I was reluctant to do that, for I knew that Rose would have supper on the stove, but I decided to wait for half an hour in the expectation that Amos might have a surprise for me. In my naivety I even thought that he might bring me a red rose or some such pretty thing as a token of his love, since the feast of St Valentine was just around the corner.

Flying with Angels

So I sat and chatted to Bessie and Myfanwy in the kitchen, and after the passage of half an hour I shrugged my shoulders, said something rude about men in general and Amos in particular, and set off. I had not gone two hundred yards from the Plas when I saw a figure rushing towards me in the gloom, shouting "Grandma! Grandma! Come quickly!" It was Rose, rushing uphill as fast as her legs would carry her, with little Levi strapped to her back and wailing lustily. She was exhausted, poor thing, and so I took her child and sat her down on a hedge bank while she recovered her breath. At last she blurted out: "Grandmother, we must get help immediately! Henry has gone chasing after them and I fear that they might kill him.........."

"Oh my God! But who are they, Rose? Who on earth are you talking about?"

"Five riders in black cloaks and hats, Grandma. And all masked. I think I know who they are, and I fear that one of them might be Thomas Watkins -- I am sure I recognized his voice."

"But what has this to do with Henry? Why is he chasing after them?"

"Oh, Grandma, they have taken Amos," said the poor girl, bursting into tears.

With Rose and little Levi both wailing, I was overcome by a cold fear, and for a few seconds I almost lost the ability to think clearly. Then I realized what had to be done, and dragged Rose and Levi back to the Plas. With my mind racing, I rang the great bronze bell adjacent to the kitchen door. That is something that I have never done before on a black winter's evening, and the sound echoed round the *cwm*. I knew that the bell would attract friends and neighbours from far and wide, and sure enough I heard running footsteps within a couple of minutes as Will and Gerallt appeared from the cowshed and as my tenants Gomer and Gwyn sprinted up the hill from Penrhiw and Gelli respectively. Ioan and Benjamin came panting up from Brithdir. Before long there were more than ten men assembled, and I passed on to them everything that Rose had by now told to me. "My dear friend Amos has been taken by five masked men," I said. "Rose thinks that one of them might have been Watkins Ffynnonddofn, and we can probably assume that they are all from the Society of Sea Serjeants. Henry has gone after them, and Rose thinks that they mentioned Tycanol before they trussed Amos up and threw him across the back of a horse........."

376

Flying with Angels

"Bastards!" said Ioan, taking control. "Right, boys. They have got too much of a start, but in the darkness horses will be more of a hindrance than a help. Grab whatever weapons you can from the barn, and follow me! We will go down over Pantry Ford, and that will save almost a mile. Martha and Rose, you stay here! Myfanwy, straight down to town if you please, and summon the constables!"

And with that, the men grabbed axes, pitchforks and billhooks and went down the hill at the trot, with their breath swirling in clouds behind them, dimly illuminated by the light of their candle lanterns.

I tried to remain at the Plas, but I could not sit still for a second, and at last I sprang to my feet and asked Blodwen to get on her cloak and bonnet and to follow me. "But Mistress," she spluttered, "Master Ioan said........"

"You do not take orders from Master Ioan, Blodwen! Nobody tells me what to do in my own home!"

So I lit another candle lantern and off I went, as fast as my legs would carry me, with Blodwen trailing reluctantly behind. Periodically walking, running and pausing to take in great gulps of the cold night air, we at last reached the ford and climbed up the hill on the other side towards the three Fachongle farms. I remember thinking that I was too old for this sort of thing, and that it would be ironic if I were to collapse and die through sheer exhaustion in the course of trying to save Amos. When we reached the edge of the wood we paused again to catch our breath, and listened intently. We could hear nothing, other than the cry of a tawny owl somewhere in the distance. I think that I knew then that we were too late, and as we trudged wearily into the wood that was confirmed in the most terrible fashion when we saw some bobbing lights moving towards us. "Henry? Ioan? Is that you?" I called, in a voice made feeble through fear.

At last we confronted the lights that were moving towards us, and made out the outlines of five or six men including Gomer and Ioan. For a moment my heart was lifted in expectation, but then I saw that one of them carried a heavy burden across his shoulders, and that the men were walking in total silence. Ioan recognized me at once, and enfolded me in his embrace. "I thought I asked you to stay at the Plas?" he asked, with resignation instead of anger in his voice. "No matter, no matter. I fear that we were too late, Martha. Amos was already dead before we could reach him."

Flying with Angels

From that point on I have few recollections of what happened, and Blodwen told me today, as gently as she could, that I screamed "Oh no! No! Dear God, let it not be true! Why could it not have been me?" before collapsing in Ioan's arms. They had to carry both me and the body of Amos into the farmhouse at Fachongle Uchaf, and I was given some sedative by Mistress Prickett, the farmer's wife. Later on, Will and Gomer fetched the chaise and the gambo from the Plas, and we all returned in a miserable procession back to that beloved place. They tell me that as we travelled I refused to be parted from Amos's body, and sat with his head in my lap, stony faced and looking without seeing towards the dark mountain and the starlit western sky.

ΩΩΩΩΩΩΩΩΩΩΩ

14th February 1855

Another day has passed, and I have recovered my composure enough to continue my narrative. Writing things down is not easy, for there is a considerable commotion here at the Plas, with people coming and going, and my family attending to me as if I was an incapable and doddery old crone. That was hard for me to cope with, in the midst of a terrible grief, but I suppose that they all meant well.

Coroner Will Daniels would not let Amos's body lie here at the Plas, and because of the circumstances surrounding his death he insisted that it should be taken to the mortuary on the Parrog for a post-mortem examination, prior to the inquest which will be held tomorrow. That sounds reasonable enough, but I am afraid that the air stinks of corruption, since neither George Havard Medical nor Shemi Wizard is allowed to examine the body on the grounds that the former is too closely related to the deceased and that the latter is a long-standing personal friend. They are both outraged by this decision. So is Master Daniels, who is not a bad man but who is weak and easily pressurized by those around him. Ifan Hipkins Medical has already travelled over from Cardigan to conduct the post-mortem. He can be counted upon to say whatever is required of him,

Flying with Angels

and George tells me that he is a long-standing member of the Society of Sea Serjeants. God only knows what his report on the death will contain. And to make matters worse, there are rumours from town that the Coroner is finding it almost impossible to find his jury for the inquest. That means that it will be packed, and that the verdict will bear little or no relation to what actually happened in Tycanol Wood.

So what did happen? I have been able to piece things together from the information given to me by Rose, Henry, Ioan and the others.

Rose and Henry were at home, waiting for me, when they heard a great commotion outside, on the hill leading down to the ford. They both went outside, and they were greatly surprised to hear Amos's voice. He was shouting something like this: "I know you are there, you miserable swine! Lurking behind that hedge like pathetic cowards, lying in wait for an innocent woman who has done you no harm! Come out and face me if you will! I know who you are -- Watkins, Owen, Huws, Laugharne and Jobbins. If you will, I will shout your names from the rooftops until you are brought face to face with your Maker. Come and face me! I demand it!"

Then, as Rose and Henry watched in horror in the gathering gloom, five masked men dressed all in black rushed out through a gate at the top of the hill and grabbed Amos. One of them -- they think it might have been Watkins -- shouted: "Damn you, Jones. Now you really have gone too far!" Rose says that Amos did not struggle very much. They tied him up, then pulled their horses out from their hiding place and threw him across the saddle of one of them. He was not a big man, and that would not have been too difficult. At this point Henry, having run up the hill, flung himself at Amos's assailants and tried to rescue him; but he was kicked and beaten, and fell to the ground. He was almost trampled beneath the hooves of the horses as the black riders wheeled round and galloped down the hill, passing within a few feet of Rose before splashing across the ford. She is sure that she heard one of them shout "Left! Left! Tycanol!" They wheeled left and rushed along the lane towards Caersalem Chapel and the woods. She is also sure that there were five horses, and that one of them was a smallish dappled grey mare. Henry struggled to his feet, shook his head, and immediately set off in pursuit on foot, reckoning that if he had tried to saddle up a horse the kidnappers would have been long gone. He shouted to his wife: "For God's sake, Rose! Go and tell your Grandmother! She will know what to do!"

Flying with Angels

Henry never saw Amos or the riders again. When Ioan and his little group of twelve men reached the wood they heard horses in the distance, and knew at once that the horsemen who had taken Amos were at the far end of the wood and would escape towards Pentre Ifan or Brynberian. It was now pitch black, and they found Henry wandering about, having lost his way without any lantern to guide him. They joined forces and followed the fresh horse tracks into the wood, and at last came to a clearing. In the light of their lanterns they saw a body there, with a noose around its neck, dangling from the low branch of an oak tree. It was obvious that it was Amos. They rushed up, supported the body and cut the rope, but he was already dead. During a quick conference, the youngest and fittest of the men, including Henry and my grandsons Benjamin and Owain, agreed to follow the tracks of the horsemen to see if they could catch up with them or at the very least find out from the hoofprints which way they had gone. The others picked up Amos's body and slowly retraced their steps back towards Fachongle; and it was on the woodland track, a little later, that they met Blodwen and me.

In spite of Myfanwy's pleading, the two new constables in town refused to come out to Trefelin or to the Plas, or to hunt for the kidnappers in the darkness. That was not surprising, for they were both new to the job, having started on their tour of duty not much more than a month earlier. They finally got to Trefelin and into the wood in the middle of next day, and although Rose and Henry both gave them sworn statements, as did Ioan and all the other members of the pursuit party, they refused to make any link between the black-cloaked riders and the death of Amos. Ioan, who accompanied them into the wood and showed them everything, including the cut rope still dangling from the tree, says that they were both incompetent and very frightened. He is clear in his own mind that they were under strict instructions from some senior magistrate -- possibly Laugharne Pengelli -- to find no evidence of any crime. So they made lots of notes, bumbled about for an hour or two, and then went back to Newport, muttering "Very sad business indeed. Oh dear oh dear! Very disturbed, he must have been."

Tomorrow, there will be an inquest. I will not attend, for I truly cannot face the trauma of it, and nor can I trust myself to control my emotions if -- as I suspect -- the occasion turns out to be as rotten as an egg left in the summer sun.

Flying with Angels

But I now know, from what has happened, that Amos has sacrificed himself for me. Those men were lying in wait for me behind the hedge at the top of the hill near Trefelin. They knew that I would pass that way on that day and at that time. Somehow, Amos got to know about the ambush, and sent a message to the Plas to delay my departure. Then he turned up in my stead, challenged those monsters with total disregard for his own safety, and paid the ultimate price. Perhaps he knew that that was his fate. But oh, what love and what courage! And he went to meet his God without saying goodbye.

Why, *cariad*, did you do that to me? Why? Why?

ΩΩΩΩΩΩΩΩΩΩΩ

15th February 1855

Last night I could not write another word because of my tears and because of the terrible realization of the manner in which the prophet had gone to his doom in order to save a miserable sinner like me. I wept for a long time, and have a vague recollection of my dear Bessie coming in and gathering me in her arms, and whispering, in the midst of her own tears: "There now, Mistress. Let go now, and let the tears come. There now. There now."

The inquest has been held in the Royal Oak, and as I expected it was an outrage. The Coroner, Will Daniel, has tendered his resignation in protest against what happened, and the town is talking of nothing else. As expected, the jury of ten was packed, and every single member belonged to the Society of Sea Serjeants. Nobody else was prepared -- or invited -- to serve. The Coroner had also received instructions (from some unknown higher authority) that he must not on any account allow any evidence that might relate to the investigations of the constables or to the allegations of "interested parties." And it was widely known, even before the start of the proceedings, that the jury would walk out together if any person associated with Jones Minor Prophet was allowed to speak. Ioan tried to speak, as did Will, Henry, Rose and Benjamin, and they were all ruled out of order.

Flying with Angels

During the proceedings, the tame doctor from Cardigan blandly pronounced that he had conducted a post mortem on the body of Master Amos Jones, that he had found no evidence of violence against the person, and that the cause of death had been asphyxiation associated with a noose tied tightly around the neck. He then, quite improperly, said that he had it on good authority from certain medical colleagues that Master Jones had been a very unstable and erratic person who had been involved in a certain great scandal in the community and who had lost his livelihood as a result. He had also lost his beloved wife some years since under the most tragic of circumstances. So, concluded Doctor Hipkins, Master Jones had every reason to wish to bring an end to his miserable life, and to go into the very wood associated with the great scandal in order to achieve his baleful objective. When Hipkins Medical sat down, there was pandemonium on the public benches, for every person in the room knew his statement to be a travesty of the truth. Ioan told me afterwards that the Coroner looked appalled, but was too frightened to conduct a cross-examination or to ask for further details. Then without further ado the foreman of the jury, our old friend John Thomas, stood up and said: "Master Daniels, we have reached our verdict."

"What? Already?" spluttered the Coroner. "You have not even retired for deliberations. I wish to ask for further evidence, and to give you guidance."

"We do not need it, sir. This is a cut and dried matter, and we all have work to do."

The Coroner sat back, and nodded, with a look of utter despair on his face. "Very well, Master Thomas. Give me your verdict."

"We find, your honour, that the deceased, Master Amos Jones, took his own life by hanging, while the balance of his mind was disturbed."

Again there was uproar, and members of the public started to throw bits of paper, coins, and a good deal of verbal abuse at the jury members. There was a grave danger that somebody might get hurt, for the constables were nowhere to be seen. The Coroner shouted "Order! Order!" to no avail, and then had no option but to bring the proceedings to an end. Shouting above the jeering and swearing of furious townspeople, he repeated the verdict of the jury as being the proper finding of the inquest, and ended by saying: "The body of Master Amos Jones is now released. This inquest is concluded!"

Flying with Angels

By common consent, the inquest in the Royal Oak was the most blatant and cruel miscarriage of justice in the town for fifty years or more, and I feel sure that what has been a simmering resentment against Laugharne Pengelli and his cronies will now boil over. Amos was, after all, greatly loved, even if he was considered something of an eccentric. Everybody knows that he was kidnapped and executed in cold blood, and the names of the five men responsible are also common knowledge.

Those who administer local justice are all in the pockets of that foul secret society, and the constables and the Coroner have clearly been intimidated, threatened and in effect battered into submission. However, evil men will not, on this occasion, have it their own way, and the community has now been pushed too far. News has come from town this very evening that the *Ceffyl Pren* is out on the road, and that it is not playing for laughs.

And while a host of grim and black-faced men don disguises and march out with lighted torches, Amos is back at the Plas, cold and quiet on a table in the parlour, with lighted candles at his head and feet.

ΩΩΩΩΩΩΩΩΩΩΩ

16th February 1855

Last night, between the hours of midnight and three o'clock, and having been comprehensively betrayed by a system of justice that is not worth the name, the people of Newport took their revenge. By all accounts there were almost two hundred men involved, all black-faced and dressed in female garb, and driven by an iron resolve. There were no charades, and there was no laughter. Twenty-five ricks went up in flames, and the justice of the *Ceffyl Pren* was imposed with terrifying efficiency. Three of the squires in the neighbourhood -- namely Owen, Jobbins and Huws --were chosen for execution. They were hunted down by delegated groups of black-faced "women" and strung up naked from the branches of trees on their own estates. When they were found and cut down by their own servants in the light of the dawn, their grotesque and pathetic bodies were covered with white frost, and each one had a note hung around its neck on a piece of string. This one, around the neck of Mefin Owen, was typical, and it said: *I hereby declare that I took my own life. Please believe me! Signed Sq Mefin Owen Gelli Fawr, 19th Febry 1855.*

Squires Dafydd Laugharne and Thomas Watkins were also taken and, for some reason that I cannot fathom, were spared. They were stripped naked on a freezing cold night and their clothes were burned. Then they were tried (in the manner of the *Ceffyl Pren*) for the murder of Amos Jones, and found guilty within two minutes. They were paraded through the town shortly before dawn in a torchlight procession, with a blaring of trumpets and a banging of drums sufficient to wake the inhabitants of the churchyard. Scores of townspeople tumbled out of their beds and joined the procession, which made its noisy way to the Parrog. There, the two men were tied into the ducking stool and subjected to the most cruel ducking in the icy water of the estuary that anybody can remember. Apparently Watkins almost died, and had to be resuscitated. Then the two men were taken to the town lockup, unable to stand because they were in deep shock, and were blue with cold. They were dumped on the doorstep. The two miserable constables who had signally failed to do their duty in the collection of evidence at the scene of the crime, or elsewhere for that matter, were then dragged from their beds and forced to open up the cell door. Laugharne and Watkins were flung inside, and then the mysterious foreman and jury of the *Ceffyl Pren* locked them in and made off with the keys, making it clear that if either man was released before being charged with murder, they would return and administer their own form of natural justice.

In other developments, the ten members of the infamous inquest jury have been hounded out of their homes, and some of them have been beaten up. And ex-Coroner Will Daniels, who following his resignation will not have to deal with the inquests for the three dead squires, has finally found courage from somewhere. He has put up a notice on the church door, apologizing to the people of Newport for his failure to resist intimidation from the members of the Society of Sea Serjeants, saying that he does not agree with the findings of his own inquest into the death of Master Amos Jones, and expressing the view that Master Jones was unlawfully killed. In those circumstances the new Coroner, when he is appointed, may have to reconvene the inquest or at the very least declare its verdict null and void.

Flying with Angels

So the prospect opens up of a protracted re-examination of the evidence relating to Amos's death. I will not allow it to delay the placing of the dear man in his final resting place, but this morning, following the discovery of Will Daniels' note, I asked both George and Shemi to examine the body and to make signed statements as to what they found. They obliged, and told me afterwards that they were both of the view that Amos was beaten black and blue before he was killed, that he had many bleeding injuries, and that suicide could be entirely ruled out.

But suicide was the recorded verdict of the legally convened inquest, and that meant that Amos could not be buried in consecrated ground. I knew that Rector Llewelyn Thomas would not have him, and neither would the pastors of any of the Nonconformist chapels. By his own request, he did not even have a coffin. I refused to have him buried in an unmarked grave in unconsecrated ground, since he was after all a man of God. But he had been dead for four days, and as the one charged with disposing of his body, I could delay no further. This afternoon, as I sat quietly in the parlour, taking my turn in the non-stop watch over him, I had a sudden inspiration. I rose and looked at his dear battered face for the last time, and kissed him. I knew at once that I had approval from his blessed spirit.

So it was that on a cold afternoon lit by a low February sun, a small procession set off from the Plas, with four men -- Shemi, Ioan, Wilmot and Brendan -- carrying a home-made bier. On it lay the body of Amos Jones, wrapped in a white shroud. I walked at the head of the procession, and behind the bier came my two daughters and their husbands, and all of my servants. Slowly we made our way up the mountain slope, in total silence. We stopped at Ffynnon Brynach, and I sprinkled some of the holy water onto Amos and read out a little passage from the Book of Amos. Then we continued to climb upwards, treading carefully on the old blue rocks and following familiar sheep tracks. Only I knew where we were going. The others probably thought we were heading for the summit, but then I led the procession to the left, scrambling over huge boulders, squeezing through narrow gaps in the rocks, and sidling along narrow ledges. Not even Will had been here, in all his days as a shepherd on the mountain. The only one who had was Daisy, when she was a small child, many years ago -- and I knew that she had no recollection of it.

We came to my cave just as the sun was beginning to set. Wilmot read out a shortened version of the burial service used by Amos himself in his days as a pastor, and with due reverence we placed him in his tomb. I said my last farewell, as did the others. Then the men found the largest boulder which they could move, and manhandled it across the cave entrance. I knew that I would never visit it again. We all embraced, and tears were shed, and all those present swore that they would never reveal to another soul the precise whereabouts of Amos's last resting place.

We were back at the Plas shortly before the last glimmer of dusk was obliterated by the spreading darkness. Now it is late, and after another day of turbulent emotions I am covered by a cloak of peaceful acceptance. I thank God that Amos, the blessed man who gave his life for me and his friends, is finally at rest. And he is in the most sacred place I know, on the mountain where angels dwell.

ΩΩΩΩΩΩΩΩΩΩΩΩ

20th February 1855

On the day after we placed Amos in his tomb, Bessie came up to my room shortly after breakfast and handed me an envelope. "Mistress, this is a letter from Master Amos."

"But Bessie, Amos is dead."

"Yes yes, Mistress. But he gave it to me on the day before he died, with strict instructions that it should be passed to you after his death and after he had been laid to rest."

"So he knew he would die, Bessie?"

"I assume so, Mistress. At any rate, he said goodbye to me."

"But not to me, Bessie," I whispered, with tears welling up in my eyes. "He should have done that........."

Bessie came and put her arm around my shoulders, and gave me a kiss on the cheek. "He knew it himself, Mistress. But there was a reason, take it from me. Just you read his letter."

So Bessie curtsied and left me. With shaking hands I opened the envelope and read the Last Epistle of Jones Minor Prophet. This is what it said:

Flying with Angels

Garfeth, Shrove Tuesday 1855

My beloved Martha

I love you more than life itself, and that is my great joy. When you read this I will be with the angels. I am not afraid, and although we are now separated by a heavy curtain and a great mystery, I rejoice that we will soon be together again. I will wait for you with a smile on my face.

I regret, cariad, that I have not said farewell, but as you know, hasty and ill-considered departures are in my nature. I will explain.

You have suspected it, without ever discovering the truth, but for the last ten years you have been surrounded by -- and protected by -- a considerable conspiracy. Your family, your servants and your friends have all been involved at some stage, although in truth many of them did not become conspirators until quite recently. It is a minor miracle that between us we have managed to keep you alive for so long.

I am sorry if I appear to be talking in riddles. Around Easter in the year 1845 you were sentenced to death by the Society of Sea Serjeants. I am still unclear as to the precise details, for that organization is difficult to penetrate, but it appears that certain families (for example, those bearing the names Howell, Watkins and Rice) have long since blamed you for their misfortunes, and have sworn vengeance. All of the men of those families were, and are, members of the Society. You have seen most of them to their graves, and few have grieved for them. Then, at the time of the Rebecca Riots, you humiliated Richard John Rice and Squires Jobbins and Huws, and caused old Squire Owen of Gelli Fawr to go to the gallows. They were all members of the Society, which is a crude and vicious organization. It does not retreat, and it does not forgive.

The passing of the death sentence was not just a silly game played by grown men. It was accompanied by an oath made with the mingling of brotherhood blood, and it placed an absolute duty upon the members of the Society to carry it out within the span of ten years. So terrible is this duty that if it is not performed, then those members deemed to have failed are themselves liable to be "eliminated." This is how discipline within the organization is maintained, and certain members are charged with the punishment of backsliders and offenders. Fear is their weapon. Those evil fellows Rice and Howell, who died last year, were not executed by the Irish rebels but by the Society's Irish disciplinary unit, which had become

Flying with Angels

displeased with certain of their activities and with their tendency to act without authority. That is why the assassins were never even pursued, let alone brought to justice.

Elijah Collins knew of the death sentence passed upon you, and I understand that he tried to warn you, on more than one occasion, in an oblique sort of way. He did not want to see you afflicted by nightmares of persecution. He had friends within the organization who were prepared to talk but were too frightened to resist the evil men who were in charge. He also had a death sentence passed upon him, for being too vociferous in his opposition to the Society, and was then executed by four men chosen for the task. I suspect that in secret he was also involved in supporting Irish opposition to the Society, and that he worked closely with his cousin Seamus -- but I cannot be sure of that.

As for you, my beloved Martha, I found out about the death sentence from Elijah Collins shortly before he died. He warned me that as time passed, the greater would become the danger. Squire Laugharne and his cronies tried, I suppose, to frighten you out of your wits with their little notes and signs, and they were of course delighted about our misadventure in the woods since that, they hoped, might hasten your demise and therefore save them from their unpleasant task. They did everything that they could to increase our misery, as you will remember only too well. Then they hoped you would die from the typhoid sickness, and you refused to oblige. You have behaved, my dear Martha, with the greatest possible lack of consideration for their interests. Their fury was certainly increased by your attempts to help the starving Irish peasants, for it is a central canon of their beliefs that Papists are to be despised and wiped off the face of the earth. They were even more angry when you took in the O'Connells, and it is rumoured that they were preparing to execute you some six or seven years ago; but then the Society fell into disarray, and Laugharne and the others discovered that the O'Connells had connections with certain very unpleasant fellows on the other side of the water. So they backed off, and decided to bide their time.

Why then, cariad, did nobody tell you about the death sentence passed upon you, when we all knew about it? The answer to that is quite simple. We discussed it a great deal, and came to the view that if you had known you might have plunged into a deep trough of melancholia, as you have done before in your life on more than one occasion. We thought that

Flying with Angels

that might kill you. The other matter which we discussed was equally worrying -- and that was the possibility, or even the probability, that you would have gone out into battle against the forces of evil dressed in your shining armour like Joan of Arc, and that like her you would have hastened your own demise. Many others who love you would have gone down with you, and there might well have been open warfare in the town. That would not have been civilized. We did not want you burnt at the stake, or put to death in some other horrid manner, and so we decided to protect you and allow you to live out your days in ignorance. You have had to cope with enough suffering as it is.

We are sorry for that deceit, cariad, and I now ask for your forgiveness. But we all thought it was for the best.

Then there are other things for which I take full responsibility, having discussed them with nobody else. I took the decision some years ago to seek to divert the attention of the Society from you onto my own person. So I set out to provoke Laugharne and Watkins and the others through my preaching and my actions. I still do not understand my own heart in this matter. Perhaps I wanted to live dangerously, as a sort of penance for our misdemeanour in the woods and for my other sins (which are many); and perhaps I wanted to do something noble for you, as a manner of expressing my love. I am not very clever at such things, as you may have noticed......... At any rate, I did attract their slingshots and their arrows, leaving you relatively unscathed, and that gave me a sort of pleasure.

Then I saw and heard the tolaeth, and knew that the end was near. You told me on the very same day that you had seen the aderyn y gorff, and so we spent that special time together during which we came to terms with our fate. Your calm dignity and acceptance was something which deepened my love for you to the point where it became unbearable, and in the silence of my own heart I determined that if it should be given to me to influence the course of events I would go before you, and allow you to die in peace rather than violence. One small sacrifice, Martha, as a means to a noble end......

News came to me, from a certain contact I have within the Society, that ten years had almost passed since the death sentence was placed upon you, and that those in authority were exceedingly displeased about the delay in disposing of you. Their displeasure was increased by the

389

realization that your tally of victories over Society members (such as Llewelyn Drover) was going up year on year. They were even beginning to be afraid of you, in the belief that you were indestructible, or protected by some supernatural force! I knew that a last play would come soon, and then my contact told me that you would be ambushed on the hill near Trefelin by Laugharne and his fellows, as you made your way to Trefelin on the day after the cnapan game. They planned to take you to Tycanol Wood, to try you for all your terrible crimes, and then to string you up from a tree, making the death appear as a suicide.

I decided to take your place, and now as I sit here scribbling away on this letter, that is what I will do. I trust that m y actions will lead to the conviction of evil men and to the destruction of the Society of Sea Serjeants. So I will ask the little O'Connell boy to go with a message to you, and to divert you for a while. Then I will confront those monsters and see what happens. If you receive this letter, dearest heart, I want you to know that I did my best for you and my God, and that I have gone to my fate.

God bless you, cariad, and all whom you love. We will be together soon, of that I am sure.

Your beloved
Amos

I have received many terrifying and crucial letters in my time, and some of them have contained great brutality and even confessions of crimes committed. This letter from Amos is in some ways the most terrifying of all, for it relates to the conflict between good people and those who do evil by lurking in the dark. But it is also the most humble and yet noble letter I have ever received. I was numbed when I read it, and I am numbed again now as I transcribe it into the pages of my diary. I thought that there were no more tears to weep, but I was wrong.

ΩΩΩΩΩΩΩΩΩΩΩ

Flying with Angels

23rd February 1855

There has been a certain amount of unfinished business for me to attend to. Justice has almost been done, but not quite, and two murderers are held in the Newport lockup without, as yet, any charges being brought against them. Laugharne and Watkins will not get away from there, since there is a picket of townspeople outside the front door for twenty-four hours of every day. But they killed Amos, and I want them in court, where justice will be done and will be seen to be done. I want it demonstrated to the wider world that these evil men, who are both squires and who have in the past manipulated, ruled and terrorized the people of the town, are not above the law.

I feel utterly exhausted after all this brutality meted out by men against other men, and I fear that I am also afflicted by some ailment. I know that Shemi and George are concerned about me, but I will not seek their advice, for I want neither cures nor a slow decline into decrepitude. There are still some things that must be done.

Today I managed to find enough reserves of energy to welcome Ioan, Wilmot and Shemi to the Plas. I asked Bessie to join us. We five old friends sat together in the parlour on a ghastly day, with rain lashing against the west side of the house and with a mad wind rattling the slates. But it was warm inside in front of the blazing fire, and since I was surrounded by love I contrived to feel moderately cheerful. We talked of Amos, of course, and blessed his memory, and then we turned to the matter of justice for Laugharne and Watkins. The first thing that I did was to ask Wilmot whether he would make charges against Laugharne and Watkins and pursue the matter through the courts until such time as they faced a judge with a black cap on his head.

"I will, Martha. That is a promise."

"You are not frightened?"

"The Society of Sea Serjeants is finished, Martha, at least in this area. I wish that certain of its members had been dealt with more gently, but your local *Ceffyl Pren* is a fearsome beast when it is unleashed after a long time spent in a cage. I know for a fact that there are twenty squires in the neighbourhood, and countless townspeople, who will give testimony against Laugharne and Watkins. I am not afraid."

"Thank God for that, Wilmot. You are a true friend. And Shemi,

Flying with Angels

will you help too?"

"All done and dusted, Martha," said Shemi with a grin on his face. "I have more than enough evidence to convict all five of the men who killed Amos, and those who killed Elijah Collins, had not fate intervened by sending three of them to early graves........"

"How can that be, Shemi?"

"A simple matter of observations and contacts, Martha, as I was taught by Master Joseph Harries many years ago. I was aware of the death sentence placed upon you some years back, and I have been observing Laugharne and his cronies very closely ever since, with a view to protecting you. I have in my possession the black cloaks and the masks used by Laugharne and Watkins on the evening of Amos's abduction and murder. The cloaks both have blood on them."

"What? How did they come into your possession?"

"Very easily, Martha. Remember that cruel men tend to be hated by their own servants. I simply asked for them, and they were provided. As soon as I heard from Amos that an attack on you was imminent I was set upon warning you. Amos begged me not to destroy your innocence, and said that he would take care of things. I reluctantly agreed, with a great sense of foreboding, for careful planning was not one of his strengths. So I took certain precautions, knowing that they would bear fruit after the event if not before. My friends in the stables of Ffynnonddofn, Pengelli and the other squires' residences made certain cuts with files on the horseshoes of their masters' favourite horses. Each cut was quite distinctive. Then they gave me access to their stables when their masters were out and about, and I made casts of the said horseshoes with a sort of plaster of Paris developed by Joseph many years ago. Each cast was carefully labelled and documented, and I have signed testimonies from the stable lads relating to what I did."

"They will appear in court if we want them to, Shemi?"

"They will. As soon as I got news of the tragic abduction and death of Amos, I rushed to Trefelin to talk to Henry. My instinct was to rush to the Plas so as to be by your side, Martha, but I decided on this as a priority since I was afraid it might rain. In the middle of the night, by torchlight, Henry and I went into the field at the top of the hill by the ford, where the murderers had lain in wait. We found all of the hoof impressions that we wanted, and took plaster casts. Then Henry took me into the wood, to

Flying with Angels

the place where Amos had been executed. We found where the horses had been tethered, and sure enough found all five of the necessary hoof impressions again, after a considerable amount of searching. Again we took plaster impressions and made detailed notes. It is all available as evidence and exhibits, Martha, and will be used in court."

I could not help smiling, and shook my head in disbelief. "Oh Shemi, how I love you! Your old master would no doubt have been glowing with pride."

"And that's not all, Martha!" said he with a glowing face. "Do you want me to tell you about the horse-shit?"

"Thank you, Shemi, but I would prefer not to know. Keep it for the magistrates and the judges, who will appreciate it. Now let me show you my evidence. Bessie, would you please give Wilmot the notes made by Billings Scrivener?"

She smiled, fetched a pile of paper from the drawer in my office desk, and handed it to Wilmot. For five minutes there was silence as he glanced through the papers and passed them round to Shemi and Ioan to read. Then there was a chuckle from deep in Wilmot's throat, and he looked at me and winked. I blushed, and he could not restrain himself any longer. A loud guffaw echoed around the room, and I dare say round the whole of the Plas, and soon we were all rolling about in uncontrollable laughter. So the sound of mirth returned to the Plas, and with a vengeance. At last we all calmed down.

"Oh dear, may God forgive us," moaned Wilmot, holding his sides and trying to wipe the tears from his eyes at the same time. "And may dear Amos forgive us from his place with the angels. This is really no laughing matter. But now we have them, Martha. Signed by Billings and witnessed by you. Will he appear in court?"

"He has given me his word."

"When this evidence is put together with Shemi's plaster casts and piles of horse-shit, no court in the land could fail to convict. Do not doubt it, Martha -- justice will be done."

And that was that. We talked, and drank tea together, and ate slices of a most wonderful chocolate cake that Bessie produced from the pantry. And, without articulating any great and noble thoughts we celebrated the facts that life goes on and that virtue prevails.

Flying with Angels

25th February 1855

I am so tired that now I want to sleep, and sleep to the end of time. But I have to dig deep into my reserves, and find the energy to write just a little more.

The Petty Sessions have been held in the Black Lion, with Squires Mostyn Gittins and Solomon Edwards presiding. Wilkins Legal appeared for me, but the charges were brought by Wilmot and Ioan. Laugharne and Watkins were charged with conspiracy, the abduction and murder of Master Amos Jones, and the murder of Master Elijah Collins. There were other charges as well -- including extortion, grievous bodily harm, bribery, theft and so forth -- brought by assorted townspeople, but I dare say that these will never be properly considered by a court since the murder charges will take precedence. There was no defence, and the magistrates declared that there was a case to answer. The two charged men were remanded in custody and were taken in chains to Haverfordwest Gaol to await trial at the Spring Assizes. They will certainly hang. May God have mercy upon their souls.

After the hearing, Shemi called by on his way home, and I took the opportunity to ask him about the last two things that have been taxing my brain. "First, Shemi," I said, "I am intrigued by the payments sent by Laugharne in bulky envelopes to Seamus Collins in Ireland. What was that all about?"

Shemi laughed and gave me a kiss on the cheek. "Mistress Morgan," he grinned, "you are quite impossible! You never did like loose ends lying about. That was quite simple. Collins was in possession of a written testimony which proved that Laugharne and the others were behind the death of his old cousin. It was straightforward blackmail. Pay up, and I keep quiet. Fail to pay up, and the evidence goes to the Lord Lieutenant and you get killed anyway. Laugharne decided to cooperate, since Collins was too well protected for the Society in Ireland to get at him. Rough place, Ireland."

"How do you know all of this, Shemi?"

"I know more than you think, Martha. At any rate, thanks to certain Irish friends that testimony is now in my possession, and will be used in evidence at the Assize Court."

"And those letters between you and Brynach? I know about them."

Flying with Angels

"Yes, I am aware of it. That was careless of me, leaving them lying around. Brynach knew about your death sentence almost as soon as he landed in America, from a Cardigan apothecary who belonged to the local branch of the Society before he emigrated. Brynach baled him out of some difficult situation, and when he was on his deathbed the poor fellow gave Brynach a written testimony saying that he made up a highly concentrated potion of digitalis for Squire Laugharne shortly before Elijah's death which had the effect of simply stopping the heart and leaving no traces. He knew it was for Master Collins, and he admitted that he was an accessory to the murder. I have suspected digitalis all along, but have had no evidence to go on. At any rate, I am now in possession of that testimony too, and also other material about the Society's activities in Pembrokeshire which has come from other emigrants. Brynach has been terribly worried about you, as you might imagine, but we agreed, in the course of much correspondence, to protect you from the truth. He wanted to come back home to see you, more than once, but we discouraged him on the grounds that the truth about this whole grubby business might come tumblin g out, thereby causing both you and him -- and the rest of us -- to be caught up in violent conflict with the SSS. But he was reassured, I know, by the promise that you would be well looked after by your family, your friends and your angels. Your son has been a valuable asset in the fight against evil in West Wales, dear Martha, in spite of the fact that he lives across a mighty ocean."

At twelve noon, I embraced Shemi on the doorstep and said farewell to him, trying to hide from him the fact that I would never see him again. He sensed something, and we stood for some minutes holding hands and gazing deep into one another's eyes. His eyes filled with tears, as did mine. No further words were exchanged, for neither of us had the right ones for the occasion. As I fought to keep my composure, he kissed me with infinite tenderness on both cheeks. Then he jumped onto his pony and trotted off onto the common without looking back.

ΩΩΩΩΩΩΩΩΩΩ

395

Flying with Angels

26th February 1855

My affairs are in order, and I will not run about the place saying my goodbyes. I could not stand that, and neither could anybody else. I am not well, and am so tired out as a result of the happenings of past weeks that I hardly have the energy to pull on my dress or to lace up my boots.

But I am happy and composed, and now it is my wish to join David, and Owain, and Iestyn, and Joseph, and Amos. They are all waiting for me. This morning I wrote my final letters to Brynach and my sisters Elen and Catrin. I have also written a note to Daisy, Betsi and my special granddaughter Rose, asking for a good Christian burial in the family mausoleum in Cilgwyn Churchyard.

I will give one small concession to any of my enemies who may be left alive, in that I will not die in my bed. But neither will I die in some vicious confrontation or cowardly attack.

It is two o'clock in the afternoon, and it is all planned. I will now put down my pen, and close my book, and lock it inside my tin box. I will quietly tidy up my room, for I abhor untidiness. Then I will leave a note for Bessie, asking her to keep my diaries safe and away from public view so long as it is in her power so to do. I will embrace each of my servants and tell them I am going for a walk. They will look at me with love and concern in their eyes, but they will not try to stop me, for I have done this countless times before.

Then I will leave this beloved house and climb -- with some difficulty -- to the summit of the mountain, and lie down at dusk as the frosty stars begin to sparkle. I will do this as serenely as may be, in the knowledge that I have done all that I wished to do with my life and that I have experienced a good deal more happiness than pain. That is the truth, in spite of future interpretations that might be placed upon my diaries. One regret is that I will never again sit on the summit of this blessed mountain beneath a golden sun and drink in the unutterable and unbearable beauty of the place. Another is that I will never again hold a sleeping child in my arms...........

I will not harm myself, but I will close my eyes and go to sleep enfolded in the gentle arms of my mountain. And I will not wake up. Do not grieve for me. I will be flying with my angels.

Flying with Angels

The Cambrian, Saturday 5th March 1855

A SINGULAR OCCURRENCE IN NORTH PEMBROKESHIRE

Our correspondent in North Pembrokeshire has reported a most singular occurrence on the mountain of Carningli, approximately one mile from the Ancient Borough of Newport.

At about two o'clock in the morning on the 27th day of February 1855 a considerable earth tremor was experienced in the town and in the surrounding countryside, causing some structural damage and panic among the local populace. At the time of the cataclysm it was a frosty and starlit night with a full moon. Many people rushed into the streets, fearing for life and limb; but it is reported that there were no deaths or serious injuries in the town. Some people who lived on the flanks of the mountain reported hearing a great crashing and tumbling of rocks close to the summit, and indeed it was confirmed with the arrival of daylight that the profile of the mountain had been greatly changed.

It is also reported that when a party of men from the nearby hamlet of Cilgwyn climbed to the summit shortly after dawn they found the body of an elderly lady on a grassy patch near the topmost rocks. It was identified as that of Mistress Martha Morgan, who resided at Plas Ingli on the southern slope of the mountain. Foul play is not suspected, and the men who found the body have reported that she appeared to have died calmly, lying on her back and fast asleep. A post-mortem examination by the local doctor has led him to the conclusion that Mistress Morgan died of natural causes early in the morning, at approximately the time of the tremor.

Three further matters relating to the morning of 27th February have caused much discussion in the Newport area.

First, the men who recovered the body of Mistress Morgan reported that as they carried her down the path from the mountain summit they were watched from close quarters by six fully grown ravens, perched side by side on a large boulder and showing no fear at all. This might not be considered to be of any note, except that according to shepherds who work on the mountain there have been no ravens in residence on the mountain this winter.

Second, a considerable crevice has opened up to the south of the main peak, revealing the remains of a human being. Investigators have found bones and scraps of clothing and rope, and it is thought that the remains are those of a tall man who died many years since. The back of his skull was severely fractured, and local magistrates suspect that the man might have been hit from behind with a blunt implement. It is therefore assumed that the man was a murder victim, although there is little chance after the passage of so many years of establishing his identity.

Third, the inhabitants of Cilgwyn and the Cwm, to the south of Carningli, have remarked that following the earthly convulsion the mountain ridge has taken on the profile of a sleeping female. Our correspondent can vouch for this, and after looking at the mountain from a number of different viewpoints he confirms that it is possible to recognize the head, breast, rib-cage and stomach, and finally the raised knees of a woman lying on her back. Master William Owen, one of Mistress Morgan's servants and one of those who found her body, says that when he and his colleagues found her she had exactly the same profile as does the "rearranged" mountain ridge.

On Thursday morning the new Coroner for the Newport district will conduct two inquests -- one for the late Mistress Martha Morgan, and the other for the mysterious murder victim whose bones were found not fifty yards away from the place where she died.

We extend our heartfelt condolences to Mistress Morgan's family and to her extensive circle of friends. A full obituary will be published in our next edition. It is anticipated that following a funeral at Cilgwyn Church, Mistress Morgan will be interred in the enclosure of the Morgan family of Plas Ingli.

ΩΩΩΩΩΩΩΩΩΩΩ

Acknowledgements

I thank my wife Inger for her endless help and support with this book, and for encouraging me to complete the *Angel Mountain Saga* by writing, publishing and marketing five full-sized novels in five years. As ever, she has acted as referee, reviewer and proof-reader, and specialist adviser on the female psyche. I am grateful to Irene Payne, Ian Richardson, Robert Anthony and Lorna Hipkins for refereeing and commenting upon earlier versions of the text. As ever, Irene has been particularly supportive, providing practical advice on all manner of technical, historical and chronological matters as well as undertaking detailed editing. Finally I must express my appreciation to the hundreds of faithful readers who have followed the adventures of Mistress Martha with huge enthusiasm, who have contacted me by phone, letter and Email, and who have pushed me to complete this project. Thank you, one and all; this book is for you, and I hope that it will bring you many hours of reading pleasure.

Readers' Comments

"A magnificent achievement. Well up to the standard of previous books; pacy, racy and full of dramatic and romantic incident."
"The Introduction is original, touching and full of humanity. Thoroughly believable."
"The book has a very interesting story line, and as ever the narrative moves along at a cracking pace."
"Quite an episode -- a real tear-jerker........"
"Well done! A lot of loose ends are very neatly tied up."
"This book features some delightful and refreshing new characters."
"It's good to see that in spite of everything Martha has not lost her sense of humour -- the book is full of striking images and witty one-liners."
"Martha is as feisty and sensuous as ever, and grows ever more eccentric."
"I really love the way you handle the winding-down at the end of the book. The final pages could have been sentimental, but I found the writing sparse, economical and very effective. I wept."

About the Author

Brian John was born in Carmarthen in 1940 and brought up in Pembrokeshire. He is married and has two grown up sons and two grandsons. He studied at Haverfordwest Grammar School and at Jesus College Oxford, where he read Geography and obtained his D Phil degree for a pioneering study of the Ice Age in Pembrokeshire. He then worked as a field scientist in Antarctica and spent eleven years as a Geography Lecturer in Durham University. He has travelled widely in the Arctic, Antarctic and Scandinavia. In 1977 he and his family moved to a smallholding near Newport in Pembrokeshire, and since then he has made his living as a writer and publisher. He is also actively involved in environmental and community organizations. He has published hundreds of articles and around 60 books, and among his publishers are Collins, Pan, Orbis, Aurum Press/HMSO, Longman, David and Charles, Wiley and Edward Arnold. His published output includes university texts, walking guides, coffee table glossies, and books of popular science. Many of his titles have been published by Greencroft Books, and have been of particular interest to readers in Wales -- for example tourist guides, books of local jokes, walkers' handbooks, and titles on local folklore and traditions. *Flying with Angels* is the fifth and final novel in the Angel Mountain Saga. The four previous books have received wide acclaim for their narrative skill, their strong sense of place, and their historical authenticity. Much to Brian's surprise, the Saga has been a runaway success, and the heroine, Mistress Martha Morgan, now has a cult following of readers from all over the world. The series has now been sold to Transworld Publishers, and the books will be republished as from 2006 under the Corgi imprint.